Indiscretions of the Queen

Due to illness, Jean Plaidy was unable to go to school regularly and so taught herself to read. Very early on she developed a passion for the 'past'. After doing a shorthand and typing course, she spent a couple of years doing various jobs, including sorting gems in Hatton Garden and translating for foreigners in a City café. She began writing in earnest following marriage and now has a large number of historical novels to her name. Inspiration for her books is drawn from odd sources – a picture gallery, a line from a book, Shakespeare's inconsistencies. She lives in London and loves music, second-hand book shops and ancient buildings.

Jean Plaidy also writes under the pseudonym of Victoria Holt.

Jean Plaidy

Indiscretions of the Queen

Pan Books London and Sydney

First published 1970 by Robert Hale & Company
This edition published 1978 by Pan Books Ltd,
Cavaye Place, London SW10 9PG
© Jean Plaidy 1970
ISBN 0 330 25509 6
Printed and bound in Great Britain by
Cox & Wyman Ltd, London, Reading and Fakenham

Contents

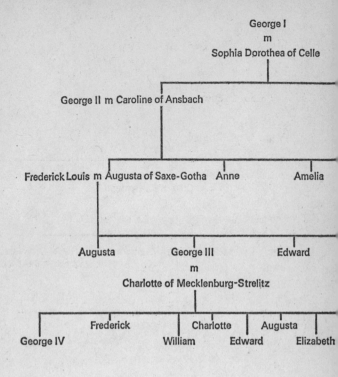

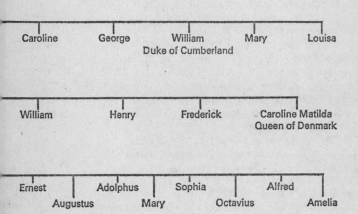

Sophia Dorothea

Caroline   George   William   Mary   Louisa
                      Duke of Cumberland

William   Henry   Frederick   Caroline Matilda
                                        Queen of Denmark

Ernest   Adolphus   Sophia   Alfred
     Augustus   Mary   Octavius   Amelia

Bibliography

National and Domestic History of England
   William Hickman Smith Aubrey
In the Days of the Georges   William B. Boulton
The Years of Endurance   Sir Arthur Bryant
George III – His Court and Family   Henry Colburn
The Life and Times of George IV   The Rev George Croly
The Good Queen Charlotte   Percy Fitzgerald
The Life of George IV   Percy Fitzgerald
George the Fourth   Roger Fulford
The Trial of Queen Caroline   Roger Fulford
England in the Eighteenth Century   R. W. Harris
Memoirs of George IV   Robert Huish
The Great Corinthian   Doris Leslie
George the Fourth   Shane Leslie
Loves of Florizel   Philip Lindsay
George III   J. C. Long
The First Gentleman of Europe   Lewis Melville
An Injured Queen: Caroline of Brunswick   Lewis Melville
Queen Caroline   Sir Edward Parry
The Four Georges   Sir Charles Petrie
The House of Hanover   Alvin Redman
Caroline, The Unhappy Queen   Lord Russell of Liverpool
George, Prince and Regent   Philip W. Sergeant
The Dictionary of National Biography
   edited by Sir Leslie Stephen and Sir Sidney Lee
Portrait of the Prince Regent   Dorothy Margaret Stuart
The Four Georges   W. M. Thackeray
The First Gentleman   Grace E. Thompson
British History   John Wade
Memoirs and Portraits   Horace Walpole
Memoirs of the Reign of George III   Horace Walpole
The Reign of George III   J. Steven Watson
Mrs Fitzherbert and George IV   W. H. Wilkins, MA, FSA
George III, Monarch and Statesman   Beckles Wilson

A wedding in Brunswick

The Court of Brunswick was preparing to celebrate the marriage of Princess Charlotte Georgiana Augusta to Frederick William, Prince of Würtemburg. The Princess was sixteen years old but quite ready for marriage, for life at the Court of Brunswick was free and easy; and both she and her sister, Caroline Amelia Elizabeth, had never suffered the restrictions which were considered necessary in most royal courts. The girls had run wild, mixing with servants and villagers; and they already knew what obligations marriage entailed.

The Princess Caroline was in the schoolroom thinking about her sister's marriage, wondering when there would be a similar occasion for her, and plaguing her governess, the Baroness de Bode, with questions.

'Now, Baroness,' she was saying, 'whom do you think they will select for *me*?'

'Your Highness knows that that day is some years distant.'

'Some years?' demanded Caroline. 'But why, pray? If Charlotte can marry at sixteen, why not I?'

'The Princess Charlotte is two years older than you.'

'Two years? What is two years?' Caroline narrowed her eyes and peered at her governess. 'I should like you to know, Madam Baroness, that I am not lacking in experience.'

The Baroness gasped with horror, which made Caroline laugh. She is deliberately trying to *shock* me, thought the Baroness. Of course she is an innocent girl. Or is she? Oh, this family! They are all so . . . odd. Sometimes I wonder . . . And when I consider her brothers . . .

Caroline watched her governess as she guessed the woman's thoughts. She tossed back the long fair curls which hung over her shoulder and raised her light eyebrows; she was pretty and her figure was already well developed.

The Baroness thought: She has too much freedom. They all have too much freedom.

'I beg of you,' said the Baroness, 'not to talk so freely.'

'But I would be *free*. Why should I be caged . . . like a pris-

9

oner? I shall always be free. I shall do exactly what I want and when I have a husband – in two years' time, because if Charlotte has one why shouldn't I – I shall see that he is aware of this.'

'You talk in a most unbecoming manner.'

'I say what I mean. Is there anything wrong with that?'

'There could be a great deal. You should pray more.'

Caroline made a face. 'Oh come, Baroness, everyone has a right to an opinion. You must admit that. I will never be anyone's puppet. If I allowed myself to accept everything that I am told without reasoning I should be like a field that would not grow a single blade of grass. Have you always done everything that was expected of you? Have *you* always been so good?'

'Indeed not. I fear I have often been wicked.'

'Why?'

'Why, Your Highness. I suppose because an evil instinct impels me to do wrong.'

'But why allow yourself to be impelled?'

'I suppose because I could not overcome my bad nature.'

The Princess laughed aloud. 'Then you are like a piece of clay, Madam. That is all – a piece of clay, and therefore I do not think you are very wicked to allow yourself to be moulded.'

'You must not think that whether we should be good or bad does not rest with ourselves.'

'But you have just said, Baroness, that you cannot help being bad. It is true. We are all bad – very bad. But that was how we were created.' She smiled mischievously. 'So you see, Baroness, it is no use your chiding me for this and that, for I just cannot help it. *I* have no say in the matter. It is simply the way I was made.'

'You talk too much.'

'Of course,' agreed Caroline. 'Do I not do everything too much? But you will admit, Baroness, that it is better than not doing enough?'

'You are determined to argue.'

'And what better occupation? For how can we exercise our minds without arguments? But how did this start? Simply because I said that it will soon be my turn to have a husband.'

'We cannot be sure—'

'We can be sure of nothing in this world, you will tell me. But I *am* sure – about many things. I am sure it is good that Charlotte has a husband for she is the kind of girl who needs a husband . . . early.'

'Your Highness!'

The Princess opened her eyes very wide and then laughed that rather wild laugh of hers which the Baroness always found a little alarming. And she added: 'So am I.'

'I hope—' began the Baroness.

'It is always good to hope,' interrupted the Princess. 'You even get what you hope for . . . sometimes.' She shut the book on which they had been working with a final bang.

'Now I really must go and fit on my dress. It must be ready for the wedding, must it not? We cannot have the bride's sister – soon to be a bride herself perhaps – not looking her best. Who knows – there might be suitors for my hand at my sister's wedding.'

She had gone, leaving the Baroness staring after her, asking herself if the Princess's behaviour was a little more than odd. Or was it due to high spirits? When one considered the others . . . one wondered.

From an upper window of the palace Caroline's father, Duke Charles William Ferdinand, saw his daughter cross the courtyard and come face to face with a young English boy who was being educated in Germany and living for a while at the Court of Brunswick-Wolfenbüttel.

He watched the young man pause, bow deeply and stand gazing at Caroline. A pretty picture, thought the Duke affectionately. In his eyes Caroline was charming; she was so full of vitality, so natural and very pleasing to the eye, with those long fair curls. She had grown in the last few months and it might have been a woman standing down there. After Charlotte was safely launched it would be Caroline's turn.

Not yet, he thought. He would keep Caroline at home as long as he could. He had admitted to his mistress, Madame de Hertzfeldt, that Caroline was his favourite child.

She was obviously flirting with young John Thomas Stanley down there, but if she had known that her father was watching she would have been alarmed, for he was the one person of whom she was in awe. Sometimes he wished that it were not necessary to inspire fear in his children; but of course it was particularly so with children such as his.

He frowned and turned away from the window as Madame de Hertzfeldt came into the room.

Approaching him she slipped her arm through his.

'You're anxious,' she said, and glancing out of the window saw Caroline in the courtyard with the English boy. 'Yes,' she went on. 'It will be her turn next and perhaps we should not delay too long.'

Her face still seemed to him the most beautiful he had ever seen; it was many years since he had noticed her and fallen in love with her. He thought now, as he had thought so many times before, how different everything would have been if he could have married her.

'Charlotte is happily settled,' she reminded him, and drew him away from the window.

'A good match,' he admitted. 'You think she *will* . . . settle?'

'Now that she has a husband she is more likely to.' She did not add that Charlotte's passing from his care to a husband's was a relief to them all; but he knew she thought this for there were no secrets between them.

Tall, stately, beautiful and dignified, devoted to him and the affairs of Brunswick, she was in all but name his queen. *Their* son was the boy he would have liked to be his heir. A soldier, handsome and, in his father's eyes, noble in every way, already making a brilliant career for himself – and like his mother, serene. Oh, God, he thought, how he admired serenity! It was because of that taint which sometimes he thought had smeared all his legitimate children.

'I think,' he said, 'that Caroline will want a husband now that her sister has one.'

'Caroline is a child yet.'

'Do you think so? You saw her down there . . .'

Madame de Hertzfeldt was silent for a moment. Then she

shrugged her shoulders. 'Like her sister she has matured early. But you won't have to raise the money for her wedding for a few years.'

'It might not be easy. Her brothers—' A look of pain crossed the Duke's face and his mistress hastened to console him.

'There is nothing wrong with Frederick William and the girls.'

'Oh, my dear, what an affliction! My eldest son almost an imbecile, my second completely so and the third blind. What is wrong? Why should I be so cursed? If I had married you—'

'We have been happy together for all these years.'

'What should I have done without you?'

'Why ask – when you have never been obliged to ... and as long as it rests with me never will.'

He looked at her beautiful face and was reconciled to everything – an unhappy marriage with his English wife, even the fruit of that marriage which had caused such grievous disappointment. All these years they had been lovers – even before his marriage to Augusta, and he had refused to give her up when Augusta had arrived from England and found her installed as mistress of his household. And so she had remained in spite of Augusta's protests and she had behaved with such dignity that in time even Augusta had come to accept her value.

'If our son—' he began, but she silenced him.

'You have your legitimate heirs,' she reminded him. 'There is no gainsaying that.'

'Only private people can expect happiness,' he answered bitterly, 'because they can choose their mates. The marriages of royalty scarcely ever result in happiness because they are not founded on love. They become embittered and often this is disastrous to the children of the marriage. They are often unhealthy in mind as well as body.'

She sought to comfort him. 'Charlotte seems happy,' she reminded him.

'My dearest, I know you seek to comfort me. Charlotte is excited. She is like Caroline. They crave constant excitement. It is a sort of madness ... no, no. It is a kind of compulsion they have. I pray God Charlotte will be happy when the excitement is over.'

'The excitement will go on for a time and perhaps she will soon have a child and that will sober her.'

'Determined as ever to look at the brightest side, I see.'

'Well, let us at least enjoy that while we can. In any case there may not be another side. Who shall say?'

He pressed her hand. 'You are right as usual.'

She smiled at him, her eyes still a little anxious. Since he had inherited the dukedom some two years before, life had been less carefree. His father had been a spendthrift and Charles had taken over an almost bankrupt country. He had determined to bring his country to prosperity and practised economy as far as he could; but that was not easy and he had been trained as a soldier rather than a statesman. But Madame de Hertzfeldt was as good as any minister; he rarely made a move without consulting her and he had proved again and again that this was wise. She it was who had helped to arrange this match for Charlotte; and she would do the same for Caroline when the time came. She had suggested that the Princesses be brought up with religious freedom so that they could in due course become either Protestant or Catholic according to the religion which their future husbands might follow. This, she had pointed out, would make it so much easier to find husbands for them, since many good matches were lost through a difference in the religion of the parties.

What a duchess she would have made! And he had to be content with Augusta who was constantly reminding everyone at Brunswick how much better affairs were managed in England under the rule of her brother King George III.

'So,' she said, 'we will think only of the wedding celebrations and deal with future problems when they present themselves.'

The Duchess was talking to her daughter Charlotte, soon to be a bride.

'Of course I could have wished we could have had an *English* Prince for you. My brother's son, the Prince of Wales, would be ... let me see ... Twenty, would it be? Yes, I should think twenty, and surely it is time he married, but do you think they would marry *him* to a Princess of Brunswick-Wolfenbüttel? Oh no! The very suggestion would give my sister-in-law an apoplectic fit. How I hated that creature. She – Queen Charlotte – was one of the reasons why I was anxious to get away from England.'

'Well, Mamma,' said Charlotte pertly, 'it is no use repining for the loss of the Prince of Wales now that I have my Frederick William. Würtemburg will have to do. And as the marriage is to take place within a day or so even if my wicked old aunt Queen Charlotte relented and sent me your nephew the Prince of Wales it would be, to say the least, a little awkward.'

'Charlotte, you really are impertinent,' said her mother mildly.

'What do you expect when I am named after that wicked sister-in-law of yours?'

'You happen, Charlotte, to be speaking of the Queen of England.'

'And so, Mamma, were you a moment ago and every bit as disrespectfully. Confess it.'

Oh dear, thought the Duchess. She would never be able to control these children of hers. It was the same with Caroline. The girls had their own way. But what can I do? she asked herself. *I* am not in command here. It is always Madame de Hertzfeldt. *She* is the Duke's confidante. *She* decides all matters, even those concerned with *my* children. What a situation! I wish I'd never left England.

She shivered. Fancy being there, with George expecting her to live with her sisters like nuns in a nunnery. No, this was preferable, even though she had an unfaithful husband who cared little for her, and children whom she could not control. Her children alarmed her. She could not bear to be in the company of her eldest boys. They seemed a continual reproach. Was it her fault? What had she done to produce those three boys who would never be able to rule? The youngest boy, thank God, was normal; and his father doted on him, and was terrified that some harm was going to befall him – his only normal son. He cherished the boy almost as much as he did Madame de

Hertzfeldt – though not quite. No one could be quite as important to him as that woman. Then there were the girls who were so wayward that they always seemed to get the better of her. They are so German, she decided; and I am so English. Sometimes she felt it was not such a bad thing that she had a strong-minded woman like Madame de Hertzfeldt to help her control the girls. That woman, thought the Duchess petulantly, would control anybody.

'Mamma,' Charlotte was saying, 'I have matters to which I must attend. So you must give me permission to leave you.'

The Duchess nodded and shaking her head sank down on to her sofa and stared blankly before her. How she had disliked this room! When she had first seen it it had seemed so primitive after the apartments of St James's, Hampton Court and Kensington Palace. But she had grown accustomed to it. And she had not really been sorry to come here. After all, a woman must marry – and they might have given her a less attractive husband. Charles had at least been a hero when he had come to England to marry her. Not that he had been quite as handsome as she had pictured him but the people had liked him. She remembered how they had been cheered at the opera while George and Charlotte were received in silence. What a triumph! Serve them right. It was all jealous Charlotte's fault, she was sure. George would never have had the gumption. Their mother had completely dominated him at that time, and he had done everything that she and Lord Bute told them.

But Charles had talked freely on English politics, which had angered them, and so instead of lodging him at one of the royal palaces they had put him in Somerset House and made their disapproval very clear to him as he was obliged to stay there without a royal guard. She too had been in disgrace for attempting to meddle in state affairs. And she had too! To think that she had helped to break up her brother's romance with Sarah Lennox and as a result he had had Charlotte. Not such a good move really – although Sarah Lennox was a silly little thing and if she had married George would probably have been no friend to the Princess Augusta.

All past history – but one could not help recalling it at times like these when there was a wedding in the family. And so she had come here and been horrified to see what a poor place the palace was and even more so when Charles had made it clear that he had no intention of giving up his mistress because he had acquired a wife and that the latter was of no great importance in his life – although he would endeavour to give her children – while the other woman remained supreme.

What a position for a proud princess to be forced into – and an English princess at that. But she had succumbed and done her duty and produced her sons – two mentally deficient, one blind, then her daughters and another boy – all of whom seemed brilliant in comparison with their brothers.

At least I have my children, though I have no control over them, she thought fretfully. They take no notice of what I say, and it is all due to the fact that they know who really rules here with the Duke. One would have thought he might have become tired of her by now. But that would not do. Who knew what arrogant upstart might take her place? The Duke alas was a very sensual man and was not entirely faithful even to Madame de Hertzfeldt; but of course none of his other peccadilloes was serious or long lasting; and on more than one occasion she had reported them to her great rival in order that they could be brought to a hasty conclusion. She supposed that she accepted Madame de Hertzfeldt, who was such an admirable woman in so many ways, and while she took command of affairs she always openly paid the correct respect to the Duchess.

So the Duchess must be content with her lot for she would have been far less happy in England, she knew, living a life of dreary spinsterhood. She had realized that in February 1772 when she had gone back to England at the time of her mother's death; but for the fact that her mother had wished to see her and they could not ignore her dying wish, Charlotte and George would have prevented her coming. As it was they had given her a little house in Pall Mall instead of lodging her at one of the royal palaces.

She recalled her anger and how she had almost returned to Brunswick before the funeral.

It would seem that she was to be slighted everywhere. How

strange when she considered what a forceful young woman she had been at home in England as the Princess Royal.

But Charles had changed her. From the moment she had realized he intended to be master and had accepted her inability to prevent it, she had sunk meekly into her place, had borne his children – and the fact that the three boys were abnormal had perhaps contributed to her meekness – accepted Madame de Hertzfeldt and even allowed her children to have some respect for the woman.

Now she sighed and thought of Charlotte soon to leave her home for a new life with a husband.

'I pray,' said the Duchess, 'that she is more fortunate than I.'

Charlotte was a dazzling bride, for she was very pretty.

'When she has gone,' Caroline told the Baroness, '*I* shall be the prettiest princess at the Court because being the only princess I must be the prettiest.'

'You occupy your mind with matters of no importance,' she was reproved, at which she retorted that her beauty *was* of great importance. Did the Baroness forget that one day – very soon – she would have to please a husband?

The Baroness sighed and reminded her of the serious little girl she had been and how when she had been asked in what country the lion could be found replied stoutly: 'In the heart of a Brunswicker.'

'I have heard the tale many times,' said Caroline, yawning. 'What a horrid little creature I must have been – even worse then than now.'

'It was a good answer,' replied the Baroness, 'and I trust you will never forget it.'

'Ah,' retorted Caroline, 'there is a sequel to the story. You've forgotten how I escaped from you all at carousel and rode round and round on the horses which was very dangerous you said and for which I should be punished, until I pointed out that fear was something a Brunswicker knew nothing about so how could you expect me, a Brunswicker, to be aware that I was causing you anxiety.'

'You have always—'

'Talked too much. So you have already told me. And I will repeat that when Charlotte has gone I shall be the prettiest princess in Brunswick.'

But never, she thought when she was watching her sister at the wedding ceremony, as pretty as Charlotte.

She gazed at her father standing erect beside the bride ready to pass her over to her prince. Dear Papa, he is the greatest man in the world, I believe, she thought; neither of us will ever find a man to compare with him.

And she began to picture herself standing there, all eyes on her, in her bridal gown with the shadowy figure of a bridegroom beside her.

Later at the banquet in the great hall the bridal pair sat at the place of honour and Caroline continued to watch them. Charlotte was very gay, almost hysterically so. I know exactly how she feels, thought Caroline. For I should feel exactly the same.

How she would miss Charlotte! She turned to her brother Frederick William and said to him: 'There are only really the two of us left now, for you can't count the others.'

Frederick looked rather shocked, but she laughed at him. It was silly to pretend. Everyone knew that their brothers were shut away from the rest of the family because of their affliction, so why pretend?

Her eye caught that of John Stanley, the English boy who clearly showed how much he admired her. She would take the first opportunity of talking to him.

When the dancing began she went to him smiling. His eyes were full of admiration. 'Of course,' she said, 'I am not supposed to talk to you in this way.'

'N . . . no, Your Highness.'

'But who cares for rules and etiquette? Do you?'

'Not if you do not wish me to.'

'Let us join the dancers. Then we shall be less conspicuous. Then I can talk to you. You will find that I talk a great deal. You come from England, do you not? As you know the Duchess is English. She cannot forget it and nor are we allowed to. Oh, you are shocked. How delightful! Do you think I am so

19

very shocking? But of course you do, and it would be foolish of you not to, because I am. Shocking and indiscreet.'

'Your Highness, I think you are—'

'Yes, come along. Don't hesitate. I dislike hesitation.'

'I think you are very handsome.'

'You think my looks are handsome but that my speech is forward and immodest and just what a princess's should not be?'

'I think that only sweet words could flow from such lips.'

'Oh, what a charming compliment. I do believe, John Thomas Stanley, that you have fallen in love with me. Oh, don't deny it. It is all very right and proper, for if my sister has a lover, why should not I?'

John Stanley was overcome with dismay and pleasure. The Princess Caroline was not only the most beautiful girl he had ever met, she was the most unusual.

Her conduct was noticed.

What can one do with such a girl? sighed her mother to herself. She is wild – like all of them. We can only pray that she is not *too* wild.

Her father promised himself that he would reprimand her later, but she would be sad missing Charlotte, so let her amuse herself a little on Charlotte's wedding day.

Madame de Hertzfeldt was asking herself how much like her brothers Caroline might be and what was the right treatment to mete out to such a girl. A great responsibility rested on her guardians she felt sure. She must choose an opportunity to speak to the Duke about his younger daughter when matters of state were less burdensome.

So Caroline flirted openly with John Thomas Stanley; and when it was necessary to say goodbye to Charlotte the young man did much to reconcile her to the parting.

'What I shall envy Charlotte most,' declared Caroline to the long-suffering Baroness de Bode, 'will be her children. Oh, Baroness, how I *long* to have a child.'

The Baroness folded her hands together and looked up to the ceiling.

'Now, Baroness, what is wrong with that?'

'It is an immodest subject.'

'Nonsense. How could the world go on without children?'

'It is immodest for a young girl to . . . to . . .'

'To talk of adding to the coming generations? But surely that would be a benefit to mankind. Admit it, Baroness.'

'Your Highness, I do not know what will become of you. I tremble to think.'

'Then you should think more, Madam, and it would, with practice, become less of an effort. That might cure the trembling. A little baby . . . a dear little baby . . . ! What a miracle! When shall I have a husband? How tiresome, that one must have a husband before one can have a baby, for do you know, Baroness, I think I should almost prefer the latter to the former.'

The Baroness put her fingers to her ears.

'Pray remove your fingers,' cried Caroline. 'I promise you I will no longer assault your ears. Instead I shall go to see my children.'

Caroline flounced out of the schoolroom, leaving the Baroness murmuring to herself: Should I speak to the Duchess? But of what use? It will have to be to Madame de Hertzfeldt. And what can one expect in a household where the wife takes second place to the mistress?

Meanwhile Caroline rode out of the palace. She should have taken a groom with her, but she had no intention of doing so. First of all she would call on the newest arrival – a baby boy three weeks old. He had been a little sickly at birth and was improving now. She had ordered the cooks to send food to the household, for if the baby were to thrive the mother must be well fed.

There he was in his crib. She lifted him out. 'I think he knows me. Look, he is smiling.'

She was happy, sitting in the old wooden rocking-chair holding the baby. How they adored her, these cottage people. They called her 'Good Princess Caroline'. Good, she thought, for doing what I want? How easy it is to be good.

She told the mother that food would arrive the following

day and she would see that the baby was properly clothed.

And after that she went on to see her next protégé. The people cheered her as she rode through the town. They had all heard stories of her love for children and how households containing them benefited. Any mother in distress only had to ask help from Princess Caroline and it came – not as they had been accustomed to receiving help from royalty, not an impersonal steward distributing a few comforts at Christmas time, but with genuine interest. It did one good, many had said, to see the Princess Caroline come into a humble room and take a child upon her knees.

She never did so without saying to herself: 'Oh, if only I had a child of my own.'

Caroline cannot go to the ball

The months flew by – one year, two years. There was little news from Charlotte, except that she had given birth to a child. Lucky Charlotte!

'*When* will there be a suitor for me?' Caroline demanded not only of the Baroness de Bode but of her older governess, Baroness von Münster.

'When the time is ripe your parents will answer that question,' replied the Baroness von Münster.

'Then I pray it may be soon,' replied Caroline, and was silent, for she dare not bait the elderly Baroness as she did poor Madame de Bode.

To the latter she remarked that if her parents did not provide a husband for her soon she would have to find one for herself.

John Thomas Stanley was no longer at the Court. In any case she had not been seriously concerned with him. She began to look about her. There was the young Count Walmoden who had royal blood in his veins because his grandmother had been the famous mistress of George II of England. And there was another descendant of George II, the Count von Schulemberg, who was reputed to be very rich indeed, having inherited some of the vast wealth which Ermengarda von Schulemberg, Duchess of Kendal, had amassed during her long reign as king's favourite.

Would such young men be considered suitable consorts? Of course not. How exasperating to be a princess and have to *wait* until a husband was chosen for one! If she were a commoner – not like the people in the cottages, of course, but a baroness like Madame de Bode – she could go to the ball next week and perhaps there meet a man, fall in love, marry and have children. What bliss!

The Baroness de Bode decided that she must really speak to someone about Princess Caroline, and that meant of course speaking to Madame de Hertzfeldt. The Duchess was too vague; moreover she was English and somewhat at odds with her children's governesses because she was constantly reiterating that they should be educated in the English way, which seemed absurd. How could the Princess be educated in the English manner without English tutors? And of what use would such an education be since she was German? And what, the Baroness asked herself, *was* the English method of education? If the Duchess was an example of it, then, for the sake of the Princess, she should be educated as a German.

What a household, where one must speak to the father's mistress rather than the mother of one's charge! But there was no help for it and no matter how resentful a good and somewhat puritanical woman like the Baroness de Bode felt when contemplating the situation, in the presence of Madame de Hertzfeldt she could have nothing but respect for that lady.

She was granted an audience immediately, for Madame de Hertzfeldt considered the bringing-up of the Duke's daughter a matter of great importance.

'I am disturbed, Madame, by the Princess Caroline,' began the Baroness.

Madame de Hertzfeldt sighed. Were they not all disturbed by the royal children?

'She speaks constantly of marriage . . . men and children.'

'It has been so since the Princess Charlotte married?'

'Yes, Madame.'

'She is now approaching the age her sister was when she married.'

'That's true, Madame, and I am a little fearful. I was wondering whether her freedom should be restricted a little.'

Madame de Hertzfeldt was thoughtful. One would have to go very carefully. She said: 'Thank you, Baroness. This is a matter of some importance. I will speak of it to the Duchess.'

The Baroness retired, knowing that the admirable Madame de Hertzfeldt would speak to the Duke and together they would decide what should be done; then they would give the Duchess her instructions as to what orders she was to make known to the Princess's governess.

It was, of course, admitted the Baroness, the discretion one would have expected from Madame de Hertzfeldt and this discretion was no doubt the reason why she reigned supreme in the Court of Brunswick.

'Not go to the ball,' cried Caroline, her eyes flashing. 'And why, pray?'

'Because,' replied the Baroness, 'it is decided that you shall not go. You are too young as yet to go to balls.'

'I . . . too young . . . when I have been at balls since before Charlotte's marriage. Am I growing younger then, Madam, that I have suddenly become too young?'

The Baroness said that there was no point in discussing the matter further for the orders had come to her and she had obeyed them.

'So my mother has decided this, has she?'

'It has been decided,' replied the Baroness.

'Stop talking like a silly old oracle. I tell you I will go to the ball . . . I will . . . I will . . .'

When Caroline talked like that she was really alarming; her eyes seemed to grow black and her face flushed scarlet.

There was nothing the Baroness could do but leave her.

*

Caroline lay on her bed biting her fists in fury. 'I must go to the ball,' she murmured. 'Perhaps tonight will be the most import-ant night in my life. Perhaps tonight I shall meet my lover. I will go to the ball. I *will*. Why should they stop me? There is Char-lotte – married at sixteen. And I am nearly sixteen and not allowed to go to the ball. I won't have it. I won't.'

But what could she do? The realization of the futility of this increased her anger. I have no ball dress? Nonsense. Nonsense. I'd wear an old one. I'd go in anything – I'd go as Aphrodite. I'd go as anybody . . .

The laughter started to bubble up, uncontrollable laughter. Imagine her entering the ballroom as Aphrodite. She would demand they announce her. 'My lords and ladies, the Princess Caroline is unable to attend owing to parental tyranny and in her place Aphrodite has risen from the sea . . . to attend the ball.'

And there she would be – stark naked. Imagine her mother's face!

'Oh, my dear, how shocked they will be at the English Court if they hear of this!'

And why? she would like to know. Cousin George, Prince of Wales, was rather a shocking young gentleman himself. He, too, chafed against restrictions. How frustrating parents were! How they spoilt their children's lives!

No, even she could not do such a thing. But she would do something. Her invention would not desert her. She would think of a way of punishing them for not allowing her to go to the ball.

From her window Caroline saw the carriages. The people had lined the streets to see the guests arrive in their splendid gowns and glittering jewels. One of the most elaborate balls ever given at the ducal palace and the Princess Caroline not there to enjoy it!

She pictured her father and mother at the head of the great staircase receiving their guests. Deep curtsies; sweeping bows; and in command – Madame de Hertzfeldt, whom everyone would know was the *real* hostess; and if they wanted any favours it was to the mistress they must go, not to the wife.

And she, Caroline, should have been there, standing beside her parents, receiving the bows and the curtsies – homage due to the daughter of the house.

None of the children would be there. She and Frederick William were the only ones who could be, and Frederick William certainly was a little young.

'But I am sixteen,' she cried. 'It is cruel and wicked to stop me from going to the ball. And I'll make them sorry for this.'

She started to laugh, contemplating the plan which had been in her mind all day. She had felt it was far more workable than the Aphrodite one and would cause them even more distress. And serve them right!

Her father would now be opening the ball. Now was the moment. She undressed, flinging her clothes about the room; then she took a pot of paste from her cupboard and smeared it over her face. The effect made her chuckle. It was horrible. It made her look like a ghost. She raised her eyes in an expression of agony. Wonderful! She looked like a girl about to breathe her last.

She got into bed and began to scream.

Two of her serving maids came running in. 'I ... I think I am going to die,' she said. 'Pray ... go ... quickly. Bring the Duke and the Duchess.'

Her maids stared at her as she fell back on her pillows, making queer rattling noises in her throat. Terrified, they ran off.

Caroline pictured the scene in the ballroom: the frightened maids appearing suddenly, forgetting all etiquette in view of the startling news they had to convey.

'Oh, my God,' said the Duchess, and looked as if she would faint.

But the Duke was beside her. 'We will go to her at once.' He glanced at Madame de Hertzfeldt who could always be relied on in a crisis.

As they hastily left the ballroom he heard her explaining to the guests that the Princess Caroline was indisposed and that this was the reason for the temporary absence of the ducal pair.

The whole ballroom was abuzz with the news. The Princess Caroline taken suddenly ill. What an unfortunate family. Those three boys . . .

Meanwhile in Caroline's bedroom her parents were gazing in dismay at her livid features distorted into an expression of agony.

'My child!' cried the Duchess. 'Where is the pain? Pray tell us – if you can.'

Caroline could scarcely keep back her mirth.

'I – I cannot hide it any longer,' she said. 'I – I am in labour. Pray send at once for an *accoucheur*.'

'Oh my God!' cried the Duchess again.

The Duke had turned pale. 'It is not possible—'

'Yes, yes,' cried Caroline. 'I fear so. I am about to give birth to my child . . . and if you do not send for an *accoucheur* immediately I shall die . . . and the child with me.'

The Duke turned to the Duchess. 'Get one . . .' he said. 'For God's sake call the *accoucheur*.'

Caroline groaned and cried: 'My pains . . . they are coming fast. Make haste . . .'

The Duchess turned, but she did not have to speak. The maids who had been hovering in the doorway immediately ran to fetch an *accoucheur*.

It was impossible to keep such a fact secret. All the guests were aware that the *accoucheur* had been sent for that he might attend the Princess Caroline, who was in labour.

What a shocking affair! How unlucky the Duke was in his family! Those idiot boys . . . the blind one . . . and now the Princess Caroline was about to present the Duke and Duchess with an illegitimate grandchild. If she could have done so secretly – well, this kind of misadventure was not so uncommon – but during a ball, so that all the guests should know! What a spicy piece of gossip! No wonder they could talk of nothing else. Indeed they would remember this ball all their lives.

Madame de Hertzfeldt heard the talk but what could she do? She had not a chance. If she could have prevented the news seeping out she would have done so, but it was too late.

27

It was not possible to continue with the ball while the Princess was in her apartments giving birth, and the whole Court knew it.

With dignity Madame de Herztfeldt addressed the company. The ball could not go on, she explained, owing to the indisposition of the Princess Caroline.

So the guests departed and Madame de Hertzfeldt went at once to the Princess's bedroom.

There an extraordinary scene greeted her.

The *accoucheur* had arrived and when he prepared to examine the Princess she had leaped out of bed, wiped the paste from her face which then appeared to be its natural colour and began dancing round the bedchamber.

Then she came and bowed low before her mother.

'That, Madam,' she announced, 'will teach you to keep me from another ball.'

What could one do with the Princess Caroline?

Could she be punished? In what way?

The Duke and Madame de Hertzfeldt discussed the matter at great length.

'A whipping?' suggested the Duke.

But Madame de Hertzfeldt was unsure. With unbalanced characters sometimes corporal punishment could be dangerous.

She must soothe the Duke though. 'She is too high-spirited,' she said. 'I think we must try to understand . . .'

'You mean,' replied the Duke sombrely, 'that we must remember her brothers.'

'I am sure,' answered Madame de Hertzfeldt, 'that Caroline is good at heart. She has a bright intelligence; she has wit. Her spirits are too high most certainly and she is a little . . . eccentric. But it is no more. Oh, my dear, let us do all in our power to see that it does not *become* more.'

The Duke gave his mistress a grateful look.

'I shall leave it to you,' he said. 'Perhaps you will discover how best to treat her and advise the Duchess.'

And he thought once more: What should we do without her?

*

Caroline was overcome with glee and thought with pleasure of that incident for months afterwards. She forgot that the guests had all been aware that on the night of the ball an *accoucheur* had come to the palace to attend her.

'Of course,' said rumour, 'we have not been told the truth. The *accoucheur* came to deliver a child which naturally was smuggled out of the palace.'

Others, who were sure that there had not been a child and the whole affair had been arranged by Caroline as a protest, were certain that she had not escaped the family taint of madness.

So the rumours had begun in earnest. Caroline, Princess of Brunswick, was either the mother of an illegitimate child or she was mad.

Caroline in love

The Princess Caroline was past twenty and still unmarried. The Prince of Orange had been a possible choice and so had the Prince of Prussia. But Caroline, who had been so eager for marriage, decided against them for she had made up her mind that when she married it would be for love.

There had been strange and mystifying news of her sister Charlotte. No one at Brunswick was quite sure what had happened to Charlotte, but Caroline's dramatic imagination supplied her with violent pictures.

Where was Charlotte? She was at the Court of Russia where her husband had left her, and he had taken her three children from her. To be deprived of her children! thought Caroline. What a bitter tragedy! And why had Charlotte allowed that to happen? Because she was powerless to stop it, was the answer.

Charlotte had been an unfaithful wife, it was said. That was possible. Her husband had put her under the care of the Empress Catherine of Russia, that woman whose amours were notorious throughout Europe. And Charlotte had simply disappeared.

How she would like to go to Russia, to discover what had happened to her sister, to travel and be adventurous! But all the same the affair of Charlotte made one wary of undertaking a marriage which would send one among strangers far from home.

She told her father so when they walked together in the grounds about the palace, for as she grew older so did the affection between them strengthen and he was the only member of the household with whom she could discuss her innermost thoughts. Her mother was a silly woman, she decided, and although she accepted the virtues of Madame de Hertzfeldt, the fact of her supremacy in the household did make an uneasy position, in spite of the fact that none of them knew what they would do without her. If Madame de Hertzfeldt had been the Duchess and her mother, then she could have confided in both her parents. Moreover, with such a mother might she not have been more serene, more what they called balanced? Who could say? But there was her father, and when he was not away from home fighting his battles under the command of his friend and patron, Frederick the Great, or was not engaged on state matters at home, he had time for his daughter. The only son who could possibly rule after him was learning his business as a soldier, and Caroline was like an only daughter now that Charlotte had gone.

He often brooded on the boys living out their lives in darkness; on Charlotte who, he was certain, had been murdered in Russia; and asked himself why he and his futile wife had produced such a brood. Then he turned to gay, lovely and pretty Caroline – for in his eyes she possessed all these qualities – and told himself that at least he had this daughter. And since that affair of the *accoucheur* she had become less wild. He had been the one who had explained to her the folly of such actions and how they grieved him, and he was a little comforted to see that it was the latter which had made most impression on her.

She had put her hand shyly in his – for in spite of all her bravado she was a little afraid of him – and had said: 'Papa, I would not wish to make you sad.'

When he had reported this scene later to Madame de Hertz-feldt she had been pleased, and said that the way to mould Caroline was through affection and it was her father who could guide her because there was no doubt that she loved and admired him; and what was perhaps most important of all, respected him.

So when her father sent for her and told her that the Prince of Orange was asking for her hand in marriage she went quietly away and considered all she had heard of the Prince of Orange and decided against the match. Then she returned to explain her feelings to her father. 'I wish to be married,' she explained, 'but I do not wish to be unhappy as my sister must have been. There is much unhappiness in marriage and I would approach it very cautiously.'

'That's a wise attitude, I have to admit,' replied her father.

'Dear Papa,' she went on, 'he would have to be a very at-tractive bridegroom to make me want to leave you.'

Yes, he had succeeded with her through affection. He had a nightmare picture of her being forced into marriage. What dis-aster would that bring forth? He dared not speculate for he believed that his unwelcome marriage was the reason why he had three afflicted children. They had found the way to treat Caroline: affection, restraint only when necessary and applied with the gentlest hands, and just a dash of fear – or perhaps respect would be a more apt description. In any case, the Duke had inspired her with enough admiration and affection to be able to guide her.

'My dearest daughter,' he told her, 'I want you to know that I shall never force you into marriage. You shall only go away from home if you wish it.'

He was rewarded by her response.

'Dearest Papa, you put me in a quandary. I wish to marry. Above all I wish to have children. Yet I know I shall never wish to leave you.'

'You will one day. It is natural for you to marry. The day will come. But I want you to know that you will never be forced to accept a marriage which is distasteful to you.'

Oh, yes, it was certainly right. There was a rare softness in her eyes subduing the habitual wildness. This was the way to treat Caroline. And they must employ this method or they would have another tragedy like Charlotte's.

So she declined the Princes of Orange and Prussia.

The Duchess was excited and came to her daughter's apartments to tell her why. Caroline's servants were there but the Duchess never worried about servants; she looked upon them as though they were pieces of furniture, and it never occurred to her that they possessed ears and tongues and might be as fond of gossip as she was herself.

'What do you think, Caroline? My nephew is coming to Brunswick.'

'Not . . . the Prince of Wales!'

'Oh, how I wish that were so! Not quite . . . my dear. But the next best thing. His brother, the Duke of York. I am most excited.'

'Oh, Mamma, you think everything English is better than anything else.'

'So it is! So it is! If I could only make you *see* the Court . . . Not so much as my brother made his but my grandfather's Court. Everything would have been so different if my father had not died before he could come to the throne. Just think of it, Caroline, now I am the daughter of a Prince of Wales whereas I might have been the daughter of a King.'

'Well, Mamma, you were of the same family.'

'Not quite the same, Caroline. Not quite the same. And oh – the intrigue that went on. My mother and – er – her friend on one side . . . the King on the other.'

'Tell me about your mother's . . . friend, Mamma.'

'I certainly shall not.'

'There is no need really so I'm happy to relieve you of the necessity. I know already. Lord Bute became the lover of the Princess of Wales after the Prince died.'

'Where do you hear such wicked scandals?' demanded the Duchess.

Caroline smiled demurely. 'From you, Mamma.'

The Duchess made an impatient sound with her lips. 'Oh, everything here is so *drab*. So different from England. One must enliven the days if only with memories. I was a person of some account in England, Caroline.'

Caroline regarded her mother quizzically. Was she? Could she ever have been? Caroline had a picture of her mother, the Princess Royal of England, vainly attempting to meddle in Court politics – ineffectually of course. Caroline softened towards her mother then and hoped that she would never be like her. Of course she would not. She would be like her father – a Brunswicker with a lion in her heart.

'Mamma,' she said gently, 'you were telling me about the Duke of York.'

'Oh, yes, he is coming here to see us. He is a great soldier, you know, and has been distinguishing himself on the Continent. He is a year younger than the Prince of Wales and I have had letters from my brother about him.'

'That, Mamma, must have made you very happy – to have letters from the King of England.'

'Very gratifying. It may well be, Caroline, that His Majesty is sending his son here for a purpose.'

Caroline nodded. She was on her feet, parading about the room, and turning to her mother she curtsied. Then she strolled about looking over her shoulder at the Duchess. 'Will I suit, Sir Duke? Am I worthy to be the consort of a Duke?' Then with an English accent: 'We will see. We will see. I am an English Duke, do not forget. My brother is the Prince of Wales.' She pretended to take a quizzing glass from her pocket and held it up, continuing to make comments in that voice with the ridiculous English accent.

Caroline was almost choking with laughter but the Duchess was not amused.

'Stop it, Caroline. You are most – most – improper.'

But Caroline would not stop. She was carrying on with this ridiculous charade in a manner which clearly showed her mounting hysteria.

Oh dear, thought the Duchess. I cannot manage her. If the Hertzfeldt woman were here now what would she do?

'Caroline,' she said sharply, 'stop it. If you go on like this you will never get a man to marry you.'

It was evidently the right thing to have said for Caroline

stopped and looked at her mother, and seizing her opportunity the Duchess went on: 'You are not so very young now that you can afford to play these childish games. I think you should be a little interested in your cousin's visit.'

Caroline had suddenly seen herself growing old at the Court of Brunswick. The eccentric Princess Caroline! And she was wise enough to know that those antics which in the young could be viewed with tolerance and considered amusing, in the middle-aged would be boring, eccentric and perhaps mad.

She did not want to stay at Brunswick all her life. She wanted to see the world; and she would never do that if she remained unmarried living always in her father's Court.

Her mother was right. She should be interested in the arrival of the Duke of York.

'What do you know of him?' she asked.

'That he is very handsome and attractive, has distinguished himself on the field of battle, is amusing, clever and witty.'

'He sounds like a god rather than a cousin.'

'I am sure you will think him so,' said the Duchess triumphantly.

So it was what they wanted, thought Caroline. They were hoping for a match. Marriage with the Duke of York. One would go to England, her mother's country of which she talked as though it were some El Dorado – and yet her mother had not been nearly so happy living there as she had believed herself to be when she left it. That's natural enough, thought Caroline, for that's how life always seems.

Yes, she would like to see England. She would like to see Uncle George, who had always seemed to be led by the nose by his mother and that lover of hers – and Aunt Charlotte who was the villainess because her sister-in-law, now Duchess of Brunswick, had so disliked her.

'Tell me about them, Mamma,' she said. 'Tell me about the King and the Queen.'

'It is long since I saw them,' said the Duchess comfortably, because there was nothing she enjoyed like a gossip and a gossip of the old days was the best kind. 'George was really quite handsome – in his way. Fair hair, blue eyes, rather heavy jaw and kind – very kind. He always wanted to please everyone. He was very startled when he found himself King of England. Grandpapa, of course, was very old and Papa was dead so George was the next in the line of succession, of course, but we all thought Grandpapa would go on and on. Then one day he went into his closet and died instantly. And so George was king and he was exactly twenty-two – not much older than you.'

'Was he pleased, do you think?'

'Pleased! He was terrified. He wouldn't move a step without Mamma and Lord Bute. Of course there was a real scandal about *that* affair. They used to call him the Scotch Stallion. The people hated him. They jeered at him when he went out in his carriage. In fact there was a time when they actually tried to do him a mischief. But Mamma was faithful to him for years . . .'

Caroline looked slyly at her mother. Trust the Duchess to explain everything which a moment before she had suggested it was improper to discuss. One could wheedle anything out of Mamma, thought Caroline, provided one employed the right tactics.

'The Scotch Stallion,' cried Caroline, suddenly unable to restrain her mirth. 'I like that. I like that very much.'

'My dear Caroline, I beg of you! You should not speak of such things. What next I wonder.'

'And what of Queen Charlotte, Mamma? Tell me about her.'

'A horrid creature. I disliked her on sight. Little and thin – very thin. Such a flat nose . . . such a big mouth. Really she looked like a crocodile. She should have been humble . . . very humble. To come from a little court like Mecklenburg-Strelitz to marry the King of England.'

'It was rather like Brunswick-Wolfenbüttel, I expect, was it not, Mamma?'

The Duchess looked cautiously at her daughter. 'Yes, but smaller,' she said. 'Of less consequence. And we soon made her realize this. I reported her actions to my mother, and we soon put her in her place. I remember an occasion when she did not want to wear her jewels to church and we made her. It was symbolic, you see. If she had had her way about that, she would have tried to exert her power over the King in more important ways. Sometimes I wondered whether it wouldn't have been better to have let him have Sarah Lennox after all. Oh dear, he was *mad* for Sarah Lennox. You would call her a pretty creature. But flighty. And that has been proved. She left Bunbury, you know. For she married Bunbury when she knew she could not have George. And there was a child – not her husband's. Most scandalous. And that was Sarah Lennox for you. And meanwhile everyone said Charlotte might be a dull, plain little German *hausfrau*, but she was fertile – oh, very fertile. Fifteen children. Just imagine! No sooner is one delivered than she is pregnant again. Serve her right. It was all she was fit for.'

'I should like to have fifteen children. I wonder if I ever shall.'

'You will have to get married soon to have so many.' The Duchess laughed suddenly. 'There has to be a small breathing space between, you know. Not that Charlotte asked for much. Or perhaps George wouldn't let her.'

They laughed together – the Duchess maliciously, Caroline wildly.

'Thirteen of them left, because they lost Octavius and Alfred. Thirteen out of fifteen is not a bad score though, is it? Thirteen. Very nice. Seven of them sons. Oh, yes, Charlotte provided the right proportion. Nine boys there were and two boys dead makes seven, does it not? Seven husbands for seven princesses.'

'So Queen Charlotte was a benefactor to mankind after all,' commented Caroline. 'To royal mankind anyway. Just imagine all the princesses who would have had to go without husbands if she had not so zealously done her duty.'

Caroline began to laugh; and the Duchess was always disconcerted – as everyone else was – by that too-wild laughter.

'It is something for you to remember,' said the Duchess severely. 'And now the second son is coming to see us. Frederick, Duke of York! I confess it is a long time since I was so excited.'

'How much more excited you would have been, Mamma, if it had been the first son, the Prince of Wales.'

'Well, my daughter, we cannot hope for miracles. The Prince of Wales would never be allowed to leave England. If ever it should come to pass . . .'

'You mean if a miracle should come to pass, Mamma?'

The Duchess looked sternly at her daughter. 'When the Prince of Wales decides to marry, it will be the King's envoy who conveys the news to his chosen bride's family.'

Again that demure look crossed Caroline's features. 'Well, Mamma, I will endeavour to be duly excited by the proposed visit – but not too excited because it is only Uncle George's second son, and he is coming himself. Now if it were Uncle George's envoy instead of his son I should be capering with glee, should I not?'

'Caroline, sometimes your talk is most improper.'

'I own it,' said Caroline. She wanted to add: 'It is a trait I have inherited from my dear Mamma.' But that would be unwise. To let the Duchess know how indiscreet she was might put a curb on conversations such as this which could mean that Caroline might become far less knowledgeable about the scandals of Europe.

The Duchess looked pleased. 'Remember it,' she said sternly. 'And as soon as the Duke of York arrives you should greet him with charm and . . . propriety.'

Caroline was thoughtful when she left the Duchess. A possible suitor? This was clearly what her parents and Madame de Hertzfeldt had in mind. Well, she would inspect the young man and if she did not like him she would not have him. Had not her father said that she would never be forced into marriage?

Crossing the courtyard she paused to watch the soldiers on duty. How smart they looked in their uniforms. She was sure Cousin Frederick of York would not be half as handsome as the soldier who was now coming towards her.

He saluted.

'Good day,' said Caroline in the familiar manner in which she spoke to everyone.

'Good day, Your Highness.'

'It *is* a good day.' She smiled up at him. 'Are you often on duty here, er—'

'I am Major von Töbingen at Your Highness's service.'

'At my service, that is nice; and a little reckless, Major von Töbingen, for what if I should *ask* a service of you?'

'It would be the greatest pleasure of my life to render it.'

What charm! thought Caroline. And he looked so earnest, as though he really meant it.

'I shall remember that,' she told him; and she walked on, but when she had gone a few paces she paused to look over her shoulder. He was looking after her.

She laughed and ran into the palace.

'Major von Töbingen,' she said aloud. 'A delightful man. I'll swear he's far more handsome than the Duke of York.'

When the Duke arrived Caroline continued to think so. By that time she had had many conversations with Major von Töbingen. In fact she was beginning to make plans which included him. She thought what delightful children he would have – that was if they grew up to look and behave as he did.

The Duke of York was a tolerably good-looking young man, a little arrogant. Were all the English arrogant? she wondered. He was light-hearted, gay and ready for a flirtation with his cousin Caroline, but she suspected that he might not wish it to go beyond that.

She liked him moderately. Perhaps if she did not constantly compare him with Major von Töbingen she might have considered him as a husband, for after all if she were going to get her big family, as her mother said, she must not delay too long.

When he found that she was not prepared to treat him as a potential lover, the Duke was philosophically resigned; one might say relieved. His cousin Caroline was not ill-looking; she was bright enough; but she did not appeal to him as a wife or mistress. He was longing to get back to England; he had been away a long time but when he thought of Englishwomen they seemed so much more desirable than any he had met on his travels.

He had a clear memory of Mrs Robinson, the very handsome young actress with whom his brother, George, had been in love. What a goddess she had seemed! And he had left England before that affair had come to its conclusion.

He often laughed to think of George in love, for when George fell in love he did so wholeheartedly. He remembered how he had accompanied his brother out into the gardens at Kew to that spot where Essex – who was then Lord Malden – had brought the beautiful actress, George's Perdita. And there George and she had embraced under the trees while he kept watch on one side and Malden and Perdita's lady's maid on the other. What a creature Mrs Robinson was! He had not seen anyone to touch her for beauty since he had left England. And the lady's maid was a beauty, too. He was longing to be back; and he hoped before very long he would be. Why should he be exiled from home just because the King thought that a Guelph should take his training in a German army? But one must be fair to the old man. There was fighting on the Continent and that gave him a chance to take part in a real battle. But oh, how he longed to go home and talk to his brother George and find out what he was doing now. For of one thing he could be sure, the Prince of Wales would be doing something exciting.

How much truth was there in this rumour that he had married a Mrs Fitzherbert? If he had ... by God, there would be trouble. But there always would be trouble around George. That was the one thing he could be sure of. Oh, indeed, what joy to be home, to share his brother's adventures, to be on those old terms of intimacy. For George was his friend as no one else ever could be.

And now here he was at the Court of Brunswick. Aunt Augusta was not in the least like her brother. In fact, Frederick was sure his father would heartily disapprove of his sister. He always had; but at the same time the King felt that his niece, the Princess Caroline, should be the wife of one of his sons.

Not this one, thought Frederick. I should soon tire of Madame Caroline. And she would never make a docile wife. Still, it amused him to ride with her, talk with her, dance with her – in fact behave towards her as a very good cousin.

She wanted to hear about England; and as they rode out with a party he would bring her horse close to his and talk to her.

Did they ride much in England? she wanted to know.

'All the time. I reckon we have some of the finest horses in the world.'

Trust them, thought Caroline. They had the finest everything.

'And your brothers and sisters – they enjoy riding?'

'My brother, the Prince of Wales, is devoted to the exercise. Not only does he ride but he drives his own phaeton and carriages. He is said to be one of the best horsemen in the country.'

'People will pay royalty such compliments.'

'What do you mean, cousin?'

'That princes and princesses are always the best this and that. They only have to have one good feature and they are beautiful. Take me, for instance. I have been called the beautiful Princess of Brunswick. What do you think of that?'

'That is not untrue.'

'Courtier!' she laughed. 'You don't mean it. You think I am just tolerable as a cousin. Oh, do not think, Master York, that I am inviting flirtation. I am not. If I wished to flirt there are many ready to oblige.'

'I am sure of that.'

'And I should not wish to bother my lord Duke, and even if he felt so disposed I might discourage him.'

'How unkind!'

She laughed aloud. 'Very glib. And I have no more desire to marry you than you have to marry me. So set yourself at ease on that score.'

'Marriage?' gasped the Duke.

'Let us be honest. Whenever the son of a king visits a princess the intention is always there. Your visit, sir, is in the nature of an inspection. I am not asking you to deny this. I am only putting your mind at rest.'

She whipped up her horse and rode on; the Duke stared after her. What a strange creature! What did she mean? Was she coquettish? Was she chiding him for not making advances or warning him off lest he did? He attempted to follow her; then he saw her making for a tall soldier on horseback.

She joined him; she threw a glance over her shoulder at the Duke. Nothing could have told him more clearly that she had no wish for him to join them.

The Duke fell back and rode with the rest of the party. Life was conducted in a very strange manner at the Court of

Brunswick, he thought, and the strangest part of it was the behaviour of the Princess Caroline.

A messenger arrived from England with letters and a package for the Duke of York and to his astonishment, when he opened the packet, he found a necklace and ear-rings set with splendid diamonds.

The Duke read the letter which accompanied them and which was signed by his father.

The King thought that the Duke of York might wish to make a present to his cousin Caroline and for this purpose he had sent him the diamonds.

The Duke looked at them speculatively for some minutes. He took out the necklace and examined the stones. To give them to Caroline would be tantamount to making her an offer of marriage. So that was clearly what the old man had in mind. It was quite out of the question. He had no desire to marry her. Moreover, he might well be refused and that would not please the King. Would she be allowed to refuse an offer from England? She had hinted in one or two of the conversations that her father had told her she should never be forced into marriage.

He shook his head, put the necklace back into its case and carefully rewrapped the package.

He sat down and thought of returning home and the kind of woman to whom he would present the necklace. He fancied she would be rather like Mrs Robinson; and she would be English.

The Duke of York had left the Court of Brunswick. Many shook their heads. Was Caroline going to reject all her hopes of marriage? What a strange girl she was! It seemed very likely that she would never marry at all.

Caroline knew they whispered of her. 'Let him go,' she said to the Baroness de Bode. 'He's a pleasant enough young man but not for me.'

The Baroness said: 'He is the son of the King of England.'

Caroline pouted. 'The second son.'

'Good heavens, is Your Highness hoping for the Prince of Wales?'

Caroline turned away with a laugh. Let them think so. Let them imagine her to be ambitious. She was ambitious . . . for a home with the man she loved and a large family of happy children.

And she was in love.

Under cover of dusk she slipped out to meet her Major. He was a little alarmed – for her, of course. He had declared frequently that he did not care what happened to him.

'Silly man,' she cried fondly. 'My father understands me. He knows he could never force me into marriage. He will let me marry where I will.'

Then if this was so why not disclose their plans to the Duke? That was what Caroline thought; but Major von Töbingen begged her to keep their secret a little longer.

She gave way. But, she warned him, not for long.

He was there waiting in the shadows – tall, mysterious in his long cloak.

She threw herself into his arms and hugged him in the unrestrained manner which while it delighted him alarmed him too.

'I have a present for you, my dearest,' she said. 'It's a token.'

She gave him the large amethyst pin which she had had made for him from one of her rings.

'I shall expect you to wear it . . . always,' she told him.

She began to talk rapidly of the future. She would speak to her father and they would be married.

'It will never be,' he told her in despair. 'They will never allow a princess to marry a mere soldier.'

'A mere soldier! You – a mere soldier! There is nothing mere about you. I love you, do you hear. I love you. That means that my father will give his consent.'

He whispered that they must speak quietly or they would be overheard.

'Let them hear!' Her voice rang out. 'What does it matter? I want the whole Court to know. Why should they not? *I* have made up my mind.'

She was exuberant and impatient. Marriage with her Major would be perfect bliss, she told him.

'Children – do you want children? But of course you do. Dear little children. All our own. Every time I go to the village to see my adopted ones I say to myself: "They are lovely. I adore them. But soon I shall have little ones of my own." I cannot wait. Why should I? I am no longer a child. I must speak to my father. I must. I must. I *will*.'

But he begged her to wait a little longer and because she loved him she agreed.

Major von Töbingen was seen to wear a big amethyst pin. Sometimes his fingers would stray to it and linger there lovingly. The Princess Caroline constantly contrived to be where he was; and her eyes were seen to rest on the pin. It is her gift to him, was the general comment.

It was impossible not to be aware of the Princess's emotions. She had never been one to hide them at any time; and Caroline in love was at her most emotional.

How like the Princess to reject the Princes of Orange and Prussia and show the Duke of York quite clearly that she had no wish to marry him – and then to fall besottedly in love with a major in the Army.

The rumours grew fast. She was already with child, it was whispered. Well, it wouldn't be the first time. That other occasion was recalled when during a ball an *accoucheur* had to be called to the palace.

A fresh scandal was about to break.

Madame de Hertzfeldt consulted with the Duke and as a result one day not very long after she had presented him with the amethyst pin Caroline went to their usual trysting place where she waited in vain for her Major.

He had gone, and when she had demanded of his fellow officers where he was they could not tell her. He had been there one morning and by afternoon had disappeared. There was simply no trace of him.

She had stamped her foot; she had raged. 'Where? Where? Where?' she had cried.

But they could not help her.

One of them suggested that her father the Duke might be able to explain.

She went to her father's apartments. Madame de Herztfeldt was with him – and they were expecting her.

'My dear child—' began her father and would have put his arms about her but she cried out: 'Where is Major von Töbingen?'

'Major von Töbingen's duties have taken him away,' said the Duke gently.

'What duties? Where?'

The Duke looked surprised. Even his dear daughter could not speak to him in that manner.

'Suffice it that he is no longer with us.'

'No longer with us. I tell you I shall not be satisfied with that. I want to know where he is. I want him brought back. I am going to marry him. Nothing ... nothing ... *nothing* ... is going to stop me.'

The Duke looked at Madame de Hertzfeldt who said gently: 'Caroline, you must realize that a princess cannot marry without the approval of her family.'

'I know nothing of other princesses. I only know what I myself will do. I will marry Major von Töbingen.'

The Duke said: 'No, my dear, you will not.'

She turned on him. 'You said that I should not be forced to marry against my will.'

'I did; and you shall not be. But I did not give you permission to marry without my consent.'

'So you have sent him away.'

'Caroline,' said Madame de Hertzfeldt, 'it was the only thing we could do.'

'The only thing *you* could do. And who are you, Madame, to govern me? Be silent. If I have to listen to my father I will not to you. I shall not stay here.' She began to pace the room. She was like a tigress, thought Madame de Hertzfeldt. How peaceful we should be if she would marry and go away from the Court.

The Duke was about to protest when Madame de Hertzfeldt signed to him not to do so on her account. She was sure that they must try to reason with Caroline gently. She was always afraid on occasions like this that Caroline's delicately poised mind would overbalance and she knew what great grief this would bring to the Duke.

The Duke said: 'You must have realized the unsuitability of such a match.'

'It is suitable because we love each other. What more suitable? Would you have me make a marriage such as yours? Would you give me a mate whom I must despise as you do yours?'

The Duke clenched his hands. She was shouting and he knew that her words would be overheard.

'Don't try to silence me. You have taken my lover from me. He is good and kind and handsome . . . but that would not do. You would marry me to some ill-formed monstrosity – just because he is a royal. That would be suitable – suitable – suitable . . .'

Madame de Hertzfeldt had slipped out of the room. The Duke guessed that it was to take some action. In the meantime he tried to quieten his daughter.

'Caroline, I will not have you shout in this manner. I will have you remember your place here. If I cared I could arrange a marriage for you entirely of my choosing. Do not imagine that because I have so far been lenient with you I shall continue to be so. So much depends on your own conduct.'

That quietened her. It was true she was a little afraid of him. She did realize that she owed her free way of life to him; that she was not treated as so many princesses in her position would have been.

'Papa,' she said. 'I love him.'

'I know, my dear, but it could not be. You must realize that.'

'Why not? It seems so senseless. Why should we have to be made unhappy when we could be happy, when we could have healthy children and bring them up in a happy home.'

'It is the penalty of royalty.'

'But we ourselves make those penalties! Why? Why? Why cannot we be free? Why do we pen ourselves in with our misery merely to preserve our silly royalty?'

'Pray do not speak in that way, daughter.'

'So I may not even speak as I will!' Her eyes flashed with sudden rage. 'I will not endure this treatment, I tell you. I will make my own life. I will go and find him – I will renounce your precious royalty for the sake of love.'

Madame de Hertzfeldt had returned; she was carrying a cup.

'Caroline,' she said, 'you know you have my sympathy. Pray do as I say.'

'What is that?'

'Drink this. It will help you to sleep for a while. You are distraught; and when you have recovered a little from this shock you may talk with your father.'

For a moment it seemed as though Caroline would dash the cup out of Madame de Hertzfeldt's hand; then that tactful woman said: 'You will feel calmer. You may be able to convert him to your ideas – or even accept his.'

The hopelessness of her situation was brought home to Caroline. The walls of the apartment seemed to close in upon her. Shut in, she thought, imprisoned in royalty.

The Princess Caroline was ill. She would eat nothing; she could not sleep. She lay hollow-eyed in her bed.

She had received a letter from Major von Töbingen in which he said goodbye to her. He begged her to accept their separation which in his heart he had known was inevitable from the beginning. She must not try to find him, for even if she did – which was not possible – he could not marry her. To do so would be an act of treason; she must realize that. He would never forget her. He would love her until he died. If she would occasionally think of him with tenderness that was all he would ask of life.

She wept bitterly over the letter and kept it under her pillow to read again and again. The dream of love and marriage with the man of her choice was over. She was listless; and they feared for her life.

It gave her a savage pleasure to see their concern. Her father came to her room each day; he was very tender. If there was anything she wished for – except that one thing which was all she wanted – she might have it.

'Nothing, nothing,' she murmured and turned her face to the wall.

But she was grieved to see his unhappiness. He had been a good father to her, and she loved him.

For his sake she ate a little and tried to feel resigned. And after a while she was well enough to leave her bed.

The Duke suggested a change of scene and she left Court for a while, and when she returned she was a little more like her old exuberant self.

But when Prince George of Darmstadt made an offer for her hand she refused him.

'Although I am not allowed to choose,' she said firmly, 'at least I am permitted to reject.'

The miracle

She was twenty-six. It was said of her: 'She will never marry now.'

She began to think so herself. She was often in the houses of her father's subjects; if a new baby was about to be born she expressed great interest, and each day she drove out to visit 'her children'.

She often thought of Major von Töbingen and wondered whether he had married; the thought of his being the father of lovely children was almost unbearable. Perhaps she had been foolish; since they would not let her have the man she loved it might have been wise to have taken one of those whom they thought were so suitable. She might at least have had her baby by now.

She was more subdued than she had been. The affair with Major von Töbingen had changed her. It did not worry her that there was scandal about her and that many malicious people said that she was unmarried because she had led an immoral life. They credited – or discredited – her with having given birth to at least two illegitimate children and they quoted as proof the occasion of the ball when the *accoucheur* had come to the palace and the time when she had left Court after the Töbingen affair. What did she care? She had grown listless about such matters.

All the same she was weary of life at Brunswick. She was fond of her father, it was true; but she was conscious of her mother's jealousy of Madame de Hertzfeldt and the latter's toleration of the Duchess. It was an uneasy situation at the best and Caroline could enjoy no satisfactory relationship with either of them.

She began to grow a little morbid. I shall end my days at Brunswick, she thought, always longing for the children I never had. I have been a fool. I should have accepted marriage with one of the men who were offered to me.

Then the miracle happened.

Her father sent for her one day and all unsuspecting she went to him to find her mother present. The Duke looked very solemn; the Duchess was needing all the little restraint she possessed to prevent herself shouting the news to her daughter.

But it was the Duke's place to acquaint his daughter with the news and this he did. 'Caroline, I have something of great importance to tell you. I think it is very good news. I have a letter here from your uncle the King of England. The Prince of Wales is asking for your hand in marriage.'

'The Prince of Wales!' A great joy came to her. She thought: I am not too late then. I waited and now I have the biggest prize.

'It is a great honour,' said the Duke. 'Of course, the Prince is your first cousin and this is an opportunity which I am sure you will not want to miss.'

'Of course you will not want to miss it.' The Duchess could contain her excitement no longer. 'Think of it, Caroline, you'll be the Queen of England. Imagine it. You – Caroline – a Queen!'

'Yes,' said Caroline slowly, 'if I married him I should one day be Queen of England.'

Her father looked at her almost fearfully. He laid a hand on her shoulder and looked into those eyes which could suddenly grow so wild. 'I would never wish to be rid of you or to send you away,' he said gently. 'But if you wish to marry, daughter, you will never have an opportunity like this again.'

'It's true, Father,' she said.

'You realize it, do you not?' cried the Duchess. 'Oh, the Prince of Wales! My dear, dear nephew! The First Gentleman of Europe. I have heard that he is the most fascinating creature. And handsome – so handsome! Caroline, you are the luckiest of young women – and when you think that you will soon be twenty-seven, it is a God-given chance. I think I should write to my brother at once. I think there should be no delay. I think—'

'Madam,' said the Duke coldly, 'it is Caroline who is to marry – not yourself.'

The Duchess opened her mouth to protest. It was humiliating – the way in which she was treated. And before her children too. He would never speak like that to the Hertzfeldt woman. Oh, no, her advice would be sought . . . and considered.

She flashed her husband a look of hatred, of which Caroline was acutely aware. It would be pleasant to get right away.

'My dear,' said the Duke, 'you need time to consider.'

'I have considered,' said Caroline. 'I will accept the Prince of Wales.'

The Duchess was clasping her hands in ecstasy. The Duke looked relieved. As for Caroline she stood very still, in a mood of rare calmness.

'My child,' said the Duke, 'you have made a wise decision.'

She looked at him steadily and then threw herself into his arms. His sternness relaxed and he held her tightly. The Duchess looked on but she was not thinking of them; she was seeing the wedding preparations; the marriage; and she was exulting because this difficult daughter who had been such a trial to them was now going to be the Princess of Wales.

*

Caroline returned to her apartments and found there the Baroness de Bode who had realized that something of great importance was afoot, and since she had seen the messengers from England she guessed it might be an offer of marriage for the Princess.

Caroline said: 'Well, you have come to hear the news.'

'I trust it *is* good news.'

'That,' replied Caroline, 'I shall not be able to tell you until I am on my deathbed.'

'What does Your Highness mean?'

'That only at the end of a marriage can one say whether it was good or bad.'

'Marriage!'

'Now do not look so surprised because you are not in the least. You guessed it was an offer, did you not?'

'From England?'

'How strange that everyone should be more excited about my wedding than I am.'

'Pray tell me which of the sons of the King of England.'

'The eldest, Madam. You should not be shouting questions at me in this manner. Rather you should be treating the future Princess of Wales and Queen of England with the greatest respect.'

'Then it is indeed? Oh, what a great day this is!'

'You are all to be relieved of the presence of your tiresome Princess.'

'I did not mean that. I meant that it was an excellent prospect. Oh, Your Highness, you will . . . take care. You will always remember to profit from your past mistakes.'

The Princess regarded her governess slyly. 'What is gone is gone,' she said. 'It will never return; and what is to come will come of itself, whatever I do.'

The Baroness was about to protest when Caroline held up a hand.

'I want to be by myself to think,' she said. 'I have accepted the Prince of Wales whom I have never seen but of whom I have heard much. I have accepted him because I am growing so tired of my life at Brunswick.'

'Your Highness—'

The Princess shook her head. 'I am catching at the crown and sceptre as a drowning wretch catches at a straw.'

'Do not speak so. It is dangerous ... If it were to reach the Prince's ears—'

'The Prince of Wales.' Caroline was laughing suddenly, the old wild laughter. 'He has never seen me – yet he will take me for his wife. Don't you think, Baroness, that his feelings about this marriage will be similar to mine?'

The Baroness was silent.

Caroline cried: 'Don't let us be so glum. This is a time for rejoicing. The Princess of Brunswick is now about to be betrothed to the Prince of Wales.'

Frederick, Duke of York, called on the Prince of Wales at Carlton House, where he was received in the Prince's apartments overlooking St James's Park.

The Prince was elegantly clad in a coat of pearl grey, the diamond star flashing on his left breast; his buckskin breeches fitted tightly to his shapely if somewhat plump legs; his neckcloth was a masterpiece of artistry of blue and grey tints worn in the fashion he himself had made because of a slight swelling in his neck; his abundant fair hair was frizzed and curled; his white shapely fingers were adorned not ostentatiously but noticeably with diamonds; and his entire person smelled of a delicately applied fragrance.

'Now, Fred,' said the Prince, 'I want the truth. What is she like?'

Frederick thought back to those visits he had paid to the Brunswick Court, and tried to remember his cousin Caroline. Quite pretty, he had thought; he had not wanted to marry her, but would it have been such a tragedy? He could not have done worse than he had. When he thought of the woman with whom he had blithely entered into matrimony – for the same reason of course that George was compelled to contemplate it now ... debts – any woman seemed attractive.

'She's a pretty creature, as far as I remember.'

'Yet you might have married her and did not.'

'Pray don't talk to me about marriage – mine at least. It's been a fiasco from start to finish.'

'You seem to have arranged matters to your satisfaction I notice.'

'Merely by refusing to live with the creature.'

'And since,' said the Prince, 'you have chosen to do this and there is therefore no hope of your marriage proving fruitful, I am forced to consider my obligations to the state.'

Frederick laughed. 'You'll admit, George, that it is your concern rather than mine.'

'I thought one of you might have taken on the task.'

'With a woman who turns the house into a zoo? I tell you this, George, Oatlands Park is no longer a human habitation. It's one big cage of animals. Bitches with their puppies in the beds; monkeys climbing the banisters; parrots screeching. It's a nightmare, George. And the fleas . . . and the smells . . .'

'Spare me,' begged the Prince, taking a white lace-edged kerchief from his pocket and holding it to his nose as he sniffed its fragrance.

'Well, I am explaining, George, that after marriage to my Duchess *any* woman seems desirable.'

'Even Caroline of Brunswick?'

'I did not say that. I thought her a pleasant creature. A little short in the legs perhaps and I fancy she does not carry herself as gracefully as she might – but then she was young and a bit of a hoyden. Doubtless she has grown out of that. She has an abundance of fair hair and fine eyes I believe.'

The Prince was obviously relieved.

'So, George,' went on his brother, 'you will do well enough.'

'I heartily wish this marriage need never take place.'

The brothers regarded each other sadly.

The proposed marriage was drawing them closer together than they had been for some time. In the days of their boyhood they had been inseparable. They had stood by each other and shared adventures and punishments. Frederick had patiently kept guard during the Prince's assignations with Mrs Robinson; many a time he had incurred his father's anger in order to protect his brother, and the bond had been strong between them. The main reason why they had resented Frederick's being sent abroad was because it meant they must be parted; and when he had come back they had resumed their friendship as though it had never been broken.

The Prince had introduced his brother to Maria Fitzherbert, whom he was then treating as the Princess of Wales, and Frederick had been charmed by the lady. She had become fond of him too although she did deplore the wild horseplay in which he indulged with the Prince, and she blamed Frederick for this because on his return the Prince had reverted to the practical joking and wild ways in which he had indulged before his association with her. But a rift had come through that wife of Frederick's – that German Princess Frederica Charlotte Ulrica –who although she filled her house with different breeds of dogs, although she was indifferent to their fleas and habits, was a very haughty personage and determined to uphold her position as Duchess of York. She had therefore refused to accept Maria Fitzherbert's right to any rank but that of mistress of the Prince of Wales – a fact which had humiliated Maria and infuriated the Prince; and as he was at that time deeply in love with Maria, he had pettishly blamed Frederick for not having more control over his wife.

Frederick had considered this unfair, for he himself had always shown the greatest respect towards Maria – but the rift between the brothers widened; and it was an indication of the depth of the Prince's feelings for Mrs Fitzherbert that on her account the lifelong friendship with his brother could be impaired.

But now, Frederick no longer lived with his wife – and no one blamed him – and the friendship between the brothers was resumed, although it was clear to them both that it would never be quite the same again.

'Cheer up, George,' said the Duke. 'Lady Jersey will comfort you.'

'That's true,' replied the Prince dubiously. His affairs were indeed in a tangle. Lady Jersey – that dainty, gadfly of a woman who while she fascinated him at the same time repelled him – was his consolation for this marriage with the German woman ... and the loss of Maria.

Ah, Maria. He could never quite succeed in banishing her from his thoughts. Sometimes he wondered whether he ever would.

He thought now that if instead of marriage with this stranger he was going back to Maria how delighted he would have been. But that could not be; and another horrible thought had struck him: What was Maria, who considered herself married to him, going to say when she heard he contemplated marrying another woman?

He sat down on a gilded couch and, covering his face with his hands, wept.

Frederick was not unduly disturbed; like all the Prince's associates he was accustomed to his tears. The Prince had always wept most effectively – and in fact, thought Frederick cynically, it was quite a family accomplishment. We Guelphs are a weeping family, he mused – but none of us can perform so artistically as the Prince of Wales.

The Prince applied the scented kerchief to his eyes which like his complexion had not suffered from the display of emotion.

'Fred,' he said, 'the truth is I shall never love another woman as I love Fitzherbert.'

'Still, George?'

'Still and for ever,' cried the Prince vehemently.

'And yet—'

'It's money, Fred. How am I going to pay these damned debts without it? And the price ... marriage with a German *frau.*'

Frederick nodded grimly. 'The price of royalty, George.'

'Why do we accept it? What would I not give for my freedom.'

Well, considered Frederick, suppose he had resigned his rights. Suppose he had made a public announcement of his marriage to Fitzherbert instead of allowing Fox to make a public denial of it in the House of Commons? Could it have been different? He would not have been wearing that magnificent diamond star, the insignia of his rank of course; he would not have been living in this splendid residence – this grand Carlton House with its scintillating chandeliers, its gilt furniture, its exquisite porcelain, its priceless pictures. George should consider all that, for there was nothing he enjoyed as much as taking a derelict house and transforming it into a palace. Look what he had done at his Pavilion in Brighton. And here in Carlton House the state apartments were far more grand than anything in gloomy old St James's, tumbledown Windsor and homely Kew. Even Buckingham House suffered in comparison. Trust George to see to that. Consider the Chinese parlour, the blue velvet closet and crimson drawing room, the silver dining room – and most magnificent of all, the throne room with its gilded columns displaying the Prince of Wales's feathers. Even what he called his own intimate apartments – these facing the park – were fit for a king as well as a Prince of Wales. No, George was too fond of his royalty to give it up even for Fitzherbert. George was above all self-indulgent; his emotions were superficial and even the affection he bore for the incomparable Fitzherbert had not prevented his deserting her for the momentarily more alluring Lady Jersey. He was not the man to resign his hopes of the crown for the sake of a woman. Imagine George, wandering about the Continent in exile – an impecunious prince whose debts would never then be settled by an understanding if somewhat tutorial parliament; and how could George live but in the most extravagant manner? He was born to elegance; he was a natural spendthrift; he could never understand the value of money. He was only aware that he wished to surround himself with beautiful things and that as Prince of Wales and future King of England he had a natural right to them.

And who was Frederick to criticize his brother? Had he not been forced into marriage for the very same reason?

So now he sought to comfort George by embellishing his picture of Caroline.

She was really quite charming, and bright and intelligent, he thought. To tell the truth he might have decided to marry her himself, but she wouldn't have him. Of course he was not the Prince of Wales. He remembered particularly her beautiful hair. It was very light and abundant. The Prince was very fond of beautiful hair, was he not?

The Prince nodded and thought of Maria's abundant honey-coloured curls. She had never powdered it although it was the fashion to do so; but had worn it naturally. But then of course few women had hair to compare with Maria's. The fact was in all ways no woman could compare with Maria.

He would always think of her as his wife.

Oh, damn these debts. Damn cruel necessity which snatched Maria from him and gave him in her place a German *frau*. Yet it was Lady Jersey who had driven him from Maria.

But it was not serious, he told himself. I never meant it seriously. It was Maria, who had taken it so.

But the Duke of York had comforted him considerably. His betrothed was not a monster, it seemed; she was not hideous like poor Fred's wife; she was not marked by the pox like that arrogant creature; and she would not bring an army of animals to perform their disgusting functions on the gilded couches of Carlton House.

Frederick, seeing that his mission had been accomplished and that he had succeeded in bringing some relief to his brother, took his departure.

The Prince sought further comfort from Lady Jersey, but he did not find it. How different, he was thinking, it would have been with Maria.

Frances was beautiful, there was no doubt of that. She was small, slim almost to girlishness and he was fond of fleshy women; but she was widely experienced, for she was nine years older than he was and in that respect she resembled the type he favoured. Maria was six years older; he always found women older than himself so comforting. Not that there was much comfort in Frances, though she was exciting; and he was just a little afraid of her. The softness of Maria was lacking; so was the deep affection Maria had always had for him. But he had said goodbye to Maria and was now devoting himself to Frances.

Frances was a sensual woman; physically she excited him; she always made him feel uncertain; that was her *forte*. He always believed that she could provide greater satisfaction than any woman ever had before; and her strength was that while she did not, the promise of future eroticism remained.

That was what had attracted him and lured him from comfortable, deeply loving almost motherly Maria. And even as his heart called out for Maria he could not go and beg her to return to him because Frances Jersey stood there between them mocking, sensually alluring and, he feared, irresistible.

She did not try to placate him as so many women did. Now she said to him: 'I cannot understand why you are so glum. You have nothing to lose by the marriage – and everything to gain.'

'You are forgetting what marriage may entail.'

Frances laughed aloud. 'Dearest Highness, I have a husband, as you know. A very complaisant husband at this time who is always eager to serve his Prince so we need not concern ourselves with him. I have had two sons and seven daughters. I am even a grandmother. I confess I am a very *young* grandmother. But you cannot say that a life so worthily spent in replenishing the earth could possibly be without experience of what marriage entails.'

'But I am to marry a German woman ... I confess I don't like the Germans.'

'I obviously cannot share your Highness's aversion, for someone for whom I entertain the most tender passions has descended from that race.'

'Germans!' went on the Prince. 'My father married one. And consider her.'

'I have always found Her Majesty most gracious.'

Frances chuckled inwardly. How amusing. Prim and proper Charlotte actually approved of her son's relationship with his mistress. In fact Frances had received instructions from Lady Harcourt. She was to lure the Prince from Fitzherbert, for only then would he consider marriage – and it was high time he was married; he had to provide that heir to the throne, for his brothers were proving themselves strangely backward in doing so. The Duke of York estranged from his Duchess was clearly not going to be of any use. William, Duke of Clarence, the next son, had set up house most respectably – at least as respectably as such arrangements could be – with that enchanting actress

Dorothy Jordan, but naturally there was nothing to hope from there. Another brother Augustus Frederick, Duke of Sussex, had just emerged from a big scandal, for he had married secretly in defiance of the Marriage Act which decreed that no member of the royal family could marry without the consent of the King until he reached the age of twenty-five (Augustus Frederick had been twenty), and the marriage had been declared null and void even though the lady in his adventures was about to give birth and was of noble lineage, being the daughter of the Earl of Dunmore and claiming royal blood from her ancestors. No, there was no hope from his brothers, so clearly it was the duty of the Prince of Wales to provide heirs to the throne. The Queen had known this could not be done while the Prince adhered to Mrs Fitzherbert; so the relationship had to be broken. Since Frances had a good chance of doing that, the Queen gave her approval to Frances' activities. Which showed, thought Frances cynically, how morals could be cast aside for the sake of the state – even by the most virtuous of ladies.

But Madam Charlotte would be very angry with her dear little spy Frances Jersey did she but know how Frances had persuaded him to take this Brunswick woman rather than the Queen's own candidate from Mecklenburg-Strelitz. For the Queen had a niece from her native land, and how she would have liked to see that young woman Princess of Wales!

Alas, she was charming; she was exceedingly pretty; and she was intelligent, so Frances had heard; and if Frances was going to retain her power over the Prince – which she had every intention of doing – she naturally did not wish him to be provided with a charming and pretty wife.

So the Brunswick offering was Frances' choice. She had heard that the creature was gauche, wild and, most heinous sin in the eyes of the Prince, not very clean in her habits, washed infrequently, hardly ever bathed and rarely changed her linen. Frances intended that the Prince should be disgusted with his bride, spend enough time with her to provide the heir, and for the rest find his pleasure and recreation in the arms of Lady Jersey, for Lady Jersey loved power and next to power she loved worldly goods. The mistress of the Prince of Wales, if she were clever, could receive these in plenty; and no one – least of all herself – would deny the fact that Lady Jersey was a clever woman.

The Queen would never know that she had influenced him to take the Brunswicker. Poor Charlotte thought this was just another example of her son's determination to plague her. Silly Charlotte, thought Lady Jersey, to imagine that she would work for her! Lady Jersey never worked for anyone but herself.

'Now,' said the Prince, 'we shall have two German *fraus* at Court. I think that is two too many.'

'If you had taken the Queen's choice it would have been exactly the same. And Frederick gave a good account of the woman, I believe.'

'I wonder whether he was trying to comfort me.'

'I hope so. It is the duty of us all to do so.'

'Oh, Frances, I dread this marriage.'

'Stop thinking of it then. There are more pleasant subjects, you know.'

She was giving him one of those oblique looks of hers, and he was beginning to feel the excitement which had led him to desert Maria.

'Why should you worry.' Her voice had taken on that deep husky note full of suggestions which he always hoped to understand. 'I shall be there,' she added, 'to take care of you.' And she thought: And of our little Brunswicker.

But the Prince was completely under the spell of Frances Jersey and was, if only temporarily, able to banish the thought of the marriage from his mind.

Which was exactly what he wished to do.

Maria Fitzherbert had arrived back from the Continent with her friend and companion, Miss Pigot, who lived with her and shared all her triumphs and misfortunes.

There was no comfort to be found abroad, Maria had decided; and so she might as well return to England. She had no desire to take up residence in her house in Pall Mall (which the Prince had given her) nor in her house at Brighton. But Marble Hill at Richmond had always been her home and she had suggested to Miss Pigot that they return to it and live there quietly.

Miss Pigot understood. Dear Maria had no wish to go into society, for if she did how could she avoid meeting the Prince of Wales; and if he were to cut her (he would never do that) or if he were to be less than loving, which he undoubtedly would be since he would be everywhere in the company of Lady Jersey, how could Maria endure to meet him? For in Maria's eyes the Prince of Wales was her husband; according to the laws of her church this was so; it was the state – due to that Royal Marriage Act brought in by the Prince's own father – which would consider that the ceremony that had taken place on 15 December of the year 1785 – a little less than ten years ago – was no true marriage.

Miss Pigot often thought how much happier Maria might have been if she had gone to the country after the death of Mr Fitzherbert and stayed there; then the Prince of Wales would never have met her, never have made up his mind that he could not live without her; and Maria would doubtless have married some pleasant country gentleman who would have adored her and made her comfortably happy for the rest of her life.

She had said this to Maria who had shaken her head sadly. 'At least I had those happy years, Piggy. I suppose I should be grateful for them. And you're fond of him too. You know you are.'

Miss Pigot admitted that this was so. He *was* charming; and when he kissed one's hand or bowed he did it so beautifully that he made one feel at least like a duchess. And when he thanked one for some small service the tears were often in his eyes as he spoke of his gratitude or affection. Who could not be affected by such charm? Not Miss Pigot. Nor indeed Maria.

And my goodness, thought Miss Pigot, Maria had stood out against him. It was only when he pretended to kill himself . . . Hush; she must not say that. Maria believed he really *had* tried to kill himself. She often spoke of it now, remembering how much in need of her he had been. Dear Maria, let her believe that, if it gave some comfort. Poor soul, she needed all the comfort she could get.

As for Miss Pigot she believed he had been over-bled. His

physicians were constantly bleeding him because when he became too excited and gave vent to violent passions he was apt to fall into a sort of fit which bleeding seemed to alleviate. An over-bleeding, thought the practical Miss Pigot, and the blood on his clothes and the pallor of his face ... well, if he said that he had tried to thrust a sword into his side and kill himself because Maria refused him – why shouldn't she believe him? But after that she had gone away and stayed abroad for a year; and then she could stop away no longer. And he had remained faithful to her all that time, which, Miss Pigot conceded, must have demanded a great deal of restraint on his part – knowing him – or a great affection. The affection was there.

Our dear charming Highness loves Maria as much as he can love anyone, Miss Pigot said to herself. That is why it is such a pity that this has happened.

For whom else would he have gone through that ceremony in Park Street? There was a real parson to perform it and so it was a true marriage. And hadn't he treated her as his wife? Everyone who wished to please him had been obliged to recognize Maria as the Princess of Wales. He had been devoted to her. But then of course there were other women.

How could he manage without women – different women? The two things in life he loved best were women and horses; and women were a good length ahead. That clever Mr Sheridan had said of him that he was too much the lover of all women to be the lover of one.

How true! How sadly true!

But Maria – clever maternal Maria – had understood her prince. She had accepted his infidelities, not happily of course, but as a necessity, until Lady Jersey had come along. Who would have thought that that ... grandmother, nine years the Prince's senior, could so enslave him! But Lady Jersey was a clever woman. She had no intention of taking second place to Maria; she had therefore set out to destroy Maria's influence with the Prince. And she had succeeded.

But it won't be for ever, Miss Pigot was sure. He will be back. I feel it in my bones.

And Maria, wounded as she never had been before, had

made no protest. How like Maria. She was always so dignified. A queen if ever there was one, thought the loyal Miss Pigot. She had not raged against him as most women would have done. She had taken her *congé* with outward serenity. If he no longer wants me, then I will remove myself from his life – since that is what he wants.

Miss Pigot had believed that he would come back; that he had written that letter telling her that he would not see her again on an impulse when he was under the influence of that wicked woman. But Maria had accepted it. Miss Pigot would never forget the day she came back from the Duke of Clarence's house with the letter which had been delivered to her there. She was like a sleepwalker. Stunned, that was it. Oh, how could he be so cruel – so wicked! What had made him do such a thing? To write to her there so that she must receive her dismissal before all those people; and when she had no notion of what was to happen either? Hadn't he been writing to her only the day before as his Dear Love?

He had dismissed Perdita Robinson in the same way – by letter. But that was because he hated scenes and Mrs Robinson according to hearsay had made scenes at the end of their relationship. True, Maria and he had quarrelled. A woman would have to be a saint not to quarrel with such a publicly unfaithful husband, for whatever the state said Maria believed him to be her husband. So perhaps that was why.

And she had gone abroad.

'You should have stayed,' she had protested at the time.

'What!' Maria had cried. 'Stay ... like a dog waiting for a whistle from its master?'

Oh, yes, Maria was proud. But what comfort was there abroad? Maria could not bear to stay in France – that tortured country which had been like a second home to her because she had been educated there; but it was all so sadly changed since the Revolution and she could not find there the peace and solace she sought. So they had come back to Marble Hill and here they were.

Maria had always been particularly fond of Marble Hill – a fine house which had been built by Lady Suffolk, one of the mistresses of George II, as a refuge for her old age when she should no longer please that monarch. It had delightful grounds which had been planned by Bathhurst and Pope, and the flowering shrubs, particularly in the spring, were charmingly colourful. Maria loved the lawns which ran down to the river and were bounded on each side by a grove of chestnut trees. From the grotto, a feature of the garden, there was a very pleasant view of Richmond Hill. One glance at the house explained why it had received its name; perched on an incline it really did look as though it were made of marble, so white was it; and it owed its graceful appearance to those excellent architects Pembroke and Burlington.

Maria was sitting in her drawing room, a piece of embroidery in her hand, but she was not sewing; she was looking wistfully out over the lawns to the river. Miss Pigot came and sat beside her, and Maria forced herself to smile.

'How dark it is getting . . . so early,' said Maria. 'The winter will soon be with us.'

But she was not thinking of the weather.

'You might as well say what's in your mind, Maria,' said her faithful companion. 'It doesn't do any good to bottle it up.'

'I suppose not.'

'If you're thinking of him you shouldn't try to pretend you're not. Is there something on your mind?'

Maria was silent. 'It can't be true,' she said. 'No, of course it's not true. And I *am* thinking of him. I thought going away would help to cure me, but I fear I never shall be cured.'

'He'll come back,' said Miss Pigot firmly. 'I just know he will come back.'

Maria shook her head. 'I would not have believed it possible that he could have written to me in that way – so cold – after all these years – after . . .'

'It was done in a bad moment, Maria, my dear. He's breaking his heart over it now, I shouldn't be surprised.'

'I should, Piggy, very. He is at this moment with Lady Jersey, not giving me a thought – or if he is to congratulate himself for being rid of me.'

'Now you don't believe that any more than I do. He'd never feel like that. He's had a little flash of temper. And you know, my dear, you have lost yours once or twice. In your quarrels you haven't always been the meek one, have you?'

'Find excuses for him, Piggy. You know that's what I want you to do.'

She looked so forlorn, so tragic sitting there that Miss Pigot went over and kissed her.

'Dear Pig, at least I have you. That is something to be grateful for.'

'I'll be faithful till death.'

'Those were exactly his words.'

'And he meant them – in his way.'

'In his way?' said Maria bitterly. 'I know what that means. Words . . . words and no meaning behind them.'

She was silent for a while and Miss Pigot did not attempt to break that silence; then Maria began to talk of that ceremony in her drawing room in Park Street.

'I would tell no one but you. I promised it should be a secret and I have kept my word. I should have known what to expect, shouldn't I, when Fox stood up in the House of Commons and denied that we had ever been married? And the Prince let it pass.'

'You left him then. Remember how unhappy you were? But you went back to him, didn't you?'

'He was my husband, whatever Mr Fox said. I didn't forget that.'

'If he was then, he is now. So you shouldn't forget that either.'

'*He* has chosen to forget, and I shall not remind him. What use would it be? But I can't stop thinking of those happy days. I think the happiest were when we were most poor. Poor! What he thought of as poor. Do you remember when there were bailiffs at Carlton House and the King would not help and so the Prince sold his horses and shut up the state apartments at Carlton House and we went down to Brighton? But we were determined to economize; we determined to settle his debts gradually ... and so we took that place in Hampshire. I think those days at Kempshott were the happiest of my life, Piggy. If he had been simply a country gentleman like my first and second husbands, I think we should have been happy. I understand him as no one else does. I could make him happy . . . but he does not think so.'

'Of course he does. This Jersey affair will pass like the others, Maria. He's a boy – rather a spoilt boy I admit – but we love him for what he is. He'll be back.'

'I see that you have not heard the rumours.'

'Rumours? What rumours?'

'He's in debt again. His creditors have to be appeased. The King and Mr Pitt have put their heads together and are offering him a condition.'

'Them and their conditions! They always make conditions!'

'This time it is marriage.'

'Marriage. How can he marry? He's married already.'

'The state would not say so.'

'Then the state would be lying. Have you and he not made your vows before a priest?'

'We have, but if the state does not recognize them . . . Remember the case of the Duke of Sussex. He had made his vows but the courts decided he was not married.'

'I know. It's wicked.'

'But it's fact. I am only the Prince's wife while he acknowledges me as such.'

'That's nonsense.'

'I know that in the eyes of God and my church I am the Prince's wife. But he does not accept that. That is why he has agreed to marry.'

'Agreed to marry. It's lies.'

'So I told myself, but rumour persists.'

'There'll always be rumours.'

'But this rumour is on very firm foundation. I even know the name of the Princess of Wales elect.'

'What?'

'Caroline of Brunswick. Niece of the King.'

'It's all a pack of nonsense,' said Miss Pigot.

But Maria only shook her head.

'It's true,' she said. 'And it's the end. I have really lost him now.'

In the Queen's Lodge at Kew the Queen was having her hair curled and reading the papers at the same time. She supposed now there would be a spate of lampoons and cartoons about the Prince's proposed marriage once it was announced. At the time it was, of course, a secret; but it would not be so much longer.

She sighed. She did hope that nothing would happen to upset the King; since that last illness of his ... she shuddered. One could scarcely call it an ordinary illness. All those months when his mind had been deranged and she had suddenly come into power had been most uneasy. It was not that she did not wish for power; she did. She was beginning to grasp it, and she had the King's condition to thank for it – if thank was the right word in such circumstances. But she faced the fact that the King terrified her. Whenever she heard him begin to gabble; when she saw those veins projecting at his temples; she was afraid that he was going to break out into madness – and violent madness at that.

Dear little Kew, as she always thought of it, had lost its serenity. She had been delighted with it from the first day when she had gone to live in the Queen's Lodge which was really one of the houses on the Green. The Dutch House was close by and there the Prince of Wales had lived before he had his own establishment – first apartments in Buckingham House and then with greater freedom in Carlton House. There across the bridge along Strand-on-the-Green many of the members of the household lodged. Certainly Kew was not like living at Court; it was even not like a king's residence. Perhaps that was why she and the King had always been so fond of it.

But Kew had changed; it was full of memories. She remembered how they had brought the King from Windsor when it had first been known that he was mad, and sometimes at night in her sleep she was disturbed by the sounds of that rambling voice going on and on, growing more and more hoarse; she thought of that occasion when the King had seized the Prince of Wales by the neck and tried to strangle him and how the hatred had shone in those mad eyes of his; she remembered a time when he had embraced their youngest daughter Amelia until the child had screamed aloud in terror because she thought he was going to suffocate her. And that was love! She would never forget the agonized look in those poor mad eyes when his beloved child had been dragged from him and they had tried to force him into a strait-jacket.

Memories of Kew! The King walking the grounds with his doctors, shouting himself hoarse, beating in time to imaginary music, shaking hands with an oak tree which he thought was the Emperor of Prussia. This had changed the face of dear little Kew.

And, thought the Queen, how can we know when it will break out again, and if it does and there should be a Regency the Prince will do everything he can to curb my power.

But she would not let him because Mr Pitt was on her side and Mr Pitt was Prime Minister and cared little for the Prince of Wales. The Prince had allied himself with Fox and the Whigs and that was enough to make Pitt stand against him.

Mr Pitt and I will rule between us, thought Queen Charlotte; and she wondered how she could have come to hate her eldest son so much, he whom, when he was a baby and a young boy, she had idolized. The others altogether had not meant half so much to her as her first-born; and now she hated him.

Strong feelings for a mother— and such a plain little woman. Ah, but then it was because everyone had thought her plain and insignificant for so many years that now she saw the chance of exerting her power she seized it.

The King who had determined to keep her in her place – which meant constantly bearing children – had had his way since their marriage. She had given him fifteen children. Surely she had done her duty? But now he was a poor shambling creature – older than his years, living in constant fear that his madness would return.

And this had given the Queen her chance.

But the Prince was determined to flout her. He must marry, and he had chosen Caroline of Brunswick when her brother's charming daughter was available.

Was it possible even yet to get him to change his mind?

She glanced at her reflection in the mirror. They had now placed the triangular cushion on the crown of her head, and had started to frizz her hair and build it up round the cushion.

How ugly it is! she thought. And nothing they can ever do to me will beautify me. And what does it matter if they did. I am an old woman in any case.

'Your Majesty, we are ready for the powdering . . .'

The powdering robe was wrapped about her and they began.

The powder seemed to get up her nose and into her throat today. It was all so tiresome.

But now she was ready and she would go to her drawing room where the Princesses were waiting for her.

The Princesses were there – all six of them. They curtsied and her sharp eyes took in every detail to see that they did so in the approved manner. Twelve-year-old Amelia was not as graceful as she should be; but one did not reproach Amelia; she was her father's favourite and he could not bear her to be scolded. And considering the soothing effect she had on him, thought the Queen, I suppose we should all be grateful to the child and forgive her her small weaknesses.

The Princess Royal was looking discontented. Poor Princess Royal, she was a disappointed young woman. Young woman . . . well, she would not be that much longer. She was twenty-nine and still no husband had been found for her. And where *could* they find a husband for her when there was such a dearth of Protestant princes? The great difficulty was that any husband for the Princesses must be both Royal and Protestant. It was a grave handicap. And when one considered that there were five others all waiting hopefully for husbands . . . Oh dear, how depressing! What a fearful problem marriage was. The sons did it where they should not and the daughters looked for it in vain.

Perhaps it was not so clever to have had quite so many of them.

The Queen looked along the line of faces. Her little girls. She loved them. They were so much more amenable than their brothers. They did not defy her and the King. But perhaps they would if they had the opportunity.

'My snuff box,' she said sternly, looking at her eldest daughter, for it was Princess Royal's duty to present her with her snuff box on occasions like this and to see that it had been adequately replenished.

The Princess Royal presented it with a curtsey and the Queen took a pinch. Ah, that was better! There was nothing like a pinch of snuff to revive the spirits.

'Who is going to read to us this morning?' asked the Queen, looking round. 'Is it going to be you, Gouly?'

Miss Goldsworthy – Gouly, to the royal family – replied that since it was Her Majesty's wish she would be happy to begin the reading; and the work was brought out, the Princesses and their ladies seated and the reading began.

How utterly boring! thought Charlotte, the Princess Royal. And this is how it goes on day after dreary day. And it will never change . . . unless the miracle happens and I escape. There was only one way in which a princess could escape – through marriage, and who knew what that would bring! Well, let it come whatever it was. Anything was better than this complete and utter monotony.

She was twenty-nine years old and she had been twenty-six before she had been allowed to meet anyone who had not been presented by the Queen. Now having exceeded that ripe age she was allowed what they called a little freedom. She might speak to people without Mamma's consent. What freedom! It was enough to make a young woman take the first lover that came along. And, thought Princess Royal, soon I shall become so desperate that that is what I shall do. At twenty-six she had been permitted to select the books she wished to read; before that she had been allowed only those which had been chosen by her mother. She had never forgotten how humiliated she had felt when she had discovered Fanny Burney, the novelist who had for a time been a member of her mother's household, censoring Swift's *John Bull* for her. And meanwhile her brothers . . . Oh, her brothers! George most of all with his women and all the country asking: Is he married or is he not? And whispering the name of that woman, Maria Fitzherbert. And before that he had had that affair with the actress known as Perdita Robinson who had threatened to publish his letters and had had to be bought off with a pension for life. And all this before *he* was twenty-one. Now there was this scandal about Augustus; and there was William, not caring for the disapproval of his parents, setting up house with a play actress. All this for the boys, while the girls were treated like nuns in a convent. Small wonder that she was exasperated.

Soon I shall be thirty, she mourned. Thirty . . . forty . . . fifty. Who would be a princess at the dismal Court of George III?

The Princess Royal glanced at her sisters. Augusta was less conscious of their plight. She was in any case two years younger; she was careless too of the manner in which she dressed – a little bit of a hoyden. She did not care so much for the restrictions as Princess Royal did but shrugged her shoulders and accepted.

Twenty-five-year-old Elizabeth had a drawing block on a little table beside her; she was sketching the group and was oblivious of Charlotte's dissatisfaction. Elizabeth wanted to be an artist; and although this was not taken seriously by the King and Queen, they saw no harm in her pursuing her little hobby. The King kindly often asked to see her drawings and congratulated her on them.

Mary and Sophia – nineteen and eighteen – were just beginning to fret under restraint; and Amelia at twelve had not begun to be aware of it. Papa's darling, she felt herself to be a very special member of the household and seemed quite content with her fate. She had not yet discovered the boring routine to be so tiresome: walking with the dogs, bringing them into the Queen's drawing room, taking them out, making sure that Mamma's snuff box was always filled each day and that it was placed on the table beside her. Oh the inanity of it all! The parade on the terrace in the evening when the public came to look at them. There they were specially dressed for the occasion, fluttering their fans and smiling and bowing to the occasional expressions of approval. All eyes were on Amelia, of course. That child would become quite conceited. And she furled and unfurled her fan and went through her special antics for their benefit; and if Papa were there he would be unable to take his eyes from her. She was never subjected to the harsh criticism which had come the way of the others.

One almost longed for Thursdays which was Court Day when the King and the Queen had to be at St James's. Not that there was anything exciting about that; its only virtue was that it was different. Then Mamma would be dressed with special ceremony and travel to London with her tippet and ruffles in a paper bag, as she said, to prevent their getting dusty on the way. She behaved like some humble squire's lady instead of a queen. And we are expected to endure this life just because it is their way of living. If the Prince of Wales were king, what a different Court that would be! She had heard Frederick say that George had once told him that one of the first things he would do when he came to the throne would be to find husbands for his sisters.

She believed he would. For at heart, in spite of the gay and romantic life he led, George was kind; and while he wanted to enjoy his own life to the full and that was doubtless the main purpose in it, he did like to see those around him enjoying theirs. Whereas with Papa – boredom was synonymous with goodness.

Oh dear, what a life we lead! And I am nearly thirty and see no hope of escape.

'Princess Royal, take the dog out.' The Queen's voice sounded severe. She should have noticed, of course. 'And Gouly, your voice sounds tired. I think Miss Planta might care to read now. You may take over her sewing.'

When the Princess Royal returned to the apartment it was to find that a paroxysm of coughing had seized Amelia.

'Pat her back,' commanded the Queen, which Sophia who was nearest immediately did. 'There, is that better?'

Amelia said it was, but a little later she began to cough again.

She had got that nasty cough and it was a mild source of anxiety to the Queen. She would grow out of it, she told herself; but what did terrify her was that if the King should hear the child's coughing, it would upset him so.

Amelia was now herself – small and dainty and very pretty. The word frail came into her mother's mind. Oh, no, Amelia was well enough. If she could throw off that wretched cough . . .

But she would and the most important thing of all was that the King should not hear it. If he did he would begin to fret; he would make something out of it. Nothing must touch his darling Amelia and he would remember that Octavius and Alfred had had unpleasant little coughs before they died.

'Are you better now, Amelia?' asked the Queen sternly.

'Yes, Mamma.'

'Don't cough when you are with Papa. He does not like coughs.'

Amelia would do her best. It was a breach of etiquette in any case to cough or sneeze in the presence of royalty. The ladies-in-waiting grew quite hilarious explaining the methods they employed to stop a sneeze. The favourite one was to place the finger horizontally beneath the nose. That was if one felt it coming in time. Coughing could be restrained more easily. What silly rules! thought Princess Royal. How happy I should be if some prince offered for my hand. I should not let them refuse for me . . . not in any circumstances. Anything would be better than this boring life at Kew.

It was time now for the Queen to retire to her apartments so she rose. The Princesses rose too and dropped their curtsies as their mother passed out of the room.

She went to the King's apartments and found him seated at his table poring over state papers. This was something she would not have dared do before his illness. Now she was in command for he recognized himself as a feeble old man who had once suffered a bout of madness; and the fear of its return was never far away.

He consulted her now. She and Pitt were the powerful ones. Although some would like to see the Prince and Fox in that position.

'The Prince is now eager for the negotiations to go forward,' said the King. 'That is a good sign, eh, what?'

'To Brunswick?' said the Queen hastily.

'To Brunswick. My sister will be pleased, I am sure.'

'She should be. The daughter from an obscure little Court to become the wife of the heir to the throne of England. Very pleased indeed.'

Charlotte remembered the excitement in as small a Court when the news had come to Mecklenburg-Strelitz that the Prince of Wales – now King of England and this poor man seated here at his table – had asked for her hand.

'Very pleased. Keeping it in the family, eh, what? I'm relieved he is thinking of settling down at last. It's not before it's necessary either. Perhaps he'll soon have children. That should sober him.'

'If anything could sober him,' retorted the Queen. 'I am wondering if this Caroline is the best choice . . .'

'There is only a choice of two – my niece or yours. And he has made that choice. It is to be mine.'

The Queen's mouth tightened. He had done it to spite her. He had passed over beautiful intelligent Louise of Mecklenburg-Strelitz for the sake of this creature from Brunswick. And there was nothing she could do about it.

'I am writing to Malmesbury at Hanover,' said the King. 'The time has come for him to go to Brunswick and there make the formal offer for the hand of Princess Caroline.'

So, thought the Queen, it *is* too late then.

She remained with the King while the letter was written and sealed.

Then she left him and went to her own apartments. She thought of the Princess who would be coming to the Court; she imagined how gauche she would be, for had she herself not been exactly so on her arrival? The English Court was certain to be quite different from the poor little one of Brunswick. She herself had been very young – only seventeen – and Caroline was twenty-seven, so she should at least be more mature. But was that a point in her favour? A young girl would have been easier to mould.

The Queen remembered those first weeks at her young husband's court when one of her biggest enemies had been her sister-in-law the Princess Augusta who had determined to make her life as unpleasant as possible. Waspish and angry, doubtless because she was unmarried, she had tried to make trouble between the new young Queen and her mother-in-law, the Dowager Princess of Wales, and the latter had been nothing loath, for she had meant to keep her hold on the King and not have it slackened by the young bride – Queen though she might be.

I hated my sister-in-law Augusta, thought the Queen now. Arrogant mischief-maker. How pleased I was when she married and went off to Brunswick. And once she had gone she was never welcomed back.

Nor shall her daughter be, Charlotte promised herself. I already hate the creature.

The Prince of Wales looked up from his writing table and across St James's Park.

He then sighed and read through what he had written.

'And I don't mean a word of it,' he said to himself, and taking his kerchief flicked it across his eyes. But it was a half-hearted gesture as there was no one there to witness it.

He quickly read through the letter. 'Whichever way the Princess is to come, I am clear it should be determined on instantly . . .'

Instantly, he thought. That meant that in a few weeks she would be here.

'The very thought of it makes me feel ill,' he murmured. 'Yet it has to be. There is no other way out.'

When he was married an adequate allowance would be his. Even his father and Pitt could not deny him that. And his creditors were clamouring for payment now. He was so deeply in debt that he dared not calculate how deeply. He had always had debts from the time he had been old enough to accumulate them but never thought of them very seriously until the reckoning came. Parliament settled them. It was one of the duties of parliament. How could they expect a Prince of Wales to live like a pauper?

They realized this but they did come along with their damned conditions and he had been obliged to give way and agree to marry this German woman; at one time it had seemed the reasonable and only solution; but the closer he came to it the more the idea sickened him.

Frances kept assuring him that all would be well. He would still have Frances, and she continued to fascinate him; but deep in his heart he wanted Maria ... not urgently but rather to know that she was there in the background of his life, to return to again and again, to confess, to repent and to be forgiven. Only Maria could fill that need in his life; and in his heart he knew that Maria was the woman he loved, the woman he regarded as his wife and that that ceremony which had taken place ten years ago in Park Street was a true ceremony of marriage.

Maria was his wife – and now he proposed to marry a German princess because parliament, the King and Mr Pitt demanded it. *They* did not accept his marriage to Maria because the King had passed a law saying that no member of the royal family could marry without his consent. That was the law; and any ceremony which ignored that law – even though a priest had officiated, even though the marriage vows had been taken – was null and void. A court had proved it with Augustus. So it was clear enough and Maria must understand that it was not his fault. He had been bludgeoned into this for the sake of the state. Oh, what a burden it was to be heir to a crown! He let his thoughts wander back to the early days with Maria. His passion for her, that wild uncontrollable passion when he had believed that he would do anything – just anything – in order to marry her.

I'd crowns resign
To call thee mine.

he had sung, and meant it.

Oh yes, he had meant it. And he would have given up everything then and left England with her. They could have had a pleasant little house on the Continent, in France say. No, not France, that unhappy country, which had so bloodthirstily rejected monarchy ... not France, which had brought home to him how uneasily crowns sat on royal heads; and this very precariousness had made them seem infinitely desirable. Infinitely, yes – and he had reassured himself there was no need to give up his crown for Maria, because he could have them both.

So the marriage had been denied by Fox in the House of Commons and it had been shown to him that although he and

Maria considered themselves husband and wife, the state did not. So all was well, which it would not have been if the marriage had been accepted by the state – for not only was Maria a commoner but a Catholic. And on the grounds of the latter alone he could have lost his crown.

I'd all resign,
Except my crown.

might have been a more accurate expression of his feelings.

Maria must understand. She must.

Maria was unlike other women. Most would have stormed and raged – at least made some attempt to get him back. He remembered Perdita's futile endeavours for which he had despised her. But Maria made no such attempts. Maria left England; she did not answer his letter but meekly accepted his decree – as though she did not care.

But now she was back in England, how he would like to see her again. To reason with her, to explain: See my difficulties, Maria. I have to marry this German woman. I know I am going to dislike the poor thing. But I have to marry her. We have to have heirs. I shall endeavour to do my duty and when it is done ... I need never go near her. Frances Jersey? She's a siren. Irresistible. But I don't *love* her – not as I love you ... always have ... always will ... until death, Maria.

But Maria made no attempt to see him. And how could he return to her now? One of the conditions of this horrible bargain had been that he must give her up. Only while he behaved as though there had been no marriage with Maria could he enter into one with Caroline of Brunswick. Although the state declared the marriage with Maria was no marriage, the church accepted it. And there would be many people in the country who did.

What would the people think of a prince who, married to one woman, allowed himself to be married to another?

It was quite clear – Frances aside – that he dared not return to Maria now.

But he did not want her to think he had forgotten her. He wanted her to know how sad this situation had made him.

He decided that he would go without delay to see the King.

The King received the Prince of Wales with a show of affection.

How the old man has changed! thought the Prince. By God, he looks as if he could lose his reason again at any moment.

But there was one benefit from the change: he had grown more mellow; he was more inclined to see reason.

The Prince's manner was more gentle towards his father than it had been in the past and this helped to subdue the animosity between them. The King was sad rather than angry. How many sleepless nights this son of mine has given me, he thought. But he was young and now he is beginning to realize his responsibilities. He'll do his duty now.

'Your Majesty, I have today written to Malmesbury telling him to expedite matters over there.'

The King looked pleased. No sign of truculence. After all these years of resistance to doing his duty, the Prince was now prepared to take this step. Excellent, eh, what? thought the King.

'I hope she proves as fertile as your mother.'

God forbid, thought the Prince. Surely even his father realized that thirteen – and there might have been fifteen – was more than enough with which to burden the state.

'I feel optimistic that we shall not disappoint Your Majesty.'

The King inclined his head and, determined to come to the point while he was in this tolerant mood, the Prince said quickly: 'There is one matter on which I should like to consult Your Majesty.'

'Yes, what is it, eh?'

'Your Majesty will know that I had a connection with a certain lady which . . . er . . . no longer exists.'

'I am glad to hear it no longer exists. It *must* no longer exist, for if it did that could provide very grave consequences you understand, eh, what?'

The Prince kept his temper and went on: 'I know this full well, Your Majesty. The connection no longer exists but I feel certain obligations towards the lady.'

The King grunted but the Prince hurried on: 'During this

connection the lady received three thousand pounds a year which I intend to continue although my connection with the lady is completely severed. But I should like Your Majesty's assurance that in the event of my death before that of the lady this pension should be continued.'

The King interrupted him. 'I know ... I know ...' Then he softened. 'This lady is Maria Fitzherbert, a comely widow.' The King's mouth slackened a little; he was looking back over the years before he had been ill; he was thinking of all the temptations which had come his way and how he had resisted them. They would be surprised, these people who surrounded him, if they knew that in his way he was as fond of women as his sons were proving themselves to be. Sarah Lennox making hay in Holland House. What a little beauty she had been! And he would have married her. He certainly had it in his mind to do so. And before her there had been Hannah Lightfoot, the beautiful Quaker girl. He had better not think of her. But he had done what he had thought right and married plain homely Princess Charlotte and tried to shut other women out of his mind. Elizabeth Pembroke ... what a beauty! There was a woman he could love. She was at the Court and he had to see her every day and he had to remind himself that he was married to Charlotte and that it was his duty to set an example. Duty. Always duty. Plain Charlotte instead of beautiful Sarah Lennox. Fifteen children and not an illegitimate one among them. There had been Hannah of course – but that was before ... that was all in the past. Since his marriage he had been a faithful husband – except in thought, of course. But how could a man help his thoughts?

And because of his own feelings he could understand the Prince's. This Maria Fitzherbert was a good woman by all accounts. Pity she had not been a Protestant German Princess instead of a Catholic English widow. He believed she would have had a good influence on the Prince. In fact he knew she had had this because she had urged him to live less extragantly, to gamble less, to drink less, to give up his more disreputable friends.

Oh yes, this Maria Fitzherbert was entitled to a little

consideration. And he, remembering certain incidents from his own past, would be the first to admit it.

'Your ... your sentiments do you credit,' said the King. 'I think this lady has a right ... to such consideration. I believe she has always behaved in a ... a very admirable manner, eh, what?'

'It's true ... true,' declared the Prince fervently.

The King nodded. 'Then we will settle this matter. But it had better come through Loughborough. The Lord Chancellor is the man who should deal with it. Tell him to bring the matter to my notice. Have no fear. I find these sentiments do you credit.'

'I thank Your Majesty with all my heart.'

The King laid his hand on his son's shoulder and his eyes filled with tears. There were tears in the Prince's also.

How pleasant – and how unusual – for them to be friends. He's changed, thought the King. He's settling down at the prospect of marriage. More amenable. More reasonable. We shall get on now.

The Prince was thinking: His madness has changed him. Made him mellow, reasonable. Perhaps we can be more friendly now.

Within a few days the Prince received a letter from Lord Loughborough in which the Lord Chancellor wrote that he had presented the Prince's problem to the King concerning the provision he had thought proper to make to a lady who had been distinguished by his regard, and asking that in the unfortunate event of his death His Majesty would see that it was provided. His Majesty wished to convey that His Highness need have no anxiety on this account.

The Prince was delighted.

He wanted Maria to know that he had not in fact deserted her. He wanted her to know that although he could not see her she was in his thoughts.

He could not write to her because he had given his word that he had broken off all connection with her. But he did want her to see that letter.

He had an idea. He would send it to his old friend Miss Pigot, who would certainly show it to Maria.

He sat down at his desk immediately and dashed off a letter.

Miss Pigot could not curb her excitement when she saw that handwriting on the envelope. And addressed to her! It could only mean one thing. He wanted her to make the peace between himself and Maria.

She opened the envelope and the Lord Chancellor's letter slipped to the floor. She picked it up, looked at it in astonishment, and then turned to the Prince's.

He did not wish his dear friend Miss Pigot to think he had forgotten her. His thoughts were often at Marble Hill; and he sent her the enclosed letter so that she should show it to one whom it concerned which would in some measure explain the regard he had for that person.

Miss Pigot re-read the Chancellor's letter, grasped its meaning, and rushed to Maria's bedroom where she was resting.

'Oh, Maria, my dear, what do you think? I have heard from the Prince.'

'*You* ... have heard?'

'Oh, it is meant for you, of course. That's as clear as daylight. Here's a letter from the Chancellor about your income.'

Maria seized it and her face flushed angrily.

'I shall not accept it,' she said.

'But of course you'll accept it. You've debts to settle, haven't you? Debts you incurred because of him. Don't be foolishly proud, Maria. He wants you to have the money.'

'Is he paying me off as he did Perdita Robinson?'

'This is entirely different. She had to blackmail. You didn't even have to ask.'

'I shall not take it. You may write to His Highness and tell him so, since he sees fit to correspond with you about affairs which I had thought should be my concern.'

Miss Pigot left Maria and went to her room to write. She did not however write to the Prince but to Mr Henry Errington, Maria's uncle, telling him what had happened and advising him to come to Marble Hill to make Maria see reason.

He arrived within a few days and talked earnestly to Maria.

Had she settled her debts? She had not. And did she propose to do so from the two thousand a year which she had inherited from Mr Fitzherbert? It was impossible, she realized.

'Maria,' said Uncle Henry, who had been her guardian since the days when her father had become incapacitated through illness and who had indeed introduced her to her first and second husbands, 'will you leave this matter to me? What has happened was inevitable. You should emerge from that affair with dignity. This you cannot do if you are to be burdened with debts for the rest of your life. You must accept this pension, which is your due. Settle your debts in time; and then return to a solvent dignified way of living. It is the best way. Don't forget I am your guardian and I forbid you to do anything but what I suggest.'

She smiled at him wanly.

'Uncle, I am sure you are right.'

'Then will you allow me to settle these financial matters for you?'

'Please do, Uncle. I do not wish to hear about them.'

Henry Errington kissed her cheek and told her that he was glad she had such a good friend as Miss Pigot to be with her.

'I have much to be thankful for I know, dear Uncle,' said Maria. 'And don't worry over me. I am recovering from the shock of being a deserted wife.'

But when she was alone, she asked herself: Am I? Shall I ever?

How different life would have been if Uncle Henry had introduced her to a steady country gentleman like Edward Weld or Tom Fitzherbert. Then she would have settled down to a comfortable middle age.

But what she would have missed! That's what I have to remember, she told herself. I have been ecstatically happy. I must remember that. And remember also that in the nature of things that kind of happiness does not last.

Then she laid her head on her pillow and wept quietly, for recalling that happiness reminded her afresh of all she had lost.

And this talk of a pension seemed to her a finality.

*

On 30 December the King announced to both Houses of Parliament:

'I have the greatest satisfaction in announcing to you a conclusion of a Treaty of Marriage between my dear son, the Prince of Wales, and the Princess Caroline Amelia Elizabeth, daughter of the Duke of Brunswick.'

The whole Court was buzzing with the news while the Prince grieved in the privacy of Carlton House.

'There is no turning back now,' he mourned.

And in Marble Hill Maria heard the news and said to Miss Pigot: 'This is the third time that I have become a widow.'

But Miss Pigot still refused to believe that it was all over.

'He still loves you,' she insisted. 'Look at the way he worried about your pension. I won't believe it till that woman's here and married to him.'

'Then you will believe it very soon,' retorted Maria.

'Never,' cried the indomitable Miss Pigot. 'For he can't ever be married to her, can he? Because he's married to you.'

But there was no comforting Maria.

Departure for England

James Harris, first Earl of Malmesbury, had come as speedily from Hanover to the Court of Brunswick as the frosty roads would allow.

He was a man of much experience for he had been the King's ambassador in foreign courts for many years; now close on fifty, he was still handsome, somewhat debonair and extremely astute.

He had come to make an offer for the hand of the Princess Caroline; a delicate task, he considered this, for if the Princess should not please the Prince of Wales on her arrival in England he would doubtless be made to feel the Prince's displeasure; and if he discovered the young lady to be not all that he would expect the Prince to admire, what could he do?

The precise instructions from His Majesty King George III were not to comment on the lady's charms, nor to give anyone any advice on the matter. His duty was solely to make an offer for the lady's hand and to see that thereafter the arrangements concerning the betrothal were carried out in a correct manner.

Poor Princess, thought Malmesbury. She had not much chance of keeping His Highness's affections if she should ever gain them. He remembered how the Prince had come to him at the time when he was courting Maria Fitzherbert and had wanted to resign his hopes of the crown and follow the lady to Europe.

He had then advised a caution which His Highness had not seen fit to adopt, but by his tact and dignity had contrived to retain the Prince's respect and friendship. He was in fact, like many people, fond of the Prince; but that did not prevent his being aware of the weaknesses of His Royal Highness and he could feel only pity for the young woman who was destined to marry him.

Malmesbury was a diplomat by nature. He was a Whig in politics but at the same time a friend and confidant of the King's; and while he served the King and attempted to bring about an easier relationship between him and the Prince he remained the Prince's friend – which was no small achievement.

When he arrived in Brunswick he was welcomed warmly by the Duke and a palace of the late Duke Frederick was put at his disposal. He was adequately supplied with servants which included three footmen, a valet, a concierge and two sentinels to guard the palace night and day. A carriage and horses were also put at his disposal; and everything was done to make him comfortable.

A sign, he told himself, that my mission will be a success. He was at once invited to the ducal palace where he was presented to the Duchess and her daughter; and an audience with the Duke was arranged for a few days ahead when he would present to him his master's proposals.

The Duchess was a talkative woman and no stranger to him, for he had known her in England – and known her for being a meddler in affairs, a gossip and in many ways a foolish woman. According to his first observations she had not changed for the better. But he was not concerned with the mother nearly so much as with the daughter.

Caroline. The future Princess of Wales and Queen of England! He saw a girl – no longer young – but pretty – though not softly so; her figure was not good; her legs were too short though her bust was full and well-shaped; her eyes were pleasant; her hair fair, abundant and her best feature; her eyebrows were too light however and her teeth though good were already decaying. If she had been a little taller . . . if her teeth had been good . . .

But this was how she was and he did not think the Prince, such a connoisseur of beautiful women, would be pleased with her. Malmesbury thought of the dazzling beauty of Perdita Robinson – one of the loveliest creatures to tread the stage; Maria Fitzherbert – perhaps less beautiful than Perdita, but with what dignity and of course great charm; and Lady Jersey was another beauty, though much older than the Princess Caroline, but everyone knew the Prince preferred grandmothers to virgins.

An absurd jingle that he had heard somewhere came into his mind.

I've kissed and I've prattled with fifty Grand Dames
And changed them as oft, do you see.
But of all the Grand Mammies that dance on the Steine
The widow of Jersey give me.

Yes, he was well known for his love of experienced women older than himself. So what was he going to think of this gauche creature whose background had been the somewhat backward Court of Brunswick? Malmesbury tried to picture Caroline at Carlton House or Marine Pavilion.

The result was an immense pity for her. The Prince would find plenty to console him for disappointments.

*

At the Duchess's dinner he sat on her right hand.

'Such a pleasure,' she sighed, 'to see someone from England.'

He had not, he reminded her, come straight from England. He had been in Berlin and Hanover.

'But you are English and so am I, my lord. And never shall I forget it. My dear brother! I often think of him. And his terrible ... *terrible* illness. So sad. But there is the dear Prince – my handsome nephew. I hear *such* reports of him.'

Malmesbury looked disturbed, visualizing what that could mean.

But she hurried on, 'He is so fascinating, I hear. He leads the fashion. And Carlton House is a positive *mine* of treasure. They say he has the most excellent taste and is extremely clever.'

It was not the moment of course to refer to the proposed match since he had not yet made the formal announcement to the Duke, but the Duchess managed to talk all round the subject and she made it quite clear that she was delighted.

At the ball which followed he danced with the Princess. Close proximity brought a rather alarming discovery. She was clearly not meticulous regarding her personal cleanliness. A dreadful discovery. He thought of the Prince, with his scented linen, his frequent baths, and general fastidiousness. This could be a major calamity; and one which an ambassador such as himself could scarcely deal with, particularly when he had had the King's instructions to offer no advice, but merely to set the negotiations in progress.

Poor girl! he thought. And she is so clearly excited by the prospect before her.

In due course he was able to present the proposal to the Duke who received it with the utmost pleasure; and now there was no reason why the matter should not be discussed openly.

There was an air of intense excitement throughout the Court of Brunswick. As the days passed Malmesbury became more and more sorry for the Princess. When he had first met her he had believed that the Prince would turn from her in disgust and as the girl was obviously beginning to have romantic dreams about what awaited her in England, he wanted to disillusion her without hurting her. Oddly enough he was growing fond of her. There was about her a naturalness that appealed to him. She had little restraint, he could see that; and she had a great deal to learn; but she was intelligent and he believed would be able to grasp the position if it were presented to her. And who could present it to her? Who but Malmesbury?

No, no. It was outside his duty as ambassador. But it was just possible that a little guidance might save her much unhappiness.

He much deplored the influence of her mother who was now beside herself with excitement. Her daughter the future Queen of England. It was one of the greatest positions any princess could aspire to, and to think that her Caroline after all these years of waiting should have secured the prize.

She prattled on to Malmesbury. 'That it should be Caroline. But then why not? The King is my brother. So why should it not be Caroline? My brother was very fond of me before my marriage. Dear George! He was a very *good* man – kind-hearted but not very wise. Alas! But he was always devoted to the family and particularly to his sisters. But of course that's years ago and he married that woman. I never liked her. I am really afraid of how she will behave towards Caroline.'

Malmesbury assured the Duchess that the Queen would behave towards her daughter as a mother.

'Ah, my lord,' cried the Duchess, 'you forget I know that woman. I was at Court when they were married. I shall never forget her. I disliked her on sight and she hated me. My dearest mother, the Dowager Princess of Wales, shared my opinion of her. Do you know when she arrived she would have liked to *lead* George. My mother soon put a stop to that. Charlotte was immediately put in her place.'

Malmesbury raised his eyebrows which was as far as he could go in expressing disapproval, while he wondered what effect such a mother must have had on her daughter.

He tried to divert the conversation from Queen Charlotte but the Duchess was obsessed by her and insisted on continuing. All Malmesbury could do was reiterate: 'I am sure Her Majesty will do what she considers her duty towards her daughter-in-law.'

Conversations with the Duke were more helpful.

'I am a little anxious about my daughter's future,' said the Duke. 'I have tried to impress upon her the importance of the position which will be hers. I have tried to make her aware of her responsibilities.'

'The Princess will realize this when she arrives in England,' replied Malmesbury.

'I have talked a great deal to my daughter, constantly impressing on her that she is not going to England merely to dance at banquets and enjoy life. She will have great responsibilities. Perhaps Your Excellency could make her acquainted with what she should expect at the Court of England. I am sure that you can do so better than anyone.'

Malmesbury bowed and said he would do everything in his power.

He found conversations with Madame de Hertzfeldt the most illuminating. Here was a sensible woman who understood Caroline; and he had quickly realized that the Princess had more respect for this woman than for her own mother, although she was made uneasy by the *ménage à trois*. If Madame de Hertzfeldt had been the Princess's mother, reasoned Malmesbury, his task might have been easier and the Princess might have been more ready to become Princess of Wales than she was now.

'She is by no means unintelligent,' Madame de Hertzfeldt told him, 'though not exactly clever. She is good hearted – very good hearted; but she has a quick temper and is completely without tact.'

Malmesbury looked grim and the lady hurried on: 'But she would respond to kindness. She wants affection . . . she needs it. She is very fond of children. In fact her love of them amounts to a passion. I believe that if she can have children she will be happy and the union will be a success.'

'Madame,' replied Malmesbury, 'I can speak frankly to you. What I fear is the first impression. You have heard rumours of our Prince and your knowledge of the world will have given you some indication of what sort of man he is. He is a leader of fashion. He has been called the First Gentleman of Europe. I can say to you that I fear he may find the Princess somewhat lacking in that – er ... charm – and shall I say mystery – which he expects in a woman.'

'I understand perfectly Your Excellency's meaning and I fear with you. I am fond of Caroline. But the situation here—' She spread her hands and Malmesbury nodded sympathetically. 'We have tried to do what we thought best for her – the three of us. But in the circumstances it has not been easy. The children of the marriage are all ... unusual.'

Malmesbury again nodded sympathetically.

'I think one would have to be a little strict with Caroline. She has been allowed a great deal of freedom, perhaps too much. And she is of course no longer a young girl so that it is difficult to impose it now. I think she needs a great deal of advice and it will have to be given frankly.'

'You, Madame?'

She shook her head. 'No. It is not easy ... in my position.'

'Her father perhaps?'

'She is very fond of him, admires him greatly but she is afraid of him. She hides this but it is there. She feels he is a little severe. It is because he has tried to impose some discipline which has been lacking in other directions.'

'Not her mother!' cried Malmesbury in alarm, visualizing the blundering effects that lady's garrulous 'advice' might have.

Madame de Hertzfeldt smiled reassuringly.

'No, most certainly not the Duchess. I speak with complete frankness, Your Excellency understands, because I consider this matter of vital importance. The Princess has no respect whatsoever for her mother. In fact I have seen a faraway look come into her eyes when her mother speaks to her and I know she does not listen to half that is said. There is only one person at this Court who can help the Princess.'

'And that is—?'

'You, Your Excellency.'

Malmesbury was taken aback. 'Madame, I have had instructions from my royal master that my sole duty is to make these arrangements.'

She nodded rather sadly. 'Your duty to your King, Excellency. But what of your duty to this poor blundering girl? You see her as she is. You know the man who will be her husband. Will you not put out a restraining hand to stop her plunging headlong to disaster?'

'Madame, you put the case very strongly.'

'Am I wrong then, Excellency? You know the Prince of Wales. I can only judge by hearsay.'

He was silent for a few moments; then he said: 'It would exceed the duties laid down to me by my King but . . .'

Her face was illuminated by a smile and he thought: She is a beautiful woman. And a wise one. What a sad fate for our poor Princess that this woman was not her mother.

'I will do what I can,' he said, 'to prepare the Princess for what she will find at the English Court.'

In her apartments Caroline was talking to Mademoiselle Rosenzweig who listened attentively. She was a clever woman who spoke English fluently and it was for this reason that the Duke had selected her to serve the Princess in the role of secretary and that it had been planned that she should accompany Caroline to England.

'He is such a charming man,' Caroline told her secretary. 'If he were just a little younger, I could almost wish he were the Prince of Wales. He is so kind. And do you know I think he likes me quite a lot. Sometimes he looks at me almost sadly. Why do you think that is? Is it because he is wishing he were the Prince of Wales? Wouldn't that be odd? Suppose the ambassador were to fall in love with me.'

Caroline seated herself on her bed and rocked herself to and fro in her merriment.

Mademoiselle Rosenzweig remembered the instructions she had received from Madame de Hertzfeldt to curb as much as possible the Princess's frivolity, and said: 'Scarcely odd, Your Highness, but a little inconvenient to the gentleman perhaps. I am sure your father would not think it seemly to speak of such a supposition, even if it were true.'

'Dear prim Rosenzweig! But you are right to be prim.' She laughed aloud. Then she was sober; 'I shall try to be more serious, dear Madam Secretary. I really shall. And if I am a good wife I shall be rewarded by ... children. I want lots of them. Ten would be a pleasant number, do you not think so? Wicked old Queen Charlotte had fifteen, I discovered the other day. Two of them died. But thirteen, that is quite a quiverful, is it not?'

'Perhaps it is also unseemly to discuss this matter,' suggested Mademoiselle Rosenzweig.

'How fortunate that you are here to remind me, my dear. But I must not call you "my dear". It is too familiar. I have to remember all the time that I am to be the Princes of Wales. I shall start practising now. So don't expect any more familiarity. Oh, I am so glad you are coming with me. It won't be quite so strange, if I have some of my own people around me. And dear Lord Malmesbury will be there. Do you know, my dear ... I must not, must I? But you are my dear you know ... so I shall say it when we are alone – I am looking forward in a way to leaving Brunswick.'

'It is time you married.'

'Time indeed. I am no longer a child, am I? I have had such charming letters from the Prince of Wales. He writes – beautifully – in German and in French and I expect in English – if I could understand it. Such rounded phrases. I am filled with admiration. I am marrying a very *clever* man, dear Rosenzweig.'

'The Prince of Wales is noted for his erudition.'

'It is a pity I have not more.'

'Your Highness will acquire it.'

'You are beginning to talk like my dearest Malmesbury. I hear my uncle the King is a good kind man. I love him already. Yet ... I am afraid, Rosenzweig ... very much afraid.'

The gay mood had passed and Caroline's expression reflected her melancholy. 'I esteem and respect the Prince of Wales, but I cannot love him with ardour yet, can I?'

'You will not be expected to. That will *grow*.'

'Dear, dear Malmesbury, for you sound just like him!' She stood up and drawing herself to her full height clasped her hands together and tried to draw her features into an expression resembling Lord Malmesbury's. She said in a voice which was a fair imitation of his: ' "Your Highness cannot be expected to feel passion as yet, but that will come. That will come. And you will in due course . . . but in due course, Your Highness, have your ten children." Ah, but I should not poke fun at his dear lordship, should I, for I love that man. I do really. Ah, if he were but my Prince of Wales . . . But he is a little old, and perhaps he would not be able to give me those children – not all ten of them.'

'Your Highness!'

'Yes, yes. I will try. You see, Rosenzweig, while I am not averse to my marriage, I think I am *indifferent* to it. I shall try to be happy, but my joy will not be enthusiastic. I once loved a man. Did you ever hear of Major von Töbingen? But they took him away from me. How happy we might have been! But they sent him away. He was there – and then he was gone. He was not good enough, they said. He was only a Major, and I am a princess. Princesses must marry princes – more's the pity. Oh God help me, Rosenzweig, it is my Major whom I want.'

Mademoiselle Rosenzweig was alarmed; she feared the Princess was going to have one of those hysterical fits of which she had heard.

'Your Highness, I beg of you do not say such things. If it were to come to the ears of my Lord Malmesbury, he might feel it his duty to report it to the King of England.'

'Let him. Let them bring back Major von Töbingen. Let them give him to me – and I will gladly hand them back their Prince of Wales.'

'Your Highness, Madam, you are not thinking what you are saying.'

Caroline was silent for a few moments; then she said sadly: 'No. I am not, am I; and must. All the time I have to think. I have to remember what I have been told. I must not do this. I must do that. Oh, you, my dearest secretary, will be kind to me, won't you? You will listen to my ravings, won't you? You will let me talk to you sometimes of my darling Major if I feel that if I do not I shall go mad . . . mad . . . mad . . .'

'Hush, Your Highness! Hush!'

Caroline threw herself against her secretary and clung to her. Mademoiselle Rosenzweig soothed her. 'It will be all right. I shall be there with you. You can tell me whenever you wish and whatever you wish. It shall be our secret. No one else shall know that we talk of these things.'

'I will tell you how I loved him. How we planned to marry. I gave him an amethyst pin and he wore it always. He said that when he died it should be buried with him. He loved me – oh, he loved me.'

They were silent for a while and then Caroline said: 'But I must do my duty, must I not? Dearest Lord Malmesbury would tell me so. He is anxious that everything should go without a hitch and I must please him, must I not? So, dear Rosenzweig, I shall endeavour to study the English language and I shall in time speak it fluently. I shall do all I can to make my husband happy.'

'That is wisely spoken, Princess.'

'I shall try to please him. I shall try to interest him in my favour, for the Fates have decided, have they not, that I am to be Princess of Wales.'

A few days later Major Hislop arrived at the Court of Brunswick. He brought letters from the Prince which expressed His Highness's urgent desire to see his prospective bride in England. For Caroline there was a portrait of the Prince.

She ran with it to her bedroom and summoned Mademoiselle Rosenzweig.

'Look,' she cried. 'He must be the most handsome man on earth. Tell me, my dear, did you ever see one more handsome?'

'I never did,' declared the secretary.

'Look at that beautiful hair. Look at his blue eyes. And the star on his coat. Do you think that is velvet or very fine cloth? And what a beautiful shade of blue. My bridegroom is a very exquisite gentleman, is he not?'

Mademoiselle Rosenzweig said that she had always heard the Prince was very handsome.

'He is the Prince of princes,' said Caroline.

She kept the picture by her bed so that 'the first thing I see on opening my eyes is my Prince beside me.' Then she laughed for she saw that Mademoiselle Rosenzweig thought that a rather improper remark for a woman to make before her wedding.

But she was often discovered examining the picture; and after receiving it she seemed to grow more and more reconciled to the marriage.

A few days later the proxy marriage took place. A royal carriage drove Malmesbury from his palace to that of the Duke and the ceremony began. The Duchess was weeping throughout; the Duke looked stern but anxious; but Caroline, though pale, gave her responses in a firm voice.

In half an hour it was over and Caroline was declared Princess of Wales. The party drove to the palace of the Duke's mother, the Dowager Duchess, where a banquet was waiting for them.

Malmesbury was relieved. His duty towards his royal masters was accomplished. But he could not rid himself of the feeling that he had a duty towards the new Princess of Wales. He saw her as a forlorn creature doomed to tragedy, and partly because he believed her to be the most unsuitable wife that could have been chosen for the Prince of Wales he felt an irresistible urge to help her.

The following day the marriage treaty was drawn up in French and Latin and the signatures of all concerned added to it.

Now, thought Malmesbury, the time has come for us to leave for England.

The Duchess took the first opportunity of speaking to him.

'I hope,' she said, 'that the journey will not be long delayed. I shall not be happy until I know that my daughter has taken her marriage vows with the Prince beside her.'

'The weather is somewhat inclement for sea travel,' Malmesbury pointed out. At the back of his mind was a thought that if they waited until January and February were over Caroline would have time to improve her English and her manners.

'December is not so bad,' declared the Duchess. 'It is January, February – and the March winds which are intolerable. I think that you should start out now.'

'I cannot make those arrangements until I receive the instructions to do so from my king,' Malmesbury pointed out.

The Duke had a different attitude.

'I do not wish my daughter to embark on the seas until I hear that an English fleet has arrived to conduct her to England,' he said.

'There is nothing to be done until I have those instructions, sir,' replied Malmesbury. 'I expect them at any time now.'

'We will await them,' said the Duke, 'and in the meantime such a marriage should be celebrated with rejoicing.'

So there were the banquets and balls and visits to the opera – which occasions gave Malmesbury many opportunities of conversation not only with the Duke, the Duchess and Madame de Hertzfeldt, but with Caroline herself.

He took one of those opportunities at a masquerade which was being held at the Opera House.

He had been turning over in his mind how he could warn her of what was in store for her without betraying his acute anxieties and make his meaning plain to her without stepping too far outside the language of diplomacy. For instance, how could he possibly advise her to pay more attention to her personal toilette?

Sitting in the balcony at the Opera House Caroline turned to him and said: 'I wish to learn *all* about my future husband. People talk so much of him. They talk of him all the time – and yet when I come to picture him I do not see him very clearly. He is handsome, I know.'

'He is considered good looking.'

Caroline clasped her hands together. 'So many princesses are forced to accept the ugliest bridegrooms. Mind you, there are disadvantages with handsome men. I hear that the Prince is very fond of the ladies.'

'He is an extremely gallant gentleman.'

Caroline tittered. 'Well, when I arrive I must put a stop to that, must I not.'

Malmesbury gave an embarrassed cough. 'I think Your Highness would best please the Prince by being very tactful. He is a man who admires ... finesse ... in conversation and behaviour.'

'Finesse. I have always believed it to be a virtue to be open and honest. I see I shall have to change things at Carlton House if they go in for finesse there.' She laughed shrilly. 'And I see too that I have pained you, my lord, and that is the last thing I wish to do. I want to please you for you have been kind and I took a fancy to you the moment I saw you.'

She touched him playfully with her fan.

My God, thought Malmesbury, what would the Prince think of such behaviour.

'I have heard talk of Lady Jersey,' went on Caroline.

Malmesbury groaned inwardly, but she continued artlessly: 'I believe she is a very scheming woman of the Court who meddles and intrigues though she is quite old and a grandmother. One would think she had better things to do. I hear she has had two sons and seven daughters. Would you not think they would be enough to occupy her?'

'I think you should be particularly careful in your behaviour towards ladies such as Lady Jersey.'

'Why?'

'Because they are much older than you and have had more experience of – er – the Court. Lady Jersey and ladies like her will frame their conduct towards Your Highness according to yours towards them.'

'But should not the Princess of Wales set the pace?'

'I think the Princess of Wales should act very cautiously for at least six months after her arrival that she may see what is expected of her.'

Caroline regarded him solemnly. 'Lord Malmesbury, I believe you are a very wise man.'

'I am honoured by Your Highness's high opinion.'

'And you know now that when I say something I mean it. I lack that ... finesse.' Her laughter rang out. Far too loud and quite unmusical, thought Malmesbury; but there was at least honesty behind it. She went on: 'Lord Malmesbury, I am very ignorant, am I not? Perhaps you could help me to be less so.'

'If Your Highness feels I can be of the slightest use to you I am always at your service.'

'I don't speak English very well,' she said, 'do I?'

'You have a strong German accent.'

'Which you don't find very attractive.'

'Your English will improve with practice.'

'And there are so many English words which I do not know. How strange, my lord, many German princesses were taught to speak English fluently in the hope that they might marry the Prince of Wales. I was the one who was not. Is that not odd?'

'And unfortunate,' agreed Malmesbury. 'But do not fret too much about the language. The present Queen of England arrived in England from Mecklenburg-Strelitz with a very poor knowledge of the language; now she speaks very well indeed.'

'Ah, there is another matter which troubles me. The Queen of England. She is bound to hate me. My mother says so.'

'With all respect to the Duchess I say that is nonsense.'

'You see, she and Mamma were enemies and she doesn't want me there. There is a Princess of Mecklenburg-Strelitz who is *her* niece. She would have preferred her naturally.'

'Her Majesty will welcome the bride her son has chosen,' said Malmesbury glibly.

She looked at him trustingly and he thought: I fear I cannot be as honest as you, my poor Princess and remain a diplomat.

'Pray give me the benefit of your advice. What must I remember when I arrive at the English Court?'

'I think you should not be as familiar with your attendants as you are here. Be affable but never forget that you are Princess of Wales.'

'I am to smile and be friendly and yet not friendly—' she grimaced. 'Go on, my lord.'

'If any of them attempt to gossip do not allow yourself to listen; and don't allow them to influence your opinion.'

'I want them to like me,' she said wistfully.

'Popularity was never gained through familiarity.'

'I am really afraid of the Queen. She sounds such a grim old lady and I have a feeling that she will hate me.'

'All the more reason why you should be on your guard and make sure that your behaviour is always correct.'

'But how should *I* know whether I am correct or not? I have often been very *in*correct here in Brunswick.'

'That is because you have been thoughtless. In England you will be constantly on your guard.'

'I have heard that the Prince is – how do you say *léger*? It is as well to know it. I shall never show him that I am jealous – even if I am.'

'I trust that you will never have cause; and I am aware that Your Highness knows that should there be a ... slackening of the Prince's affection it is more likely to be rekindled by affection and tact than by reproaches.'

'Tell me, when do the King and Queen hold their drawing rooms?'

'On Thursdays and on Sunday after church.'

'Does the Prince go to church?'

'He will doubtless go with you.'

'But if he does not care to?'

'Then Your Highness must go without him and *tactfully* let him realize that you would *prefer* him to acocmpany you.'

'What a solemn conversation,' she cried. 'This is masquerade, my lord.'

'It is a pleasant subject, for what could be more agreeable than Your Highnesses going to church together.'

Caroline leaned forward to watch the dancers.

She looked, Malmesbury noticed, more at ease as a result of their conversation.

The Duke sent for his daughter.

'Caroline,' he said, 'I have today received dispatches from England. It is not the wish of the Prince of Wales that Mademoiselle Rosenzweig should accompany you to England.'

'Not accompany me! But she must. She is my secretary. How am I going to understand the English without her? Who is going to write my letters? How can I manage without her?'

'Caroline, pray do not become so excited. You must remember that the Prince of Wales is your husband now and you must obey his wishes.'

'But he does not know Mademoiselle Rosenzweig. Why should he object to her? I shall take her – no matter what he says.'

'Caroline, pray be reasonable.'

'I be reasonable! What of the Prince, my gallant husband!'

'You are going to the English Court. You must remember that ours is small compared with it. There may well be rules you do not understand. You should remember always to obey your husband.'

'But it seems so senseless. He has never met Mademoiselle Rosenzweig. Why should he object to someone he has never seen unless it is to spite me?'

'You are talking nonsense.'

'*He* is talking nonsense. He is being unreasonable. I will not part with Rosenzweig. I *will* take her with me.'

'Caroline, control yourself.'

'You yourself said that my English was so bad that I needed a secretary.'

'I know. I know. Perhaps I might put this case to His Highness. Perhaps I could explain to him. He may not realize that you write English even worse than you speak it.'

'So you will tell him that I insist on bringing her?'

'I will put the case to him and ask him to allow you to bring her.'

Caroline laughed suddenly. 'It is the same thing,' she said.

Her father looked at her anxiously; and thought of her sister Charlotte who had mysteriously disappeared in Russia. How had she behaved to attract such a fate? What was wrong with the children he had had by the Duchess – born of dislike and indifference. Oh, God, he thought, we royal people are to be pitied because we are forced into marriages which are repugnant to us; and not only do we suffer but our children also. And what would happen to Caroline? Looking at her now, seeing the stubbornness in her face, hearing that wild laughter, he wondered.

But he would at least endeavour to explain to the Prince of Wales that his daughter needed the help of a secretary.

The Duchess sent for her daughter. When Caroline arrived her mother was lying back in a chair in a most dramatic attitude, a letter held in her hand.

'Caroline! My daughter!' she cried. 'Shut the door. Make sure no one is listening.'

Caroline regarded her mother with distrust, but there was no doubt that the Duchess was genuinely agitated.

'I have a letter here from – I know not whom – but it is most distressing. I don't know what to make of it. But if it is true it . . . it horrifies me.'

'What is it?' asked Caroline, seating herself inelegantly on her mother's bed.

'It is unsigned. It tells me that Lady Jersey is the mistress of the Prince of Wales, that she is treated as the Princess of Wales and that he will continue to treat her as such after your arrival.'

'What?' cried Caroline and snatched the letter from her mother's hand.

'Oh dear, your manners! What will they think at the English Court . . . and if this is true . . . and I really believe . . .'

But Caroline was not listening to her mother; she was reading the letter.

The Prince of Wales doted on Lady Jersey; he spent most of his time with her; she was received at all the greatest houses as though she were Princess of Wales. The letter purported to be a warning to the Princess against Lady Jersey who, it was said, would do all in her power to undermine Caroline's position in England. She would almost certainly attempt to find a lover for the Princess, and aid her to continue the intrigue.

'What will become of you,' moaned the Duchess, taking the letter from her daughter and starting to read it again.

'No one is going to lead me into a love affair if I don't want to go,' declared Caroline.

'You don't understand how clever these people can be. Even if you were not tempted—' The Duchess looked knowingly at her daughter as though she were sure she would be – 'that woman would make out a case against you. Oh, I am terrified – truly terrified.'

'Nobody is going to make out cases against me,' declared Caroline.

'I fear, my child, that you are going among wolves.'

'You forget that I have the Brunswick lion in my heart.'

That might be, thought the Duchess, but it was a somewhat wild animal.

'I will speak to dear Lord Malmesbury about the letter,' said Caroline. 'Pray give it to me, Mamma.'

'I am not sure.'

'I am,' said Caroline, and snatched the letter.

'I think you should be very careful, Caroline. Lord Malmesbury is, you must remember, working for the King.'

'No,' said Caroline almost gently, 'he is working for me.'

Her mother looked after her helplessly as she went out.

'Pray, my Lord Malmesbury, tell me *all* you know about Lady Jersey.' He was taken aback, she saw. So there *was* something in it. 'Is she the Prince's mistress? Come, be frank.'

'The Prince has many friends and in a cultivated society friendship between members of opposite sexes does not necessarily indicate a love affair. Why does Your Highness ask?'

Caroline brought out the letter. He read it and could not hide his dismay.

Then he said: 'An anonymous letter! One should never take such letters seriously. It may well be some milliner who is disappointed not to have obtained a post in the household that is being made ready for you. Some maidservant . . .'

'Do you think such people would have *intimate* knowledge of my husband's affairs?'

'I see that there is much you have to learn of the English scene. There is constant gossip in the chocolate and coffee houses concerning people in high places. Royalty does not escape. Rather is royalty treated more scurrilously than most. That is why it is always so important to live exemplarily. The writer of this letter has clearly been listening to gossip. She – or he – shows a complete ignorance of affairs. This letter should be immediately destroyed and forgotten.'

'So you mean I should not be on my guard against Lady Jersey?'

'Your Highness should be on guard against everyone.'

'But not specially Lady Jersey?'

'Especially against those members of the Court with whom Your Highness will be in close contact.'

'But it says she will attempt to lead me into an affair of gallantry.'

'Complete nonsense. She could do no such thing.'

'And why not, pray?'

'Because, Your Highness, no man would dare make advances to the Princess of Wales.'

It was then that Malmesbury felt more than a twinge of uneasiness, for the Princess actually looked disappointed.

'Why not?' she demanded shrilly.

'Because, Your Highness, anyone who presumed to love you would be guilty of high treason, which as Your Highness will know is punishable by death.'

'By death!'

'But certainly. It is a universal law. The King's own sister, Caroline Matilda, who was Queen of Denmark, took a lover. He was executed; and she would have been also but for the intervention of His Majesty. She was imprisoned and died in prison when she was about Your Highness's own age.'

The Princess Caroline had turned pale, and Malmesbury pressed home his advantage.

'So you see, this is the letter of a person who is unfamiliar with the ways of the Court. It should be destroyed. I am surprised—' He stopped himself in time. He had been about to say that he was surprised that the Duchess should show it to her daughter. His friendship with Caroline was making him forget his diplomatic manners.

'It is addressed to my mother,' she said. 'I will take it back to her and tell her to destroy it.'

'Destroy and forget it,' admonished Lord Malmesbury.

She almost flounced out. What lack of grace! he thought.

What will the Prince think of her? Lady Jersey's task will not be difficult, I fear, and of course she will call attention to these *gaucheries.*

Poor Caroline! What can I do to save her from unhappiness?

In the Duchess's apartments Caroline was saying: 'So you see, Mamma, this is merely the spiteful letter of a disappointed servant. Lord Malmesbury says that no man would dare attempt to be my lover, for if he did he would be punished by death.'

Caroline's eyes gleamed. How exciting – to face death for a lover. If Lady Jersey were in truth the mistress of the Prince of Wales and she wanted a lover she would most certainly not hesitate. Why should she? If he could be unfaithful, so could she. She would have faced death for dearest Töbingen. Could there be another like him?

The Duchess was thinking: Death to love the Princess of Wales? Could that really be the law? It certainly had been flouted in the case of her own mother. She remembered the Dowager Princess of Wales who had been so enamoured of Lord Bute that she had been unable to keep her devotion secret. She had never heard any suggestion that they should be sentenced to death – although everyone knew of the connection. He used to visit her openly; he behaved like a father to young George – and it was a very cosy comfortable arrangement. The people had not liked it, of course. But that was because they had not liked Lord Bute – it was not due to the fact that he was the Princess's lover but that he was a Scotsman who had wanted to rule England.

Oh, yes, the people had murmured against the lovers. The Duchess remembered the shouts of 'Jackboot' – a play on Bute's name – and 'Petticoat' which used to be shouted in the streets. But they were amused by them, and there were lampoons and caricatures. No one had suggested treason.

She knew that the English were the most tolerant people in the world. They liked their royalty to amuse them and a little scandal was very palatable.

In her frivolous way she was about to tell Caroline this; but even she realized the effect it might have on her daughter.

So she said nothing; and held the offending letter in the flame of a candle.

As soon as Christmas was over preparations to leave went on at great speed, and when a message came from the Prince of Wales to say that in spite of the Duke's intercession on her behalf he forbade Mademoiselle Rosenzweig to accompany her mistress, Caroline was thrown into a fury of rage. 'Why, why, why?' she demanded. Lord Malmesbury with his customary tact managed to calm her.

There was doubtless a reason, he told her, but he could not tell her because he did not know it. He begged her to be patient. He would be her friend and counsellor in all things; and he believed she would find him as useful as a secretary.

'The dear man,' cried Caroline afterwards when taking farewell of Mademoiselle Rosenzweig, 'I could have flung my arms about his neck when he said that. And he does, my dear Rosenzweig, comfort me a great deal for my loss of you.'

There was no time for grieving; the journey was about to begin and it was by no means the best time of the year for travelling; the roads would be icy; and it might even be dangerous. Caroline was not put out at the thought. At least it would be exciting.

On 29 December 1794, at two o'clock in the afternoon, they left Brunswick.

The Duke said his goodbyes to his daughter very tenderly; and she wept a little. Dear Papa, she thought, he really was very good to me; and I suppose next to Major von Töbingen I love him best in the world.

He had been stern often and she was a little afraid of him but he had always been concerned for her, though never so much as now.

'Goodbye, dearest Papa,' she said.

'Caroline, my dear child, try to be happy.'

'It shall be my purpose in life, Papa.'

'And please listen to the advice of older and wiser people.'

She promised she would. She got into the carriage where her

mother was already seated, for the Duchess was accompanying her to Hanover.

Then the Duke took his leave of Lord Malmesbury and begged him to be a second father to his daughter until that time when she should be under her husband's care, which Lord Malmesbury promised he would do and in a manner so fervent that the Duke's fears were considerably appeased.

The cannons on the ramparts of the palace were fired; and the carriages began their journey. Through Brunswick the people came out to see it pass and to cheer their dear Princess who had always been good to them and their children.

Long life to her, they shouted. She, Princess of Wales – their own Caroline, who would one day be Queen of England.

When the cavalcade reached Osnabrück there was grave news waiting for them. Malmesbury had planned to travel through Holland, but according to the dispatch, the enemy of England, the French, had marched into Holland and that country was in danger. It was impossible therefore to contemplate taking the Princess of Wales by that route and the squadron of ships under Commodore Payne which was to be sent to convey the Princess to England had, in view of the situation, returned to England. There was nothing to do but call a halt at Osnabrück and consider the next move.

This was irksome, for without the influence of the Duke and Madame de Hertzfeldt, both mother and daughter became very unstable. The Princess openly flouted her mother; the Duchess gossiped incessantly; and the improvement which Lord Malmesbury believed he had begun with the Princess seemed to have evaporated. Caroline was a little truculent. She did not take his veiled criticisms so readily as she had at Brunswick. She was far too familiar with her attendants and called them her dears, her little ones, her darlings; and when Lord Malmesbury reminded her of the need to combine affability with dignity, she was a little haughty with him as though reminding him that he was merely the King's ambassador while she was the wife of the Prince of Wales.

There is going to be trouble, thought Malmesbury.

The Duchess, having heard that the French were not far off, was thrown into a panic.

Caroline found her preparing to depart and reported this to Malmesbury, at which the Earl went at once to the Duchess and remonstrated with her.

'Madam,' he said, 'you cannot surely wish to leave your daughter unchaperoned.'

'Nonsense!' said the Duchess. 'She is surrounded by women and she has you here to look after her. If the French were to come here, I don't see why I should be here to be captured. They've always hated the English and they'd remember I am one.'

'Madam, I crave your pardon, but I am in charge of the Princess and I cannot allow you to leave Her Highness until her ladies arrive from England.'

'And when will this be?' demanded the Duchess.

'That, Madam, I cannot say, since our plans have been frustrated by the advancing French armies.'

The Duchess could do nothing but obey for it was true that the Earl of Malmesbury was in charge; and it was in any case her duty to stay with her daughter.

Caroline cried: 'If you wish to go, go. I do not want you to stay with me if you prefer not to.'

They wrangled together; and Lord Malmesbury was more concerned with their behaviour than with the advancing French.

What will become of her in England? he asked himself.

He made up his mind that it would be better to retreat to Hanover and stay there until he could be sure of conveying the Princess safely to England. From there he sent dispatches to the King and the Prince and settled down to wait for action.

Perhaps, he thought, this enforced stay at Hanover was not such a calamity. The Princess was most certainly not ready to be presented to her husband. He had a few weeks' respite – and because he was fond of her, he was very anxious to help her all he could.

He had been shocked – but at the same time touched – when

as they prepared to leave Osnabrück she had suggested he ride in the carriage with her.

'For to tell you the truth, my lord,' she said in her most confidential and somewhat coquettish manner, 'I am heartily sick of my mother's company and feel sure I should not only enjoy yours more, but profit from it.'

'Quite impossible,' he had retorted coldly. 'It would be most improper.'

This had sent her into peals of that uncontrolled laughter which he always found so alarming.

'Your Highness,' he had told her, 'must really take greater care in your behaviour towards your servants.'

'But I do not regard a noble lord like you as my servant,' she had cried mischievously.

It seemed to him that she had learned nothing.

Oh, yes, they needed this stay in Hanover.

All through February they remained there, the Princess being lodged in the Bishop's Palace. Malmesbury suggested that she read English for several hours each day and that he and she should converse in that language, which was an excellent idea because she improved considerably. She even tried to curb those gushing displays of affection towards her attendants of which the Earl had warned her; and he grew pleased with her once more. But there was one matter which continued to worry him. This concerned personal cleanliness.

What, he asked himself in exasperation, could a man do in such circumstances? It was too embarrassing to be spoken of – but warned she must be, for no sooner was she taken into His Highness's presence than he would be aware of her lack of cleanliness.

He could no longer delay and however delicate the matter must find some way of making the Princess aware of what offence she would cause.

The opportunity came when he was talking to her after dinner.

'The Prince is a most fastidious gentleman,' he explained, 'and pays great attention to his *toilette*.'

'So I have heard. Diamond buckles on his shoes! He invented a buckle of his own, I was told, and when he first took his seat in the House of Lords he wore satin and spangles. What a sight he must have been!' The Princess giggled, half with admiration, half derision.

'I was thinking rather of personal cleanliness,' said the Earl hastily.

'Oh?' Caroline was surprised. What did that mean? she wondered.

'The English nobility pay attention to bathing; in fact the *toilette* is a ritual – not to be hurried over.'

Caroline laughed. 'Oh, I never waste much time on washing. Madame Busche says she has never known anyone get through that performance as speedily as I.'

'That,' replied the Earl sharply, 'is nothing of which to be proud.'

Caroline looked startled and the Earl plunged in.

'Your Highness must forgive me. I speak for your own good. It is obvious to me – and it would be to His Highness in particular – that you do not spend enough time at your *toilette*.'

'My lord, what *do* you mean? Why should I waste my time going through a ceremonial dressing?'

'I did not mean the ceremony, Your Highness. I meant the actual performance. It is necessary to wash the body all over and with care.' This was most embarrassing and he admitted with any other member of a royal family but Caroline it would have been impossible. But that very familiar quality which he so deplored did at least have the effect of allowing him to speak freely. 'And,' he added, 'to change one's linen frequently.'

Caroline burst out laughing. 'Oh, you mean I'm dirty!'

Malmesbury remained outwardly unperturbed.

'It may be,' he said, 'that I exceed my duty, but Your Highness knows that more than duty prompts me. In England we pay more attention to matters of personal freshness than is the custom in Brunswick. The Prince is a gentleman of high fashion. His linen is kept in scented presses; he bathes each day and would expect Your Highness to do the same. He would, I fear, be aware immediately if you failed to do so.'

Caroline was astonished. 'Bathe!' she cried. 'What an odd idea. Is it not a little eccentric? Even in France they do not bathe. I was told that there is only one bath-tub in Versailles and that they grow flowers in it.'

'I am sure you have not heard the truth. But I must explain to you that in England bathing is considered of great importance.'

'What a strange people I am going among.'

'And a gentleman such as the Prince is of course greatly addicted to the habit.'

Caroline looked at him mischievously, sensing the embarrassment which was lurking behind his dignified manner.

So I am not clean, she thought, and he has been wondering for a long time how he can tell me so. He really does care about me or why should he bother? If I did not love my dearest Major von Töbingen, if I were not going to be the wife of the Prince of Wales, I could love this man.

'I will take advice from you, my lord,' she said, 'though I do not like it from others.'

His words had some effect, though not enough. Caroline was not fond of washing and she thought her dear Earl was being over-anxious.

He was relieved that he had been able to talk to her on such a subject without mortally offending her; but he could see that the matter had not ended with that conversation.

Perhaps he should approach one of her women. It would certainly be easier to explain to her. He sought out Madame Busche, one of her very personal maids who seemed to be a sensible woman.

'Madame Busche,' he said, 'I know I can speak to you frankly. And this is a matter of some delicacy so that I must know also that I can trust to your discretion.'

'You may rely on me, my lord.'

'It concerns the Princess's *toilette*. Frankly she does not pay enough attention to it and this is noticeable. The Prince would immediately be aware of it and as I know him well I know that he would find it repugnant – more so than most of us, because he is a very fastidious gentleman. I fear that if the Princess were presented to him as she is today, he would be – quite frankly – a little disgusted.'

Madame Busche was indeed a sensible woman. 'I am aware of this, my lord. We find it very difficult to get the Princess to bathe or to change her linen. She says it is all a waste of time. In fact she prides herself on the small amount of time she spends at her *toilette*.'

'This must be rectified before she meets the Prince.'

Madame Busche sighed. 'I will do my best, my lord. You will understand—'

'I have already spoken to the Princess and I think it has had some small effect, but there must be more of a change before we reach England. What kind of linen does she wear?'

'Coarse petticoats and shirts, my lord, and thread stockings. I put fresh ones out for her, but often she does not change them.'

'Madame Busche, we must do our best to make her realize the importance of cleanliness.'

Madame Busche promised that she would do her utmost.

But the fact was, Malmesbury reminded himself, that the German idea of personal hygiene was not the same as that of the English, and English nostrils therefore would be far more sensitive to unpleasant odours.

Soon Mrs Harcourt would be coming out from England to take up her part as Lady of the Bedchamber to the Princess of Wales. He would be able to speak to her and perhaps something effective would be done then.

He might have spoken to the Duchess. Perhaps she was the obvious person to whom he should have spoken. But she was a foolish woman – and he was surprised that with her English upbringing she had not noticed this failing in her daughter. But while she followed the habits she had been taught in England she had made no effort to instil them in Caroline.

It was not until March that news came from England that the fleet which was to escort Caroline to England had arrived.

The waiting was over. Malmesbury was relieved yet apprehensive. It was perhaps foolish of him to feel the latter, because no one could find fault with the manner in which he had so far carried out his commission. But it was impossible to have come to know Caroline so well and not to feel affection for her – and the apprehension was for what would happen to her. He could not imagine how the Prince of Wales could possibly be attracted by her.

The arrival of Mrs Harcourt was a comfort. She was, he believed, a sensible woman; she was English; she would understand the need for an improvement in the Princess's *toilette* and Lord Malmesbury could talk to her frankly.

Caroline was at first suspicious of her and resentful that her ladies-in-waiting should be chosen for her when she was not allowed to take her secretary Mademoiselle Rosenzweig with her. So she received Mrs Harcourt as though she disliked her, for there was no finesse about Caroline.

Mrs Harcourt – a friend of Lady Jersey who had planned with that lady that the Prince should marry not the fascinating Louise of Mecklenburg-Strelitz, niece of the Queen, but the less attractive Caroline of Brunswick – was a woman of experience.

At the moment it was necessary for her to find her way into the Princess's good graces, so she ignored the churlish reception and very soon Caroline's temporary dislike had passed.

Malmesbury took the first opportunity of talking to Mrs Harcourt and telling her of his fears. Mrs Harcourt had, of course, been aware of Caroline's failing and she told the Earl that she was doing all in her power to lure the Princess to cleaner habits.

'Pray do so,' begged the Earl, 'or I fear for the results.'

'My lord Earl,' replied Mrs Harcourt, 'I think your anxiety over these matters has made you a little blind to our Princess's virtues. I am sure the Prince will love her. She is so affectionate and good-natured. And you will agree that her desire to please everyone is most engaging.'

'I recognize these virtues and I hope they will make up for the defects.'

'Oh, but she is so lovable. And have you noticed a slight resemblance to Maria Fitzherbert – when Maria was young, I mean? I am sure it is there. That in itself would endear her to His Highness.'

'I had not noticed,' replied Malmesbury. 'And certainly there is a great difference in the characters of these two ladies. If Her

Highness possessed one half the dignity, the regality of Mrs Fitzherbert—'

'Ah, but she is so sweet-tempered and affable. I am sure she will please everyone.'

There was one person who would be very pleased, Mrs Harcourt was sure, and that was Lady Jersey. But it was impossible to be with the Princess without feeling sympathy for her and Mrs Harcourt genuinely did find her affable and affectionate.

She was well aware that these qualities would not carry her far with His Royal Highness the Prince of Wales. But the more she saw of the Princess the more Mrs Harcourt liked her and by the time they set sail for England she shared a little of Malmesbury's desire to launch the Princess happily.

The Duchess clasped her daughter in her arms.

'Goodbye, my daughter. May happiness be yours. Tell the King of England that I think of him often and I remember the happy days when we were children together. Tell him how happy I am to see my daughter heir to the throne – Princess of Wales . . . Queen of England.'

'It would be scarcely kind to mention that, Mamma, because he has to die before I can be, hasn't he?'

'Don't be so frivolous, Caroline. The King won't like it. Remember he said he hoped you had not too much vivacity and would be prepared for a quiet life.'

Caroline pouted. 'I shall be myself and His Majesty will have to put up with me.'

'Oh, my dear child, when will you learn. Well, you are married now and nothing can alter that and you are going to my dear . . . dear England. How I wish I were going with you! Oh no, I don't. I'm sure I should soon be quarrelling with Charlotte. You will have to beware of Charlotte. I never liked her. She is sly and cunning and she will naturally hate you.'

Lord Malmesbury interrupted with apologies. It was time they left.

Caroline was not sorry to say goodbye to her mother, and she felt her spirits lifted a little. It was a relief that the waiting was over. Very soon now she would see her husband and since she had heard so much about him she was beginning to feel eager to start her married life. He was obviously a very fascinating personality; and she was determined to do everything that would please him, even endure a thorough bathing and changing her underclothes every day. They all seemed to insist on that and though it seemed rather foolish to her, to please him she would do it. Often she looked at the picture which had been brought over for her. He is undoubtedly very handsome, she thought. It will be pleasant to be Princess of Wales and we shall have children.

Yes, she was beginning to look forward with pleasure to the prospect.

The cavalcade arrived at Stade and there they spent the night. Next morning, at dawn, they sailed down the river to Cuxhaven where the English fleet lay in residence. Caroline was touched to realize that these magnificent ships had come from England to carry her to her new home.

As she boarded the *Jupiter* a royal salute was fired.

The journey to England had truly begun.

The meeting

After three days at sea the *Jupiter* arrived off the coast of Yarmouth. Caroline, who was a good sailor, and had not suffered from seasickness as some of the company had, was on deck to get the first glimpse of her new country but all she saw was mist and the Captain told her that they could not land in such a fog but must wait a few hours before proceeding to Harwich. She had chatted familiarly with him throughout the voyage and he, like all the other officers on board, found her charming.

'There's nothing haughty about the new Princess of Wales,' was their comment.

Lord Malmesbury looked on and saw much of his training dispensed with. Often he heard her shrill laughter, noticed her coquettish glances at the men, deplored her habit of making what he called 'missish friendships' with her attendants and the habit into which she had slipped once more of calling her maids, 'my dear', 'my heart', 'my love'. It pleased them perhaps – but it was not royal. And he heard too that Lady Jersey had been appointed as one of the ladies of her bedchamber. This was a cruel action on the part of the Prince, but he supposed His Highness had been cajoled into it; and knowing something of that lady, Malmesbury saw great trouble ahead for his Princess.

The Prince, however, was almost certain to be a little interested in his bride. His love of women would surely arouse in him a certain curiosity and if he found Caroline just a little to his taste he would be ready to be her lover, if only for a brief time.

The fog lifted and the *Jupiter* was soon sailing past Harwich; they anchored at the Nore and then next day sailed on to Gravesend.

There Caroline said goodbye to the captain and officers of the *Jupiter* in a most affectionate manner and boarded the royal yacht *Augusta* for the journey up the Thames to Greenwich.

Malmesbury was beside her as they came up the river, eager to see the effect the country had on her. The sight of those green fields touched him deeply. Nowhere on earth, he believed, was the grass so green. Caroline thought it beautiful and for once seemed to find nothing to say as she gazed at those fields, shut in by their hedges, and the graceful houses with their gardens coming down to the river's edge; and as they came to Greenwich she could see the city's buildings on the skyline dominated by the dome of St Paul's Cathedral.

Now, thought the Earl, there should be members of the Prince's household waiting to greet his bride. He looked for them in vain.

So the Princess of Wales stepped ashore at Greenwich and found no one to welcome her.

As she sat in her carriage on her way to Greenwich Lady Jersey was complacently smiling. We shall be at least an hour late, she thought, and that is exactly as I would wish it to be.

She had in fact arranged that it should be so. Madam Princess would have to learn quickly that the lady who ruled the Prince's household was his mistress and there was going to be no change in that arrangement now that he had a wife.

She was sure there would be nothing to fear from Caroline – if her information was correct. The young woman was gauche, without grace and not particularly clean. How that had amused her! To think of Malmesbury – that most urbane of diplomats – finding it his duty to warn the Princess that she should take more baths!

One day she would amuse the Prince with an imaginary account of the scene. But not yet. She must tread carefully for a while. Let him learn that the creature disgusted him without – as he thought – her help.

She had whispered all sorts of information to him, gradually damning Caroline, just as she had when she had had Maria Fitzherbert to deal with. Maria, aloof at Marble Hill, gave her greater cause for anxiety than the Princess of Wales, for she knew that the Prince thought often of Maria. However, she herself could still enthrall the Prince and she was going to keep a tight hold of the leading reins by which at the moment she held him.

With her she had brought a change of costume for the Princess which she herself had had made. She had had many descriptions of the Princess's physical appearance and had decided to dress her in white which would, Lady Jersey felt, be the most unbecoming; she had brought with her a tightly fitting hat which would hide Caroline's hair because by all accounts it was beautiful. Lady Jersey had it all cleverly planned.

She was amused now to see the discomfiture of her companions, Lord Claremont and Colonel Greville, both of whom had been commissioned by the Prince to meet the Princess and, with an escort of the Prince's Own Light Dragoons, escort her to St James's.

How they fidgeted; and they knew in their hearts that Lady Jersey had deliberately delayed them so that the Princess might have the humiliation of being kept waiting.

The Governor of the Hospital at Greenwich, Admiral Sir Hugh Palliser, received Caroline and the company with the utmost grace, but he could not hide the fact that he was uneasy because the escort had not arrived.

Malmesbury was deeply conscious of the reason for the delay and thought it augured no good for Caroline's future. He was glad that he had warned her to be on her guard against women such as Lady Jersey.

He was not displeased with the Princess who, since she had stepped ashore, had behaved with some decorum. This might have been due to the fact that she was nervous, but it was still admirable. She had been far too noisy on the *Jupiter* but it was true that she had endeared herself to the officers; and if she could win the approval of the people through her free manners perhaps they had some virtue.

She looked charming, too. In fact he had rarely seen her look so well. The clothes which she put on for this occasion had been chosen by Madame de Hertzfeldt and Malmesbury was thankful for the good taste of that lady. Madame de Hertzfeldt had made Caroline promise that she would wear these clothes for her entry into England and although Caroline had thought them too quiet, she had promised.

Madame de Hertzfeldt had chosen well. The muslin dress over the blue quilted satin petticoat was the most becoming colour she could have chosen; it gave a touch of blue to Caroline's rather protruding pale green eyes which was attractive; but it was the hat which did more for her than anything else. It was black beaver trimmed with blue and black feathers; it shaded her face; it subdued the rather too high colouring; and it showed her pretty hair to advantage.

Presentable, thought the Earl. I wonder whether she thought to change her linen.

She stood at the window with the Earl beside her.

How much longer! he wondered. This is disgraceful. They should have been an hour early to make sure of being here. I am sure the Prince would be most displeased.

Sir Hugh was doing his best to entertain the Princess and she was already becoming friendly towards him. She was quite comfortable, she said. She liked looking around. And seeing some of the crippled pensioners in the courtyard below the

115

window, many of them having lost a limb, she said with a little laugh: 'Tell me, do all the English lack a leg or an arm?'

Malmesbury saw Sir Hugh flinch and his lips tightened as he said with the utmost severity: 'Do not joke on such a matter, Madam, I beg of you.'

Caroline was silent for a few moments, and then to his relief he saw that the first carriage had arrived. Lady Jersey alighted and came into the Hospital to greet the Princess on behalf of the Prince of Wales.

Caroline was all eagerness to see this woman of whom she had heard so much. She was astonished. She had imagined some monster and there curtseying before her, with the utmost display of homage, was the daintiest creature she had ever seen.

How pretty she is! thought Caroline.

Lady Jersey was raising the most beautiful eyes Caroline had ever seen, smiling charmingly. Could it be possible that she was a grandmother! How did she remain so slender, so beautiful?

'Your Highness, I have come to serve you.'

The Princess nodded and Malmesbury closed his eyes because he could not bear to look.

Lady Jersey was thinking: She is more attractive than I had been led to believe. But it is that hat. It would make anyone look attractive. That must be discarded.

'Madam,' she said, 'there has been some unaccountable delay . . .'

Unaccountable, fumed Malmesbury inwardly. Very accountable, I should think!

'If you would give your permission for us to proceed with the dressing immediately—'

'Why yes, yes, of course,' cried the Princess.

'Then if you will allow me to conduct you to a room where we can thus serve Your Highness . . .'

'Come along,' cried Caroline.

Lady Jersey and Mrs Harcourt left with the Princess. Malmesbury looking after them thought: She has learned nothing – nothing.

*

'I have here, Madam, the clothes which have been especially designed for your journey to St James's.'

'Clothes!' Caroline was eager to see them. 'White?' she cried.

'Yes, Madam. The symbol of purity.'

Caroline laughed aloud, and Lady Jersey looked surprised.

'Your Highness is amused?'

'Just a little.'

'Indeed, Madam.'

'My father's mistress used to say that white never suited me.'

'White not suit you! But Your Highness has the most beautiful colouring. Such *freshness*. White, if you will pardon me, Madam, is for ladies like Your Highness.'

Lady Jersey – herself so elegant – must know, thought Caroline. Madame de Hertzfeldt had seemed elegant, but that was in Brunswick. She could not compare with this dainty creature.

'It is the most beautiful satin available. Pray touch it, Madam. There, do you not long to try it on?'

'I never saw such satin,' admitted Caroline.

'No, Madam, I daresay not. I ordered it especially for you. Nothing but the best would be worthy of Your Highness and I chose the best dressmakers in London. Would Your Highness try it?'

Caroline removed the beaver hat. Her hair is lovely, thought Lady Jersey. That must certainly be put out of sight. That turban will be excellent.

Caroline took off her muslin dress and put on the white satin.

'It couldn't be better,' cried Lady Jersey. 'Do you not think so, Mrs Harcourt?' Mrs Harcourt, whose position in the Princess's household depended on Lady Jersey, must agree with her, so she did, but reluctantly, for she had grown fond of the Princess and had been pleased to see her look so well in her muslin gown. Nothing, thought Lady Jersey complacently, could have brought out the coarseness of that ruddy complexion better than the harsh white satin.

She picked up the hat. 'It is charming for some purposes,' she admitted. 'A ride in the country perhaps. But this is Your Highness's first ride through the capital, and we need something more fine.'

She produced a turban trimmed with white satin and decorated with white feathers. This she placed on Caroline's head, making sure that her hair was hidden.

The result was too much for Caroline to accept. It was quite hideous. It accentuated the deep colour of her cheeks while taking all the colour from her eyes.

'It's ugly,' cried Caroline.

'Your Highness, it is the height of fashion.'

'Then the height of fashion is not for me.' Caroline tore off the turban and threw it across the room. She shook out her hair and put back the beaver hat. The effect was ruined by the harsh white satin dress.

Lady Jersey was disappointed, she had reckoned on discarding that hat, but she saw it would be unwise to press the point. And in any case the beaver hat with the white satin was quite ridiculous.

'At least Your Highness will wear the dress,' said Lady Jersey anxiously.

Caroline smoothed down the folds. She had never felt such soft material. Oh yes, she loved the dress.

'Then you must allow me to touch up Your Highness's complexion . . . just a little. The ladies of the Court do, you know. It's the fashion.'

Caroline looked at Lady Jersey's delicately tinted cheeks. She really was a little beauty. It would be pleasant to look like that.

Caroline sat down and Lady Jersey applied rouge to the florid cheeks. The effect was startling but it seemed to please Caroline as much as Lady Jersey.

She was ready for the journey, so putting on a green satin cloak trimmed with gold loops and tassels she allowed herself to be conducted to the coaches.

Lord Malmesbury was horrified by the change in her. He should have prevented this. He should have foreseen what that wicked creature, Lady Jersey, would do to his innocent Princess. For innocent she undoubtedly was and was almost ready to treat the woman as a friend in spite of what she had heard of her. At any moment she would be calling her my love.

Caroline got into the first coach and Lady Jersey was about

to take her place beside her when Lord Malmesbury pointed out that the Princess should sit facing the horses and her ladies opposite her. No one should sit beside the Princess.

Lady Jersey put her hand over her eyes. 'I feel sick when I sit with my back to the horses.'

'How unfortunate, and you a Lady of the Bedchamber! I should have thought such a disability would have disqualified you from taking such a post; but since it did not I suggest that you ride in the second coach with me which will give me great pleasure and prevent any unfortunate occurrence.'

'But who will ride with the Princess?' demanded Lady Jersey.

'There is the second lady-in-waiting.'

'It would be most improper for Mrs Ashton to ride with Her Highness,' declared Lady Jersey. 'My place is in the first carriage and I will take it . . . no matter what the consequences.'

The Princess was about to offer to change places so that Lady Jersey might be comfortable, but a stern look from Lord Malmesbury stopped her.

'The Princess must sit facing the horses,' he said firmly. 'Anything else is unthinkable.'

The horses were whipped up and the journey began.

Caroline thought: So this was his mistress. Could it be that she had wanted to sit in the place of honour to show that she was of more importance than his wife? Still, she had been kind to her; she had had this beautiful dress prepared. Perhaps they could be friends.

How gauche she is! How unroyal! thought Lady Jersey. Simple, too. He will loathe her on sight. And that dress is quite hideous. I must compliment the dressmakers on making exactly what I wished for.

She does give herself airs, thought Caroline. Of course she is very pretty. But she must be quite old – yet I admit beautiful and very experienced. They say the Prince admires experience.

'You should not think that I am an innocent girl,' she said suddenly.

'Your Highness?'

'I am not so young, you know. Do you think I have lived like a nun in a convent?'

'I had not thought of the matter, Your Highness.'

'I love a Prussian officer. He is very handsome. I would give a great deal to be going to marry him. I love his little finger better than the whole person of the Prince of Wales.'

'Is that so, Your Highness?'

Lady Jersey was finding it difficult to suppress her laughter.

How amused the Prince will be to hear of these confidences! she thought.

They had arrived at St James's and the old palace loomed up before her. There was a crowd of people come to cheer her.

She alighted from her coach. In the Prince's Light Dragoons which had led the cavalcade from Greenwich, Ensign George Bryan Brummell watched the arrival.

'My God,' he thought, 'what a fearful sight! I feel quite ill to see a woman who could be moderately attractive look so inelegant.'

The Prince drove from Carlton House to St James's. The moment was close at hand, what will she be like? The reports he had heard of her, thought not effusive in her praise, at least conjured up visions of a not unattractive woman. Perhaps he could educate her, teach her to be cultivated and beautiful.

In his heart he was a little tired of Lady Jersey. He wondered if he had ever been in love with her. Certainly not in the way he had been with Maria. And what was Maria doing now? What was she thinking? She would be in her drawing room at Marble Hill – how well he remembered it! And he thought: How I wish I were there now!

But at least a new woman was waiting for him, and he confessed to a certain amount of curiosity. And if she were not too unattractive he might grow fond of her. It was his duty in any case to provide heirs to the crown.

He was dressed in his Hussar's uniform which was very becoming, he thought; the gold lacing suited his hair. He was a little too florid though, and had put on weight. He weighed seventeen stone which was really too much. He was perhaps too fond of drink, but he did take plenty of exercise. It's a family failing, he thought; and touched the swelling at his neck, carefully hidden, of course.

And now he must go and meet his wife.

Yet all the way to St James's he could not get Maria Fitzherbert out of his mind.

In the reception room of the palace Caroline was waiting. Malmesbury would present her to the Prince, and protocol demanded that no one but the three of them should be present for it was the ambassador's duty to deliver Caroline of Brunswick to George Prince of Wales.

Caroline had begun to feel nervous. Malmesbury was whispering last-minute instructions. 'When the Prince approaches, you must kneel – immediately. You understand?'

Caroline nodded – for once too overawed for speech.

'Listen. He is coming.'

The door was thrown open. Caroline caught a glimpse of a large glittering figure. She knelt. The Prince was standing before her and as he raised her a shudder he could not repress ran through him.

This – this – *thing* they have dared bring to me! This over-rouged, repulsive, ill-smelling object!

Caroline looked at him. He was flushed, not nearly as handsome as the portrait she had received, and fat – so very fat. She smelt the perfume that clung to him; she saw his short nose wrinkle in disgust.

Her hands were damp and hot. He could not bear the touch of them. He dropped them quickly and turning to Malmesbury said: 'Harris, get me a glass of brandy quickly. I feel ill.'

Caroline stared at her future husband in dismay.

Malmesbury replied: 'Your Highness, would you not rather have a glass of water?'

'No, by God,' cried the Prince. 'But . . . no matter. I must go to . . . the Queen.'

With that he turned and walked from the room.

Caroline looked at Malmesbury who, for once, was overcome by confusion. Poor child, he thought, how gauche, how unattractive in that dreadful white satin gown! And she had not changed her linen. The Prince's delicate nostrils would have detected this at once. It was the reason he had flown. He was always inclined to turn his back on what he considered unpleasant and that was clearly what he was doing now.

Caroline was recovering herself. She had visualized this moment many times since the proxy marriage but never had she imagined anything like this. She was angry. He did not like her. Well, she did not like him either.

She said in her shrillest voice: 'My God, is the Prince always like this? I found him very fat and not nearly so handsome as his portrait.'

Malmesbury had recovered himself. 'His Royal Highness is a great deal affected at this first interview. His feelings were too much for him so . . . he retired.'

'It seems very strange behaviour. I thought I had to be so careful of mine. He does not seem to be of his.'

'You will find him very different at dinner.'

'I should hope so,' cried Caroline.

'I will see that you are conducted to your apartments now. I expect the King and Queen will wish you to visit them.'

'Then I trust,' cried Caroline, 'that they have better manners than their son for I do not much like his.'

Malmesbury flinched.

I would to God, he thought, that I had never taken part in this unfortunate affair.

The unwilling bridegroom

He hates me, she thought. He could not have expressed it more clearly than if he had stated it in words. If they had let us meet before this and he had treated me so I would never have married him. She felt so alone. Her only friend was the Earl of Malmesbury and she knew that, in a way, while he deplored the Prince's behaviour he understood it. Why should this fat Prince find her so repulsive when Major von Töbingen had loved her so much?

Life was cruel to princesses; but one thing she had learned and that was that self-pity was of no use to anyone. She had to face them all at dinner – the dinner to celebrate her arrival – when the Prince would entertain all those who had brought her to England.

There was only one course open to a woman of her nature, and that was to show them that she did not care for their opinion, not even her husband's. She might have known what to expect. Had he not insulted her before he had met her by appointing his mistress a lady of her bedchamber?

She was not quite sure afterwards what happened at that dinner. All she was aware of were the disgusted looks of the Prince, the shocked ones of Lord Malmesbury and the delight of Lady Jersey which she scarcely took the trouble to hide. At least they should discover that she was not a meek nonentity. If they were going to be unpleasant to her, she would treat them in the same way.

She accused Lady Jersey – in a mischievous way – of being the Prince's mistress. She laughed loudly and continuously; she chattered in her own brand of French which was very different from the elegant manner in which the Prince expressed himself in that language. And as she drank and ate without restraint her laughter grew louder, her comments more risqué. The company was half amused, half horrified. The Prince alone felt no amusement, only dread.

And in the midst of her banter she had suddenly felt so lonely. She had wanted this man who was to be her husband to be interested in her and at least to give her a chance to please him. She thought of the children she had always dreamed of having. And this man would be their father.

Why should he prefer that old woman–the mother of all those children–to the young woman who was his wife? She had youth; she was not as unattractive as he believed her to be. Her hair was quite lovely and she had heard that he greatly admired beautiful hair. It was, someone had said, Mrs Fitzherbert's cascades of bright curls and waves which had first attracted him to her.

123

And that woman sitting there now saying little but unable to hide her smirks of satisfaction had tried to make her wear a turban which would have hidden her beautiful hair!

On impulse she removed the combs from her hair and it fell about her shoulders.

There was silence at the table. The Prince looked at her in astonishment. Is the woman mad? he was thinking. My God, what have I done to be burdened with such a creature? Lord Malmesbury was looking embarrassed. He was upset which meant of course that she had done the wrong thing again.

She laughed louder than ever; she made some crude jest.

They were talking together, ignoring her.

She did not need the sad looks of Lord Malmesbury, the furtive pleasure of Lady Jersey, the scarcely veiled horror of the Prince to tell her that she was a dismal failure.

When her maids helped her to disrobe that night she continued her wild chatter, but when she was alone she lay quietly thinking of the future.

What will become of me? she wondered. There was no point in pretending to be defiant in the darkness of her room. She was afraid; she had to remind herself that she was a Brunswick lion and they never showed fear.

'He hates me,' she whispered. 'Why, I did not expect him to love me . . . so soon. But he *hates* me. I disgusted him – so much that he could not hide it. Suppose he refuses to marry me? Nothing would please me more!'

Then she pictured her return to Brunswick – defeated, the Princess who was sent on approval and found unacceptable! She imagined her mother's diatribes which would go on and on for the rest of her life, for no other Prince would want to marry a Princess who had been rejected by the Prince of Wales. There was her dearest Töbingen. Oh lucky people who were not royal, and free to marry where they loved!

But whatever the next few days held for her, she must face it. And there was only one way she knew how to act. It was how she had acted tonight. She had been coarse, vulgar, ribald, mocking, indifferent to their scorn. It made dear Lord Malmesbury sad.

But what can I do? she asked herself. What other way is there?

She knew of none.

The Queen received Lady Jersey in private.

It was a difficult position, mused the Queen, for she had no wish to encourage immorality in the Court; and the Prince's love affairs were most public. But Lady Jersey, reasoned the Queen, was doing the country a service. She had separated the Prince from Mrs Fitzherbert and so made a marriage possible for him, for while he continued with that woman he would never have married because she convinced him that she was his wife. Sometimes, the Queen reminded herself, it was necessary to waive one's principles for the good of the country.

Lady Jersey's manners were impeccable. She swept a deep respectful curtsey and the Queen signed for her to rise.

'Pray be seated, Lady Jersey.'

Lady Jersey humbly thanked Her Majesty and waited for the questions.

'You have recently come from the Princess Caroline? Tell me, how is she?'

'Your Majesty, I greatly fear—' Lady Jersey stopped herself.

The Queen said graciously: 'You may proceed.'

'Your Majesty will think me presumptuous but because Your Majesty asks for truth—'

'Yes, yes. I want the truth.'

'I fear Her Highness has not been bred for the high honour for which she has been brought to England.'

'Tell me what happened.'

Lady Jersey told, stressing the *gaucherie*, the uncouth manners, the effect her appearance had on the Prince, his horror.

'Do you think he may refuse to go on with the marriage?'

'Oh, but he must go on with it now, Your Majesty. Or perhaps I am wrong but—'

'If he refused to go through the ceremony he could do so.'

Lady Jersey was secretly alarmed. She knew how the Queen's

mind was working. It was not too late for him to give up Caroline of Brunswick and take Louise of Mecklenburg-Strelitz.

Never! thought Lady Jersey. Caroline might not suit the Prince but she suited her purposes perfectly.

'It is for him to say,' went on the Queen triumphantly.

'Madam, what are your instructions regarding the Princess?'

'Watch her. If she writes to her home I should like to see the letters before they are sent. I should like to have reports of her conversation. I gather she is a very indiscreet young woman.'

'Alas, Your Majesty, that's very true.'

'We shall see what happens. In the meantime keep me informed. And if the opportunity arises to advise the Prince, you may be able to make him aware that it is not yet too late.'

Lady Jersey said that it was her great pleasure to serve Her Majesty.

The Prince paced up and down his silk-lined drawing room and declared: 'I cannot marry the woman. The very thought of it makes me ill.'

Lady Jersey looked at him sadly. 'You could never draw back now.'

'Why not? Why should I not?' . . .

'The proxy ceremony has taken place.'

'A pox on the proxy ceremony! *I* have not made any promises to the woman.'

'It would be an international incident if she were sent home now.'

'Little Brunswick! Need we fear that petty little place?'

'There are your debts.'

'I would take another wife if necessary, but not this one.'

Lady Jersey's eyes narrowed. Another wife? The alluring Louise. It was just what the Queen was hoping for. Her own niece to form an alliance with her – the wives of the King and the Prince would rule together. The poor, kind, weak-minded King whose mind often went wandering and the pleasure-loving Prince of Wales to be ruled by the ladies of Mecklenburg-Strelitz. And what of Lady Jersey? How would an attractive young wife deal with a mistress who for all her charms was an ageing woman?

She knew the Prince. If he succeeded in throwing off Caroline he would think her successor desirable and beautiful merely because of the comparison.

My God, she thought, what a trial I have to keep my place! Did Fitzherbert go through all this?

But she was wily and she enjoyed the game really. It was a great pleasure to work with the Queen – or to allow the Queen to think she was working with her – when all the time she was playing her own game.

Then she said: 'And what of the people?'

'The people. What have they to do with my marriage?'

'Everything that concerns their future King concerns the people. They are already showing sympathy for the Princess.'

'Why should they?'

'You know what the people are. They imagine someone is in distress and out comes the sympathy. I think that if you sent Caroline home you would make her into a martyr and in doing so you would become very unpopular.'

That startled him. He longed to be popular. He often thought of the old days when he had been Prince Charming and so handsome, the days before he grew so fat. Everywhere he went the people had cheered him. He longed for a return of that popularity.

Lady Jersey smiled secretly.

She had struck the right note. He would go through with this marriage for he realized how right she was.

The people would be against him if he treated Caroline so churlishly.

He looked grim. He could see that there was nothing to be done but marriage and yet . . . Who knew, some miracle might happen.

Caroline lifted her eyes to the protruberant ones of her uncle. There at least she saw kindness.

'Welcome to England, my dear,' he said in German, which was comforting. 'We are happy that you are joining the family.'

She could have hugged him and almost did – until she remembered that he was the King. This was the brother of whom her mother had talked so often – George who had a kind heart and addled head.

And now the Queen. Caroline was startled by the venom in the face of the little woman who was Queen of England.

She *is* ugly, thought Caroline, and they were right when they said I should beware of her, for she hates me.

She was bidding her welcome in English but that was no welcome. Queen Charlotte had no friendliness, no warmth to offer the stranger. Caroline had come without her blessing and she had no intention of pretending that it was otherwise.

And there were the Princesses who quite clearly took their cue from their mother.

This is my new family, thought Caroline.

The Prince called on the King and Queen to express his feelings forcibly.

'The thought of marriage with Caroline fills me with horror,' he declared. 'She is the most unattractive woman I ever saw.'

'She seems a pleasant sort of young woman,' said the King. 'I thought she was good looking . . . in a way. Surely you exaggerate, eh, what?'

The Queen watched her husband and son slyly. The Prince was really distressed, there was no doubt about that, and she was glad: he would refuse to marry the girl and then they could bring Louise over.

'I feel I cannot go on with it.'

The Queen put in: 'You know, George, it is for you to say whether you can marry this Princess or not.'

'I cannot marry her,' said the Prince.

'The King will tell you that it is for you to say,' reiterated the Queen.

The King nodded. 'No one can make you marry if you do not wish to. But you have to consider the reason for the proposed marriage. It is a condition of the parliament, eh, what? No marriage – no payment of debts. What are you going to do then, eh? Creditors getting impatient? They'll be in Carlton House if we say no marriage. It will only take that.'

'I cannot marry her. I cannot.' The Prince was striking his

forehead dramatically. But the thought of those debts, the total of which he dared not contemplate, and the effect his jilting of the Princess would have on the people, made him realize that there was no other way out.

He talked to his friends. He could not stop talking. They all knew of the revulsion the Princess Caroline aroused in him and in the clubs the betting against the marriage's taking place was high.

'He won't do it,' they said. 'He can't face it.'

And the Prince said to himself, 'Can I face marrying her? Can I face *not* marrying her?'

There was one, of course, who might have decided for him. He thought of her often. Maria. Why had she not understood that he had not meant it when he had said he would not see her again? She should have wept and stormed. It was what he had expected. Instead, that silence, and then her leaving the country.

But she was back now. She was at Marble Hill. She was his sweet lass of Richmond Hill as she had been in the old days – and always would be.

He could have talked to Maria as he never could to Lady Jersey. He had never loved Frances Jersey. She had fascinated him – still did to a certain extent – but it was Maria he wanted.

He sent for his phaeton and rode out. He drove wildly and the horses were heading for Richmond.

Miss Pigot saw the well-known phaeton.

'Maria,' she called, 'he has come. He is here.'

Maria came running into her drawing room crying: 'What are you saying?'

'He rode past just now. I saw him clearly.'

'He rode by,' said Maria sadly.

'He will come back. He has ridden by in the hope of seeing you.'

Maria took her stand at the window – to the side so that she could see and not be seen.

'Are you sure?'

Miss Pigot nodded. 'Poor, poor darling. He is so unhappy. All he needs is a sign from you.'

Maria shook her head. 'It is I who need the sign.'

'This is it. He is coming back to you. He has come to tell you so.'

'Then why ride by?'

'Because he wants that sign from you. He wants you to bid him come in, to make him welcome.'

'He was never so coy before, my dear.'

'He is begging you to take him back.'

'I have not noticed it. A strange way to beg. To become betrothed when he already has a wife.'

'Oh, Maria, don't turn your back on happiness.'

'I tell you it is for him to say. Have not the decisions always been his? As for myself, I must just wait.'

'He is coming again. He is coming back. I can hear the horses.'

'Stand away from the window.'

'It is for you to stand there. To beckon him as he passes.'

Maria stood very still, hidden from sight. She did not move. The phaeton drove past but she was aware that the pace of the horses slackened as they approached.

Was he in truth waiting for that sign?

I cannot give it, she thought. How can I? I am his wife. What does he want? For me to go back to him, to acknowledge myself his mistress?

'He has gone,' said Miss Pigot. 'But perhaps he will come again.'

He did – twice past the house; and on each occasion Maria stood at the window waiting, hoping, but not showing herself.

She gave no sign and he rode back to Carlton House.

But she kept thinking of him, riding out to Richmond. Surely it must have been because he hoped she would welcome him to her house. She thought of the vows of eternal fidelity he had made to her. She believed herself to be his wife. Did he believe her to be?

She would know the answer to that question in a few days' time. If he refused to marry the Princess Caroline she would know that he considered he had a wife already, and since he had come to Richmond could that mean that he wished the world to know it?

The Prince had had a sleepless night, but when he awoke on that Wednesday morning of the eighth of April he knew he must go on with the marriage.

While he was being dressed in his splendidly embroidered blue velvet coat and his elegant knee breeches he called for a glass of brandy. He drank it quickly and felt a little better. But by the time he had put on his high-heeled buckled shoes and was ready to leave for the Chapel Royal at St James's, he needed more brandy to sustain him in his ordeal.

Lord Moira, who was to accompany him, asked the Prince very cautiously if it were wise to take so much brandy before this important event.

'I need it, Moira,' he declared with tears in his eyes, 'for I do not think I can go through this ceremony without it.'

Lord Moira was sympathetic, but he could not agree that more brandy was what was needed.

'My dear friend,' said the Prince, 'you see before you the most reluctant bridegroom in the world.'

'Your Highness takes this too badly.'

'How otherwise can one take a bad business?'

The carriage was at the door and the resplendent bridegroom took his place in it, Lord Moira beside him.

As they rode from Carlton House to St James's, he said mournfully: 'It is no use, Moira. I shall never love any woman but Fitzherbert.'

Caroline was being dressed in St James's, whither she had come after the family dinner at Buckingham House. What an ordeal with those sly-looking Princesses watching her all the time, and the Queen showing her disdain. If I had known what it would be like I would never have come, she told herself. My father would never have forced me. Oh, how I wish I was home in Brunswick. And the Prince hates me. He shows that clearly. More and more every day he hates me.

There was only one member of the family who was kind to

her and that was the King. His hands shook as he embraced her and he kissed her as though he enjoyed doing so. She almost wished that she had come as *his* bride instead of his son's. At least he would have been kind.

When she had left Buckingham House he had taken her into his arms and kissed her fondly.

'This is a happy day, my dear,' he had said rather mournfully, and the rest of the family showed quite clearly that they considered it a calamity. The Prince and the Queen hated her – and those silly parrot-like Princesses followed their mother.

She looked at her white satin dress with the pearl embroidery. It was beautiful; and she, who liked flamboyant clothes, should have been pleased with it and the big cloak of crimson velvet which covered it. But she was very apprehensive as she left the apartment for the Chapel Royal.

The Prince swayed as he walked into the Chapel Royal. The two unmarried dukes on either side of him moved closer for they thought he would totter. A fine thing it would be if the Prince had to be carried to the altar because he was too drunk to walk there.

Caroline, who had entered the chapel on the arm of the King, had decided that she would hide her true feelings from all those who had come to watch her married and consequently appeared to be unbecomingly gay. Walking down the aisle with the King she smiled and nodded to people as she passed. The King did not appear to notice her odd behaviour but everyone else did.

There was a hushed silence throughout the chapel and all attention was focused on those two brilliant figures. The Prince swayed a little, magnificent in his blue velvet and Collar of the Garter but, as many noticed, looking confused and uneasy; and Caroline, shimmering in her bejewelled white satin with the diamond coronet on her head, looked a true princess.

But the Prince could not bear to look at her and kept his face turned from her. He was thinking of that other ceremony which had taken place in Mrs Fitzherbert's house in Park Street. That was a real marriage; this was a farce; and he yearned for Maria, whom he knew he should never have left – and he had done so for the sake of Frances Jersey! If he had left her for marriage to this woman it would have been a different matter, for this could be blamed on the exigencies of state. But he had deserted her for Lady Jersey whom he was discovering to be worthless in spite of her fascination. He was a traitor to Maria. He despised himself and he longed for an opportunity to tell her so.

And here he was at the altar about to be married to a woman he hated. Yes, he did hate her; he hated her fiercely. He could see no virtue in her. To him she was utterly repulsive and even the fumes of brandy which dulled his brain and his senses could not free him from the horror he visualized in the marriage bed.

How different that ceremony in Park Street and the ecstasy which had followed!

Oh Maria, Maria, you have deserted me.

But that was wrong. He had to admit it. It was he who had deserted Maria.

Is it too late? But of course it was too late. Here he was at the altar and Dr Moore, the Archbishop of Canterbury, was about to conduct the ceremony.

He knelt while the Archbishop began to say those words which had been said before in a house in Park Street, when he had made his responses with a joy as great as the revulsion he now felt.

The Prince was feeling dizzy; the brandy was having its effect though it relieved his feelings very little. He heard the Archbishop asking if anyone knew of an impediment why they might not be lawfully joined together in holy matrimony; and in that moment he saw Maria's reproachful eyes begging him to remember.

He stumbled to his feet. He must get away. He could not go on with this. There was a sudden silence in the chapel. All eyes were on the Prince of Wales; all wondered what drama they were about to witness.

Then the King rose from his seat and stepped up to stand beside the Prince.

'For Heaven's sake,' whispered the King, 'remember what this means.'

'I—' began the Prince, his face creased in his misery, the ever ready tears springing to his eyes.

'It's too late – too late . . .' whispered the King.

Wretchedly the Prince nodded and once more knelt beside the Princess.

Dr Moore was aware of the cause of the Prince's distress. Who in the chapel was not? Everyone had heard of the marriage with Mrs Fitzherbert.

The Archbishop proceeded with the ceremony and when he came to the injuction to the bridegroom to forsake all others but his wife he repeated it.

There was a tense expectancy throughout the chapel. Until the ring was on the Princess's finger many believed that the Prince would stop the ceremony.

But at last it was over, and the Prince of Wales had been married to Caroline of Brunswick.

Organ music filled the chapel and the choir began to sing:

For blessed are they that fear the Lord.
O well is thee! O well is thee! and happy shalt thou be.

And the chorus:

Happy, happy, happy shalt thou be.

The wedding night

The bells were ringing all over London; from the Park and the Tower the guns were booming; people stood in little knots in the streets and talked of the marriage of their Prince of Wales. Many had seen the huge wedding cake which had been driven to Buckingham House and which was so enormous that it filled a whole coach.

The Prince, whose antics never failed to cause comment – although lately it had been adverse comment – was married at last to a German princess who would one day be his Queen. Now the heirs would come along and if he were anything like his father and the Princess of Wales like the Queen, there would be plenty – and to spare. Jokes were made – coarse but friendly. The Prince was pleasing them more today than he had for a long time.

And what asked some, of Mrs Fitzherbert, the lady who had caused such a stir when the great question in everyone's minds had been: Is she or is she not married to the Prince?

The Queen held a drawing room and it was seen that she was noticeably cool to the bride. Caroline was going to get no help from her. It was also noted that she received Lady Jersey graciously, which was strange on such an occasion.

That lady was pleased with the way everything had happened, although there had been that horrible moment in the chapel when everyone thought that the Prince would refuse to go on with the ceremony. Now he was safely married to a wife whom he loathed. What could be better? This would give her complete ascendancy – particularly as the fact that he had been publicly married was a death blow to his liaison with Mrs Fitzherbert – the rival whom Lady Jersey most feared.

But Caroline had looked rather splendid in her glittering wedding dress; and the Prince must spend the night with her.

Alarming thought! For who could say what might happen in the privacy of the bedchamber? The Prince's revulsion might turn to acceptance – which it must of course – and suppose he came to like the woman a little!

Lady Jersey was determined to make the Prince's revulsion complete on that wedding night; she was reminded of something which one of the ladies of Charles II's seraglio had done when she feared a rival. Was it Nell Gwyn? She believed it was. That was a more ribald age of course but for that very reason the Prince of Wales might be less amused than King Charles had been. She gave orders that the pastry which was to be given to the Princess of Wales should be impregnated with a very strong dose of Epsom Salts, explaining to the cooks that there was an old maxim that if the bride were a virgin this ensured conception.

135

And so the family supper party took place. The Princess, plied with too much spirits – as arranged by Lady Jersey's spies and servants – was brash and over-excited; the Prince looked on sombrely and drank steadily throughout the banquet.

He had eyed his bride mournfully and declared to his neighbour that the only manner in which he could face the ordeal before him was through a haze of intoxication.

The ceremony over, it was time for the bride and groom to leave for Carlton House.

The King, with tears in his eyes, embraced his new daughter-in-law; with deep feeling he wished her well. The Queen kissed her cheek coldly and muttered her wishes perfunctorily, but her eyes, Caroline noted, were as cold as a snake's.

She was glad to be rid of them all at Buckingham House and in the coach with her highly intoxicated husband.

Mrs Fitzherbert sat in her drawing room at Marble Hill where she had remained all during the morning. Miss Pigot looked in every few minutes, her eyes anxious.

This was his wedding day.

Miss Pigot knew that in her heart Maria believed that the wedding would never take place. How could it when he already had a wife?

Miss Pigot was not so sure. She kept thinking of that occasion only a day or so ago when he had ridden by the house several times, hoping for a sign from Maria. If she had given that sign, Miss Pigot knew that everything would have been so different. He had wanted Maria's support then and she had not given it.

Miss Pigot shook her head. She regarded these two – the Prince and Maria – as her very dear wayward children who could have been so happy together and yet were constantly hurting each other.

'Come and sit with me,' said Maria. 'You fidget me – wandering about like that.'

Miss Pigot sat down.

'He'll never do it,' said Maria. 'I'm sure he never will.'

Miss Pigot shook her head. She thought of all the arrangements, the ceremonies in the streets. Was it possible to bring over a foreign princess, after she had undergone a proxy marriage, and then refuse to go on with the ceremony?

Yet he would have done that, she was sure, if Maria had just given that one sign.

'He can't,' went on Maria. 'It would be a bigamous marriage.'

Not in the eyes of the state, Miss Pigot wanted to say sadly. Dearest Maria, you are not married to the Prince in the eyes of the state.

But Maria believed she was married to the Prince no matter in whose eyes.

Miss Pigot knew that Maria was hoping that a messenger would come to her here at Marble Hill with the news that the ceremony had been stopped. That was what she was waiting for.

'Had you lifted the curtain, had you shown him yourself standing at the window ready to welcome him—' began Miss Pigot.

'I could not. The first move had to come from him.'

'But it did. Didn't he show that he had come out to Richmond to see you?'

'How could we be sure that he had come to see *me*?'

Miss Pigot laughed. 'Why else should he come riding out here like a madman?'

'Oh, Piggy, this could be the end.'

'It won't be, my dear, Whatever happens it won't be.'

'She will be the Princess of Wales – the Queen of England. Well, I could never have been that, could I?'

They were silent; ears strained for the sound of horses' hoofs.

'They would be at St James's now,' said Maria. 'The ceremony would be beginning . . . Do you think—'

'We shall hear,' soothed Miss Pigot.

They sat listening. Miss Pigot was aware of an intense melancholy. How could it be otherwise? How could he refuse to go through with this ceremony? She knew him, for she loved him even as she loved Maria. He was her splendid boy – spoilt, selfish and lovable. And now he was unhappy, she was sure of that. Oh, why had he been so foolish as to leave Maria for that wicked Lady Jersey! But then he had always been foolish, always impulsive, always acting in a way which would bring sadness to himself and those who loved him.

No two people could have been as happy as he and Maria had been – in the beginning. She had shared in that idyll; she had wanted to preserve it for the two people she loved best in the world. And they had smashed it between them like two petulant children, for Maria was not entirely blameless with her dignity, her determination not to give way and finally those outbursts of temper. Such a melancholy spectacle it had been to see that union disintegrate; and there was that dainty monster, that wicked Jezebel, Grandmamma Jersey waiting to step in.

And now . . . this.

They would hear soon. They must.

Yes, those were horses' hoofs. Maria was sitting tense, her face alight with hope. She really did believe he had refused to marry this Princess, and that he was coming back to her.

Miss Pigot was at the window. She saw the horses pulling up; the carriage was stopping at Marble Hill.

'It is my Lord Bradford,' she said to Maria, who still remained seated, a rapt expression on her face. Lord Bradford, who had been Orlando Bridgement when as a young man he had taken part in that ceremony at Park Street! The Prince had commanded him to stand outside the door and warn them if anyone approached because Prime Minister Pitt would have had the power to stop the ceremony if he had heard it was taking place.

It was appropriate that Bradford should come now.

The footman was at the door.

'My lord Bradford—'

Maria rose and held out her hands. Miss Pigot took one look at Bradford's face and knew.

'The Prince of Wales has been married to Caroline of Brunswick,' said Bradford.

Maria swayed a little. Miss Pigot ran forward and caught her.

'She has fainted,' she said to Lord Bradford.

*

Caroline surveyed the bridal chamber in Carlton House.

'It's grand enough,' she said.

The bridegroom looked at her disdainfully.

'Well,' she cried, 'you'll have to like me a little bit tonight, won't you?'

She recoiled before the look of loathing in his eyes.

'You're drunk,' she said. 'And *I'm* not so very much in love with *you*.'

He swayed about the room. And she thought of how she had dreamed of her wedding night; it should have been with Major von Töbingen but that was all over. Instead she had this man of whose attractions she had heard so much – and he had turned out to be a fat drunken creature who hated her.

'I doubt many have had a wedding night like this one,' she said; and she began to laugh.

But duty must be performed. Even he was aware of that. He asked himself if it were possible. The sooner the better, he told himself. When she was with child he need never share a room with her again.

Such a thought was stimulating.

He turned to her. She was laughing her loud vulgar laughter.

'Oh, changing your mind?' she asked.

So the consummation took place.

She is even more repulsive than I believed possible, he thought. Oh God, why was I ever lured into this?

She was sitting up in bed shaking the hair out of her eyes.

'It's all so romantic,' she mocked.

He staggered out of the bed. He could not bear her near him.

'Ah,' she said, 'where are you going? To Madame Jersey?'

He did not look at her. His one thought was to get away from her as quickly as possible. The room was whirling about him. Too much brandy, too much wine. He felt sick and ill.

He wept, thinking of that day in Park Street; it was winter and they had ridden off to Richmond together; the roads were icy and they had had to pause at Hammersmith – a romantic inn, supper by candlelight. Maria, Maria, why are you not with me? Why have they married me to that vulgar slut in the bed.

He had reached the fireplace. How his head ached! He felt so dizzy.

He put out a hand to the mantelpiece to support himself, missed it and fell, his head close to the grate.

He was too intoxicated to get up. He did not care. He preferred the hard floor to a bed shared with Caroline.

She had got out of bed and stood looking at him.

'All right, you drunken sot,' she cried. 'Stay there. Spend your wedding night under the grate.'

A child is born

'So,' said Caroline, 'they call this a honeymoon!'

They had travelled down to Windsor from Carlton House and there spent two weeks. The Prince, having made up his mind that as soon as Caroline was pregnant his duty towards her and the state ended, had one purpose in mind; and only the thought of the freedom which would come with success gave him the necessary enthusiasm to achieve that end.

Caroline was deeply wounded. She would, if it had been possible, have attempted to make their union a happy one but she had no notion how to please him, and when she tried to do so only succeeded in making herself more repulsive in his eyes.

He hated her. Every time he looked at her he remembered that he had been a traitor to the woman he really loved. He tried to forget Maria by becoming more and more attentive to Lady Jersey, who was enjoying the situation and had no idea how often Maria Fitzherbert was in his thoughts. Her attitude towards Caroline was haughty as though she were the Princess of Wales and Caroline her lady-in-waiting. Caroline had never been meek and such a situation was scarcely likely to curb her impulsive eccentricity.

The Prince decided that he would take his bride to Kempshott Park and with him should go some of those friends who would amuse him most and lift him out of his gloom.

Perhaps Kempshott was not a very good choice with its memories of Maria. It was here that he had spent many happy times with her and although she had never actually lived in the house, for with her usual discretion she had occupied a cottage on the estate, she had chosen the décor for the drawing room and had planned much of the gardens. He had been very happy with Maria at Kempshott and he took a savage delight in remembering those days and comparing the woman he thought of as his true wife with the one who bore the title of Princess of Wales.

But he also had at Kempshott one of the best packs of foxhounds in the country and there he kept his best hunters. He could at Kempshott play the country squire as his father used to enjoy doing at Kew and Windsor – but whereas the King had dressed and behaved like a country gentleman, the Prince was never anything but the Prince of Wales.

The country people were less fickle than those of the capital. They did not joke so much at his expense. There were no lampoons and cartoons, no bawdy and disrespectful gossip such as that which went on in coffee and chocolate houses.

He was married and that seemed a good thing to the country folk. As for the Princess of Wales she was a pleasant lady always with a smile for any who looked her way; and often she would stop and talk to the children in a manner which showed she loved them.

Caroline thought: If it had happened differently I should have been happy here. We might have made a good royal marriage.

If she could have had some of her friends with her she would have felt more at ease. Why had he been so cruel as to deny her the company and skill with English of Mademoiselle Rosenzweig? If only she could have had someone just to talk to. But she was unsure of all these English women who surrounded her, because they all seemed to be under the influence of Lady Jersey.

She talked a little to Mrs Harcourt, who was inclined to be sympathetic.

'The Prince hates me,' she said. 'Why does he hate me so much?'

'Your Highness is mistaken. The Prince needs a little time to grow used to his marriage. He – er ...'

Caroline burst out laughing. 'The more used to it he grows the more he hates it. Though I daresay few people here have ever seen a bridegroom try to turn away from the altar just at that moment when the Archbishop is about to make him and his bride man and wife.'

'Your Highness finds this amusing?'

'Very amusing,' cried Caroline, speaking in her racy French. 'I wonder if it has ever happened before to a Princess of Wales? If not I shall be remembered for it, shall I not?'

'If it were true, Madam, which I am sure it is not, it would best be forgotten.'

Mrs Harcourt, for all her sternness and her loyalty to Lady Jersey, was sorry for the Princess and somehow conveyed it.

'You need not be sorry for me,' cried Caroline. 'It is the fate of princes. My father used to talk of it. He was forced to marry my mother and was in love with another woman. He regretted he could not have married her. He always believed that if he had, his children would have been different.' Again that shrill laughter. 'Oh you are thinking that I am a little mad like my brother? Perhaps you are right. Perhaps I am. Oh no, no. I am very wise. I know that this is a *mariage de convenance*. Are not all royal marriages? But this one particularly so. I would never have been brought over here if the Prince had not been in debt. I was the victim of mammon. The Prince of Wales's debts must be paid and poor little I's person was the pretence.'

'Your Highness!' murmured Mrs Harcourt, shocked.

'Oh, Your Highness! Your Highness!' mimicked Caroline. 'You know the truth of this as well as I do, madam. Parliament would vote supplies only for the marriage of the heir apparent. A Protestant princess must be found so they fixed on the Prince's cousin. I hate it all. I tell you God's truth, I hate it all!' She threw back her head and beat her hands on her heavy breasts. 'But I had to oblige my father. He wished it. My mother wished it. And what could I do?'

'It is like so many royal marriages, Your Highness. But these are often happy. The King and the Queen—'

'Have fifteen children. Shall I? I think the Prince will be content with one – for when he has one he no longer needs to sleep with me. I tell you, this is what he waits for. He wishes to say: "I have done my duty. Now, I need do no more. It is enough." And I shall be glad. I do not love him. Let him go to his Jersey woman. The moment I saw that woman with my future husband I knew how it was with them and I shrugged my shoulders and knew I did not care.'

Her eyes were glazed with a sudden emotion; she was thinking of Major von Töbingen with the amethyst pin with which he had said he would never part while he lived.

'Oh mine God,' she cried, 'I could be the slave of the man I love. But one I did not love and who did not love me, that is a very different thing – that is impossible.'

'Your Highness should not talk in this way.'

'Do not, I beg you, tell me how I should talk. I talk as I wish, Madam. And I say this: very few husbands love their wives and when a person is forced to marry another it is enough to make them hateful to each other. If I had come over here just as a princess on a visit . . . Do you know that that was what Mr Pitt wanted me to do? Oh, it was before there was talk of marriage; but I think Mr Pitt wanted the Prince to marry and he thought that if I came over on a visit the Prince might have liked me a little. Do you think he would?'

'I feel sure he would.'

'Yes, he would have liked me – and perhaps I should have liked him. We should have been good friends. It would have been very different . . . perhaps.'

She began to laugh. 'But do not be sorry for me, my good Mrs Harcourt. All the Prince gives me in trouble shall be repaid. If he does not want me, believe me I do not want him. Once I am with child, once I have my baby, I shall be ready to say "Go away. Your presence is offensive to me." ' Her laughter was more wild. 'Oh, you are shocked. Be shocked. It amuses me to shock people and if I am not to have love let me at least have amusement.'

The Princess of Wales was indeed very strange, thought Mrs Harcourt.

When they could no longer curb their hatred of each other they allowed it to break out and seemed to take a great delight in hurting each other.

The Prince would wrinkle his nose in disgust when he looked at her. Caroline, deeply wounded, determined not to show her hurt, would give vent to mocking laughter or sometimes she would try to discountenance him with her ribaldry. Her intention was to show him that she did not care for him any more than he cared for her and that the marriage had been forced on her no less than it had been forced on him.

One evening when there were guests at Kempshott and it was necessary that they dine together with their guests, he looked distastefully at her. Her appearance was always too flamboyant; her clothes – no matter who was her dressmaker – managed to look vulgar in his eyes as soon as she put them on. She was always over-rouged although her cheeks were naturally highly coloured; her dresses never seemed to fit. Her bust which was magnificent – and he thought of Maria's fine bosom every time he looked at her – gave her a pearshaped look which he found repulsive in the extreme. She loved finery and would wear too many jewels of clashing colours in which she managed to look slovenly; and the greatest crime of all was that she refused to bath frequently.

The Prince shuddered and as he could not bear to look at her face, he fixed his gaze on her feet.

'Well,' she cried truculently, 'you seem to find my boots very interesting.'

'I find them extremely clumsy.'

'Oh, so you do? Well then you go and make me another pair. Yes, you go and make me a pair of boots. And then bring them to me and perhaps if I consider them good enough I may wear them.'

The Prince turned away.

Although she might shout and mock she was bitterly wounded.

It was a comforting thought to know that the Prince had invited her old friend Malmesbury to dinner that night. What joy it would be to see him. She would never forget how he had tried to help her. He, who knew the Prince so well, must have realized what would happen when she came to England. No wonder he had been so anxious for her, so eager to help her – dear good Malmesbury! If only they had brought her over to marry him instead of the Prince, how different it would have been.

I believe, she thought, that I hate my husband.

Among the guests were Lady Jersey and Colonel Hanger. She hated them both. Lady Jersey now made no secret of her contempt for Caroline. She wanted everyone to know that she was the true mistress of the house. What an insult to have his mistress as Lady of the Bedchamber when she had not been allowed to bring her own friends from Brunswick. And Colonel Hanger was a coarse man, a player of practical jokes, and she wondered that her fastidious husband could have such a man for a friend. But his tastes were not all that refined it seemed. He could gather together the most vulgar companions at times. It was all very well to be so elegant and wear such beautiful clothes and to bow in such a manner that it was the admiration of all who saw it. But what about some of these vulgar friends of his like Colonel Hanger, Sir John and Letty Lade, and the Barry brothers? They were always playing their silly practical jokes and of course she was the butt for most of them; they invaded the house and it was made noisy by their horseplay. And how they drank! They were almost always drunk and she would often find them sleeping on the sofas with their boots on – snoring.

Not so elegant, she thought grimly.

At dinner the Prince was attentive to Lady Jersey and kept pressing her hand and looking at her with great affection.

Still, she thought, he doesn't feel quite so affectionate to her as he pretends to be. It's all to anger me. And the woman was wearing pearl bracelets. She knew those pearl bracelets. They were hers. They had been part of the jewellery which had come to her on her marriage. How dare he take them away from her collection to give to Lady Jersey!

There is surely a limit to what I need stand, she thought.

Malmesbury was looking sad, now and then catching her eye as though he would warn her. Warn her! Shouldn't he warn the Prince? Who had set the pace? Had she or the Prince? When she had come here she had been ready to be a good wife to him, to build up some family life, to give him some affection.

If only I could go home, she thought. If I could explain to my father that this life is so wretched that no good can come of it! But that is impossible. Royalty must come before happiness. Royal people had no say in their destinies – royal princesses that was. The Prince was determined to have his way, and even though he had been obliged to marry – which was really because of his debts – he still intended to keep on Lady Jersey.

The meal over, Colonel Hanger lighted the great pipe which he affected. Everyone laughed at George Hanger who did the most eccentric things; and no one dreamed of protesting even at that big ill-smelling pipe of his.

The Prince was smiling at Lady Jersey who was talking animatedly to him. He took her glass and drank from it. It was a token of the state of affairs between them.

In a sudden rage Caroline snatched the pipe from Colonel Hanger's mouth and putting it in her own, puffed smoke across the table into the Prince's face.

There was a hushed silence about the table. She was aware of the Prince's blank stare, of the glitter of Lady Jersey's snake-like eyes.

Caroline burst out laughing. She had to do something to put an end to that awful silence.

Everyone was embarrassed; the Prince looked helpless; then ignoring her completely he began to talk of the play which was running at Drury Lane. Caroline knew nothing of the play. She could not join in.

She sat smiling to herself. She was not going to let any of them know how unhappy she was.

The Prince had sent for the Earl of Malmesbury who came to him rather sadly, guessing that after that strange exhibition at the table the Prince was going to criticize his consort and because Malmesbury had brought her over to blame him.

He saw at once that the Prince was really angry. 'Well, Harris,' he said, 'you have seen that extraordinary display of bad manners. How do you like this sort of thing?'

Malmesbury murmured that he did not like it at all, but he thought that the Princess was in a strange country and was not yet sure of herself.

'Not sure of herself!' echoed the Prince. 'My dear Harris, what antics do you think she will perform when she is? Why on earth did you not write to me from Brunswick and tell me what sort of woman you were bringing over?'

'Your Highness, there was nothing of which to complain against the Princess's moral character.'

'You could bring this ... this woman over, knowing what you did. I do not consider you served *me* very well.'

'Your Highness, His Majesty sent me to Brunswick not on a discretionary commission but with the most positive commands to ask the Princess Caroline in marriage.'

'I see,' said the Prince bitterly. 'You were obeying the King and you did not see it as your duty to warn me.'

'Your Highness,' replied Malmesbury somewhat sharply, 'while I knew that the Princess had much to learn I did not conceive that Your Highness would make up your mind so to dislike her.'

The Prince looked exasperated. 'You see what she is like. Do you think she will ever inspire respect in my friends?'

'I think, with encouragement, she will improve.'

'With encouragement. Harris, you are always so discreet and diplomatic, are you not?'

'It is my business, sir, to cultivate these qualities.'

'You manage well, I do assure you. But that has not helped me very much I fear. I see nothing but disaster through this marriage – nothing but disaster. This woman is ... impossible. She revolts me. She is not even clean.'

Malmesbury looked hurt. He understood, of course. Had he not tried to instil in her the importance of 'freshness'; had he not warned her of the extra-fastidiousness of the Prince? And she had lightheartedly refused to consider his advice. He was exasperated with her, but desperately sorry for her too.

And through her he had lost the confidence of the Prince who could never quite forgive those whom he thought considered his father before himself.

'And what do you think will be the outcome of this marriage which you, Harris, have arranged?'

'I think the outcome will depend on you, sir, and Her Highness. And I must remind Your Highness that it was His Majesty who, with your consent, arranged the marriage. My commission was merely to go to Brunswick and make a formal offer. This, sir, I did to the best of my ability.'

The Prince shook his head mournfully. 'I know, I know. But a word of warning, Harris. One word of warning. What disaster might have been averted then!'

Malmesbury could only look regretful; but as he left the Prince's apartment he knew that he was expected to take some share of the blame for the marriage and the Prince would always remember it against him.

He saw the Princess.

'I would to God, my lord,' she said, 'that I had never come to England.'

'Your Highness will grow accustomed to your new life.'

'I will never grow accustomed to life with him. Nor shall I have to. Because I tell you this, my lord: As soon as I am with child, he will never see me again. That is what he waits for. The best news I can give him is that I am with child.'

'It is the best news you can give the nation.'

'Oh, my dear ambassador, who is always so correct – and therefore so different from me. Yes, it will be good news. If I can provide the heir the nation will be pleased. But he will be pleased – not so much because I have given them the heir but because he can then be rid of me.'

'Your Highness, you remember when we were in Brunswick I implored you to be discreet and calm.'

'You implored me to do so much, you dear, good, kind man.

But you could not change me, could you? But I love you for trying.'

Malmesbury flinched. She would never learn. She would go on making wild and reckless statements, but she would not wash as she should; and she would never please the Prince of Wales.

'You see, my dear lord, I shall never change. I shall always be your naughty Caroline of Brunswick.'

'I believe that if you would try very hard to behave in a manner which would not shock the Prince—'

'Shock him. He is the right one to be shocked. You know, don't you, that he sleeps with that Jersey woman?'

Malmesbury turned away, his expression pained. What could he do to help such a woman? Had he not done his utmost; and all his efforts had clearly been in vain.

There was nothing he could do, thought Malmesbury.

The marriage was doomed.

The King was equally concerned for the marriage. The Prince disliked his bride and that was bad; but whatever happened appearances must be kept up.

The Queen came to his apartments. How their relationship had changed, thought the King sadly. In the days before his illness she would never have dared to come without an invitation. Now, of course, she was so necessary to him. A good wife, he thought. And he remembered all the children who had given him so much cause for anxiety: The girls who ought to have husbands found for them for they were growing restive and in a few years would be too old for marriage; the boys with their wildness. But there was always dearest little Amelia, the light of his life, he called her. His dearest youngest daughter who was yet too young to cause him any concern; he would like her to remain a child – a lovely innocent child for ever. And even she worried him because of that cough of hers. He himself prescribed her cough mixture and always impressed on her the need to take it; and when she put her arms about his neck and kissed him and called him dearest Papa, everything that he had suffered, the years of marriage with a woman who did not greatly attract him, everything seemed worth while.

He still had the verses which Miss Burney composed on his recovery after that frightful illness and which darling Amelia had presented to him. He remembered how sweet the child had looked and how she had spoken her piece which was:

The little bearer begs a kiss
From dear Papa for bringing this.

He would always treasure the memory. And whatever happened he had his darling Amelia.

Now he asked the Queen how Amelia's cough was and when he heard that it was better he was much relieved.

'I must bring up this matter of George's debts to parliament,' he said. 'I suppose they will be generous.'

'It is the price he has to pay for his marriage.' The Queen's big crocodile mouth widened in a smile. 'I daresay he is thinking the price a high one. Well, we all have to pay for our follies.'

'You think he cannot take to the young woman, eh, what?'

'I am sure he cannot. You will admit that she is a – spectacle.'

'I thought she was a handsome enough young woman.'

'Not handsome enough for George, evidently.' The Queen gave a quick laugh.

'Poor child,' said the King compassionately. 'It is not easy.'

'Scarcely a child. I was some ten years younger when I came here.'

'I know it. I know.'

'I feel Louise would have been a better choice. Well, it is too late now. I can feel almost sorry for George.'

The King frowned. 'I hope there will be no troubles about these debts. They are enormous. Some £620,000. How did he ever manage to let them grow to that extent, eh, what?'

The Queen shrugged her shoulders. 'George will have the best of everything.' She laughed again; but the King did not feel in the least like laughing. He was worried. It was not so long ago that the French had taken their king to the guillotine and cut off his head. When such a mighty conflagration as the Revolution was raging across the Channel a neighbour so near as England could not expect to remain aloof. The execution of a king must stir up feeling against all monarchies. Are we so safe over here? wondered the King. And one of the most unpopular members of the royal family was the Prince of Wales.

'If they go on like this,' he said, 'there'll be no kings left in Europe. Eh, what?'

The Queen was accustomed to the manner in which the King's thoughts strayed from one topic to another and she knew how much events on the other side of the Channel had preyed on his mind. If the King were incapacitated again she was going to make sure that she had a say in affairs and if George became Regent she would conspire with Pitt to put a limit on his powers.

'George's behaviour does not help to make royalty popular,' she observed. 'And now this marriage of his. If he had listened to me ...'

'When has he ever listened to either of us?'

The Queen lifted her shoulders. 'Well, he married that his debts should be paid and it is high time that they should be. I hear that some of the trades-people involved are getting very restive.'

'Something must be done – must be done. Don't want trouble, eh, what? Must speak to Pitt. Should not be too much delay.'

'Yes, speak to Pitt. It is a well-known fact that the Prince entered into this marriage for one reason only – and that was because he was in debt to such an extent that it could not longer go on.'

The Queen smiled. Lady Jersey reported to her regularly.

Between them – and with the help of the Prince, of course – they would make Caroline wish she had never heard of the Prince of Wales.

Mr Pitt was not inclined to make life easy for the Prince of Wales. Why should he? The heir to the throne had consistently shown himself to be the enemy of Mr Pitt, had allied himself with Mr Pitt's enemies, and had made no secret of the fact that Fox was his man and on the day when he inherited the crown he would do all in his power to oust Mr Pitt from his position and set up in his place Mr Fox or one of his Whig cronies.

The Prime Minister was too much of a politician to help such an enemy. It was Pitt who forced Fox to deny in the House of Commons the Prince's marriage to Mrs Fitzherbert which had been responsible for making such a breach between Fox and the Prince that it had, Pitt believed, never entirely been healed. But the Prince was a Whig and Mr Pitt and his Tories were prepared to do as little as possible for him.

The Prince's debts seemed to be a recurring problem. How one man could manage to spend such large sums was a mystery. Should the nation be expected to pay an extravagant young man's gambling debts and those he had incurred in the pursuit of women – and Lady Jersey was one of the most rapacious of his band – merely because he was the Prince of Wales?

Certainly not.

Mr Pitt made his proposals to the House of Commons.

The Prince's debts, he explained, were once more a subject for discussion. He regretted to inform the House that they amounted to some £619,570 — a vast sum of money they would all agree. He proposed as follows: The Prince's income should be increased to £125,000 a year exclusive of those revenues due to him from the Duchy of Cornwall which he estimated as some £13,000 a year. £20,000 should be allowed to the Prince for the completion of Carlton House. He did not, however, propose to settle the Prince's debts. He believed that the best manner of dealing with this problem was for the Treasury to deduct £73,000 from the Prince's income per annum and this should be done until his debts were settled. This seemed to him the best possible solution to a delicate matter.

When the Prince heard what the Government proposed he was furious.

He raved to Lady Jersey: 'They have cheated me. I married this woman whom I loathe solely because my creditors were threatening action if they were not paid. And I went through this marriage with her – this farce of a marriage – and now I am worse off than ever. They have increased my income and will deduct £73,000 a year to pay these wretched debts. I shall be worse off than before.'

Lady Jersey was mournful. The Prince's poverty affected her deeply. She did not wish him to cut down his expenses; she was doing very well and if there was less to be gained because the Prince must be 'careful' – what a hateful word – she was far from pleased.

She tried to soothe him. 'It is not final yet. It has to be passed.'

'Pitt!' he said. 'It's always Pitt. That fellow hates me. What a diabolical plot! To deduct such a sum from my income!'

He thought of that other occasion when he had been unable to pay his debts and the King would not help him. He had economized; he had sold his horses, shut up most of Carlton House; and he and Maria had gone down to Brighton in a hired coach. It had seemed such fun then. They had enjoyed their economizing. But then he had enjoyed everything with Maria. Maria had never wanted anything; she had never craved money, jewels . . .

He looked with faint distaste at his mistress – that dainty creature who sometimes reminded him of a snake. But she still knew how to fascinate him, though not so completely as she once had done.

Yes, they had shut up Carlton House and gone down to Brighton and they had lived in a manner which he called humble – and now looking back he could believe that had been the happiest time of his life.

How different this was! His debts unpaid; his income raised and yet he would be poor because from it he would be obliged to pay his debts.

It was insulting. And it was more than that. It was infuriating, maddening and tragic because to achieve this end he had been forced to marry a woman he loathed.

He hated her more than ever now. And what consolation had he? Frances Jersey – when his heart cried out for Maria Fitzherbert.

Caroline was in despair. She had not believed that it could be quite like this. Although she had not expected her husband to fall passionately in love with her on sight, she had allowed herself to imagine that in time they would come to an understanding. But how could they, when he loathed her and made no secret of the effect she had on him.

I would have tried, she reminded herself. But, by God, if he is going to humiliate me then I shall show him that I care nothing for him!

Lady Jersey! That woman was always close to her. And he had placed her there. She would not have blamed him for having a mistress; but surely he should have had the good taste, the good manners, to keep his liaison from his wife. The First Gentleman indeed! Then God help women if he was the finest example of his sex!

'I hate him!' she cried in the privacy of her apartments. But that was in private. No one was going to know how hurt she was.

She wondered how best to hurt *him*. She found a way. She had seen Maria Fitzherbert, the woman who had once so enslaved him that he had committed the utmost folly of going through a form of marriage with her.

So that was Maria! She seemed an old woman to Caroline. She must be well past forty. And what airs! One would have thought she were indeed Princess of Wales. Handsome in a way, but with a beak of a nose. Lovely hair. Better than mine? Caroline asked herself. *I* don't think so. A good skin it was true, but fat and unmistakably middle-aged.

She told him when next she saw him: 'I met Widow Fitzherbert. What a madam, eh? "Mrs Fitzherbert", they told me, I thought she was visiting royalty – or at least a duchess. Then I hear she's plain Mrs Fair-fat-and-forty!'

He had turned scarlet with anger. How dare she attack his goddess. He gave her a look of the utmost contempt and she knew that he was comparing them and that he saw the middle-aged widow as eternally beautiful and herself eternally repulsive. He revealed something else. In his way he was still in love with the woman – more so than with Lady Jersey.

It was hurtful but gratifying in a way. It might well be that Madame Jersey would not always be at hand to torment her.

Caroline went about with a defiant air. She had given up trying to please him; instead she did her best to make him aware that she had no love for him. And yet she longed to win his affection. She had heard much about his elegance, so she tried to be elegant too, but she only succeeded in looking more vulgar in his eyes. She could never compete with the exquisite ladies of his circle; and the more she tried to, the more dismally she failed. Knowing how he admired wit, she tried to be witty; her clumsy efforts to amuse were even more pathetic than her attempts to dress with taste.

Everything she did made him despise her the more.

God damn him! she cried. Why did they bring me here? I wish they had kept their Prince of Wales.

Then she would think of Major von Töbingen, yearn for him and dream of the happy life they might have had together. She wished then that she had died when they took him from her – which she believed she almost had.

And then in the midst of her despair she made a discovery. She forgot her miseries; she even forgot the lost joy she might have had with Major von Töbingen. She forgot everything but what the future was promising her now.

That sad and sordid union was to bear fruit.

She was going to have a child.

They would go to Brighton, said the Prince. The air would be good for her condition.

She had hoped that now he would show a little interest. It was true that he was delighted. He had done his distasteful duty and got the woman with child. Now he was entitled to leave her alone. His spirits rose, although he was angry about the manner in which parliament had decided his creditors should be appeased. He always enjoyed being at Brighton; the people were so different from the Londoners; they did not criticise him – at least not openly. Perhaps they would always be grateful to him for bringing prosperity to their town.

So to Brighton where the inhabitants turned out in their thousands to welcome them and to shout their loyal greetings, not only to the Prince but also to his Princess. It was fitting that he should bring her down to Brighton. His chief residence might be Carlton House but Brighton was his home. And the Princess was pregnant so what better for her than the sunshine and the sea breezes?

It was rather a damp arrival, for the rain poured down on the Prince and his wife, but Caroline cared little for that; she smiled and waved to the people in her free manner and consequently, to the Prince's chagrin, won their hearts.

But she was soon to discover that life could be as humiliating at Brighton as at Kempshott and Carlton House. The Prince had no intention of spending any time with her; he left her alone and devoted himself to his Brighton friends who thought up all kinds of lavish entertainments for his pleasure.

Lady Jersey was constantly with the Prince and by an unfortunate irony was also pregnant. This caused a great deal of amusement and even the loyal inhabitants of Brighton could not resist fabricating jokes and cartoons about the Prince's virility.

Lady Jersey was more unbearable than ever. She constantly took the place of honour; and Caroline, often feeling sick and ill, spent a great deal of time alone in her apartments, sometimes going for walks with only Mrs Harcourt and a manservant in attendance.

Her greatest relaxation was writing home. She found that thus she could relieve her feelings. If she told her mother how right she had been, how Queen Charlotte was an ugly little woman who was determined to spoil her daughter-in-law's chances of living happily in England, she felt better. She would write cruel little descriptions of her new family; she could describe the foppish ways of her husband; the spitefulness of the Queen and the aloofness of her brood of silly daughters.

And doing this and walking now and then and dreaming of the following year when she would have her baby, she felt life was tolerable.

The Prince had left her in Brighton and gone to Carlton House. Lady Jersey accompanied him and during her stay in London was summoned to audience with the Queen, who wished for a detailed account of Caroline's behaviour in Brighton.

'So she is with child,' said the Queen. 'It has not taken long, and I believe that the Prince has not been the most devoted of husbands.'

Lady Jersey smiled sycophantically. It was clear that she herself was pregnant, and doubtless through the Prince. But Lady Jersey was a discreet woman, and Lord Jersey would accept paternity, so there was no need for propriety to be outraged.

'I congratulate you on your condition,' went on the Queen.

Lady Jersey thanked Her Majesty and said she welcomed this addition to her family.

'I trust it will not mean too long an absence from your duties.'

'I can assure Your Majesty that my desire to serve will not allow me to absent myself for longer than is necessary.'

The Queen nodded. 'And how does the Princess spend her time?'

'She walks a little, rides, and writes a great many letters home.'

'Ah. Letters.'

'Your Majesty, I am told that she sometimes laughs herself almost into hysteria when writing letters to her family.'

The Queen's eyes narrowed. 'It would doubtless be interesting to know what those letters contain.'

Lady Jersey's eyes sparkled with mischief.

'If it were in my power to inform Your Majesty of that I should believe myself to have done my duty.'

It was a dangerous subject – one which should only be referred to in the most oblique terms.

But it was clear to Lady Jersey that this was a command from the Queen.

It was Mrs Harcourt who called Caroline's attention to the fact that Dr Randolph, a member of the household, was shortly leaving for Germany.

'It occurred to me that Your Highness might have some special commission for him.'

Caroline declared that the doctor might carry some letters to her family. When was he leaving?'

In the next few days, was the answer.

Caroline sat down at her table and wrote home. This was her revenge. She would tell her mother about Charlotte, the dumpy ugly Queen who reminded her of an old duck waddling out with her ducklings following her in order of age. She told of the cool reception she had received at the Queen's hand; and that the Princesses, her sisters-in-law, were a spineless collection of old maids. They hadn't a will between them. Mamma said: 'Persecute George's wife' so they did their silly best to persecute. As for the King he was kind and she liked him, though everyone said he was mad. The Prince of Wales was a poor husband and they weren't to believe the stories they heard of his good looks. He was very fat and even the special corsets he wore couldn't hide his paunch. She could tell them that the English branch of the family would do well in a circus.

She sealed the letters and sent for Dr Randolph.

'Dear Dr Randolph.' She smiled, Lord Malmesbury would reprimand her for her freedom of address. '*Dear* Dr Randolph,' she went on, 'I have heard you are leaving for a journey and will be passing through Brunswick.'

'It is true, Your Highness.'

'Then would you please take these letters to the Court there? They should be delivered into the hands of the Duke and Duchess and Madame de Hertzfeldt.'

Dr Randolph bowed, accepted the letters and told the Princess that she could rest assured that they would be delivered with all speed.

Lady Jersey smiled at the doctor in the slightly coquettish manner in which she regarded all men.

'Dr Randolph,' she said, 'I hear that you are about to leave for Germany.'

'It is true,' replied the Doctor.

'And the Princess has honoured you with a commission?'

'She wishes me to carry some letters to her family.'

'I see.' Lady Jersey's smile widened. 'A very important person is interested in those letters.'

Dr Randolph said: 'Madam, they have been entrusted to my care. I could not lightly hand them over to any ... person.'

'Not lightly, Dr Randolph. But there might be a perfectly reasonable way in which this would come about.'

'I cannot see how this could be.'

'It is for you to decide. The personage who wishes to see the letters is of the greatest influence. She has the power to bestow rank on those who wish for it, preferment – honours of all kinds.'

'Preferment?' A bishopric dangled before Dr Randolph's imaginative mental eye. Preferment indeed! For handing over a packet of letters. The important personage was of course the Queen. One had to obey the Queen. There was not only the hope of preferment if one did, but the fear of reprisals if one did not. The Queen, who for so many years had been a nonentity, had now become a power in the land, and she was a vindictive woman who would be implacable in her revenge.

If Lady Jersey – and everyone knew on what terms that woman was with Her Majesty – went to the Queen and told her that Dr Randolph could have put the letters into her hands and failed to do so, that would be the end of Dr Randolph's hopes of advancement. Who knew, it might be the end of Dr Randolph's career.

'So ...' said Lady Jersey opening her beautiful eyes provocatively.

'Madam, you who are in the service of the great will doubtless have some suggestion to offer.'

Lady Jersey was only too willing to explain.

As the post chaise carried him out of London on the way to Yarmouth Dr Randolph was thinking of his bishopric. It was really a very simple matter. He only had to obey instructions. His great fear was that something would go wrong.

No. Lady Jersey was very efficient where her own advancement was concerned; and as this was his too, so must he be.

He alighted at the inn and there was the messenger waiting for him as had been arranged.

'Sir, there is disturbing news. Mrs Randolph has been taken ill and the doctor believes it to be very grave.'

Dr Randolph took the letter which was handed to him. He

had rehearsed the scene during the journey to the inn. He put his hand to his forehead and said: 'My God, what shall I do? What can I do? There is nothing to be done but return home.'

'While the horses are being prepared I will write a letter and I wish you to take it with all speed to Lady Jersey in Brighton.'

His hands were trembling a little as he wrote the note. He had had grave news of his wife's illness and was returning home at once. He must therefore postpone his visit to Germany. Lady Jersey would remember that he had been entrusted with a packet of letters by the Princess of Wales. He was wondering now whether he should entrust them to another traveller, who should be chosen by the Princess, or return them to Lady Jersey to hand to the Princess, and was now leaving for London where he would await Lady Jersey's instructions. He trusted there would be no delay as he was anxious to return home to his sick wife.

Lady Jersey saw that there was as little delay as possible.

She had spoken to the Princess of Wales who wished that the letters be returned to her. Dr Randolph should therefore return the packet addressed to Lady Jersey at the Pavilion. They could be sent from London to Brighton on the post-coach which set out from the Golden Cross Inn, Charing Cross.

Dr Randolph sighed with relief, put the packet on the coach-post and returned home to his wife who was spending a few days in bed which she would have found a little irksome but for the promise of future glory as wife to the bishop.

Caroline did not notice that the letters were not returned to her.

She left Brighton for Carlton House, there to await the birth of her child; and so eager was she for this event that she had little thought for anything else.

When Lady Jersey gave birth to a boy she laughed. Let her! She had already had a brood of children. What was one more? Caroline was not vindictive and if Lady Jersey had been ready to be her friend she would have forgotten everything that had gone before and have settled down to cosy chats about babies.

But Lady Jersey was determined not to be friendly. She was eager, as she said, to keep the Princess in her place. Lady Jersey had the approval of the Queen who recognized her as a good servant; the manner in which she had diverted Caroline's letters into the Queen's hands was an example of her good service. And reading those letters was not likely to make Her Majesty feel any more friendly towards her daughter-in-law. Low, vulgar creature! thought the Queen. What folly ever to have let her come into the country! Everything should be done to make her as uncomfortable as possible. As for the Prince he could scarcely bear to hear her spoken of. The Queen laughed grimly; their mutual dislike of his wife had made a new bond between them. They were almost allies.

'Your Highness seems to be carrying a girl,' Lady Jersey told Caroline.

'You would know,' retorted the Princess, 'being so clever.'

'It is the method of carrying the child.'

'Well, it is to the grandmothers we must turn to learn of these things,' replied Caroline.

Grandmother indeed! thought Lady Jersey. At least she could be more proud of her appearance than Caroline could of hers.

'Experience is always so valuable,' said Lady Jersey; and while Caroline was thinking up a suitable retort, asked leave to retire.

When she was alone Caroline thought of the baby.

'Girl or boy,' she murmured. 'What do I care? It'll be my very own child. And when it comes ... perhaps even these last months will have seemed worth while.'

Caroline lay in her bed. Her time had almost come.

Soon now, she thought, I shall have my very own baby. She had longed for this all her life. When she had visited the homes of humble people and delighted in their children she had dreamed of the day when she would have her own.

And now it was to happen. But she was in an alien land. She had a husband who did not care for her. She laughed at the expression. Did not care for her! As for her mother-in-law; she would be delighted to see her sent back to Brunswick. She was alone in a foreign land, without friends, for there was no one here whom she could trust. The King perhaps – but he was a sick old man and his position alone made him remote.

But when the baby came it would be different. She and the child would be together.

Would they? She had heard the women talking. They had said that royal children saw little of their parents. Their education was taken care of by their governors.

Nonsense! she had told herself. I would never allow it. I would fight for this as for nothing else.

And she would win. She was sure of it. There was one thing she had discovered about this precious husband of hers. He hated scenes – unless he could play the injured party, unless he could be the one who wept and suffered. He certainly did not want to partake in scenes with her. He only wanted to avoid her.

She had put this to use when she had shouted at him: 'Have your mistress by all means. But keep her out of my sight.'

He had looked as though he were going to faint with horror and had waved a perfumed kerchief before his nose as though to revive him or remove the odours of her person. But it had worked. Lady Jersey was less in attendance.

One of these days I shall insist that she leaves me altogether, Caroline told herself.

But why brood on Lady Jersey when this cherished being was already announcing, in an unmistakable manner, his or her – intention to come into the world?

A baby, she thought ecstatically. A baby of my very own!

The Prince of Wales paced up and down the chamber. Assembled there were the Archbishop of Canterbury and the King's chief ministers of church and state waiting for the birth of an heir to the throne.

Caroline's labour had been long and she was exhausted; the Prince was in terror that the child would not be healthy or would be born dead.

He kept murmuring to himself: 'There must be a child. There must be. I could never . . .'

The suspense was unendurable.

At last they heard the cry of a child. The Prince hurried into the lying-in chamber.

'A girl, Your Highness. A lovely healthy little girl.'

There was no doubt of her health. She was bawling lustily.

Caroline lying in the bed, completely exhausted, cried out: 'My baby. Where is my baby?'

They laid the little girl in her arms.

'Mine God,' she said, 'It's true then. I have a baby.'

'A little girl, Your Highness.'

'Mine God, how happy I am!'

The Prince was happy too. A boy would have been better of course; but there was no Salic law in England and the succession was secure.

He embraced the Archbishop; he shook hands with all who came near him. He was a father. He had done his duty.

I shall never be obliged to share a bed with that woman again, he thought.

The royal separation

The Prince could not hide his relief.

He explained to his friend and Master of his Household Lord Cholmondeley: 'I was terrified that something would go wrong. I cannot tell you, my dear friend, what the birth of this child means to me. If you could know all that I have suffered.'

Tears filled his eyes at the thought of his suffering, then he shuddered thinking of his wife. She seemed to him gross and vulgar and because she was so different from all that I admired in women she reminded him of the most perfect of them all: his dear Maria.

Oh, to be with Maria again, to be settled and happy; to return to her, often a little intoxicated as he used to be in the old days, to be aware of her concern, to listen to her tender scolding. Oh, Maria, goddess among women, why had she allowed him to marry this creature!

He turned to Cholmondeley: 'If you could understand—'

Cholmondeley assured his master that he did understand; and he realized therefore that the birth of this child relieved him of a hateful burden.

'I shall be grateful to this daughter of mine until the end of my days,' said the Prince. 'Pray God I never have to *touch* the woman again.'

'There should be no necessity, Your Highness. The child is healthy.'

'May she remain so. I have no intention of following my father's example and producing fifteen of them. Fifteen! It's a joke. What a pity my parents were not more moderate. They would have saved themselves a good deal of trouble.'

Cholmondeley could scarcely answer that without being guilty of *lèse majesté* so he remained silent. The Prince was however not expecting answers. He was in one of his lachrymose moods, full of self-pity; in a short while he would be talking of Maria Fitzherbert. Cholmondeley believed that Lady Jersey must be a very clever woman – a witch perhaps – to be able to cling to her position as she did considering the Prince's obsession with Maria Fitzherbert.

But the Prince was not looking healthy. His face – usually highly coloured – had a tinge of purple in it. A bad sign, Cholmondeley had noticed before. Well, it had been an emotional time; perhaps another bleeding was necessary.

'Your Highness is exhausted. It has been such a trying time. Do you not think you should rest a little?'

'I feel tired,' admitted the Prince. 'Bring me some brandy.'

Cholmondeley went to do the Prince's bidding and when he returned he found the Prince slumped in his chair. As he appeared to be suffering from one of those fits to which he was accustomed, Cholmondeley sent for the physicians.

The Prince, they said, was indeed ill, and bleeding was immediately necessary as it was the only effective way of dealing with these unaccountable turns of his.

So the Prince lay on his bed, pale from much blood letting; and rarely had he seemed so wan and feeble.

The news spread through the Court.

The Prince is seriously ill.

He felt so feeble; he had no strength left. He had never felt quite so ill before in the whole of his life.

He asked that a mirror be brought and when he saw his face lying on the pillows, so white and drawn, so unlike his usual florid complexion, he was sure he was dying.

'Leave me alone,' he said. 'I want to think.'

And when they had left him he lay thinking of the past – thinking of Maria. That first meeting along the river bank when he had known that she was the only woman who was going to be of importance in his life. He had always known it. Why had he allowed himself to be led astray?

Maria had refused him countless times. Good religious Maria, who believed in the sanctity of marriage and could only come to him through marriage. How right she was! And at last the ceremony in that house in Park Street . . . and the happy years.

He should have stayed with Maria. He should never have allowed himself to be seduced from her side. Only with Maria lay happiness. And he had broken her heart.

But all the world should know now in what light he regarded her. He was dying and he was going to tell the world.

He called for paper.

'I am going to make a will,' he told Cholmondeley, and seeing the expression on his friend's face he went on: 'There is no point in hiding the truth. There may well be little time left to me. Do as I say.'

The paper was brought.

'This is my last Will and Testament,' he wrote. And the date: 'The 10th day of January in the year of our Lord 1796.'

He wrote that he left all his worldly goods to 'my Maria Fitzherbert, my wife, the wife of my heart and soul' who although she could not call herself publicly his wife was so in the eyes of heaven and his. She was his real and true wife and dearer to him than the life which was slowly ebbing away.

Everything ... everything was for Maria. Miss Pigot was not forgotten. He had already settled five hundred pounds a year on her for the rest of his life, and it was his dying wish that on his death his family should provide a post for her perhaps as a housekeeper in one of the royal palaces.

He wished to be buried without pomp; and a picture of Maria was to be buried with him; it should be attached to a ribbon and hung about his neck; and when Maria died he wished that her coffin be placed beside his and the inner sides of both coffins removed and the coffins soldered together in the manner employed in the burial of George II and his Queen Caroline.

He finished with a loving goodbye to his Maria, his wife, his life, his soul.

Then he felt better. She would know that he had sincerely cared for her. Their parting was a piece of folly which they should never have allowed to happen. He could never be happy in life without her; and he wanted her to know this as she would when his will was read after his death.

But he did not die.

In a few days' time he had recovered from the excessive bleeding and the florid colour was back in his cheeks.

Caroline was happy. She had her baby and nothing else mattered. But there was inevitably one fear which haunted her; what if they should take the baby from her? The Prince showed little interest in the child; her only importance to him was that she made it unnecessary for him to live with her mother.

'What do I care for him!' said Caroline. 'If I can keep my baby, I care for no one.'

Lady Jersey had hinted that the child would not be left under her control.

'Let them try to take her away from me,' cried Caroline clutching the child to her breast. This made Lady Jersey smile her haughty condescending smile, and Caroline felt she hated that woman almost as fiercely as she loved her child.

The christening took place at St James's, with the King, the

Queen and the Duchess of Brunswick (represented by the Princess Royal) as sponsors. The Archbishop christened the little girl Charlotte Augusta.

'Charlotte,' laughed Caroline to Mrs Harcourt, 'after her dear grandmamma, the Queen of England, and Augusta after my own mother. I hope my little girl will resemble neither of them.'

Mrs Harcourt shrugged her shoulders. She was in duty bound to report this to Lady Jersey who in her turn would report it to Her Majesty, and Caroline would have advanced a little farther in the ill-favour of the Queen.

Yet, thought Mrs Harcourt, Lady Jersey was perhaps not so firmly established in the good graces of the Prince. True he was fascinated by the woman, but she had heard that he repeatedly spoke – and with great longing – of Mrs Fitzherbert, and now that that lady's friends had persuaded her to take a house in town and enter society, who knew what would happen? It was beginning to be said that if one would please the Prince one should invite Maria Fitzherbert. An old and familiar pattern which must make Lady Jersey uneasy, though she gave no sign of it and seemed as confident as ever of her sway over the Prince.

The Princess Charlotte could one day be the sovereign and therefore great ceremonies should attend her birth, but the Prince was smarting under parliament's methods of dealing with his debts and refused to receive the loyal ceremonies planned by the City of London.

'I am too poor,' he announced, 'to receive these loyal addresses in a manner fitting to my rank. Therefore I would ask that the speeches be written and presented to me.'

The Aldermen of the City were incensed. The Prince might have his dignity but theirs was as great. They could not depart from their old customs to please an impecunious prince. Therefore the ceremonies would not take place.

The City was indeed offended. The matter was discussed in the streets and the coffee houses.

'Can't afford it! You know what this means? He knows that *she* will have to receive the congratulations with him and he can't bear to stand beside her while she does so. He hates her.

167

And why? Because he knows she's not his true wife, that's why. He's married to Maria Fitzherbert and he can't abide this one.'

Why not? She was affable. She was German, it was true, but he was half German himself in any case.

The Prince of Wales was more unpopular with the City of London than he had ever been before. He was unhappy about this. He loathed the silences that greeted his carriage when he rode in the streets, and he thought longingly of those days of his youth when he was Prince Charming and everything he did was right. Then they loved him and hated his father; but since the King's bout of madness that had changed. Not that the King was so popular. Royalty was not beloved in this changing world. There was the grim example from across the Channel always to be remembered. Only last year there had been riots in Birmingham. Flour had risen in price; a mob in Westminster had sacked the crimping houses; and the windows of Pitt's house in Downing Street had been broken. This was how trouble had started in France. In October on his way to open parliament crowds had surrounded the King's carriage shouting that they wanted bread. Stones had been thrown at the King and to his immense consternation among them was a bullet.

There was no doubt about it. Royalty was not popular and it was unfortunate that the French had shown the world their method of dealing with it.

The Prince shuddered; but he was completely immersed in his own affairs; and his longing for Maria Fitzherbert surpassed any qualms he might have felt for the future of the monarchy.

The King was preparing to call on the Princess Caroline at Carlton House to see his granddaughter, a journey of which the Queen could not approve, but His Majesty was very worried about the situation between the Prince of Wales and his wife.

'He treats her very badly. No way to treat a wife, eh, what?'

The Queen replied that she was not altogether surprised. Caroline was certainly an odd creature, and vulgar by all accounts. They could not expect George – elegant, fastidious George – to enjoy living with a woman like that. It had been a great mistake to bring her into the country and when they considered that there was charming erudite Princess Louise whom he might have married ...

The King's eyes filled with tears. 'Nice woman,' he said. 'Can't see anything wrong with her. Pretty hair ... nice figure ... eh, what?'

He was determined to show her that at least one member of the royal family was on good terms with her.

Caroline received him affectionately, returned his kiss warmly, which delighted him. He liked to be kissed by pretty women – and in his eyes Caroline was pretty enough.

She sent for the child. What a lusty little creature!

'Reminds me of her father when he was her age. You'd have thought then there wasn't a prettier baby in the world. Ah well. Very healthy little thing, eh, what?'

Caroline held her baby in her arms and the King's eyes filled once more with tears to contemplate her. He knew how she felt. He remembered his own feelings. They were so enchanting when they were young – and then they changed. Amelia hadn't changed. She was still his darling. She would never bring him anxieties – except through her cough. He could not bear to think of Amelia's cough so he gave his attention to young Charlotte.

'Like her father,' he said gruffly. 'And has he been to see you?'

'Not to see me. I have not seen him since the birth. But he comes to see the child.'

The King shook his head. 'Bad,' he said. 'Bad. The people don't like it.'

'Well,' cried Caroline with a shrill laugh, 'my husband does not like me – which seems even worse.'

'Must stop, you know. Should live together. There should be others. Madame Charlotte should have brothers and sisters, eh, what?'

Caroline shook her head. 'He won't, you know. He ignores me. I don't exist for him.'

'It'll have to be stopped. He'll have to do his duty.'

Caroline grimaced. 'I don't like being a duty much, Your Majesty.'

'Ha,' laughed the King. 'Have to do your duty, you know. We all have to, eh, what?'

'Your Majesty should be telling him this – not me. I'm ready to live with him. He's the one who has made this separation.'

'So you would welcome him, eh?'

'Well, I wouldn't say welcome – not unless he changed his ways. He would have to treat me as a wife. He would have to recognize me as the Princess of Wales. I won't have that Jersey woman set up in my place while I'm treated as though I were one of her servants, because that's how it was. Oh, no, I should not accept that.'

'There's no reason why you should,' said the King. 'Nor shall you. Leave this to me. We cannot go on like this. It's not natural, eh, what?'

Caroline agreed that it was not natural. But it was such a delight to have a child of her own that she was prepared to forget everything else.

The Prince summoned the Master of His Royal Household and Cholmondeley saw at once that he was in a rage.

'What do you think, Cholmondeley, I have just been summoned by my father and told that I must without delay do my duty as the husband of the Princess of Wales.'

Cholmondeley sighed.

'Well,' cried the Prince, 'what have you to say? What do you think? That I should spend my life with that vulgar creature. Eh, what do you think, Cholmondeley?'

'I think,' said Cholmondeley, 'that it is something Your Highness would not contemplate with pleasure.'

'You're right there, Cholmondeley. But I shall not contemplate it. I have no intention of living with her. In the first place I loathe her; I find her the most repulsive object I ever set eyes on. And in the second place I do not accept the fact that she is my wife.'

'The Princess Charlotte—'

'Oh, they have the heir. I've done my duty – all the duty I intend to do if it concerns that creature. I am going to make this very clear to her and to everyone. I wish you to go to her without delay and tell her my feelings.'

'If Your Highness will tell me exactly what you wish I shall be happy to comply with your instructions.'

'Go to the Princess Caroline and tell her that I wish us to be formally separated. We shall each go our own way and our affairs will be of no concern to each other.'

Lord Cholmondeley looked uneasy but the Prince said peremptorily, 'Go. Go at once. I wish there to be no delay.'

Caroline was in the nursery. In fact she rarely left it. She was like a merchant's wife, said Lady Jersey, with her first child. No one would believe she was a future Queen of England.

When she heard that Cholmondeley had brought a message from the Prince of Wales she feared there would be an attempt to take her daughter from her. She had visualized it a thousand times. A visit from an important member of the Prince's household; the order that the Princess Charlotte was to be conveyed to some new residence and put under the care of a governess, and taken away from her mother.

Her florid cheeks were a shade paler as she left the nursery and made her way to the apartment where Lord Cholmondeley was waiting for her.

He bowed and she cried out impatiently: 'Yes, yes what is it?'

'I have a message from His Highness, the Prince of Wales.'

'Well, that's a change. It's not often that he honours me with his messages.' But the fear stayed with her, and her bravado could not entirely hide it.

'His Highness has commissioned me to say that he wishes for a separation. You and he shall be entitled to act according to your wishes and one shall have no duty to the other.'

Caroline's relief was obvious. 'That's fair enough,' she said. 'I can tell you, my lord, I'll be as glad of it as he will. But one thing I do want to say is that I never wish to be forced to live with him as his wife again. I'd like to say this: I would agree to this separation provided this can be promised. Even if I lost my daughter . . .' She shivered involuntarily at the idea . . . 'I would never wish to resume marital relations with the Prince of Wales. If this could be promised I should be agreeable to what he suggests.'

'I feel certain that this could be arranged, Your Highness.'

'I should want a written agreement of this, you'll understand.'

'I doubt not that His Highness would be delighted to give it,' replied Lord Cholmondeley.

In Windsor Castle the Prince of Wales sat at his bureau and wrote to his wife.

30 April 1796

Madam,

As Lord Cholmondeley informs me that you wish I would define in writing the terms upon which we are to live, I shall endeavour to explain myself upon that head with as much clearness and as much propriety as the nature of the subject will admit. Our inclinations are not in our power, nor should either of us be held answerable to the other because nature has not made us suitable to each other. Tranquil and comfortable society is, however, in our power; let our intercourse, therefore, be restricted to that, and I will distinctly subscribe to the condition which you require that even in the event of any accident happening to my daughter, which I trust Providence in its mercy will avert, I shall not infringe the terms of the restriction by proposing, at any period, a connection of a more particular nature. I shall now finally close this disagreeable correspondence, trusting that as we have completely explained ourselves to each other the rest of our lives will be passed in uninterrupted tranquillity.

I am, Madam,
With great truth, very sincerely yours,
George P.

He smiled at what he had written. There. That was the end and it was amicable.

He sighed.

Never to have to be near her, never to have to touch her again.

He felt pleased with life.

Caroline was almost as pleased when she received the letter.

She was the Princess of Wales, yet she was free. No more restrictions. She was no longer accountable to her husband.

Let her keep her child, let her live her own life and she would be very contented to have come to England. She answered the

Prince in French, accepting his terms with glee and telling him that she would never cease to pray for his happiness.

She sent a copy of the letter to the King who came to see her on receipt of it.

'So you think that you cannot live together?'

'Your Majesty will know the Prince's views on that.'

'Never heard anything like it,' said the King. 'Heirs to the throne are not expected to love their wives; only to have children.'

'The two sometimes go together,' suggested Caroline demurely and burst into loud laughter.

The King did not seem to take this amiss but grumbled to himself: 'Young people ... nowadays. When I was a young prince ...' Then he looked a little sad and went on: 'You should live under the same roof, eh, what? It looks better. The people expect it.'

'The people know the truth and I would not care to live under the same roof as my husband.'

'H'm. Have to see about it. An income you'll want, too. Wife of the Prince ... mother of the heir, eh, what?' £20,000 a year, he was thinking. Have to consult Pitt. Why was it that this family could not seem to live in peace together? And where would she live? Carlton House, eh? For a while in any case.

Children! What a worry! Better not to have them if it could be avoided. But of course that was what they married for. The Prince of Wales had caused him as many as ten sleepless nights in a row since he came of age – and went on doing it too.

It was no use trying to bring them together if they had determined on parting.

It was amazing how news of the Court reached the gossip columns; there was a scandal about letters which had been written by the Princess of Wales to her family, intercepted and taken to the Queen. The stealer of the letters was of course Lady Jersey.

Her name was in every paper; there were obscene verses and even pictures of herself and the Prince; but the chief complaint against her was not so much that she was the mistress of the

Prince and flaunted her ascendancy over the Princess, but that she was all the time acting as the Queen's spy, intercepting the Princess's private correspondence and giving it into the hands of her enemies.

Caroline had managed to win public approval. Her affable smiles and obvious pleasure in popularity delighted the people. Besides they had heard stories of her reception and they saw her as an injured woman. And why? Because of that voluptuary, their Prince of Wales, whose debts and adventures with women were a scandal; who had 'married' the good and virtuous Maria Fitzherbert and discarded her. But even more unpopular was Lady Jersey.

The comments in the press made it impossible for Lady Jersey to ignore them. Something would have to be done, she told the complaisant and long-suffering Lord Jersey, and it was for him to defend his wife's honour. His manners were too graceful for him to as much as smile at this. He was in fact noted for his beautiful manners. What would his wife wish him to do? She had only to say.

She had written to Dr Randolph asking him to explain what had happened to a certain packet of letters which the Princess of Wales had entrusted to his care and so far had received no reply. Lord Jersey should without delay write to the doctor and tell him that he insisted on an explanation.

This the obliging Lord Jersey did and in such terms as Dr Randolph dared not ignore. He explained in detail how he had set out for Germany, been called back by his wife's illness and had sent the packet of letters entrusted to him by the Princess of Wales back to her by way of Lady Jersey.

Lady Jersey wrote to say that she had not received that packet and was most uneasy about it. The fact that it had not been returned had been overlooked at the time as the Princess herself had not questioned its return. However, she would publish the correspondence and hoped that this would put an end to the cruel slanders against her.

Caroline read the papers and tried to remember what she had written in those letters. Comments on her new family. Of one thing she was certain. They would not have been very flattering.

She laughed at the affair. It was perfectly clear to her what had happened. Lady Jersey had deliberately stolen the letters and sent them to the Queen.

Then she became angry. Why should she have that woman in her household? Why should she allow herself to be spied on?

She would endure it no longer.

When the King came to see her she told him that she wished to ask a favour of him.

'I think,' she said, 'that now that the Prince and I have come to an understanding I should no longer be expected to keep Lady Jersey in my household.'

'No, indeed you should not,' declared the King. 'Too much, eh what? No, the woman shall be dismissed. You may leave that to me, my dear.'

Caroline threw her arms about the King's neck and kissed him.

Bless me, thought the King, the woman has no decorum. But it's rather pleasant to be kissed by a pretty woman, eh, what?

The King sent for the Prince of Wales.

He shook his head sadly over his son's matrimonial affairs.

'The people don't like it,' he said. 'They're in an ill mood. You should take care.'

'By God,' cried the Prince of Wales, 'I married the woman. What more do they want?'

'They expect you to do your duty. You should have sons.'

'I have a daughter. No one can prevent her from becoming Queen of England.'

'A son would have pleased them more.'

'I have pleased them enough. I now intend to please myself.'

'A Prince can never please his people enough.'

'So it would seem. But nothing will induce me to return to her. That is settled. Your Majesty has seen the correspondence?'

'Yes, yes. And it seems to be a matter on which you are both in agreement – she as well as you, but there is one matter I have to discuss with you. She asks for the removal from her household of Lady Jersey and in view of the unfortunate position that lady holds in your affections I must ask you to dismiss her.'

'And if I refuse?'

'Then I shall be forced to dismiss her myself. You understand, eh, what?'

The Prince's face had flushed to a deeper red than usual.

'So Your Majesty would concern yourself with my wife's household?'

'The lady whom you have repudiated, remember? Someone must protect her. I have decided to do that.'

The Prince narrowed his eyes. He was not going to fight for Frances. Why should he? He was tired of her. Perhaps she would realize if he made no attempt to keep her in Caroline's household, that he wished to be free of her.

'Am I to understand that these are Your Majesty's orders?' he asked.

'You may take it so.'

The Prince bowed and retired.

'And so,' he told Frances, 'I had no alternative but to accept.'

'So you are not allowed to choose the members of your own household?'

'You are a member of the Princess's household.'

'But surely you, as the Prince of Wales, could insist—'

'Madam,' said the Prince coldly, 'I am not the King; and it is on his orders that you are to leave.'

She was too angry to see the warning lights in his eyes.

She would not forget this insult, she declared. She would make that creature sorry for this. She had carried tales of her to the King and this was the result.

She was indeed angry. Now she would be of no use to the Queen, and the Queen would quickly withdraw her favour from one who could not serve her. This was going to make a great deal of difference to Lady Jersey's power, and power was money of which she was very fond. She had had a good picking from the Prince but there were all sorts of perquisites which came the way of a lady who was on good terms not only with the Prince but with the Queen who, since the King had become feeble-minded, had the power to bestow all sorts of honours.

Yes, Lady Jersey was very angry.

She left the Prince in no doubt of her ill temper, but she did not care. She believed she had the power to subdue him when she wished to, and it was Caroline against whom she vented her anger. That gauche ridiculous creature. Lady Jersey burst out laughing remembering her in the hideous white satin she had had made for her first meeting with the Prince. Stupid creature, did she think she could get the better of Lady Jersey?

She got into her coach and as it passed down St James's she was recognized by passers-by. One called her a lewd name. The people nowadays were becoming more and more insolent. Examples should be made of them. She sat back against the upholstery pretending not to see those grinning faces which looked in at her.

Mud splashed against the window. Someone threw a stone.

It was too bad. She was most displeased.

In the privacy of her own house she sat down to write to the Princess of Wales, telling her that she had that day obtained permission from the Prince of Wales to resign her position of Lady of the Bedchamber. She considered that she had suffered persecution and injustice in Her Royal Highness's service but she had the satisfaction of knowing that through her silence and forbearance she had given proof of her loyalty to His Highness the Prince of Wales and to the royal family; as for gratitude and attachment to the Prince, that would only cease with her life. She was, with all *possible* respect Her Royal Highness's humble servant.

When she read the letter Caroline shrieked with laughter.

'At last I am rid of her,' she cried. 'First I rid myself of him and then of her. This is triumph. Now I can live in peace as long as my darling Charlotte is left to me.'

Caroline was happier than she had been since she had come to England. She was free of the Prince and the odious Lady Jersey; she had her child; and the King was her friend.

But Charlotte was a princess and an heir to the throne so she must be treated as such. She was no humble child to be cared for solely by her mother. Caroline could have access to her child; she could spend a greater part of her day in the nursery, but Charlotte must have her own establishment and Lady Elgin was put in charge of the royal nursery, with Miss Hayman second in command. Caroline took a fancy to Miss Hayman who was a very sensible young woman and interested in music; she played the piano with great skill and was lighthearted, and if she was not as polished in her manners as Lady Elgin she was all the more to Caroline's taste.

So they were very happy together in Carlton House while the Prince was away at Brighton and scarcely ever called to see his daughter, the King coming often to show that he at least liked his daughter-in-law.

'As for Madam Queen,' said Caroline to Miss Hayman, 'she is very welcome to stay away – and her band of spinster daughters too. I am very pleased to be rid of them. His Majesty is my friend and to tell you the truth, my dear love, I think he is a little in love with me. Oh, it would have been a very different story I can tell you if I had come over here as bride to the father instead of the son. My blessed Charlotte would be well on the way to becoming the sister of my next, I do assure you. Ha! Ha! But it was not to be.'

Miss Hayman laughed and was amused by the free and easy conversation of the Princess of Wales.

The Prince fretted. To think that the odious woman was in Carlton House – *his* Carlton House – that shrine of his own talent and good taste which he had made from the old ruin with which his father had presented him when he could no longer prevent his having his own establishment.

Caroline in Carlton House; Maria keeping away from him. Cruel Maria, who knew what a failure his marriage with the Princess of Brunswick had been, who knew that he had never really cared for Lady Jersey. It had been a temporary aberration, a madness which had come upon him, a spell the wicked Frances had laid on him. In his heart he had never strayed from Maria. She should know this.

But she ignored his advances. She was not often in town; she had given up the lease of Marble Hill – ah, dear Marble Hill where she had lived when he had first discovered his Sweet Lass of Richmond Hill! And now she had retired to Castle Hill in

Ealing and was spending much time there – far too much time – with the faithful Pigot.

It should not go on. He would not allow it.

His first step must be to remove Caroline from Carlton House.

So he sent word to her that he wished her apartments to be redecorated and this would necessarily mean that she must vacate them while the work was being done.

There was a charming villa at Charlton, not far from Blackheath. She would find it a delightful spot. If she would agree to inhabit it while the rooms at Carlton House were being repainted it should immediately be made ready for her use.

And baby Charlotte? she wanted to know.

Obviously the Princess Charlotte could not be taken from the royal nursery. She would remain at Carlton House in the care of her governess and nurses. In due course the child would be reunited with her mother.

It seemed reasonable to Caroline. She prepared to leave for the villa in Charlton.

She did not know that the Prince of Wales had vowed he would never have her back at Carlton House; and had expressed the view that he had no desire for his daughter to be brought up by such a vulgarian as her mother.

Princess Royal's romance

The Princess Royal came hurrying into the apartments she shared with her sisters and there was no need to ask her if something exciting had happened; it was written clearly in her face.

'I have just seen Papa,' she cried. 'So it is true – true.'

Elizabeth looked up from the canvas on which she was drawing. 'Not,' she said, 'a husband at last?'

Sophia rose from her seat and embraced her eldest sister. 'Oh, you most fortunate of women!'

The Princess Royal acceded to this. 'Oh, how grateful I am! How tired I am of walking the dogs and filling the snuff boxes. I shall be free – free – of restraint for evermore.'

'Husbands can be more restraining than fathers and mothers,' Augusta reminded her.

'Not more than ours,' retorted the Princess Royal. 'I do believe Papa is jealous of us all. I used to believe he wanted to keep us all here ... *pure* and unsullied and that is why husbands have never been found for us until now.'

'And then only one husband!' sighed Sophia.

'It is not necessary to be pure as well as unmarried,' cried Augusta with a grimace. 'Do you think dearest Papa realizes that?'

'You should really be careful in front of the children.'

Sophia and Mary exchanged glances and laughed. 'Don't mind us,' Sophia said. 'I am eighteen and not so innocent as I'm supposed to be.'

'And I can well believe that!' replied Augusta.

'Hush!' cried the Princess Royal. 'How can you think any man will want to marry you if you talk like ... like—'

'Harlots?' suggested Sophia. 'I confess I often feel they have more interesting lives than ours.'

'They could scarcely be less so,' added Mary gloomily.

'But,' soothed Elizabeth, 'if a husband has been found for our sister perhaps we need not despair.'

'There are so many of us,' wailed Mary, 'and all getting older and older every day.'

'A fate no man or woman can escape, you must admit,' Elizabeth reminded them.

'Yes, but the nearer we spinster princesses get to the grave the farther we get from the marriage bed. I must confess it is a dreary thought.'

'Well, let us rejoice that at least one of us is to have a husband,' said Elizabeth. 'What do you know of him, sister?'

'That he is a prince.'

'Naturally.'

'That he has been married before.'

'A widower!' grimaced Sophia.

'Pray do not give me your pitying looks,' cried the Princess Royal. 'A man who has been married before is better than no man, I do assure you. And the second is likely to be your fate. The fact that he has had a wife makes me like him the better. He will be so experienced.'

'Perhaps she was a great beauty.'

'Hardly likely when she was the sister of our sister-in-law Caroline.'

'Is that indeed so?'

'I assure you it is. My Prince of Würtemburg had the misfortune to take to wife a Princess of Brunswick. She was Charlotte, too.'

'He must have a fancy for the name.'

'There are so many Charlottes in this family. Our mother, myself and now this new baby.'

'Not to mention Caroline's sister, your Prince's dead wife.'

'I wonder what Caroline will think of your marrying her brother-in-law.'

'Caroline's opinion is of no importance.'

'I know. I just wondered. Perhaps she has already met him. She surely would for she would have been at her sister's wedding, I daresay.'

Sophia looked expectant, but the Princess Royal said quickly: 'I should not dream of discussing my future husband with Caroline in any circumstances.'

'I should not dream of discussing anything with Caroline!'

'I have decided to make my own wedding gown. I am starting on it without delay. I shall sit up all night to finish it if need be for I am determined to put every stitch into it myself.'

'Have you no qualms about leaving your home and going to a strange land with your widower?'

The Princess Royal looked pityingly at her sisters. 'You should be the ones to suffer qualms,' she told them, 'for it may well be that the King has decided that none of you shall ever have a husband.'

*

Caroline heard of the proposed wedding and was saddened, remembering her sister Charlotte who had married Frederick William, Prince of Würtemburg. Charlotte had been sixteen then and she herself fourteen and how she had envied the elder sister who was starting out on her married life!

But what had happened to Charlotte? She would never really know. It was a shock, too, to learn that that same bridegroom was now coming to England to marry the Princess Royal, for she had never really believed that Charlotte was dead.

Charlotte's story was strangely mysterious. Caroline knew that her father had sent messengers to Russia to try to discover the true story. And what sort of a husband was this Prince of Würtemburg who had deserted his wife, leaving her in Russia, after taking her three children away from her?

Was it true that she had had a love affair with the son of Empress Catherine – that woman whose own life was something of a legend? Or had she dabbled in politics? How could they know? But the fact remained that Charlotte had disappeared and no one could be quite sure where.

And now her death must be accepted as a fact for how otherwise could her widower come to England to marry the Princess Royal?

What strange lives we lead, thought Caroline, when we are married to strangers.

The Princess Royal was not the least bit disturbed by the rumours. Her great desire had been to be married and escape from the thraldom of court life under the stern eye of her mother. She stitched happily away at her dress and her sisters came in to marvel at her happiness as her needle worked on the white satin making what Sophia called the most perfect little stitches in the world.

She was in transports of joy when she was fitted for her trousseau. She clasped her hands together in ecstasy over the jewellery which Forster, the court jeweller, was making for her. She listened patiently to her mother's advice on how to be a good wife, and to her father's assurances of his love for all his children. He looked upon her as a child, which might have been exasperating in other circumstances since she was past thirty, but all this she accepted in a kind of ecstasy – so delighted was she to have a husband.

'My one fear,' she confided to Elizabeth, 'is that something will go wrong and prevent the marriage taking place.'

'Can you feel so strongly about a bridegroom whom you have never seen?'

'It is marriage I want.'

'Any marriage?'

'Oh, come, sister, the Prince is handsome we hear. He is not deformed. He is not a monster.'

'He has been married before.'

'I tell you I don't care. I don't care.'

'I wonder about his first wife.'

The Princess Royal frowned. She had not heard very much about the first wife except that she had been the sister of Caroline and had had three children and was now dead. But what more did she need to know?

'Stop looking like a wise old witch,' she cried. 'I tell you everything is going to be all right.'

But was it?

The case of the diamond ring seemed like an omen.

It was to be a beautiful ring set with thirty diamonds. Forster had brought the design and the stones to the Princess's apartments to discuss the setting with her.

He then took it back to his shop and set to work on it. He had done some work on the ring and left it on his bench and while he was absent a chicken – which by some strange manner had found its way into the workshop – was attracted by the diamonds and swallowed some, even pecking one out of the ring.

Their disappearance would have remained a mystery if one of Forster's workmen had not arrived in time to see the chicken pecking at the stones in the ring and guessed what had happened.

News was hastily sent to the Princess Royal who was deeply distressed – not at the loss of the diamonds but because she feared it to be an omen. She was hearing strange rumours about the first wife of her future husband and although she was reassured that she was dead, there did not appear to be absolute proof of this.

Her demeanour had changed a little and she now no longer sang as she stitched away at her wedding dress.

But a few days later the jeweller called on her in triumph. There was the ring just as it had appeared in the design – with thirty brilliants bravely glittering.

'It's another ring?' she asked.

'No, Your Highness. We killed the chicken and recovered all the diamonds from his gizzard.'

He was looking at her, expecting her approval for his cleverness in recovering the stones; but she took the ring gingerly and slipped it on her finger.

She could not help looking on the incident as an omen.

The King summoned his daughter. He was looking worried and the Princess Royal, like all the family, felt uneasy to see him so. She would never forget that terrible day when they had first known that he was going mad, when he had caught the Prince of Wales by the throat and tried to strangle him. She remembered too the occasion when she had been going for an airing with him and he had kept getting out of the coach to give the coachman instructions, so that at last she had felt quite hysterical herself and dashed back into the palace declaring that she could not ride with Papa. She remembered too his excessive fondness for Amelia and how he had hugged the child so tightly on one occasion that they had feared he would kill her and had dragged her from him and put him into a strait-jacket. He was supposed to be cured now but there were times when he talked in that quick way of his until he became hoarse and incoherent. This was when he was upset about something. He was upset now.

'I have something very serious to say to you,' he began. 'Difficult. In a quandary. Don't quite know what it means but we shall have to discover. Can't let you marry if the bridegroom already has a wife, eh, what?'

'Already has a wife!' cried the Princess Royal. 'But she is dead.'

'So we think – so we hope. At least one should not hope for

the death of others, eh, what? But there are rumours. Some say that she is not dead ... but a prisoner in Russia ... and if she is, then that means that Prince Frederick can't take another wife, can he – because that would be bigamy and something we couldn't have, eh, what?'

The Princess Royal looked stricken. What a worry children were! thought the King. But they couldn't have bigamy in the family – although in a way they already had it, because the Prince of Wales was supposed to be married to Mrs Fitzherbert and he'd married Caroline. Oh dear, oh dear, families were difficult to control. Why could they not all be docile like himself and the Queen, who had always done their duty!

The King said: 'Well, my dear, you see what this means. You must prepare yourself for no marriage. Though it may be it won't come to that. The Prince assures me that his wife is dead. He has a letter from the Empress of Russia dated two years after he left his wife in her country, and the Duke of Brunswick also has a letter from the Empress and in both these letters it states that the Princess Charlotte of Brunswick is dead.'

'Then she *is* dead,' cried the Princess Royal. 'Why is there all this talk if she is dead?'

'Because, my dear, no one seems to know *how* she died. Some say one thing, some another. And there are some who so doubt the motives of that strange woman, the Empress, that they say the Princess did not die at all but that she was kept a prisoner and still is in prison in Russia.'

'I won't believe it! I won't believe it!' cried the Princess Royal.

'All the same,' said the King, 'it is a matter which must be cleared up to my satisfaction – and the Queen's – before we can consent to this marriage.'

'But my – my future husband is due to arrive here ...'

'Postponement, my dear. It is sometimes necessary. We have to be very sure. We have to have proof. You understand that, eh, what? Can't have our Princess Royal going off to a strange country unmarried, eh, what?'

The Princess Royal felt limp with misery.

'I feared it was too good to be true,' she sighed.

The King looked a little shocked. Did marriage mean so much to his daughter? After all this was not love for a man. How could it be when she had never seen him? It was merely the desire to be married, to escape from home.

He liked to think of his girls unsullied. He could never bear to contemplate them in the marriage bed, particularly Amelia. I shall never part with her, he thought. Nor any of the others. They are my girls – my *pure* girls. They shall never be sullied if I can help it.

He thought of the life he had led – the good pure life with his Queen – plain, unattractive Charlotte whom he had had to accept when he 'burned' for Sarah Lennox. But he had subdued all his desires in order to do his duty, and as a result he had had thirteen children – fifteen if Octavius and Alfred had lived. He had never been unfaithful to his wife in deed although he had often dreamed of beautiful women. Sometimes in his less lucid moments he thought he had mistresses – beautiful women like those favoured by his brothers and his sons who had lacked his sense of duty. He dreamed erotic dreams – but they were only dreams.

And he was anxious that his daughters should remain pure. He would keep them under his roof, growing older perhaps – but they would always be children to him.

So now, although he was sorry for his daughter's tragic looks, in his heart he would be pleased if this marriage came to nothing.

The King visited Caroline at Blackheath.

'You are happily settled here?' he asked.

'I could enjoy my stay, Your Majesty, but I miss my daughter.'

'Ah, yes, the young rogue! I was with her yesterday. She grows apace and is into everything.' The King smiled affectionately. He loved babies. Caroline smiled with him and gave him an account of young Charlotte's amazingly clever conduct in the days when she was at Carlton House with her.

'She misses her mother,' said Caroline. 'But not as much as her mother misses her.'

The King smiled. This was the sort of conversation he loved – happy domestic conversation. He discussed the food the Princess should be given and what rules should be made for her household.

Then he came to the real point of his visit.

'As you know there is a betrothal between the Prince of Würtemburg and our Princess Royal.'

'Yes, I had heard of this.'

'You will have met the Prince?'

'I met him when he came to Brunswick to marry my sister.'

'And your sister, Caroline, what of her?'

'I had never believed her to be dead. I have always felt that she was alive and there were rumours . . .'

'And your father?'

'My father believed her dead and so did Madame de Hertzfeldt and my mother. But perhaps that was what they wished.'

'Do you remember what happened?'

'Yes. There was a letter to say that my sister had died of a terrible disease which made it necessary for her to be buried without delay.'

'And you did not believe this.'

Caroline shrugged her shoulders. 'Perhaps I did not wish to believe it. I had been brought up with her. She was always so full of life. I could not imagine her . . . dead. Her maid came back to us. She said she had been dismissed by my sister and sent back home. She became my maid and she told me that my sister had fallen in love with one of the Empress's lovers.'

The King shuddered; he could not bear hearing stories of other people's profligate habits because when he was alone he could not stop thinking of them.

Caroline had no notion of this and went on, 'This maid told me that my sister had a child by this man and that the Empress had her sent away and imprisoned her. Perhaps she had her murdered in prison.'

The King did not speak and Caroline went on: 'One cannot believe these stories of someone with whom one has spent one's childhood. When I think of all the games we played together and our tricks and jokes – and then I think of her being murdered – I can't grasp it. Perhaps that is why I cannot believe she is dead.'

The King said: 'We cannot allow the Princess Royal to marry a man who has a wife living.'

Caroline thought: No. But I was married to a man who, in the eyes of some, already had a wife.

'I think,' she said, 'that it is remarkable what strange adventures can fall to the lot of princesses.'

'I shall need to have proof of your sister's death before I can consent to this marriage.'

'My father will give you a copy of the letter he received from the Empress and doubtless the Prince of Würtemburg will too. Your Majesty will consider that proof?'

'There is no other proof I could hope for.'

'And would that suffice?'

'I am not sure.'

The Princess Royal was ill; her skin had turned yellow and her eyes were tinged with the same colour.

She lay listlessly on her bed. She had felt the sickness coming on her but she would not go to bed until she had finished her wedding gown. There it was hanging in her wardrobe – like a white satin ghost.

'At least I had a wedding dress if I don't get a husband,' she said to her sister Elizabeth.

Her mother came to see her. She folded her arms and stood looking down at her daughter, her wide mouth grim. The girl was sick through anxiety, so much did she wish for marriage. Queen Charlotte thought of her own marriage – that astounding message which had come from England to say that she had been chosen for the future King of England. She would never forget it – and remembering it, she could have some sympathy for her daughter.

'You understand,' she said, 'that we must make sure he is free to marry you.'

'I understand, Mamma.'

'And when we have satisfied ourselves, there is no reason why we should not go ahead with the marriage.' She went to the cupboard and examined the wedding dress.

'You have stitched it very fine,' she said. 'I am sure the reward for such diligence will be that you will wear it for what it was intended.'

The Queen came back to the bed and looked at her daughter. The Princess Royal was indeed sick – sick with fear that she might not get a husband.

The Queen would tell the King that it was essential that the Princess Royal married. There were enough daughters at home.

The King was uncertain. He had received letters from the Duke of Brunswick and the Prince of Würtemburg. They had no doubt that the Prince's first wife was dead. 'And yet,' mused the King, 'I don't know.'

He did not in fact wish his daughter to have a husband at all; but the idea of giving her to a man who could not be her husband shocked him deeply.

'I am uncertain,' he said. 'I wish the offer had never been made. Better to have heard nothing about it, eh, what?'

The Queen replied that she did not care for the marriage either but the Princess Royal was set on it and it was hardly likely that they would find another husband for her. There were the other girls, too.

'They're happy enough at home.'

'But they should marry if it is possible.'

'H'm,' said the King.

'Princess Royal will be ill if this marriage does not take place. I could see her becoming a confirmed invalid. That sort of thing can happen. We don't want sickness in the family.'

The Queen stopped abruptly and the King looked alarmed. They were both thinking of that most terrible of all illnesses – the one to which he was addicted and which robbed him of his sanity.

'I . . . I shall accept these letters,' he said. 'We will give our consent. It all happened a long time ago. The woman must be dead, eh, what?'

'I think the woman must be dead,' said the Queen.

*

The Prince of Würtemburg had arrived in England for his marriage. The Princess Royal rose from her sick bed. She had quickly recovered although her skin was still yellow.

She put on the wedding dress and in the Chapel Royal of St James's she made her marriage vows with the Archbishops of Canterbury and York presiding, and the King giving the bride away.

She was radiant and the bridegroom seemed well satisfied; but the King was so ill at ease that many who watched the ceremony wondered whether he was sickening for another bout of his illness. Later in the Queen's drawing room he talked incessantly, and it was clear that he did not like parting with his daughter.

The Princess Royal suffered no qualms at parting with her family. She was at last married and all the fears and omens had come to nothing.

She embraced her brothers and sisters with affection; then she left St James's to spend a few days at Windsor before setting off with her husband for her new life in a strange country; and it seemed that the ghost of his first wife troubled neither of them.

Caroline who had attended the marriage remembered him from all those years ago; but he did not wish to remember.

Caroline grimaced inwardly. I'm the outsider, she told herself. The family don't want me here. But perhaps the one who was most anxious for her absence was the bridegroom from Würtemburg.

Caroline's little family

Caroline had accepted her life. The Prince would always hate her; he would, if he could, separate her from their daughter but this was not in his power while the King remained her friend. She was grateful to the King, the only member of the royal family whom she could trust, but naturally the most important, for in the end if he insisted that something be done so it must be.

He visited her often; they talked of the Princess Charlotte and he told her how worried he was about Amelia's health. Caroline always listened intently and although the King had to admit that her manners were too free and her conversation a little coarse and that she laughed too loudly and was too familiar, he always added a rider: She was affectionate and he liked to feel affection in the family.

The Queen ignored her – more than that, she would do her harm if she could. Caroline retaliated by laughing behind Her Majesty's back at her odd habits of which she read in the press. Her snuff-taking, her careful scrutiny of accounts, how she kept her tippet in a paper bag to prevent its getting dusty – as though she were some farmer's wife. But Caroline knew that the Queen was not merely a figure of fun; she was a sinister power in her life. 'The old Begum,' she would say, 'what is she up to now?'

But the days she spent with baby Charlotte made up for any disappointments in her life. How she loved to romp with the child! They would crawl about the floor together and Charlotte would give imperious orders and show quite clearly that she adored her mother.

If she could only have the child with her she would have been perfectly happy; but she had to realize that as a royal princess, a possible Queen of England, Charlotte would have to receive an education which it was not in Caroline's power to give her.

But she was a baby yet and there were happy times together.

Caroline was not allowed to return to Carlton House and Charlotte continued to live there with her governess and nurses; but the King arranged that Caroline should often visit her daughter and that Charlotte should often stay at Charlton with her mother.

'Dear old George,' said Caroline to Miss Hayman, who was a very special friend. 'A pity he had to marry the old Begum. He deserves better.'

Miss Hayman, like everyone else, thought Caroline's speech and manners very wild and free; but that did not disturb Miss

Hayman; and she often visited Caroline at Charlton to tell her what Charlotte had been doing and to repeat her clever sayings.

When the Prince heard of the friendship between Caroline and Miss Hayman he dismissed the latter from Princess Charlotte's household, so Miss Hayman went to serve that of Caroline.

The Princess was becoming extremely popular. She only had to ride out into the streets and a little crowd would gather to cheer her. When he heard of this it infuriated the Prince, for the more people liked her the less they liked him.

He could not understand why this rather slovenly, none-too-clean creature with her too ready and too loud laughter, her flamboyant manner of dressing, her tactlessness and her lack of grace should have so caught the public imagination. But the fact remained that she had.

He was ashamed of her; and while he determined to shut her out of his life as much as he could he was desperately longing to bring Maria Fitzherbert back into it.

Caroline meanwhile had moved to Montague House, near Greenwich Park, which was more suited to her rank than the little house in Charlton, and she set out to make this an inviting centre for amusing people. Strangely enough she did attract to it some of the most brilliant men of the day. The chief of these was the great politician, George Canning. This further enraged the Prince, who could not understand how such a man could find anything in Caroline's household to attract him. Other important influential people followed Canning's example and it seemed inevitable that Montague House should become a rendezvous for those who disapproved of the Prince.

But Caroline longed for her daughter and since she could not have her all the time she took up a hobby which had been hers in Brunswick and 'adopted' children from the surrounding neighbourhood. She would call at any house however humble if there were children there; and she only had to hear of an orphan to take the child into her special care.

This project filled a great deal of her time because she made it her duty to see that the children were placed in households where they would be well looked after; she founded a little school where they could be taught; she treated them as though she were their mother and no matter how poor and sick they were she cuddled and kissed them, showering her affection on them.

People were surprised to see her pick up a child with open sores on its face and tend them herself.

She loved children. She adored her own daughter; but since she was allowed to see her only occasionally she created her own little family about her.

This was one of the reasons why she was so loved by the people who saw in her a good kind woman who had been badly treated by their profligate Prince.

And so the next few years passed.

The reunion

Miss Pigot sighed deeply as she glanced at Maria. How much longer, she was asking herself, was she going on in this state of uncertainty. It was no use Maria's telling herself that she was determined never to see him again; because Miss Pigot knew that it was only a matter of time before she did.

Miss Pigot was a romantic and her two beloved children, the Prince of Wales and Maria Fitzherbert, were made for each other. She knew it. They would never be happy without each other and it was time they rid themselves of stupid pride on Maria's part, and a naughty wayward love of variety on that of His Highness, and realized that the only happiness they could find was with each other. If Miss Pigot could bring about that happy conclusion she would certainly do so with all speed.

'You should see him,' she chided now. 'What more can he do? I am sure he has been as humble as any man could be – and him the Prince of Wales.'

'For Heaven's sake stop your romantic matchmaking, Pig. I tell you I will have none of it.'

'It's a bit late to say that, is it not – when you're speaking of your lawful husband?'

'A fact which he does not acknowledge.'

'Why, bless my soul, he's telling you now that he wants to acknowledge it.'

'I want no more of the whole business. I've had enough.'

'Now, now, marriage is for life.'

'You should be talking to him, not to me. Have I broken my marriage vows to him? Have I gone through a form of marriage with someone else? Oh, have done with your foolish romantic dreams. Our marriage is over. I shall not see him again.'

'And not even answer his letters!' said Miss Pigot reproachfully. 'Sending them back unread. I never did. I reckon it's *lèse majesté* or something.'

'Forget he is the Prince of Wales and think of him as a man.'

'Well, he's sent Madam Jersey packing. And I hear he found it rather difficult to shake her off. She wouldn't take a hint and he, poor boy, wanted to let her down lightly. Well, now she knows . . . the whole of London knows, that our prince has one desire and that is to be reunited with his wife.'

'Then he had better go to Montague House.'

'Now you know he only had to do that to please the King. That's a state marriage – marriage of convenience.'

'And ours?'

'A true marriage, my love. And you know it.'

'I know, too, that when a man is married to one woman he cannot marry another. Yet he has done so and the world acknowledges that she is his wife. That can mean only one thing. I am not.'

'Nonsense. We know better than that. Oh come, my dearest Maria, don't be hard on him. Think how unhappy he is.'

'And who but himself is to blame for that?'

But she was thinking of him and his unhappiness; for in her heart she knew that he could only be truly happy with her.

Miss Pigot brightened. In time, she thought, she will relent.

Very soon more letters would be arriving. Miss Pigot knew her prince. Once he had made up his mind that he was going to have Maria back he would not stop pleading with her until she came.

At the sound of horses' hoofs on the road Maria looked up expectantly – hopefully. Oh, she couldn't hide her true feelings from her faithful Pigot.

'Who is that?' she asked.

Miss Pigot was at the window. 'It could well be a messenger from His Highness,' she said with a smile.

Maria read the appeal. She must come back to him. She was his dear wife, his angel. He did not know how she could be so cruel to him. He admitted that he had been the victim of a mental aberration when he had thought he could do without her. But she *had* been a little cross with him at times. She *had* lost her temper she would admit. Not that he did not deserve all the abuse she had showered on him. She was his angel and he was foolish and in need of forgiveness. But how could she have *believed* he had been serious when he had sent that note telling her he did not want to see her again. Why hadn't she realized it was meant as a joke? Why hadn't she laughed at him and re-fused to believe it? Did she not know that he was her faithful husband until death did them part?

Maria wept as she read the letter, recalling that period of desolation when he had left her, thinking of the happy times they had shared together at Kempshott when he was so deeply in debt that he had had to close part of Carlton House.

Could she go back? No, of course she could not. He was married to Caroline of Brunswick and that marriage was accepted in the eyes of the law, which meant of course that that ceremony which they had gone through in her house at Park Street was considered to be no true marriage after all.

'I could never go back,' she told Miss Pigot. 'It was different before this public marriage. Then I believe many people ac-cepted me as his wife. Now no one could, for to do so would be to imply that the Princess Charlotte is illegitimate.'

'These rules and regulations,' sighed Miss Pigot. 'What are

they? You know you're his wife. I should have thought that was good enough.'

'You are trying to tempt me.'

Ah, thought Miss Pigot, so she admits it is a temptation!

Miss Hayman brought the news to Montague House.

'The Prince is courting Mrs Fitzherbert very ardently.'

'Well, I hope he's successful,' cried Caroline.

'People are saying that he's as much in love with her as he was in the beginning.'

'We should drink to the success of our fat lovers,' laughed Caroline.

Miss Hayman was surprised at the Princess's attitude; but Caroline was always unaccountable.

'Come, fill a glass and drink with me. I have said that I hope he won't feel me to be an impediment to his reconciliation with the lady.'

'Your Highness has said that?'

'Oh come, Hayman, let us be honest. I don't want the man.' She shuddered. 'That wedding night of ours. He was drunk. It was the only way he could face me. How many brides do you think have a husband who spent his wedding night lying under the grate?' She began to laugh and Miss Hayman joined in, for if the Princess saw the matter as a joke she was prepared to do the same.

'I'll tell you something, Hayman,' went on the Princess. 'I've made many *faux pas* in my life as you can imagine, but the biggest one I ever made was to marry Mrs Fitzherbert's husband.'

She began to laugh immoderately.

Lord Cholmondeley did not know how to lift his master from his despair. He was continually being summoned to talk about the Prince's problem.

'Cholmondeley,' he cried, 'I am frustrated at every turn. My father denies me the right which is every other Englishman's – to fight for his country. I have offered my services and they are refused. I have pointed out that I have six brothers who could take my place if I should die in action. And what is the reply. No! No! It has always been the same. It is not the first time I have offered to fight for my country and been refused the honour.'

'As Prince of Wales, Your Highness—'

'I know what you are going to say, Cholmondeley. And how can I gainsay it? It's true I'm the heir to the throne. It's true that the state of my father's health is ... precarious. But I have brothers.'

'But Your Highness is the Prince of Wales.'

But he had not summoned Cholmondeley to talk of war but of love.

'Denied my rights as an Englishman and as a husband. Yes, my dear Cholmondeley, as a husband. Oh, I am not referring to that ... object with whom they made me go through a form of marriage but to my own dear wife, Maria Fitzherbert, with whom I can make no headway – no headway at all.'

'I am sure Your Highness will in time.'

'In time! Ever since I left the Princess Caroline I have been trying to persuade Maria to come back to me. The answer is always No.'

Cholmondeley was thoughtful. There had been Lady Jersey, of course, and it might well be that Maria Fitzherbert was not absolutely certain that that affair was ended. But he would not remind the Prince of that lady for His Highness disliked being reminded of what he preferred to forget.

'I do not think, Your Highness, that the lady will persist in holding out against you.'

'She has so far. I sent her a copy of a will I made a few days after that public ceremony. In this I left her everything I possessed and I referred to her as my dear wife, my second self, for that is how I shall always think of Maria.'

'And still she is adamant?'

'She does not answer most of my letters.'

'Perhaps she fears to offend the Princess of Wales.'

'Why should she? That woman is of no importance whatsoever.'

Was His Highness unaware of the cheers which followed the

Princess wherever she went? Was he unaware that the King was attached to her? And most important of all that the people of the country were taking sides and they were supporting the Princess against the Prince?

'And she continues to live in Ealing – Ealing, Cholmondeley – in a rather humble way when she could live in Pall Mall in splendour.'

'Mrs Fitzherbert has never been a woman to flaunt her position, Your Highness. She is I think the most regal lady I ever beheld—'

The Prince's eyes had become glazed with emotion.

'Regal, indeed. If she could have been accepted as the Princess of Wales I should have been the happiest man on earth, Cholmondeley. As it is I am thrust into this position and am the least happy. Although, if she came back to me . . .'

'I heard, Your Highness, that the Princess of Wales expressed a wish that the reconciliation you hope for with Mrs Fitzherbert be successfully concluded to your mutual happiness.'

'Did she say that? She has at least a good heart though the most repulsive body in the world. I tell you, Cholmondeley, I feel quite ill to think of it.'

'Then perhaps Your Highness should refrain from doing so.'

The Prince was smiling. 'So she said that did she? It shows does it not that it is obviously the right solution – since even she is aware of it. To think that the one who is standing in the way of my happiness is Maria. She is breaking her marriage vows. Did she not swear to be with me for better or worse? It's true, Cholmondeley, and I shall have no more of this. I am determined that she shall come back to me. And I will tell her that I command this. If she will not, I will make public the fact that I went through a ceremony of marriage with her. Her brother and uncle were witnesses at the ceremony. She is my wife, Cholmondeley, and by God, she shall be made to do her duty.'

Cholmondeley was startled, but he knew the Prince well enough to realize that it was useless to attempt to restrain him.

Maria read the letter and turned pale. Miss Pigot was beside her. 'What is it? What now?'

'You may read it,' said Maria, and Miss Pigot picked up the letter which had fluttered to the floor.

Miss Pigot gave a short whistle. 'So he'll make a public statement that he's married to you, will he. Well, I thought that was what you'd always wanted.'

'You talk foolishly. Don't you see that this would have been dangerous before the Princess Caroline came here. Now . . . it's doubly so.'

'Dangerous?'

'If he proclaims our marriage then how can he be married to the Princess Caroline?'

'That's a question a lot of people might like to know the answer to. Perhaps if he did make this proclamation we should find out.'

'You are not thinking of the consequences. Oh, he is mad – mad.'

'Mad for you, my dear.'

'You talk like a romantic fool, Piggy.'

'It's what I am, I suspect. But I should like to see you two happy together. He's a dear good man in spite of being a little naughty now and then. But think of that will of his. You see how he loves you. He calls you his wife, his angel, his soul – and that was only a few days after the birth of his daughter.'

'Oh be silent, do, Pig.'

'Well, I will if you want, but you've got to make your decision, haven't you? Think how he's always looked after me. Five hundred a year he's given me and, dear boy, thinking he might be going to die he worries about me and says I'm to have a place in one of the palaces after he's gone. You must call that thoughtful of him.'

'You were always his advocate. I suspect you of intriguing with him.'

'It would only be for your happiness, my dear, and his.'

'Oh, I know, I know. But he is driving me to distraction.'

'I always knew you loved him.'

'When did I ever deny it?'

'It would have been no use, my dear. I know you too well. Why, Maria, what's the matter?'

199

'It's just struck me. If he is such a fool as to make a public announcement of our marriage you know what will happen, Pig. We shall all be found guilty of *praemunire*.'

'What in the name of the saints is that?'

'It's offending against the church. You see we knew of the Royal Marriage Act; we knew that the state would not accept his marriage to a commoner, and a Catholic at that, and we went through a church ceremony.'

'You mean that that parson will be found guilty. What was his name?'

'Burt. He's dead so they can't hurt him. But— oh, Piggy, I've just remembered. My brother and my uncle signed as witnesses. Heaven knows what will happen to them. They will be found guilty.'

Maria had risen and Miss Pigot rose too to stand beside her. 'What are you going to do?' she asked anxiously.

Maria did not answer but hurried out of the room and into her bedroom, followed by Miss Pigot. There Maria took a strong-box from a cupboard and drew out a document.

She studied it in some emotion for a few seconds. It recorded that on 15 December 1785 George Augustus Frederick Prince of Wales had married Maria Fitzherbert.

Then deliberately she picked up a pair of scissors and cut out the names of John Smythe her brother and Henry Errington her uncle.

'Maria,' cried Miss Pigot aghast, 'what are you doing?'

'I am saving my brother and uncle from the disaster which would surely fall on them if my husband were so foolish as to carry out his threats.'

Miss Pigot could only stare in dismay at the mutilated marriage certificate.

'Why don't you give in!' she said. 'You know you will in the end.'

The Queen was sitting with the Princess Augusta and Mary while they worked at their embroidery. The readers had been dismissed because the Queen wished to talk with her daughters and she did not want what she had to say to go outside the family.

The Prince of Wales was at Carlton House; so was his daughter; the Princess Caroline was at Blackheath, but she was visiting Carlton House regularly to see her daughter and the child paid visits to her. The Queen would have liked to see Princess Caroline shut out completely from the family circle. She hated her daughter-in-law; this was only partly due to the fact that the Prince had chosen her in preference to her own niece Louise; the other reason was that she had hated Caroline's mother. When she had first come to England— a frightened inexperienced girl of seventeen – Caroline's mother had spied on her, reported her actions to her mother-in-law and had in fact been one of the main causes for all the years of insignificance which had been hers during her long period of childbearing. Now she was discovering how exciting it was to have power. She was vindictive and she enjoyed having her revenge on her enemy's daughter.

In any case, she assured herself, she disliked the Princess for herself alone; and she was irritated that the King should show such affection for her. He showed more for her than he did for his wife and was constantly defending her.

If the Prince should decide to be reconciled to her and give her more children like young Charlotte – who was, she was forced to admit, a fascinating child with a gift for charming everybody – the odious Caroline might become very powerful indeed.

Reports were that the Prince loathed her; but the creature managed to be followed by cheering crowds every time she came to London and she knew how the Prince wanted popularity. He might feel it was politic to go back to her.

It must not be. And now that he had discarded dear Lady Jersey one could never be sure what action he would take. It was true he was courting Maria Fitzherbert but the lady was holding aloof.

She looked at her daughters and sighed. It was distasteful to have to discuss such matters with them but she feared there was no help for it.

'I believe,' she said, 'that Mrs Fitzherbert now spends most of her time in Ealing, although she has taken a house in Tilney Street for her brief visits to town.'

The Princesses were alert and more attentive now than during their readings, their mother noticed grimly.

'She is a very good woman, I believe. I have never heard ill of her.'

'There has been scandal about her marriage to George, Mamma,' said Augusta, and was silenced by a look.

'I should like to see virtuous ladies more at Court.'

'She is a Catholic . . .' began the tactless Augusta.

Oh dear, thought the Queen, Augusta would always act impulsively. Mary would be more tactful. Elizabeth was so much the artist, and could scarcely be called practical.

Perhaps that was as much as she should say. Royal people must learn to be diplomatic. Her daughters should realize that she would not frown on the return of the Prince of Wales to Mrs Fitzherbert; and that anything they could do to bring about that conclusion would have her approval.

'She has never been obtrusively Catholic,' said the Queen. 'She has always behaved with the utmost decorum; and now that we have a Princess of Wales who is *far* from discreet . . .'

Her daughters had understood. The Queen wished George to return to Maria Fitzherbert; and as George wished it and his brothers had never been anything but extremely friendly with the lady, surely it was for his sisters to play their small part in bringing about the reconciliation.

Miss Pigot was triumphant. It was clear that the royal family wished Maria to return to the Prince. How could she possibly hold out against such a weight of opinion? The Prince's brothers had always been on his side so naturally since he wanted to return to Maria they would do their best to persuade her. But when the royal Princesses – whom she met at some of the houses to which she had received invitations it would have been churlish to refuse – actually approached her and hinted that the family wished for a reunion she could scarcely ignore such an approach. And when certain members of the Queen's household suggested that Her Majesty had given similar hints Maria knew that she must act.

She now answered the Prince's letters. She was moved by his

professions of devotion; doubtless he knew her own feelings; but before she agreed to return to him she must have the sanction of the Holy See as to whether she was truly the Prince's wife; and only if she were so in the eyes of the Pope could she consider returning to him.

Knowing the delays appeals to Rome entailed the Prince gnashed his teeth in impatience. But he wanted Maria and he must agree to her terms.

Each day Miss Pigot awaited the messenger from Rome. She was almost as impatient as the Prince. Maria waited philosophically and none would have guessed the turmoil within her. To go back to that early happiness? Was it possible?

She would control her temper. She would need to, for he was the most exasperating of men. It was no use deluding herself. She loved him. Probably more deeply than he loved her. His emotions had always been of a superficial nature — but they certainly went deeper for her than for anyone else in his life. She was astonished that he had waited all this time for her to return to him. She had heard no rumours of his adventures since the dismissal of Lady Jersey. And so it had been in the early days when he had been courting her so assiduously and she had run away to the Continent to escape him. Then he had gone through that very important ceremony of marriage which might have cost him his crown . . . and all for love of her.

How could she help but love such a man?

And at last the Brief arrived from the Pope himself. He had reviewed the marriage of George, Prince of Wales, and Maria Fitzherbert and he had decided that in the eyes of the Church they were married.

There was no reason now why they should not be reunited.

Maria's house in Tilney Street was decorated with white roses, for it was June. This was because the Prince of Wales had called Maria his 'White Rose', accusing her laughingly of being a Jacobite and wanting to see the end of Hanoverian rule. White roses overflowed on all the tables. London select society had been invited to meet the Prince of Wales at breakfast; and this

203

was intended to represent a wedding breakfast. It was the solemn occasion of Maria's return to the Prince of Wales.

Plump, no longer young, either of them, they were radiant. The Prince behaved like an eager boy. He could not take his eyes from Maria. All was forgiven: her temper; his infidelities. They were lovers again.

'Togeher,' said the Prince of Wales, 'until death do us part.'

The second honeymoon had begun.

Caroline laughed loudly when she heard of it.

She insisted on drinking their health.

'Good luck to them,' she said. 'Blessings on our plump pair. I am truly pleased that Maria Fitzherbert's husband has gone back to her.'

Willikin

The Prince's return to Mrs Fitzherbert was tantamount to a public renunciation of his marriage to Caroline. True she was the Princess of Wales and mother of Princess Charlotte, but everywhere Maria Fitzherbert was received with the Prince and apart from openly being acknowledged as such was in every other way his wife.

In spite of her apparent acceptance of this extraordinary situation Caroline was at heart deeply wounded. Her only friend was the King and his health was declining rapidly. He visited her now and then and she was allowed to visit him; he showed clearly that he had a firm and growing affection for her which, Caroline confided to Miss Hayman, was comforting.

She was entertaining more frequently at Montague House, and was delighted to find that there were people who were prepared to visit her in spite of the fact that they knew they displeased the Prince of Wales by doing so. It was not only the

Prince of Wales who was displeased but the Queen also; and as the King was growing stranger every day it seemed as though Caroline would not long have a supporter in the royal family.

Caroline endeavoured to show that she did not care and, gay and unrestricted, made an effort to lead her own life. She had her beloved daughter, and Charlotte loved her mother however much her relations tried to turn her against her; she had her little family of poor children whose welfare was of the greatest concern to her; and she had the friendship of the King and the affection of the people who had considered her very badly treated by her husband and always went to a great deal of trouble to show her that they were on her side.

She felt shut in in her house in Blackheath – aloof from the affairs of the world which were distinctly uneasy. There was trouble with France where a man of tremendous ambition named Napoleon Bonaparte had risen to make a nuisance of himself to his neighbours – by no means excluding the English. The price of bread had risen alarmingly and there was general discontent among the poor because of this.

One May morning the King went into Hyde Park to review a battalion of the Guards. Crowds had gathered to see the parade and all was going well when suddenly the sound of a shot was heard and one of the spectators fell to the ground. Crowds collected; the King asked to know what had happened and learned that the fallen man had been wounded by a ball cartridge. There was no doubt in anyone's mind for whom that shot had been intended.

The King was calm as always in such circumstances, having long ago assured himself that kings must be prepared at all times for sudden death. As for himself, since his illness he was haunted by the fear of going mad and he often told himself that sudden extinction would be preferable to years endured in the clouded world of insanity.

'Continue with the exercise,' he said, and went on as though nothing had happened.

People who had witnessed the incident talked of the King's remarkable courage; and that evening when he went to Drury

Lane to see the play he was loudly cheered, but as he stepped to the front of the box to acknowledge these cheers a man in the stalls stood up and fired at him.

For the second time that day the King had had a narrow escape from death, for had the bullet been a few inches nearer the mark it would have entered his body.

There was a hushed silence before pandemonium broke out and the man who had fired the shot was captured.

The King, however, preserved his miraculous calm and signed for the play to continue; he slept through the interval which was a habit of his, usually sneered at, but on such an occasion applauded.

No one could help but admire the courage of the King and during the evening Sheridan, manager of Drury Lane, wrote a verse to be added to the national anthem and sung to the King that very night.

From every latent foe,
From the assassin's blow,
God save the King!
O'er him thine arm extend,
For Britain's sake defend,
Our father, Prince and friend,
God save the King.

The King listened while the audience sang this new verse several times and there were tears in his eyes as he did so.

And when the would-be assassin turned out to be a certain James Hadfield, an old soldier who had received a wound in the head and was clearly suffering from delusions, the King was immediately sympathetic – as he always felt towards those who suffered from insanity.

Momentarily to the people he was a hero instead of bumbling old George, Farmer George, Button Maker George, the butt of the cartoonists who depicted him talking to cottagers about their pigs and inquiring of an old woman how the apple came to be inside the dumpling. They were fond of old George while they laughed at his homely ways and his concern for small matters. The man who could act so calmly after an attempt on his life was in another category.

But they soon forgot and he was old George again – parsimonious, prim, father of a large and troublesome family – poor old George who had once been mad and was likely to be so again.

Pitt resigned and Pitt had been the King's anchor ever since he had shown himself to be the ablest minister of his day and had headed a ministry at the age of twenty-five.

The King's constant anxieties about the state of Europe, that new menace, Bonaparte, and the complicated matrimonial affairs of the Prince of Wales, had their effect.

He became ill – of a fever his doctors called it. But it was well known what the King's fevers entailed. The Queen was in despair, while the eyes of the Prince of Wales were hopefully turned towards the Regency which had once almost been his and which if it had come to him would have brought him great power.

But the King recovered – although he still acted strangely.

Caroline was awakened one morning by her servants who announced that His Majesty was below and had called to see her.

Fearing something was wrong Caroline did not wait to dress, but in her unconventional manner ran down in her nightgown to greet her father-in-law.

The King embraced her with fervour – in fact in such a manner as to alarm her faintly. She had long felt that he was somewhat attracted to her.

His eyes were a little wild as he declared: 'You have been constantly in my mind. Constantly. Constantly, you understand, eh, what?'

Caroline replied that she understood and she was gratified and honoured to have been in the kindly thoughts of her dear father-in-law and uncle.

'My poor, poor Caroline, the way in which you are treated ... I think of you. I think of you. I have been ill – very ill – you understand, eh, what? and I have thought of you. I have decided to give you the Rangership of Greenwich Park. You understand, eh, what?'

Caroline sank to her knees and kissed his hand.

He surveyed her with tears in his eyes.

'All wrong,' said the King. 'All wrong. Treated like this. While he goes off with ... Always been a trouble to me. Such a beautiful baby he was, beautiful child – always fed in the proper manner – always disciplined – and then he gives me sleepless nights. I've had ten in a row. The Rangership of Greenwich Park, you understand, eh, what?'

Caroline did understand. She was triumphant. This was going to upset the old Begum. But the King, the dear crazy King, was her friend and so she had something to be thankful for.

Life was not unpleasant at Montague House for Caroline since so many interesting people were delighted to be her guests. Where George Canning was there was always brilliant conversation. Mrs Canning often accompanied him; and there was Lady Hester Stanhope, the eccentric young woman to whom Caroline was very much attracted; that able politician Spencer Perceval came; others followed these; Mr Pitt himself called on her with other distinguished Tories, for after all the Prince of Wales was notoriously Whig which meant that the Tories would support the Princess of Wales.

So Caroline delighted herself by giving lavish parties in which she dispensed with all ceremony. She would dance with her guests, laugh with them and play romping games. No one could have behaved less like a Princess of Wales; but all her guests were well aware that there had never before been a Princess of Wales like Caroline of Brunswick.

But what she most enjoyed were the times she spent with those whom she called her 'children'. She had her school which she herself superintended and where the children received a good education; not as she was determined to make sure, an education which would give them airs and graces and good manners. Oh no, theirs was to be a practical education. She wanted to equip her children, who would have no fortune, to take their places in the world with a trade behind them. She wanted her girls to learn how to manage a house so that if they married they would be good wives; and the boys should not leave school without a good trade in their hands. She, who was so wildly impractical in most things, was entirely the opposite where her children were concerned.

Each day they were brought to her and took a meal with her. They called her Mamma and had no shyness where she was concerned. They would come to her if they hurt themselves and she was the one who must bandage them or kiss and make better.

'There is only one thing I regret about my children,' she told Mrs Fitzgerald, her lady-in-waiting, 'and that is that they are not my own.'

She spoke wistfully, for in every child she saw her own daughter Charlotte and lived for the hours she could spend with the little girl.

'All my life,' she told Miss Hayman and Mrs Fitzgerald, 'I longed for a child, and when I had one it was to discover she belonged to the state and not to me. What a tragedy! But I must not complain, must I? I have my little family and I think of them all as my own – all the little children I should have had if I had been allowed to marry where my heart lay. That was with my dear Töbingen. Ah, I could tell you of my beloved Major. He was worth a hundred princes. But he was not good enough for poor little Caroline. Does that not make you laugh?'

They were accustomed now to the wild conversation of their mistress and saw nothing remarkable in it.

She was busy in Montague House; her children saw to that. She turned one of her fields into potato land so that the produce could be sold to add to the income she spent on her children.

She enjoyed walking round the field while the potatoes were being dug.

'You see,' she would say to her ladies, 'I should never have been a princess. I should have been a country woman to marry where I wished and raise children – my own – a large family all my own.'

But the happiest days were when she saw Charlotte. She would devise games to amuse the child; she showered affection on her and it was returned; and meanwhile she knew that the Prince was making all sorts of plans to keep them apart and that but for the intervention of the King he would have done so.

She discovered a gift for modelling in clay and her first effort was to make a head of her daughter.

'To remind me of you, my angel,' she said, 'when you are not with me.'

Charlotte was intrigued and sat as still as she could while her mother worked; then when the sitting was over they would play rough games – for Charlotte was a tomboy – until it was time for the little princess to go back to Carlton House.

So, thought Caroline, deprived of my own child for long periods, I must have my adopted family to keep me from grieving.

Because she thought that the sea would provide her boys with a career she made the acquaintance of Admiral Samuel Hood who was the Governor of Greenwich Hospital; and through him she met a man who was to have an important effect on her life. This was the dashing sailor, Sir William Sydney Smith, always known as Sir Sydney, a man who immediately attracted Caroline because he had the manner of an adventurer and was indeed one. He had fought many a sea battle and could tell a stirring story, so he was cordially welcomed to Montague House.

Caroline was entranced and made no secret of her interest in the sailor. He must come again to Montague House, she told him, when he was in the neighbourhood.

'That, Your Highness,' he replied, 'could be any time you invite me, because I am staying for a while in the house of my friend Sir John Douglas.'

'And that is near by?' Caroline wanted to know.

'Very close to Montague House. Your Highness has doubtless seen the house on your trips around. In fact it is the nearest to Montague House. You should meet the Douglases; they are an amusing pair. John Douglas was with me at Saint Jean d'Acre. That was when I was taking care of the defences. Those were stirring days. I could tell you some tales. It was just before I took over command of Alexandria. I remember the news coming in that Bonaparte had stormed Jaffa.'

The Princess's eyes shone with excitement. If she could not have a large family of children to care for she would like to travel about the world, see strange places, enjoy the company of exotic men and women.

'Well, my friend Douglas was with me. And now I'm ashore for awhile I'm staying with them. Lady Douglas is an enchanting creature. She has recently had the most delightful child.'

'A child.'

'A baby daughter. A pretty and engaging creature I do assure you. Your Highness would enjoy meeting the mother and child.'

'That I should,' said Caroline, 'and doubtless I will as they are such near neighbours.'

Such a cold day, thought Caroline. How she wished that she was in one of those hot and sunny spots which dear Sir Sydney talked about with such enthusiasm. Still, her destiny lay here. She had come to England to be a Princess of Wales, one day a queen – though she trusted that would be a long time hence, since it could only be on the death of the King.

She felt restless so she sent for Miss Hayman and told her she was going to walk.

'Alone, Your Highness?'

'Yes, dear Hayman, alone.'

It amused her to see the shocked look in dear Hayman's eyes. They should be used to her by now. She was not treated like a princess; she was not allowed to live in Carlton House; therefore she would behave like a country lady and go walking alone if she wished.

In her mauve satin cloak and yellow half-boots she looked very colourful. Would Maria Fitzherbert say she looked a little too flamboyant? Well, Maria my love, I am the Princess, not you!

'Now, my love, bring my sable cap and I'll be off.'

When the cap was brought she set it jauntily on her head.

'There, my dear, the Princess of Wales takes the air – unescorted – but not desolate. Because it is as she wishes and as she commands.'

'Your Highness—'

'No, my dear, I do not need your company. I am going alone.'

She left Montague House smiling as she went. She knew exactly where she was going. She would call on Lady Douglas and see the enchanting child and perhaps Sir Sydney Smith if he were there.

She found the house he had described. How did one call? Did one walk straight up to the door and knock? That was what she had done in Brunswick when she had wished to call on humble folk. But this was not Brunswick; and there she had merely been the Princess Caroline, daughter of a small ducal house. Perhaps the Princess of Wales should have a different approach.

She put her hand on the gate and hesitated; then she stopped and walked up and down along by the iron railings.

What does it matter how I get in? It only matters that I do.

An attractive young woman had come out of the house and approached Caroline. Opening the gate, she asked: 'Do you want something? Can I help you?'

'Are you Lady Douglas?'

'Yes, I am.'

'I thought you must be. I hear you are the mother of a very beautiful little girl. May I see her? I love children.'

'Madam—' began the startled woman.

'Sir Sydney told me about her. Sir Sydney Smith. He was at Montague House, you see.'

'Montague House ... but that is—'

Caroline nodded. 'Yes, of course. I am the Princess Caroline – Princess of Wales.'

'Your Highness!'

'There's no need to stand on ceremony. Ask me in, please.'

'My ... my humble house is at Your Highness's service.'

'Well, come and show me your little daughter.'

So that was the beginning and Sir Sydney was right. The child was enchanting. As for Sir John and Lady Douglas, they were delighted to have the honour of entertaining Her Royal Highness. And while they gave her refreshment Sir Sydney arrived; and then there was a joyful encounter between him and the Princess.

It was a very entertaining visit and Sir Sydney begged leave to escort her back to Montague House, which permission she willingly gave.

The Douglases were hopeful, they told her, that they might again have the pleasure of Her Highness's company and that they hoped that next time she came she would give them warning so that they might have the opportunity of entertaining her in a fitting manner.

'Nonsense!' cried Caroline. 'I've been most fittingly entertained. I want no ceremony. You shall come to my next party at Montague House. And certainly I shall come again. We are neighbours.'

When Caroline had left with Sir Sydney the Douglases looked at each other in astonishment.

'I feel I've dreamed the last two hours,' said Lady Douglas.

'I always heard she was eccentric.'

'Who would have believed that she – that woman – was our future Queen!'

'The stories we've heard must have been true.'

'What an adventure!' said Lady Douglas. She looked at her husband. He was a brave man and had not done badly; he had been given a pension after the part he had taken with Sir Sydney in the defence of Saint Jean d'Acre; but she was the strong one; she had always led the way and he had always followed.

When she had suggested that the gay bachelor, Sir Sydney Smith, should live in their house when he was ashore he had raised no objection, and if he knew of the relationship between herself and Sir Sydney he raised no objection to that either. He was no raiser of objections and that suited Lady Douglas and Sir Sydney very well indeed.

But the Princess of Wales – to call on them like some humble village woman!

' "I hear you have a beautiful daughter . . ." ' mimicked Lady Douglas in a thick guttural accent. 'What an extraordinary thing!'

'You found her – attractive?' asked Sir John.

'I would say she is an attractive proposition rather than an attractive woman,' said Lady Douglas with a smirk.

'You think this could bring good fortune to us?'

'I intend to see that it does. Good heavens, can't you imagine what it could mean to us? Friends in high places! My dear friend and neighbour is Madame Caroline. She's crazy; she's wild; she behaves in the oddest way – I grant you that. But she is still the Princess of Wales.'

'Sydney seemed taken with her.'

Lady Douglas turned away to hide the frown.

'He would have to be taken with the Princess of Wales, wouldn't he? So have you to be – and I. So have we all, if we're wise.'

Lady Douglas left her husband and went to her room as she said to think of what could come out of this.

From her window she watched for the return of Sir Sydney and when he came back and up to the rooms which had been set aside for him, she was waiting for him in his bedroom.

'Well?' she demanded.

'It's a fantastic thing. I can scarcely believe it.'

'*She's* a fantastic thing, you mean.'

'Tut tut, Lottie. You're talking of the Princess of Wales. Remember that.'

'I trust you remembered it.'

'Now what does that mean?'

She threw herself against him and put her arms about his neck.

'You know full well.'

He laughed.

'Myself – and the Princess of Wales! Come, Lottie, you're letting your imagination run away with you.'

'Mind you don't let yours run away with you where that woman's concerned.'

He laughed again and embraced her.

'Your spare time is for me,' she told him. 'Remember it.'

'As if you'd let me forget!'

'I shan't. But if you did by any chance there'd be trouble. You know that.'

'I know my Lottie,' he said.

*

The friendship with the Douglases flourished. Lady Douglas, Caroline believed, was a very exciting personality. She was full of fun, ready for the wildest games Caroline arranged for her parties; and there was the delightful little daughter of hers who had been christened Charlotte Sydney. It made a bond between them that they both had a daughter named Charlotte; and Caroline was constantly bestowing gifts on the adorable little creature.

How pleased she was that she had called on the Douglases that day!

There was a great deal of entertaining and Sir Sydney was in good form at parties; he had a talent for devising all sorts of games and they were usually games with forfeits. And the price he always demanded from the ladies was a kiss. This caused great merriment. And when Caroline had to pay her forfeit, Sir Sydney did not alter his terms and Caroline was very prepared to kiss him heartily. He was her dear friend who had helped to make her life so much more exciting.

Captain Manley came to Montague House a great deal too. He was very interested in her boys and told her that the sea would be a fine career for any of them who was suited to it.

'Why, you are like a father to my darlings,' she cried in her impulsive way; and once when he took his leave she kissed him heartily to show him how grateful she was.

She did not realize that her behaviour was noticed and commented on not only among her friends but among her servants. Nor did she know that some of the latter had been placed in her household on the orders of the Prince of Wales, that her conduct might be observed and reported.

'Dear, dear Captain Manley,' she would say. 'What a wonderful man he is! And *so* kind.'

As for dear Sir Sydney she had a great affection for him, too. He was the life and soul of any party and she enjoyed his high spirits and those occasions when he would hold them all entranced with some tale of the sea in which Sir Sydney always played the part of dashing hero.

Since she had come to Montague House she certainly was

building up a little coterie around herself which was making life very agreeable.

The King called with presents for herself and little Charlotte. She was sad because she saw that his health was deteriorating. He spoke in that rapid manner which was so alarming and he was a trifle incoherent.

'Well, well, well, so you are settled here, eh? It's wrong you know, wrong, wrong, wrong. Ought to be at Carlton House. And little Charlotte? How is the child? Are you seeing her? Glad of that, glad of that. Should be there, though. Don't like trouble in the family. My father quarrelled with his father . . . his father quarrelled with *his* father . . . and now my son . . . Who would have sons, eh? Lucky to have a daughter. Worried about Amelia, though. Do you never see the princesses?'

'I never see them, Uncle dear. I think they may have had orders to stay away.'

'Don't like it. All wrong – wrong – should all be friends. Like to see you back with the Prince.'

'He'd never have me, Your Majesty, and I don't think I'd want to go. I'm happy here. If I could have little Charlotte here I'd want nothing else . . .'

'Happy, eh? Like it here? Not suitable really for Princess of Wales. Should be at Carlton House. Don't like it.' He looked at her in an oddly appreciative way. He said: 'Pretty woman – fine bosom – should be painted. Should have your portrait painted. Has it been done since you came? Should have it done, I'll send a man to do it. You'd like that, eh, what?'

'Why yes, Your Majesty. I'd be delighted.'

'Leave it to me. Only right. I'll send a man, eh, what?'

Poor, poor Uncle George, thought Caroline when he had left. One of these days he will go completely mad.

She believed that he would forget the promise to have her portrait painted and expected to hear no more, so she was surprised when Sir Thomas Lawrence, RA, arrived at Montague House.

Caroline was delighted with the painter from the beginning. He was handsome, in his early thirties and had an extremely gallant manner. She was discovering that she liked to be surrounded by admiring men; their attentions and compliments helped her to forget the insults of the Prince of Wales, for although she pretended that she did not care and that she was no more attracted to him than he to her, her pride had been deeply wounded; and men such as Captain Manley and Sir Sydney Smith, with their perpetual gallantries and air of 'Ah, if I but dared' were a comfort to her. And now to their number was added the handsome young painter.

How should she be painted? Let them decide together. She had seen some of his portraits. Would he make her as handsome as some of his other sitters?

'If I tell the truth Your Highness will be more beautiful than them all.'

She laughed aloud; she slipped her arm through his. He was a little astonished at the familiarity but like everyone else he had heard of the eccentric behaviour of the Princess of Wales.

So there was the additional pleasure of sitting to Sir Thomas who had taken up residence at Montague House.

'I shall be sitting with Sir Thomas for the next two hours,' she would tell her servants. 'See that we are not disturbed.'

There were sly nods and winks below stairs.

'We see life,' they said to each other, 'serving such a mistress.'

She was 'a one' for the men. As if Sir Sydney and Captain Manley were not enough – now they had Sir Thomas Lawrence as well.

One morning Mrs Fitzgerald came to tell Caroline that there had been an accident. Mrs Lisle, one of her ladies, had fallen and hurt her foot.

Caroline was immediately sympathetic. She ran into Mrs Lisle's room and found her lying on her bed, her ankle very painful and swollen.

'Oh my dear, my love, does it hurt? We must call the doctor at once. Fitz dear, will you see that they send for him. Oh, my poor, poor Lisle! Now lie perfectly still and don't move.'

She asked questions about the ankle, how it had happened, how painful was it. And she would be very, very angry with her dear Lisle if she got up from that bed before the doctor had given his verdict.

Mrs Lisle thought how endearing the Princess was. It was true she behaved in a manner most unsuited to a Princess, but who else would be so concerned about a sprained ankle – or whatever ailed her. At times like this one loved the Princess.

The doctor came and diagnosed a bad twist to the ankle. Her foot was also damaged. He said she must certainly not stand on her feet more than was absolutely necessary for at least a fortnight.

'I have my duties,' began Mrs Lisle.

Caroline who had insisted on being present cried: 'What nonsense! Of course she shall stay in bed. I myself will see to it, doctor.'

'The Princess has the kindest heart in the world,' said Mrs Lisle.

Caroline said 'Nonsense!' again, but she was pleased. It was true she did love those who served her, and wanted to do the best possible for them.

Lady Douglas came that day. She was coming more frequently than ever and she and Caroline were considered to be fast friends. An added bond between them was Lady Douglas's pregnancy. 'Lucky, lucky you!' cried Caroline when she had heard; and it was this fact which made her more eager than ever to talk to Lady Douglas.

Caroline greeted her warmly. 'And how are you today, my dear? Taking good care of yourself, I trust? Oh, how I envy you. And no one attempts to keep you from *your* darling Charlotte. I saw mine the other day. What a tomboy! She is going to be a wild one. You cannot think how I miss her. And you, lucky creature, have your daughter all the time – and a new child coming. What do you hope for? A girl or a boy?'

'What does it matter?' said Lady Douglas. 'Once one has a child that child is all one ever wanted.'

Caroline clasped her hands. 'How right you are, my dear. And pray tell me how are dear Sir John and dear, dear Sir Sydney?'

Lady Douglas suppressed the wave of jealous anger which

rose in her. Sydney said there was nothing serious in his relationship with the Princess; it was merely a flirtation. Could she trust him? Not at all. He was a born adventurer and he took adventure where he found it. Had he found it here? She could never be sure. Was Caroline having love affairs with Manley and Lawrence? There was gossip enough and she saw that her servants were on friendly terms with those of Montague House. Servants were such good detectives; not only did they have opportunities but an extra sense where the scandals of the families they served were concerned. Some said yes and some said no. And I'd make her sorry if I found out there was anything between Sydney and her – Princess of Wales or not! thought Lady Douglas. And perhaps since she was Princess of Wales it would be easier than if she were not in such an exalted position.

Let her babble on about her babies, those cottage children she treated like her own! The woman was more than eccentric: she was mad – and she had said as much to Sydney.

The eternal question was: 'Is Sydney faithful to me?' What a fool she was to become so besotted about a man. It was not like her; she was usually so calm and practical. But ever since she had met Sydney . . . Oh, well, she was obsessed by the man and as long as he remembered that he was hers and that she expected fidelity all was well. But if he was the Princess's lover . . .

There sat the woman brilliantly rouged, her hair in some disorder, her bodice cut low to show too much of her voluptuous bosom. Looking at her one would say that suspicions were not unfounded.

By God, if I found out, thought Lady Douglas, while she said sweetly that one must of course take care of oneself during the waiting months for the sake of the child.

The Princess listened rapturously. One would almost think she was pregnant herself.

'Poor Lisle hurt her foot today,' she said suddenly. 'I am insisting that she lie up for a fortnight. Doctor's orders. Of course the dear soul is worrying about how I shall manage without her. It will be difficult. I do miss my ladies when they are absent.'

'They're very fortunate to serve Your Highness.'

'And I'm fortunate to have such angels to serve me. Oh – something has just occurred to me. I wonder whether you would like to come here for a fortnight as a maid of honour? It would be so amusing. We could talk and talk – and I should see personally that you did nothing to harm the precious child.'

To live in Montague House for a fortnight. That would be interesting. Then she might discover a great deal. Sydney could visit her there. It amused her to think of them being together under the same roof as the woman who might well be another of his mistresses.

'Your Highness is so good to me.'

'Would Sir John object, do you think?'

'Sir John!' She must not show her contempt for her husband for that might cloud a little the image the Princess had of her. 'Oh, Sir John, I am sure he would be delighted. He would be extremely conscious of the honour done to me.'

'Then it is settled.'

So Lady Douglas came to stay for a fortnight in Montague House.

What gossip there was and it was all of babies. Lady Douglas was present when the children came to see the Princess. She watched them all at breakfast with her, saw Caroline's devotion to them and thought her quite mad.

'Lucky, lucky creature,' she said to Lady Douglas. 'You already have one and another little darling on the way. I trust you will have a large family. Ten, no less.'

God forbid, thought Lady Douglas.

Sir Sydney came but he was reluctant to spend too much time alone with Lady Douglas in Montague House.

'What of the Princess?' he demanded. 'What if she should discover?'

'Would she be so shocked?'

'The general opinion would be that she would.'

'You probably know more of her than most people.'

That made Sir Sydney laugh.

'Do I detect a certain jealousy, my dear?'

'Do I detect a certain complacency?'

'Complacent. Why shouldn't I be complacent? I'm a naval hero, my love.'

'And the lover of the Princess of Wales?'

Sir Sydney's eyes sparkled. 'Hush. Who knows we may be overheard. That's treason.'

She took him by the arm and shook him. 'Is it true? Is it true?'

That made him laugh. She thought how maddeningly attractive he was. She longed to subdue him as she had Sir John but of course she could not and that was the man's attraction for her.

'Answer me, answer me.'

His eyes were alight with mischief.

'Ask the Princess. I should like to hear what she has to say.'

How was she to know whether it was true or not? But from that moment she began to believe it was; and her hatred for Caroline was like a physical pain. She felt a longing to destroy the Princess.

But the fortnight passed in outward harmony and Caroline had no idea of the stormy feelings she aroused in Lady Douglas.

And when Mrs Lisle was again on her feet Lady Douglas went home.

'It has been such a privilege to serve Your Highness,' she said.

'Oh, don't call it serving,' cried the Princess. 'It's been the visit of a friend.'

Shortly afterwards she was out walking in the neighbourhood when she came across a case of extreme poverty which she found most distressing.

She was first attracted by Mrs Austin who was heavily pregnant, and paused at the door of their cottage to talk to her.

'I see you are soon to have a child.'

'Worse luck,' said the woman, recognizing the Princess, for most people in the neighbourhood knew her by now and were aware of her eccentric habits and as she did not ask for ceremony they gave her none.

'My dear good woman, how can you say such a thing? You

are about to have that most precious gift – a child – and you see it as ill luck!'

'I've had too many precious gifts, Madam – more than I can afford to feed.'

Caroline's deepest sympathies were aroused.

'You should have come to me and I would have helped you. Now you are not to worry any more. I shall have food sent to you. And I shall see that the baby is looked after when it is born.'

'We all know of your godness, Madam. And I can only say we know too you'll keep your word. This was a lucky day for me.'

Caroline went on her way but she could not stop thinking of the coming child. Poor mite, to come into the world unwanted. If only she was the mother ... if she could only have a child which would be all her own and not taken away from her, how happy she would be!

She could not get the Austins out of her mind; and next day she was at the cottage with blankets and food; and it soon became clear that although she was interested in all the children and pregnant mothers of the neighbourhood, she had a very special feeling for the Austin family.

'Mrs Austin's child will be born in two months' time,' she told Lady Douglas when she called. 'I wonder whether it will be a boy or a girl.'

'I doubt she minds much.'

'She said she had had too many. Poor dear soul! As if one could have too many. It's strange that some feel this to be so and others would give years of their lives to have one.'

'Your Highness loves children so much. Perhaps other women are less motherly.'

Caroline held her arms as though she cradled a baby. She began to laugh suddenly. 'Do you know I feel as though *I'm* pregnant.'

Lady Douglas looked startled.

'Yes, I do,' insisted Caroline. 'I really do. Mrs Austin was telling me how she was feeling and I understood so well. I said to her: "Why, Mrs Austin, I feel with you. I do indeed." '

Lady Douglas looked at the strange creature sharply. Could it be? Was she? Sydney would think it all a great joke.

I believe it is so, thought Lady Douglas. There is a look about her. She's excited. I could almost be sure of it.

When Lady Douglas had gone Caroline called for her pelisse and cap. She had not told Lady Douglas yet. No, it was a secret so far. It might not happen and she had first to consult Mrs Austin, who at the moment did not want the child but women did change when their children were born. It was natural enough and God forbid that she should take a child from its mother.

Mrs Austin was at the cottage door when Caroline arrived.

She invited her in. Small and dark and insanitary, she noted. The idea of this new and precious life starting in such a place!

Mrs Austin dusted a chair for the Princess.

'Thank you, Mrs Austin. I have come to speak to you of a very . . . delicate matter.'

'Oh . . . Madam . . .'

'Don't be frightened. If you say No, I shall understand. It's that when the baby is born will you . . . could you bear to give it to me?'

'To give it to you, Madam! You mean you want to *take* it?'

'That's what I mean, Mrs Austin. I have a daughter, my own little Charlotte, but I am not allowed to have her with me all the time. I want a baby of my very own . . . to care for . . . to have with me. You said you had too many. I am asking you to give me this one.'

'Do you mean, Madam, that you'd take the baby . . . Like one of those you have in your school and look after it like, and feed and learn it things—'

'I didn't mean quite that. I want to have this baby as soon as it's born. I want to care for it myself. I want to adopt it.'

'Why Madam—'

'I quite understand if you can't bear to part with it.'

'I can bear it, Madam. Why, I can't believe it. It's too good to be true.'

'Then you will?'

Caroline came out of the cottage, her eyes glowing. In two months' time she would have her own little baby, to care for, to bring up, one who would not be snatched from her.

She came running into Montague House. Some of the servants were within earshot.

'My dear Fitz ... Lisle, my love, something wonderful has happened. I'm going to have a baby.'

Spencer Perceval, who had now become the Attorney General, often called at Montague House. Caroline knew he was a friend whom she could trust and was delighted with his growing success. She knew, too, that he was brilliantly clever; his conversation was a delight, spattered with epigrams as it was; and she heard it said that he was an unusual man, for not only had he won the approval of Pitt, who had once said that Perceval could be a future prime minister, but Fox and Sheridan had also expressed their admiration for him.

It was gratifying therefore that he should call on her; and she knew that when such men showed their friendship for her it caused a great deal of chagrin to the Prince of Wales. This in itself would have made it worth while her receiving such men; but she liked Perceval for himself and was delighted to have him as her friend.

She confided in him a great deal – what comfort to confide in a clever man! He knew about her school and the children she cared for and he applauded her for doing this social work.

So now she felt she could talk to him of the Austins, but as yet she had decided to be unusually discreet and say nothing of her plan for adopting the child. This she supposed was due not so much to discretion but the fear that if she talked too much of the project something might go wrong with it. She could never understand a mother's parting with her child and was therefore haunted by the thought that when the time came Mrs Austin would not let it go; moreover there was the dangerous affair of birth itself. If this one were lost in the process she would be heartbroken. So therefore she had a superstitious feeling that she would not speak of it until the child was actually in her hands.

But she was anxious about the poverty of the Austins.

'I have discovered a very poor family living near here,' she told Perceval. 'I know you understand my concern for these people.'

He did indeed. He wished that others of her rank shared her conscience.

'Then I know you'll help me. The father of this family is a good respectable man who had work in the dockyards until he lost it. There are several children and I have done what I could but I think that if the father could earn money himself they would all be happier for this. They do not want to live on charity. I can recommend Samuel Austin as a good respectable man. Can you do something for him?'

Perceval said that he would do his utmost and he had little doubt that he could find some form of employment for a good and honest man who was a protégé of the Princess.

In a week or so Caroline was able to carry the good news to the Austins that there was a job waiting for Samuel in the dockyards.

'You're our good angel, Madam,' said Mrs Austin.

'And you haven't changed your mind about the baby?'

'Why, Madam, do you take me for a fool? This baby's going to be the luckiest in Blackheath.'

'I'll try to make it so,' said Caroline.

Lady Douglas had had another daughter. Caroline went over to their house as soon as she heard the news, taking with her lavish presents for mother and baby.

'My dear,' she cried as she sat down heavily on the bed, 'you must be the happiest woman alive.'

Lady Douglas asked the nurse to bring the child and it was laid in the Princess's arms. Caroline was rapturous. 'What a little darling! I adore her. I would envy you except for the fact – but it's a secret. You will know in due course.'

Lady Douglas clenched her hands beneath the bedclothes and thought: Can she mean she is pregnant! Is it possible! Oh, the traitor. It is so. I'm sure of it.

She said sweetly: 'I am going to ask a great favour of Your Highness. May I?'

'Please do. I am sure it will be granted.'

'Would you act as sponsor to my new daughter?'

'Nothing would please me more.'

'And have I Your Highness's permission to name her after you? Sir John and I would like to call her Caroline Sydney.'

'I cannot think of a happier combination,' smiled the Princess.

As the birth of Mrs Austin's child became imminent, Caroline arranged for her to go into Brownlow Street Hospital and in due course a boy was born. When Mrs Austin came home Caroline went to the cottage and saw the child in his shabby cradle. She took him up in her arms but Mrs Austin said that she would have to keep him with her for a week or two.

'You are not going against your word?' cried Caroline.

'Lord love you, Madam, it's us that's frightened *you'll* go against yours.'

'Never,' said Caroline, hanging over the cradle. 'Have you named him?'

'We thought of William, Madam.'

'It's a good name,' replied Caroline. 'Little William ... my little Will. Yes, he shall be William. When am I going to have him?'

'In three weeks from now?'

'I wait with great impatience.'

As was promised the baby boy was delivered to Montague House where Caroline had already prepared a luxurious nursery for him. She covered his face with kisses; she was going to look after him herself. He was hers as darling Charlotte could never be. Her little Willie.

'My Willie,' she cooed. 'My little Willikin.'

And that made him seem like hers. From henceforth he was Willikin.

Lady Douglas was away for a few weeks and Caroline was longing for her to come back so that she could show her the baby. When she eventually did she immediately came to call and was shown ino the Princess's drawing room by Mrs Fitzgerald.

Caroline had thrown a light piece of cloth over the child so that it was not immediately visible.

'I have a surprise for you,' she cried excitedly. 'Turn your back – or shut your eyes. No – turn your back. I want you to have a really big surprise.'

Lady Douglas did so and when Caroline gave her permission to turn, saw the child lying on the sofa.

'Your Highness!' cried Lady Douglas.

'Ha. I told you I was going to have a baby, did I not?'

'You did, Your Highness, but—'

Mrs Fitzgerald who had remained in the room said quickly: 'Her Highness adopted the child. He is the son of a Sophia Austin, the wife of a dock labourer. You should have seen him when he arrived.'

Caroline had snatched up the child and was kissing him frantically.

'He has changed has he not, Fitz? Is he not now the most beautiful baby in England?'

'He should be, Madam, with all the care you give him.'

'So your Highness is looking after him yourself?' asked Lady Douglas.

'Of course, my dear. Why else should I want a baby? To give to others to care for! You shall see how I look after him. I think it is his feeding time, is it not, Fitz? I shall feed him myself. Only the best for my darling Willikin. Send in all I shall need and I shall show my dear friend Lady Douglas how I care for my child.'

Lady Douglas watched incredulously while the Princess superintended the feeding of the child and herself changed his napkin.

It's a nightmare! thought Lady Douglas and all the time she watched Willikin to see if there was some resemblance to Sir Sydney. But, she thought, a little mollified, it could be Manley or even Lawrence.

What a fool she is! And she, the Princess of Wales! Is it possible that she can't see what trouble she might be making for herself?

Lady Douglas felt very excited. What a scandal this could be. She felt suddenly powerful which was a very comforting feeling, suspecting as she did that her lover had found satisfaction with another woman.

But it could only be because she is Princess of Wales, Lady Douglas soothed herself. If I knew it were true, I'd make her wish she'd never set eyes on him.

Not long after the arrival of Willikin, Lady Douglas came to tell the Princess that she and Sir John would be going away, perhaps for some years. They were going to Devonshire in the company of Sir Sydney Smith, both the men being called away to duty.

The Princess took an affectionate farewell of her friend and a rather tearful one of her little godchild; but there was Willikin to comfort her.

No sooner had the Douglases left than Mrs Fitzgerald told the Princess that she wished to speak to her on a rather delicate matter.

It had come to Mrs Fitzgerald's ears that Lady Douglas had spoken very disrespectfully of the Princess in the hearing of her servants, some of whom had reported this to the servants at Montague House.

'And what was this?' asked Caroline.

'She spoke slightingly of Your Highness's morals and said that William Austin was in fact your own child.'

'My little Willikin! How I wish he were! But he *is* you know, my dear. He is my own.'

'But, Your Highness, Lady Douglas hinted that he was the result of an adulterous intrigue and that you had actually given *birth* to him in secret.'

The Princess was silent. 'I think they would call that treason,' she said.

'They would indeed, Your Highness. That is why I think you should know that Lady Douglas was a false friend.'

'She must have been if she spread tales like that.'

'She did, Madam, I assure you. Heaven knows what could result if she talked too freely in some circles.'

The Princess was thoughtful. Then she brightened. 'Well, she has gone, my dear.'

'She may come back. If she does—'

The Princess waved her hand. 'If she does – well then I shall not receive her. My dear, dear Fitz, you are so concerned for me. Have no fear. She is far away and if she ever comes back I shall simply not receive her. Now . . . go and bring Willikin to me if he is awake, but don't disturb the little pet if he is not.'

Mrs Fitzgerald went away to do as she was bid.

How feckless she was! She did not seem to have any idea of the trouble her conduct could arouse.

Willikin was awake and screaming to be picked up.

Willikin indeed! thought Mrs Fitzgerald. The cause of all the trouble.

The anonymous and obscene

Caroline settled down to enjoy life with Willikin and dismissed the Douglases from her mind. She rarely gave a thought to what was happening in the world outside Montague House – and great events were in progress.

Napoleon was astride Europe. Even Hanover, that stronghold of the Guelphs, was in his hands. Most alarming of all he was at Boulogne casting covetous eyes on England, and the threat of invasion was in the air.

The Prince of Wales was fretting against inactivity. He had settled down to harmony with Maria and was now looking for further adventure. He was very unpopular with the people and that wounded him deeply for he desperately wanted their approval and he felt he could win this by becoming a hero in this battle against that great bogey man known throughout the land as Boney; and he longed to take a part in the war.

He told Maria that he was going to insist on doing so.

'Why should I, a man of my age . . . be *told* that I must not be allowed to fight for my country? Did you ever hear such rubbish?'

Maria replied that as the heir to the throne it was reasonable for the King to refuse to allow him to risk his life.

'You would make a coward of me, my dear love. I shall write to him all the same.'

He sat down at once. He was always happy with a pen in his hand. Watching him Maria remembered those long impassioned letters he used to write to her – some of them thirty-two pages in length.

'Listen to this, Maria:

In this contest the lowest and humblest of Your Majesty's servants have been called upon. It would therefore little become me, who am the First, to remain a tame, idle and useless spectator.

'Very fine,' said Maria. 'But it will not move His Majesty one bit.'

'By God, I'm not allowing the people to think me a coward.'

There was excitement in the air. The country was united as it could only be at such a time of danger. Just across the Channel Napoleon had gathered together a large fleet of gun boats. He thundered threats from the soil of France. The British were defeated, he cried. It was only a matter of weeks. Who did they think they were to dare stand out against Napoleon? Hadn't they heard of his victories throughout Europe?

The answer came back: Yes, who does he think we are?

And there was the nation suddenly in arms. Farmers and fishermen, merchants and their apprentices – everyone who could carry a gun or a scythe if no gun was available.

'Come on, Master Boney,' they cried. 'We can't wait to welcome you.'

The King was growing more and more afraid. The twilight times when his mind became so clouded that he was not sure where he was, and whether or not he was a young man again, were becoming more frequent. Sometimes he would doze off and wake up to find himself talking of he knew not what, and when he tried to stop himself the voice still went on and sometimes he was not sure that it was his.

Trouble, he thought. It's all trouble ... always has been, always will be.

He had been very upset recently over the plot organized by a certain Colonel Despard.

What had possessed the man? he kept asking. Eh, what?

Despard was a good soldier. At his trial Lord Nelson himself had come forward and testified to his valour and loyalty. What had happened to make Colonel Despard plot to assassinate his King? 'Why?' he cried. 'What have I ever done but my duty, eh, what?'

It was a mad plot – to shoot the King and take possession of the two Houses of Parliament. Why? Eh, what?

And he had been discovered and executed with his fellow conspirators at the top of Southwark Jail, and there he had made his last speech in which he had declared that he believed in the end liberty and justice would triumph over despotism and delusion.

What had he meant, eh, what?

Despotism and delusion! Hadn't he, George III, always tried to be an honest man? And had he not always had the good of his people at heart?

All this trouble: George and Caroline not living together. Bickering over the Princess Charlotte. A fine way for a child to be brought up! What did she know of the trouble between her parents? A great deal– she was a knowing young minx.

And it was all wrong. Napoleon planning invasion. Voices in his head.

What next? he asked himself.

And there was that young fool the Prince of Wales wanting to go and fight.

He took up his pen. The answer was no – no, no. Couldn't he understand that, eh, what?

'I had flattered myself to have heard no further on the subject,' he wrote angrily.

Then he buried his face in his hands and asked: 'What next, eh, what?'

The Prince was furious.

'He thinks I'm a child,' he raged. 'By God, I'll make him repent that.'

'Remember,' said Maria, 'he is a very sick man.'

'That may be. But he's representing me to the people as a coward. Am I going to stand aside and see that happen?'

'My dearest, there is nothing else you can do.'

'My dear love, I have thought of something. The obvious way to let the people know the truth.'

Maria had risen, alarmed.

'Oh, yes,' he said triumphantly. 'I am going to publish our correspondence. That will let the world know that I am not the one who is holding back.'

Lord Nelson had made an attack on the fleet which Napoleon had accumulated for the invasion of England and this changed the Corsican's ideas of easy conquest. The whole of England knew that though he might conquer Europe, Napoleon was no match for Lord Nelson.

Invasion fears died a little; but the country was still in danger and its militant mood persisted even though the situation was easier, and the King still had his troubles.

When he saw the correspondence between himself and the Prince published in the *Morning Chronicle* he was overcome with rage and grief.

Once more an open quarrel in the royal family! He raged and stormed and talked perpetually and incoherently of his eldest son's treachery to him.

As Prime Minister Addington remarked to Pitt, this was enough to turn the King's brain again. They would have to be watchful.

Caroline, happy at Montague House looking after Willikin who was fast growing objectionably spoilt, was not very pleased to hear that the Douglases were back in Blackheath.

Lady Douglas lost no time in calling at Montague House and was somewhat taken aback when she was informed that the Princess of Wales was not at home.

This might have been so, but the next day she received the same answer and as she knew that this time the Princess was in residence she realized that she was being turned away.

She was furious. She raged to Sir John: Did the Princess think she could treat her in this way? She would find she was mistaken.

'I know too much,' said Lady Douglas ominously.

She called at Montague House again to receive the same answer.

'Oh, dear,' sighed Caroline when she heard. 'I shall have to tell her that I don't wish to see her.' She called to one of her women. 'Vernon, dear, I want you to write a letter to Lady Douglas and tell her not to call again.'

When Lady Douglas's reply was brought to her Caroline turned her head away. 'Send it back to her,' she said. 'I don't want to read it. I want nothing more to do with that woman. She's dangerous.'

When this letter was returned to her Lady Douglas was furious.

'Does she think she can treat me like this? She will see that she is not dealing with some humble servant. She is a vulgar woman for all that she is Princess of Wales. I'll not endure this.'

'Be careful,' warned Sir John. 'Remember this is royalty.'

But when had she ever taken his advice? She had only scorn for him.

She sat down to write to Mrs Fitzgerald, a letter which held veiled threats. The Princess of Wales had confided in her about a matter of great importance not only to herself but the country. She had respected the Princess's confidence but if Her Royal Highness were going to treat her so churlishly, why should she behave with such meticulous honour towards Her Highness? She had written to Mrs Fizgerald because the Princess refused to read a letter addressed to herself. Perhaps Mrs Fitzgerald would acquaint Her Highness with the contents of this letter.

Mrs Fitzgerald was very perturbed. She went at once to Caroline.

'You know what she is saying, Your Highness. It is that Willikin is indeed your child.'

'My precious pet! He is my child, my dear. That's how he is to me. But what this creature is suggesting is that I gave birth to him. Is that it? And that I confided this to her? What a liar she is.'

'Yes, Your Highness, but perhaps a convincing one.'

'A convincing one. What do you mean, my dear? How could she convince anyone of such a falsehood!'

How indeed? thought Mrs Fitzgerald sadly, when the Princess of Wales was so familiar in her attitude to the men who visited the house, when she had been seen kissing Sir Sydney Smith in a game and had shut herself in a room with Sir Thomas Lawrence to be painted and was always so delighted to see Captain Manley and so affectionate in her manner towards him.

Heaven help us, thought Mrs Fitzgerald, if that woman really tried to make mischief would it be so difficult?

'Tear up the letter, Fitz dear, and think no more about it. She'll stop making a nuisance of herself when she realizes that I am determined not to see her.'

But Lady Douglas was not a woman to be lightly put aside.

She had made a plan of revenge and she lost no time in putting this into action.

Caroline received another letter and this one she read. It was very short and extremely mystifying. Lady Douglas wrote that she had received the anonymous letter Caroline had sent her together with the drawing.

'What is the woman talking about?' demanded Caroline. 'What letter? What drawing?'

Neither Mrs Fitzgerald nor Mrs Vernon could throw any light on the matter but they were deeply disturbed.

Another letter followed which was signed by Sir John and Lady Douglas and Sir Sydney Smith. They asked for an audience with the Princess because they felt that in the peculiar circumstances they must have an explanation.

'What are they talking about?' demanded Caroline.

'I don't know, Your Highness,' said Mrs Fitzgerald, 'but I find it very disturbing and I think that you should get advice on how to act.'

Advice? thought Caroline. Yes, she did need it. This matter was too important to be ignored. And what was Sir Sydney Smith doing in it? She had thought he was her friend.

She could go to the King. No. He was too ill and he would be so shocked at the prospect of any scandal; moreover he had been too much worried already by his children; she did not want to add to those anxieties.

The Princes – apart from her husband – had always been friendly towards her; perhaps she could ask one of them.

Her choice fell on Edward, Duke of Kent, who was the most sober of all the Princes; he was good-natured and kind-hearted. She would ask him to come to see her and help her throw some light on this affair.

As soon as he received her invitation he came to Montague House and listened carefully to all she had to tell him. She explained how she had met Lady Douglas and had become friendly with her but how she had heard that Lady Douglas had gossiped most scandalously, after which she had refused to see her. Then had come letters and finally one referring to an anonymous letter and another requesting an interview with the Douglases and Sir Sydney Smith. Caroline had no idea what Lady Douglas was attempting to do and why Sir Sydney Smith should be involved.

The Duke of Kent looked grave.

'The matter must be examined,' he said. 'I don't know these Douglases but I have met Sir Sydney Smith. I will see him and hear what he has to say.'

The Princess thanked him and remarked to Mrs Fitzgerald after he had gone: 'My kind brother-in-law will soon get to the bottom of this affair, and that will be an end of it.'

Sir Sydney Smith called on the Duke of Kent as requested, and with him brought the anonymous letter and the drawing to which Lady Douglas had referred.

'Her Royal Highness, the Princess of Wales, has told me of some trouble in which you and Sir John and Lady Douglas are involved. She does not understand what it is about. Perhaps you could explain.'

'I can indeed,' cried Sir Sydney. 'And begging Your Royal Highness's pardon, I am sure the Princess is in no doubt as to the cause of the trouble. Would you yourself, sir, not want an explanation if *this* had been sent to a lady of your acquaintance when that lady had a husband who was your greatest friend?'

The Duke of Kent stared at the piece of paper which Sir Sydney Smith had laid before him. It was an obscene drawing of Sir Sydney Smith and a woman (Lady Douglas, Sir Sydney explained) in a compromising position.

'This is . . . disgusting!' cried the Duke of Kent.

'So think I, sir, and so thinks Lady Douglas. Why, it is enough to set Sir John and me at each other's throats.'

'And this—'

'Is the work of the Princess of Wales. It came, sir, with this letter which although unsigned I am assured is in Her Highness's handwriting.'

It did not occur to the Duke of Kent to doubt that the letter and drawing were the work of Caroline. Her eccentric behaviour was well known. The point was that however innocent she might be, it was not inconceivable that she might be guilty of the charges brought against her.

'And what do you propose to do?' asked the Duke of Kent.

'This is an attack, as Your Highness will see, on my honour and that of Lady and Sir John Douglas. I do not think Sir John is a man who will lightly allow such an insult to pass.'

'It is a shocking affair. You know the precarious state of the King's health. This would have a disastrous effect on him if it came to his ears. You will appreciate this, Sir Sydney, and I am sure that such a loyal subject as yourself would not wish to increase his difficulties.'

Sir Sydney agreed that he was indeed a loyal subject and if he could persuade Sir John to drop the matter, he himself would be prepared to do so. But of course the Princess of Wales must understand that there must be no more such attacks.

'I can assure you of this,' replied the Duke of Kent.

'Then, sir, leave it to me to persuade Sir John. I am sure I can do it.'

The Duke grasped Sir Sydney's hand. He believed he had settled, with the utmost tact, a matter which might have raised a big scandal in the family.

A few days later Sir Sydney called on him and told him that

Sir John had promised that the matter should go no further.

The Duke of Kent wrote to the Princess to tell her that the unfortunate matter was at an end but she should have no more correspondence with the Douglases. The fact was that he had been disgusted by the drawing and had readily believed that it was the work of the Princess.

He shivered, pitied his brother for being married to such a wife, congratulated himself on having skilfully handled a delicate situation, and put the matter out of his mind.

Lady Douglas was incensed. Her little plot had failed. And it was due to Caroline's having called in her brother-in-law. Who would have thought she would have had the sense!

And now Sydney, out of deference to a royal duke, had made them all agree that the matter was at an end.

Was there to be no revenge then? Was she to be insulted by Caroline?

She would not accept that. But she would have to wait awhile. After all there was the affair of Willikin, which was far more serious than an anonymous letter and a disgusting picture.

The Douglas affair

For some months Lady Douglas waited impatiently, but her desire for revenge grew rather than diminished. She was a vindictive woman; and she had hoped for great benefits through her association with the Princess of Wales. They would never be hers now since the odious woman refused to receive her. But she was going to regret that.

It seemed the greatest fortune when Sir John was given a post in the household of Augustus, Duke of Sussex. The Duke of

Sussex, fourth brother of the Prince of Wales, had had rather startling adventures in matrimony himself when at the age of twenty he had married Augusta Murray without the consent of his father. His marriage had later been declared null and void since it contravened the Royal Marriage Act, but the Duke had snapped his fingers at the law and set up house with the lady he and his brothers acknowledged as his wife.

Lady Douglas saw the opportunity she needed in this appointment and badgered her husband to tell the Duke that Willikin was the Princess's own child.

'But my dear,' protested Sir John, 'this could make the most violent upheaval.'

'That's what I want.'

'You want it? But it would be trouble – terrible trouble.'

'For those that deserve it.'

'I think we should keep out of it. You know what happened about the letter.'

'Oh yes, yes, His Majesty's health is so precarious that he must not be disturbed. In the meantime that scandalous woman can foist her illegitimate offspring on the nation.'

'But she is not foisting William Austin on anybody.'

'William Austin! He's no more Austin than I am. That's her story. And how do you know that she won't try to foist the little brat on the nation? Why, don't you see, that boy could be our future king.'

'Oh no, that's going too far.'

'I will decide what is going too far. It's your duty, John Douglas, to see that what is going on reaches the right quarters.'

'And what do you mean by the right quarters?'

'Surely you know. The Prince of Wales should hear of this.'

'You're not suggesting that I go to the Prince of Wales?'

'What I'm suggesting is that you tell his brother. That's not so difficult, is it? You are after all a member of his household. Tell him, and let him carry on from there.'

'I don't think you understand what a storm you could be raising.'

'That's exactly what I do understand. And I'm waiting for that storm. It's our duty. Are you going to stand by and see a little bastard king of this realm? Are you going to see him snatch it from our dear Princess Charlotte?'

'I don't like it. I don't like it at all.'

'Oh, but you're going to, John Douglas.'

A few days later Sir John came to his wife; he was pale and trembling.

'I have spoken to him,' he said.

'Yes – yes, and what did he say?'

'He said that he thought this matter should be brought to the notice of the Prince of Wales.'

Lady Douglas clasped her hands together in joy.

'But he says we should prepare a document which he can show his brother – setting down all the facts. Put it in writing.'

She nodded and he cried in dismay: 'Don't you realize what this means? It's all very well to *say* these things but to put them into writing! I don't know what this could bring us to.'

'Chicken heart,' she mocked. 'Leave it to me.'

How exciting it was, going back over those meetings, colouring them up, putting constructions on them which would add conviction to her story. For instance had not the Princess said: 'I am going to have a baby.' Had she not shown an inordinate interest in Lady Douglas's own pregnancy? It was easy to adjust a word here and there. It was dangerous when a Princess of Wales lived an immoral life because of the succession. Lady Douglas wrote that she had reminded the Princess of this and that Her Highness had replied that if she were caught she could put it on to the Prince of Wales because she had slept a few nights at Carlton House and he was often so drunk that he could not account for his actions. Then there was the story of Lady Douglas's calling at Montague House and seeing the baby for the first time. There was Mrs Fitzgerald's hasty explanation that he was William Austin and that the Princess had adopted him.

Oh yes, she had a very plausible story to tell.

*

The King was surprised to receive a call from his sons, the Prince of Wales and the Duke of Sussex; and as soon as he saw them he knew that something extraordinary had happened.

Not family trouble again, he hoped. There was no end to it. Both of them were offenders. Sussex marrying that woman when he had no right to and having a court case about it and then its being decided that he wasn't married. Not that he cared. They had no morals, these sons of his. There he was living like a respectable married man with the woman he called his wife and he had a family too. As for the Prince of Wales with his Mrs Fitzherbert and all that scandal – well, it was better not to think about that!

'An unexpected pleasure, eh, what?' he said grimly.

The Prince of Wales felt a momentary wave of pity for his father. How he had aged in the last few years! Those white eyebrows jutting out from the far too red face and the protuberant blue eyes gave him a look of madness. Surely it couldn't be long before he broke down again. And this matter was not going to help him. But it had to be done and while the King clung to his rank he would have to accept its responsibilities. Better, thought the Prince, for him to retire gracefully, to abdicate perhaps. And then *he* would take charge. He admitted to himself that the prospect of power pleased him.

Should he have kept quiet about this matter? Certainly he could not! It was of the utmost importance to the Crown, and at the back of his mind was a solution which pleased him as much as the thought of wearing that crown: to rid himself of Caroline.

'A very serious matter has come to light,' he said, 'and Augustus and I thought you should immediately be acquainted with it.'

Alarm shot up in the King's eyes which seemed to become a shade more prominent.

'Your Majesty,' went on the Prince, with the utmost solemnity, 'I have here a grave charge against the morality of the Princess of Wales.'

'Eh? What's this? Eh, what? Caroline you mean? What's this? Grave charge, eh?'

'I think that Your Majesty might read this accusation which has been written by Sir John and Lady Douglas. It seems that the Princess of Wales is the mother of an illegitimate child – a son – a boy who now lives with her at Montague House.'

'What? Eh? What's this? Don't believe it. Impossible. A boy, eh? What's this, eh, eh, eh?'

'If Your Majesty would read this charge.'

The King took the Douglases' statement and stared at it. His eyes boggled as he read.

He stuttered: 'But this is impossible—'

'Unfortunately, Sir, it appears to be true.' The Prince then went on to explain that his brother, the Duke of Kent, had been shown a disgusting drawing which Caroline had done of a neighbour Lady Douglas and Sir Sydney Smith. His Majesty would remember the well-known sailor who had served his country with such zeal. Sir Sydney had wanted to take action but had been dissuaded from doing so to prevent a scandal.

'Disgusting drawing! What? A *drawing* you say. What drawing?'

'Of Sir Sydney and Lady Douglas.' The Prince put his handkerchief to his eyes. 'Too disgusting, sir, to be talked of, but Your Majesty may well imagine . . .'

He could imagine. Sometimes when he was in one of his lost moods pictures came into his head. Pictures, he thought. Disgusting pictures. They'd have to put a stop to it.

'This matter,' said the Prince of Wales, 'is too grave to be dismissed. If it is true that the Princess of Wales has an illegitimate son, some action must be taken – and taken promptly.'

'There must be an inquiry,' said the King.

Spencer Perceval rode over to Montague House.

'I have heard some very grave news,' he said. 'There is to be an inquiry into your actions with regard to the boy William Austin.'

'But why should that be grave?' inquired the Princess. 'There is nothing wrong with Willikin.'

'The implication is that he is your own son.'

'I regard him as such.'

Perceval was faintly exasperated. 'Your Highness must realize the gravity of this charge. It is being said that he is the result of an indiscretion on your part and that you gave birth to him.'

'That's a lie, of course.'

'I know it, Your Highness, but we have to convince others of it.'

'We?'

'I suggest that Your Highness engages me to work on your behalf.'

She smiled at him tenderly. 'Oh, you dear good man.'

He said gruffly: 'I am a friend and a neighbour. Naturally I wish to do all in my power to refute this wicked slander. I rejoice in my position for as such I can do good service to Your Highness.'

She would have embraced him but he held her off. The most indiscreet woman in the world! he thought. And even now she does not realize that it is her indiscretions which have led her into this dangerous position.

'I must ask Your Highness to tell me the truth of this matter. Hold nothing back. Tell me, how did the child come to be in this house?'

Caroline told him of her discovery of the Austins, how he himself had found work for the child's father, how before he was born his mother had promised him to her and how he had come to her a few weeks after he was born.

Perceval nodded, well satisfied.

'We have a good case,' he said. 'We need one. But I don't think we are going to have any difficulty in proving these charges false. You have been very indiscreet, Your Highness; and I do beg of you to curb your tongue. A word in the wrong place can ruin you. I beg of you remember that.'

'I have always been told that I talk too much and without thinking.'

'I trust Your Highness will remember the truth of that.'

'I shall do my best. And I think it's – noble of you to help me. You know, don't you, that the Prince will not be very pleased with you because I believe my beloved husband is *hoping* to

prove me guilty. He can have as many love affairs as he pleases
– and he'd grudge me just one.'

Perceval sighed. What was the use of begging for discretion?

'We must do what we can,' he said sternly, 'and remember the
gravity of the situation.'

The Queen was delighted; the Princesses giggled together. It
certainly added a spice to life when such dramatic events took
place in the family. And all centred round the Prince of Wales
as was usually the case.

'So,' said Sophia, 'there is to be an investigation.'

'A *delicate* investigation,' Mary reminded her.

They laughed. 'Oh, very delicate. Really Caroline is a fool.
What do you think will happen?'

'Well, if it goes the way George wants it, she'll be divorced
and sent back to Brunswick. And then he'll take another wife
and if he has a son that will put dear little Charlotte's nose out
of joint.'

'Which I daresay will do her no harm. That child gives herself
airs.'

'What do you expect with such a mother?'

'And such a father!'

'How exciting they make life. George has had a morganatic
marriage which you would have thought was enough for
anyone. But not for George. Now he has to have a Delicate
Investigation!'

The 'Delicate Investigation' had begun. The King himself had
appointed a council to inquire into the truth of the Douglases'
allegations and this was made up of Lord Grenville, the Prime
Minister, Lord Erskine, the Lord Chancellor, Lord El-
lenborough, the Lord Chief Justice, and Lord Spencer, the
Secretary of State; and presided over by Sir Samuel Romilly,
one of the leading lights of the Bar recently, at the instigation of
the Prince of Wales, appointed Solicitor General.

There was no representation for the Princess of Wales although Perceval was at hand to help her and advise. She had in
fact not been officially warned that the investigation was to take

place although an attorney, a Mr Lowten, had been appointed to watch the case for the Prince of Wales, which meant that he was to do all he could to prove Caroline's guilt.

She had just put Willikin to bed – a task which she undertook herself with the utmost pleasure – when Mrs Fitzgerald came to tell her that a messenger had arrived with a letter for her.

She said that he was to be brought to her and when he came she read the letter and went to her desk to write an answer.

When the messenger had left with it she said to Mrs Fitzgerald: 'They are telling me that they will want the servants to appear for questioning and I have answered that they may question all they like.'

'For questioning?' cried Mrs Fitzgerald, aghast.

'Why? What's worrying you? Why shouldn't they question them if they want to?'

'If they tell the truth all should be well,' said Mrs Fitzgerald, but she was thinking of the many indiscretions – the light, frivolous flirtatious manner and conversation of the Princess. She was thinking of young Willikin upstairs in his bed.

Couldn't she see how easy it was going to be to make a case against her?

But it was not so easy. It was true that some of the servants gave the answers which they knew the Prince of Wales would want. Several of these servants were no longer with the Princess of Wales; some had been dismissed and had a grievance; others had been sent to serve her for the sole purpose of spying.

Oh yes, said these. They had seen the Princess behave very familiarly with men who came to the house. They had seen her kiss Sir Sydney Smith, embrace Captain Manley and speak very affectionately to Mr Canning; she had told them not to disturb her when she was alone with Sir Thomas Lawrence. Oh, yes, they all thought this was very strange behaviour for a Princess of Wales.

But there were other servants – good and loyal. The Princess was by nature friendly. She was warm and affectionate to everyone – even the humblest of her servants. She called them 'my dear', 'my love', 'my angel' even. It was a habit of hers.

Had she been very familiar with men who called at the house?

No more than with women. She was impulsively friendly with all.

But right at the heart of the matter was Willikin. Who was this boy? Was it possible that he was the Princess's son? This was the charge against her and if it could be proved that she was the mother of that boy then it would be possible for the Prince to divorce her, for not only would she have been proved flagrantly unfaithful, but guilty of treason to the state, for that boy could claim the throne; and this was where the matter was so serious.

The Princess had declared – and some of her servants corroborated this – that William Austin was the son of Samuel and Sophia Austin; they were near neighbours of hers and the man worked in the dockyards.

There was only one thing to be done: Call the woman whom the Princess alleged was the mother of the boy.

Sophia came – clean, respectable, a witness whom they had to admit they could trust.

Yes, she had had conversations with the Princess of Wales.

'And was she the mother of the boy who lived with the Princess of Wales?'

'If you be talking of young Willie,' was the direct answer, 'I am his mother.'

'And your son now lives at Montague House with the Princess of Wales?'

' 'Tis true that I sometimes have to pinch myself to believe it. But she's an angel, that Princess. And my, don't she love the little ones! When I was carrying Willie she came to me and I complained of having another mouth to feed. "Give him to me," she said. "I'll adopt him." There! It was as easy as that.'

'Do you swear that you are the mother of William Austin?'

'I swear it, and if you don't believe me you go along to Brownlow Street Hospital, for that was where Willie was born.'

There was no refuting evidence of that sort.

The council had reluctantly to admit that there was no truth in the allegation that the Princess of Wales had borne an illegitimate son.

They did not forget, however, that they must please the Prince. They added that, although there was no evidence to support the theory that the child, William Austin, was the Princess's and although it seemed certain that he was not, this did not mean that the Princess was not guilty of behaving in a most unbecoming manner; and in the council's opinion the morals of the Princess of Wales left much to be desired.

So her enemies were defeated. They had been proved – even by the Prince's friends – to be lying.

She had forgotten that she was only exonerated from the charge of producing an illegitimate child; it was by no means proved that the life she led was not one of immorality.

She was made aware of this when she wrote to the King with her usual exuberance and received a very restrained letter in reply in which His Majesty stated that he could not help but be gravely concerned by her conduct.

'By my conduct,' she cried to the faithful Mrs Fitzgerald. 'But I have been proved to have been slandered! Oh, my dear, dear Fitz! Was ever such a poor devil in the plight I'm in? I'm a princess and no princess. I'm a married woman with no husband – for the Prince of Wales is worse than none. This is not the end, Fitz. They've determined to make my life a hell . . . all of them. Can't you imagine the old Begum tittering away surrounded by her virgin daughters! Let them! What do I care! But I do care about the old man, Fitz. I think I loved him in a way. He tried to be so good always. And now look at this. He's gravely concerned . . . by my immorality and he isn't going to see me. I'm going to be shut away here and forgotten. But I'll tell you something, my dear, I won't have it. I won't. I won't.'

Mrs Fitzgerald looked alarmed, but Caroline burst out laughing.

'Don't be frightened, my dear, I'm not going mad. Though I declare there's enough to make me. That's for my poor old father-in-law. God bless him. But I'm not having him turned against me! I'm going to see him. And I'll keep on at him until I do. I shall write to him again and again —'

'Your Highness, why not ask the advice of Spencer Perceval? He will know what's to be done.'

The Princess was thoughtful for a moment. Then she cried: 'You're right. That dear man will know – and at least he is my friend.'

The King was decidedly worried. On all sides he heard stories of Caroline's misconduct. The Queen believed in it and constantly referred to it. Oh, they had not *proved* that she had had this child but it was quite *obvious* that she led a very wild life. All those men calling on her at odd times of the day and night! Most peculiar! And what a way for a Princess of Wales to live! What a sad day for the Prince of Wales, for the family and for England when George had taken the King's niece from Brunswick instead of the Queen's from Mecklenburg-Strelitz!

A sad day, a sad day indeed, thought the King. But she was a pleasant woman, quite handsome in her way too. Why could not the Prince of Wales give up his wild life and settle down as an heir to the throne should do?

He was sorry for Caroline, but how could he see her in the circumstances? It would be as though he gave his approval to immorality.

And he had felt life was going to be better. Nelson's victory at Trafalgar had put new heart into the nation and in him. Yet even that victory had its sadness, for Nelson had fallen and the country had lost its saviour in the moment of victory. He thought of the great hall of Greenwich Hospital into which the public had crowded to see the coffin of the naval hero, and of the funeral that followed and at which he had been represented by the Prince of Wales and his brothers. A sad occasion to follow victory. But Lord Nelson would have rejoiced because he had crippled the might of Napoleon and made England safe.

But there was constant trouble. No sooner was the threat of invasion removed than the family was at war within itself. The Prince of Wales hated his wife and this was an even sadder pattern than that set by the family when father and son were fighting together. At least he had been faithful to his Queen; George II had been notoriously uxorious in spite of infidelity. George I – ah, there had been a sad case of husband and wife who had been enemies . . .

But what was the use of thinking of the past? He dared not think too much. His head went into a painful whirl when he did so. He tried to catch at his thoughts and found them eluding him. He grew alarmed when that happened.

I must not think of it, he told himself. And I must not receive her.

On her request Spencer Perceval called to see Caroline and listened to her account of the King's refusal to receive her.

'This must not be allowed to continue,' he told her, 'or it will be said that you were guilty. His Majesty is treating you as though you are. This must be stopped at all cost or the verdict of the people will be against you. This is unthinkable, for try as they did the council could prove no case against you. The King must receive you. You should write again and request him to do so.'

This she did and it brought a reply from the King. He would see her; but before the meeting could be arranged she received a letter from Windsor in which the King said that he must postpone receiving her because he had heard from the Prince of Wales that he intended consulting his lawyer with regard to the council's findings. Until he heard the result of this His Majesty must put off the meeting.

When Caroline received this letter she was furious. She wrote indignantly to the King. It was with great pain that she had read his letter, she said. It was seven months since she had seen the King and now that nothing had been proved against her there was no longer any reason why he should refuse to see her. She signed herself 'His dutiful and affectionate but much injured subject and daughter-in-law.'

She declared that she *would* be received at Court. She was not going to be thrust aside in this way. How dare the Prince of Wales, whose own life was so scandalous, treat her in this way?

Perceval came to see her. He heard of the latest developments and said they must delay no longer. It was necessary to deliver an ultimatum. The only thing she could do was threaten to publish the findings of the council which would enable the public to know how she had been slandered and proved innocent. They were already on her side because of their dislike of the Prince of Wales and would be ready to believe her; and neither the Prince of Wales nor the King dared stand out against public opinion.

He dictated a letter which she was to send to the King.

As to any consequences which may arise from such publication, unpleasant or hurtful to my own feelings and interests, I may perhaps be properly responsible ... but whatever these consequences may be, I am fully convinced that they must be incalculably less than those to which I am exposed by my silence ...

As there was no reply to this letter Perceval arranged for five thousand copies to be printed of what was known as 'The Book'; this contained a full report of the proceedings against the Princess of Wales at the Delicate Investigation.

Then, due to a dispute concerning Catholic reform, the Government fell, and the Whig friends of the Prince of Wales were replaced by the Tories. Lord Portland was Prime Minister and Spencer Perceval was given the post of Chancellor of the Exchequer. The leading ministers were now the enemies of the Prince of Wales which meant that they would give support to Caroline. Perceval lost no time in doing all he could to reinstate her. Very soon after the new Ministry had been formed he prevailed upon Portland and other ministers, including George Canning, to put their names to an ultimatum which was addressed to the King.

Your Majesty's confidential servants humbly submit to Your Majesty that it is essentially necessary, in justice to Her Royal Highness and for the honour and interests of Your Majesty's illustrious family, that Her Royal Highness the Princess of Wales should be admitted with as little delay as possible into Your Majesty's royal presence, and that she should be received in a manner due to her rank and station in Your Majesty's Court and family.

Another letter followed this in which it was suggested that a suitable residence be found for the Princess of Wales which would be nearer to the royal palaces and enable her to be within easy access of the Court.

This was something the King could not ignore. He knew if he did so *The Book* would immediately be published and the people would rise up against the Prince of Wales – and perhaps the King – for treating the Princess so cruelly.

'She must be invited to Court without delay,' he told the Queen, who was wise enough to recognize an ultimatum when she saw one.

'It is something we shall be forced to endure,' she agreed.

'And where can she be lodged?'

'As far from Carlton House as possible, I suggest. Perhaps Kensington Palace.'

So Kensington Palace it was; but although Caroline took apartments there she kept on Montague House and declared to Mrs Fitzgerald that she was only going to Court to let people know that she was innocent of the charges brought against her, for to stay away might give an appearance of guilt. What she enjoyed most would be her stays in Montague House, when she could devote herself to Willikin and entertain her friends there in her own way without the ceremony which could not be avoided in palaces.

The King greeted her with affection and tears in his eyes. 'My dear, how glad I am to see you. It has been a bad time – eh, what, a bad time?'

'A very bad time, dear Uncle. But I hope it is over now and your feelings towards me have not changed.'

With tears in his eyes he assured her this was not so.

The Queen regarded her coldly and gave her only the barest acknowledgement while her eyes rested on the extravagant dress of too many colours, cut far too low. Caroline wanted to laugh at her; but she reminded herself that she must be on her best behaviour.

The Princesses of course followed their mother and treated her with almost cool insolence.

And then the Prince of Wales. She looked at him almost

hopefully. He was splendid, not so glittering as in the past, being under the influence of Beau Brummell who had taught him his own special brand of unobtrusive elegance.

She dropped a curtsey.

His bow was notorious. There was no one who could perform the act with such grace. There was a breathless moment when he enacted this feat for now it was especially interesting.

It was over very quickly – that most elegant bow – and then she was looking at the Prince's back. He had turned and was speaking to one of his sisters.

So ... she was to be received back at Court though ignored by the Prince of Wales, and the Delicate Investigation was over – but not forgotten.

Royal scandals

Just before Caroline had gone to Court she had had sad news from Brunswick. Her father, the Duke, had been killed while leading the Prussian army against Napoleon.

This event had momentarily made her forget her own dismal affairs. She was very melancholy. She thought of her father and all he had meant to her in the past. He had been perhaps the only person she had really loved during her Brunswick childhood. It was true that it was long since she had said goodbye to him but she had never forgotten him.

Incidents from the old days kept coming back to her: the occasion when she had pretended she was in labour; Charlotte's wedding; the day he had told her that she need never marry if she did not wish. If only she had taken his advice. But would she have enjoyed life any more in Brunswick, at the mercy of her rather silly mother and sensible Madame de Hertzfeldt? And then she would never have had Charlotte.

'Charlotte, my darling, my angel, whom I am only allowed to see once a week!' she cried.

And she decided then that it would have been one degree worse to have stayed in Brunswick than to have come to England in spite of being married to a husband who was no husband and determined to harm her.

Mrs Fitzgerald came in to tell her that Willikin was crying for his mamma and demanding to know why she wasn't there to amuse him.

'Bring him in. Bring him in,' she cried.

And there was the naughty little boy to be petted and kissed and cuddled and told that his mamma loved him and that he was her pet boy, her little Willikin.

Mrs Fitzgerald told Mrs Vernon that the change in the Princess's moods was something alarming. Rarely has she known one whose moods changed so rapidly. She would be in the depth of despair one moment and the next shouting with joy.

'That's Willikin's doing,' said Mrs Vernon.

'She's making him into a horrible spoilt brat,' added Mrs Fitzgerald.

The Prince was uneasy. He had enjoyed several years of connubial bliss with his dear love Maria, and was looking for adventure.

Women! He adored them. But he had to be in pursuit of them; and he liked the pursuit to be difficult and not to be brought to too easy a conclusion. Maria was his life, his soul, his wife; and there would always be a place for her in his heart, but he was not meant to live a placid married life which was what Maria wanted. She and dear old Pigot would have liked there to have been cosy little domestic evenings spent at home in Carlton House. But Carlton House was not built for cosy evenings; nor was the Prince of Wales.

While the Delicate Investigation had been in progress Maria had been concerned in a court case of her own. A few years previously she had taken a little girl to live with her while her parents, Lord Hugh and Lady Horatia Seymour, had gone to Madeira because Lady Horatia was suffering from galloping consumption.

Maria, one of whose greatest griefs was that she had no children of her own, doted on the little girl and wished to adopt her legally; but, on the death of the child's parents, her aunt, Lady Waldegrave, also wanted to adopt her. Maria, who had cared for the child for a few years, was determined to keep her.

The Prince of Wales had been fond of little Mary Seymour, 'Minney' as she called herself; and seemed much more interested in her than in his own daughter Charlotte. She would clamber all over him and christened him 'Prinney' to rhyme with Minney which amused him greatly; and he felt when the three of them were together they were indeed a happy family.

He had been very sorry when Lady Waldegrave claimed her; and declared that they must have a legal ruling on the matter, and was so upset to see his dear Maria heartbroken at the prospect of losing Minney that he offered to settle £10,000 on the child if she were left in Maria's care.

This case had been going on for some months, and during it the Prince became very friendly with the Hertfords because the Marquess of Hertford as head of the Seymour family agreed that he would put an end to the proceedings by declaring that he would adopt the child himself. Since he was the head of the family no one could dispute this; the case was settled and then the Marquess appointed Maria Minney's guardian.

This was very satisfactory, but during the proceedings the Prince had become infatuated by the Marchioness of Hertford.

It was not that he no longer loved Maria, he was careful to assure himself. He did love her; but Lady Hertford seemed sylphlike in comparison. He could not take his eyes from her when they were in company together; and people were beginning to notice. Miss Pigot tried to comfort Maria. The household had changed since the Prince had come back. They were, according to Miss Pigot, living happily ever after. And now they had the adorable Minney.

Maria had not noticed at first the way things were going, so immersed had she been in the battle for Minney. Now she was elated because Minney was hers.

But one day she said to Miss Pigot: 'The Prince is giving a dinner party for the Marchioness of Hertford. It's not the first time.'

'Well, I expect he's grateful to them for giving you darling Minney.'

'I don't think it's that,' said Maria slowly. 'And he wants me there – to make it seem . . . respectable. Isn't that just like him?'

'Nonsense!' said Miss Pigot. 'Of course he wants you there. Doesn't he always want you there?'

But Miss Pogot was beginning to be worried. It would be tragic if anything went wrong now that they had gained little Minney.

Caroline was settling into her new life. She gave wild parties at Montague House, to which were invited all kinds of people from politicians to poets. Lord Byron was a constant visitor and a great favourite with the Princess.

'A strange moody man,' she confided in Lady Charlotte Campbell who had come to serve her. 'Yet he can be the gayest I ever met. And so amusing. Such fun. He is two men. He is one for the people he loathes and another for those he loves – and I think I am one of those he loves. He is so good at my parties. I sometimes declare he shall come to all of them.'

Lady Charlotte listened attentively. She had been a great beauty when she was young and she had married Colonel John Campbell by whom she had had nine children. The Princess of Wales had taken to her at once, for anyone who had had nine children excited her admiration and envy. When Lady Charlotte's husband died Caroline had asked her to join her household and they had become great friends. What the Princess did not know was that Lady Charlotte kept a diary and recorded every little incident. Lady Charlotte fancied herself as a writer and had decided that when she had time she would devote herself to the art.

In the meantime she could enjoy her diary which would remind her of the Princess if ever she should cease to serve her.

Caroline had found her the perfect confidante because she listened so intently to everything that was told her and remembered too. More and more she began to confide in her while Lady Charlotte diligently wrote of the Princess's *penchant* for people whose conduct was somewhat scandalous, like Lord

Byron. She was so unconventional. When she was at Kensington she would walk in the gardens and talk to *strangers* as though she were an ordinary member of the public. Nor was she content to stay in the gardens but would wander out into the streets and enjoy what she called the 'dear people', forgetting that at any moment she might be recognized. She liked to wander about incognito; and if she saw a poor child she must immediately stop and give it money. Once she looked over a house in Bayswater which was to let and pretended that she was considering renting it. She did the maddest things.

She had taken a great interest in a family of Italian musicians, the Sapios – father, mother and son – all excellent in their profession; but Caroline became so enraptured by their talents and their company that she treated them as friends and had them to dine and walk with her and call upon her at any hour of the day.

And in addition to this eccentric behaviour there was Willikin, growing into a most objectionable boy. He was hideously spoilt, refused to learn his lessons and wanted the Princess's perpetual attention.

He was generally disliked in the household; the only one who could see no wrong in him was the Princess Caroline.

There were letters from Brunswick. The Duchess, now that she had no husband, was thinking of returning to her native land. Moreover, Napoleon had overrun practically the whole of Europe and exile was necessary. The Duchess felt that she should be in England, for there she could be near her daughter and see something of her little grand-daughter the Princess Charlotte.

Caroline was not very pleased at the thought of having her mother living in England but she saw that she must receive her graciously. Her brother also was in exile since he had been driven from his country by the invader, so he too must come to England.

It was a dreary prospect, but there was nothing to be done but bow to it. The royal family made no effort to welcome their relations so Caroline put Montague House at her mother's disposal while she herself remained in Kensington Palace. This was a hardship because the unconventional life she could lead in Blackheath was more to her taste than that in Kensington.

The King, though, was a family man, and he was sorry for his sister, who chattered incessantly and talked of the changes in England since she had left and all that she had suffered in Brunswick. And eventually he took pity on Caroline and gave the Duchess a house in Spring Gardens. It was by no means grand but the Duchess contrived to make it so; and she would sit in the dingy rooms as though in a palace and receive, for now she had returned to England she was very conscious of her royalty and wished everyone else to be so too.

Caroline ran through Montague House declaring how good it was to be back.

'Poor Mamma!' she said to that diligent recorder Lady Charlotte. 'I believe she is so happy to be here. It reminds her of the old days when she was Princess Royal. And her little Court there in Spring Gardens – it is sad, don't you think, Lady Charlotte? Court! I call it a Dullification. I have rarely been so bored as at dear Mamma's Spring Garden Court. Ah, you are thinking how sad it is that she has been driven from her home. But perhaps it is not so sad as you think. She always had to take second place, you know, when my father was alive. Madame de Hertzfeldt, his mistress, was the power in the land. Dear Lady Charlotte, you always tempt me to shock you because you are so easily shocked. Never mind. I like you. You are my dear friend, my angel. And we shall entertain now. I confess I am eager to fill this place with people who make me laugh.'

So she planned parties with amusing people and ran shrieking among her guests playing blind man's buff, a game which had always been a favourite of hers.

One day the King called. As soon as she saw him Caroline thought he looked strange. He kept telling her how pleased he was to see her, that she was a beautiful woman and constantly in his thoughts.

It was pleasant to be back on the old terms of affection which had been interrupted by the Delicate Investigation; and she told him how happy she was.

'Ah,' he said almost roguishly. 'I believe you love your old uncle.'

'But indeed I do. No one has been kinder to me. Why I do not know what I should have done without your friendship, for I have had little from the rest of the family.'

'Let us sit down,' he said and drew her onto a sofa.

She was alarmed, for his manner had become stranger and he called her Elizabeth. Then he talked incoherently of his love for her and what he would do for her and how she was in fact his queen.

Caroline realized that his mind was wandering and when he fell on her she rolled off the sofa and ran out of the room.

She stood at the door listening and peeping in she saw him sitting on the sofa, his head in his hands.

Poor Uncle George! she thought. He mistook me for someone else. He is truly going mad.

She went back into the room and when he looked up she realized that he had no remembrance of what had happened.

'It is good of Your Majesty to call on me,' she said.

He stood up and as he approached, she curtsied.

He said: 'I should like to see a reconciliation. It's not good, eh, what? The Prince of Wales and his wife living apart – not together. It's wrong. You understand that, eh, what?'

She said she did understand but it was the wish of the Prince of Wales and nothing could alter that.

When he had left she was depressed thinking of him.

He is close to the brink now, she thought. And if I lost him I wouldn't have a friend at Court.

There was always scandal circulating round the royal family and the King lived in perpetual fear of some fresh exposure. He could not understand why his sons should have this habit for creating trouble. It made him all the more determined to see that his daughters had no chance of doing so. He was glad there were no marriages for them. Only the Princess Royal had achieved it and she appeared to be living quietly with her husband. No husbands for the others, he had told himself grimly. They shall be kept here – under my eye and that of their mother.

The Prince of Wales was creating fresh scandal with Lady Hertford – another of his famous grandmothers. Not content with refusing to live with the Princess of Wales he had returned to Mrs Fitzgerald – a good woman and a beautiful one who should have been enough for anyone. But no, now it was Lady Hertford and God alone knew what fresh trouble was in store there.

And he was so anxious about Amelia, his youngest, his favourite, his darling. He used to tell himself that no matter what trouble the others caused him there always Amelia. But even she caused him anxiety for she grew more wan every day. She had developed a lameness in her knee which he knew gave her great pain.

He would weep when he saw her and embrace her, covering her face with kisses.

'Your Papa feels the pain with you, my darling. You understand that, eh, what?'

And she would nod and tell him: 'But it is not such bad pain, Papa,' just for the sake of comforting him. His angel, his darling! How different from his sons. The sea bathing at Worthing had done her good but only for a time. And he had to face the fact that as the months passed she grew no better.

She was his little invalid. He asked after her continually. 'She is better today, Your Majesty,' they would tell him: and he believed that they told him so on the Queen's orders, for the Queen was determined that the King must not be upset.

His eyes were failing and he would put his face close to hers trying to tell himself that she looked a little better than when he last saw her; and whenever he asked her, she would always say, 'Much better, Papa. Much *much* better.' And perhaps add: 'I took a little walk in the gardens today.'

So even the best of his children gave him cause to worry.

In spite of his expectations, trouble came from an unsuspected quarter.

The Prime Minister, Lord Portland, came to see him on a grave matter.

'It concerns the Duke of York, Your Majesty, and a certain Mary Anne Clarke.'

'Mary Anne Clarke!' He had never heard of the woman. And Frederick couldn't have made one of those marriages his sons were fond of making because he was married already. 'Who is this woman?'

'A woman, Your Majesty, of dubious character.'

'H'm. And what is the trouble, eh, what?'

'A question has been raised in the House of Commons, sir, by a Colonel Wardle. He brings a charge against the Duke for wrong use of military patronage which as Commander in Chief of the Army he has been in a position to carry out.'

'And what has this . . . woman to do with it?'

'She is the Duke's mistress, Your Majesty, and has been selling promotion which she has persuaded the Duke to give.'

'Oh, God,' cried the King. 'What next?'

The Prime Minister said that he feared a great scandal as the House was insisting on an inquiry which would of course expose the Duke's intrigue with this not very reputable young woman and would – if the charges were proved – result in his being expelled from the Army.

'And so – there is to be this – inquiry.'

'I fear so, sir.'

So this is the next disaster, thought the King. Can so much happen in one family? Am I dreaming it? Am I going mad?

The great topic for the time was the scandal of the Duke of York and Mary Anne Clarke.

Mary Anne was an extremely handsome woman in her early thirties who had begun her life in Ball and Pin Alley near Chancery Lane. Her mother was widowed when Mary Anne was a child and later married a compositor, the son of whose master was attracted by the pretty child and had her educated. Mary Anne in due course married a stonemason named Clarke and later went on the stage where she played Portia at the Haymarket Theatre. Here she was noticed and became the mistress of several members of the peerage. At the house of one of these she made the acquaintance of the Duke of York who was immediately infatuated, and set her up in a mansion in Gloucester Place.

The doting Duke had promised her a large income but was constantly in debt and not always able to pay it; Mary Anne's expenses were enormous and so to provide the large sums she needed she had the idea of selling promotion in the Army.

This was the sordid story which became the gossip of London. The Duke was in despair, but when Mary Anne was called upon to give evidence at the bar of the House of Commons she did so with jaunty abandon.

The Duke's letters to her were read aloud in the House and these caused great merriment. All over London they were quoted – and embellished. This was the *cause célèbre* of the day.

The King shut himself into his apartments and the Queen could hear him talking to himself, talking, talking, until he was hoarse. He was praying too. And it was clear that he did not know for whom he prayed.

Amelia was sent to comfort him; and this she did by telling him how well she felt – never so well in her life.

And that did ease him considerably.

It emerged from the Select Committee which tried the case, that the Duke was not guilty of nefarious practices however much his mistress might have been; but all the same he had to resign his post in the Army.

He broke with Mary Anne, but he had not finished with her because she threatened to publish the letters he had written to her. These were bought for £7,000 down and a pension of £400 a year.

But people went on talking of Mary Anne Clarke; and it was noticed that the King's health was even worse than it had been before.

The Mary Anne Clarke scandal had scarcely died down when another and far more dramatic one burst on London.

This concerned Ernest, Duke of Cumberland – the King's fifth son.

Ernest was the last son the King would have expected to

bring trouble. He had been sent to Germany to learn his soldiering where he had acquitted himself with honour; and when he had come back to England in 1796 he was made a lieutenant-general. Not only was he an excellent military leader but he had shown some skill in the House of Lords; he was an able debater and was regarded with respect by the Prince of Wales. The most likeable quality of the brothers was their loyalty to each other; and Ernest was determined that when George became King he would be beside him.

It was the night of 10 May. Duke Ernest had been to a concert and according to himself retired to bed in his apartments in St James's Palace. Soon after midnight his screams woke his servants who rushing in found him in his bed with a wound at the side of his head. One of the servants had fallen over the Duke's sword which lay on the floor and was spattered with fresh blood.

The Palace was soon aroused; doctors were sent for; and it was noticed that the Prince's valet, an Italian named Sellis, was missing. One of the servants went to call him and ran screaming from the room. Sellis was lying on the floor, a razor beside him, his throat cut.

What happened in the Duke of Cumberland's apartments on that fateful night in May no one could be quite sure but there was rumour enough. The Duke's story was that a noise in his room had awakened him and before he had had time to light a candle he had received a blow on the side of his head. He had started up, and as his eyes were becoming accustomed to the darkness he received another more violent blow; he had felt the blood streaming down his face as he fell back on his pillows screaming for help.

That was all he could tell them.

The public was excited. This was far more dramatic than the recent Mary Anne Clarke scandal. A royal duke attacked in his bed; his valet murdered. There would be an inquest. What would come out of that? Speculation ran wild. The valet had a very beautiful wife. Everyone knew the weakness of the royal princes where women were concerned. Why should a valet attack a duke? Why should the valet be murdered?

The King was becoming quite incoherent.

'This terrible scandal,' he said. 'What does it mean, eh, what does it mean, eh, what? This is worse than anything the Prince of Wales ever did. Ernest – what does it mean ... what can it mean?'

There was one fact which kept hammering on his mind. The valet had a beautiful wife. He kept seeing pictures of Ernest and a woman – a dark woman. Italian? Oh, God, help me, groaned the King. This family of mine will drive me mad.

The inquest was conducted with decorum and respect for the royal family. It was not easy to sort out the evidence. It seemed incomprehensible. Why should the valet attempt to murder the Duke and then commit suicide?

The public had the answer. It was discussed in all the coffee and chocolate houses. It was simple wasn't it? Sellis had found his wife in bed with the Duke, had attacked him, and the Duke retaliated by murdering the valet and making it appear as suicide.

It seemed the only logical answer. And knowing these princes, a very reasonable one.

At the inquest the verdict of suicide was brought in. Sellis, it was said, had gone mad, had attacked his master and realizing what he had done had committed suicide. That the Duke had been attacked was indisputable. The blow on his head had cut deep and could have killed him. Why the Duke's sword should have been stained with fresh blood was never answered. But the people had their verdict and they were not going to be diverted from it by a mere jury.

'What would happen to us, eh,' they asked each other, 'if we committed murder?'

'Hanged by the neck. That's what. But then we're not royal dukes.'

The King muttered to himself as he paced up and down his apartments. 'What next, eh? What next?'

The Prince of Wales discussed the state of affairs with Lady Hertford. He was most humble with the lady, as he needed to be for she made it quite clear that she would not be an easy victim. That was why he was so desperate. She was not beautiful, but her elegance was supreme. She was the best dressed woman in London and cared passionately for the cut of a gown and that the jewellery she wore should be in absolute keeping with her ensemble.

'Perfection!' the Prince would sigh looking at her. But she was frigid and made it clear that she had her reputation to consider. She had no need of the gifts he could bestow for she was the wife of one of the richest peers in the country. He might win her by accepting her advice but he was supposed to be a Whig and she was the most ardent of Tories.

This made the pursuit of her full of difficulties and the more exciting because of it.

But she was most gracious when he talked politics and if he were to ask her advice she became almost affectionate, so different from Maria. There could not have been a woman less like Maria. Was that why he was attracted? He knew he wanted them both. But he had Maria. Maria was his affectionate and devoted wife; there was no need to pursue Maria. But he was madly in love with his elusive frigid fashion plate.

Now she listened with interest to the state of the King's health.

'It grows worse, I hear,' she said. Her eyes glinted. 'It could mean that he cannot live much longer.'

A king! she thought. Power! The Tory party triumphant! That was a consideration. But while King George III was alive it was a mere dream and Lady Hertford was not a dreamer; she liked cold reality.

She would not talk of the King's death. That was unwise; and she was a shrewd woman.

'It could mean a Regency,' she temporized.

'If I became Regent,' he said, 'there is nothing I would not do that you asked. You would be at my right hand. How fortunate to have the most beautiful woman in England for my chief minister.'

And the Fitzherbert? wondered Lady Hertford. A Catholic. Inwardly she shuddered. She did not believe in the emancipation of Catholics, which of course the Prince did – at the moment. It was not only the Fitzherbert influence but he was a man of tolerance – weakness, she called it.

But if he ever came to power – through the Crown or the Regency – she would certainly feel more friendly towards him.

The Prince realized how interested Lady Hertford was in the possibility of a Regency; and he wanted her to understand that this possibility was by no means remote.

'I heard that my father remarked on his way to open parliament that he was going to begin his speech by "my Lords and Peacocks". I believe they were in a state of apprehension expecting him to carry out his threat.'

'But he did not,' said Lady Hertford. 'If he had that would have been the end.'

'He has deteriorated terribly in the last weeks. These scandals about Fred and Ernest—'

Lady Hertford pursed her lips. She did not like scandal.

The Prince had been about to tell her of an incident which had been reported to him of how when the King had inspected the royal yacht his eyes had fallen on an exceptionally pretty woman whom he had approached and regarded in a manner which was alien to what was expected of him. 'My word,' he had exclaimed, very audibly, 'what a pretty bottom! I'd like to slap that bottom.' Those watching had choked with laughter and the King had sought to embrace the young woman who had quickly extricated herself, made a quick curtsey and run off.

Such incidents in public meant that he must be near breaking point.

Poor father, thought the Prince with compassion. But if he did have to retire it would mean the Regency.

And if the Regency were his, he believed, then so would be Lady Hertford. Lady Hertford to satisfy his need for romance – always so strong in him; and Maria to go home to like a nice warm feather bed – always his great comfort in life, his wife, his soul – but to whom he had grown accustomed so that he must seek romance elsewhere.

When Caroline heard of the Prince's *penchant* for Lady Hertford she shrieked with laughter.

'He's a fool, of course,' she told Lady Charlotte. 'He'd be wise to keep to Maria. He doesn't realize when he's got a treasure. They say he sits and looks at Madam Hertford with tears in his eyes and longing in his expression. And that Maria Fitzherbert is very angry with him. They quarrel. And she has a temper, our paragon. Not that I can't understand that – married to that trying man. But it makes me laugh ... oh, it does make me laugh, Lady Charlotte my dear, to think of these fat middle-aged people behaving like young people in love.'

She wanted to hear how the romance of Mrs Fitzherbert's husband progressed. And she asked everyone who came to see her to tell her what they knew.

They could not keep the news from the King any longer. Amelia was very ill. With the coming of the autumn she contracted what was known as St Anthony's Fire.

The fact that the King's jubilee was being celebrated made this even more tragic to him. Fifty years since he had ascended the throne – fifty years of anxieties and fears which had grown greater as years passed. Looking back he could not remember everything that had happened; but two things stood out in his memory: the loss of the American colonies and the scandals of his family. He had failed somewhere. All his efforts to be a good man and a good king had not brought him success. He had become a tragic old fellow. 'More dead than alive sometimes,' he mumbled. 'And oh, God, I wish I were dead for I am afraid I am going mad.' He was half-blind, tormented by desires for women which he had never fulfilled in his youth because he was so determined to be a good husband to a wife whom he had never wanted, worried by his children, and now he faced the greatest tragedy of all: his darling Amelia was dying.

Yes, he must face it. She was going. She could not live. Everyone knew it although they were trying to keep it from him. They had said: 'Amelia can do more for him than anyone else. Amelia can soothe him, comfort him.' And so she had with her frail delicate beauty and her soothing voice and her love for him which had made all his sufferings worth while.

He sent for her physicians.

'Tell me the truth,' he cried. 'Don't try to delude me. You understand, eh, what? I want to know the truth. Is my daughter better? Is she, eh, what?'

'She is as well as can be expected, Your Majesty.'

'I expect her to be well. Is she as well as that? Tell me. Save her life. Is it too much too ask, eh, what? Go back to her. What are you doing here? You should be with her. Go to her . . . Tell her . . . Tell her . . .'

And he covered his face with his hands.

The physicians looked at each other. He needed their services as much as his daughter.

The Princess Mary came to him, her face blotched with tears. It was Mary who had loved Amelia best of all her sisters and who had scarcely left the sick room. That made him love Mary.

'What is it?' he cried as he stumbled towards her.

'Papa, she would like to see you . . . now.'

He went to her room. She smiled at him. Poor Papa, who looked so wild with his jutting white brows and his red face. But he was her good kind father who had always doted on her and been charmed by her and whom it had been her duty always to soothe and comfort.

'Dearest Papa, I am going to leave you.'

He nodded and the tears began to fall down his cheeks.

'You must not grieve for me, Papa. I have had a great deal of suffering and shall be past all pain.'

'My darling!'

'And I know you love me well enough to be glad of that. Dearest Papa, I have had a ring made for you. I have it here. See it is a lock of my hair under a crystal and set round with diamonds. Give me your finger, Papa. Will you always wear it and remember me?'

She put it on his finger. He stared at it through his tears, holding it close to his eyes that he might see it clearly.

'My darling child . . . my best loved . . .' he began.

But he could say no more. He was remembering the day twenty-seven years ago when she had been born and all the joy she had brought into his life.

'No,' he cried, 'not this – I cannot lose you. Anything ...
anything but this.'

And he kissed the mourning ring and watching him, smiling,
she sank back on her pillows.

The Princess Amelia was buried at Windsor with great pageantry.

In his apartments the King gave way to grief. He had lost his
love, his darling, and with her his sanity.

No place for Mrs Fitzherbert

The Prince of Wales had decided to celebrate his inauguration
as Regent with the most dazzling of spectacles. This was to be
held at Carlton House. Many members of the French royal
family, who were in England at this time, were to be guests; and
there was talk of nothing else but this extremely grand occasion.

Maria, melancholy in the house in Tilney Street, wondered
whether she would receive an invitation. Miss Pigot watched
her anxiously. Thank God, she thought, for darling Minney,
who made up for so much. And could Prinney be so tiresome?
What could he see in that woman Hertford? How could he
compare her with Maria?

But he was infatuated by the creature and the talk about them
was growing more and more insistent, and the more so it became
the sadder was poor Maria.

They did not discuss this in front of Minney of course, but
when they were alone Maria said: 'I doubt that I shall receive an
invitation.'

'What nonsense!' cried Miss Pigot. 'How could his wife not
be invited?'

'Quite easily because it is clear that he does not consider me
to be his wife.'

'Now that's talk I won't listen to. He's straying a bit now, I'll confess, but that's because he does think of you as his wife and he thinks he can have his little games and come back to you.'

'He could be mistaken,' said Maria with a show of temper.

But how pleased she was when she received her invitation! Her pleasure was brief, however, because she soon learned that at the fête there was to be a royal table at which the Prince would sit with his special guests including members of the French royal family. For the remainder of the guests there would be a buffet – for two thousand people had been invited – and those who used the buffet would naturally have to serve themselves.

'Of course you'll be at the royal table,' said Miss Pigot. 'How could it be otherwise?'

'It could very well be otherwise,' said Maria grimly. 'But I shall see that it is not. I am going to discover whether or not I am expected to get my own supper at that buffet.'

'How can you find out till you get there?'

'Oh, can't you see that this would be the ultimate humiliation? I have presided at dinners where that woman was the guest of honour because he wished it. But I will not consent to this. And I am going to Carlton House to ask him.'

Miss Pigot was nervous, but Maria insisted and called at Carlton House where she demanded to see the Prince.

He received her with some surprise but with a show of affection.

'I have come to ask you where I am to sit at the banquet?' she asked.

He was embarrassed. How could he explain that Lady Hertford did not expect her to have a place at the table and that he must please Lady Hertford? Maria should understand. It was not that he did not love her; but he was under the influence of the fascinating Lady Hertford and he must obey her wishes.

Maria did not make it easy. She was looking at him with cold dislike – yes, actually dislike.

He said, 'You know, madam, you have no place.'

'None, sir,' she answered curtly, 'but such as you choose to give me.'

With that she left him – uneasy, embarrassed and angry with

her for not understanding that he could not displease Lady Hertford.

She returned to Miss Pigot in a state of melancholy.

'This is the end, Piggy. This is really the end. I can endure no more.'

The Duke of York came to see her. His brother's first act as Regent had been to reinstate him as Commander-in-Chief of the Army and as he was popular and had been exonerated from guilt in the Mary Anne Clarke scandal, there was no public objection to this. He was fond of Maria and deplored the rift between her and the Prince. She must go to the fête, he told her. People would notice if she were not there. The people accepted her; did she not know that?

'Oh, what use is the people's acceptance if my husband repudiates me?'

Frederick remonstrated with the Prince who repeated what Lady Hertford had suggested. Maria must not take such a prominent place now that he was Regent, he pointed out. It was all very well for him when Prince of Wales to have a Catholic wife, but the people would not tolerate their Regent – who was in all but name their King – having one. She would have to accept this for the future.

To this Maria replied that she never would. But she did not prevent the ladies of her household from going to the fête and even provided them with new dresses so that they could do so in style.

The fête was very splendid. The Regent in scarlet and gold lace was a brilliant figure wearing the garter and diamond star. The state apartments were hung with blue velvet embroidered with the fleur-de-lis in honour of the French visitors; the gowns of the women – the costumes of the men, their glittering jewellery – nothing had been seen to rival this for years.

But there were the inevitable malicious whispers.

'Doesn't His Highness look grand? And how odd! He is a Regent with two wives – both of whom have stayed at home.'

*

Maria knew this to be the end. She was not going to be relegated to the position he had planned for her.

It was necessary for political reasons, he said; and she granted this. But it was also necessary for personal reasons. Lady Hertford wished it. That was what decided Maria.

'After all,' she said, 'perhaps we should be happier without him.'

'Oh, Maria!'

'I should have said: Perhaps *I* shall. The uncertainties of the last years have been unbearable at times. I am never sure of him. I cannot go on like that. I am his wife. I refuse to be regarded as his mistress. I am fifty-five years old. Surely that's an age when one should have some dignity. And I have dearest Minney and you. I shall step quietly out of his life.'

And this she proceeded to do. He was uneasy and unhappy when he thought of her, but the chase for Lady Hertford must go on.

It had always been so with him. The woman he was pursuing was always the all-important factor in his life.

Maria was Maria. He would always regard her as his wife and did not wish to lose her. He wanted her always there in the background, to come back to be comforted when he needed it. But Maria was proud – she had more regality than any member of the royal family – and this time Maria said no.

The Duke of York remonstrated with him. He must settle Maria's debts which had been incurred on his account; he must see that she was well provided for. It was to be an honourable settlement.

This the Prince was ready to do.

'If you only knew, Fred, I don't want her to go. If only she would be reasonable.'

But his idea of reason was not Maria's.

It was over. She would never go back to him again, she promised herself, no matter how much he insisted. She had finished with him.

She was a wealthy woman; she had no debts; and there would be no occasions to incur them in future. She had her dearest Minney and she would make the care of this beloved adopted daughter her life.

'We will manage very well without him,' she told Miss Pigot. And this time Miss Pigot knew that she meant it.

Caroline had a detailed account of the fête at Carlton House, all the glitter and splendour.

'I should have been there,' she said, faintly regretful, and for a moment gave herself up to contemplating what a life she might have had if the Prince of Wales had not taken such a dislike to her when he had first seen her. Wife to the Regent! Yes, it might have been good fun. She laughed at the description of him in his splendid uniform.

'Imagine him – well-corseted! But what's the good of corsets for a paunch like that?'

Then she started to laugh, but was soon melancholy again.

'One of her moods,' said Lady Charlotte to Mrs Fitzgerald.

'And poor Maria Fitzherbert, she was not there either,' murmured the Princess. 'I'm sorry about that. Oh, what a fool he is. He's chasing that woman and she'll never be his mistress. She's too cold. She doesn't care for him, only for the Regency. He is a stupid man, my fat husband. And the most stupid thing he ever did was to part from Maria Fitzherbert. She's his true wife – not me. He's a great big fat fool to have broken with her.'

Then she started to laugh, and Lady Charlotte tiptoed away to make an account of this in her diary.

Persecutions

A dramatic incident suddenly and most unexpectedly robbed Caroline of her most influential supporter.

The Prince Regent had not made any changes in the Ministry although his Whig friends confidently expected him to. When the Duke of Portland had died Spencer Perceval had become Prime Minister, although many had supposed this plum would fall to Canning; and during those first months of the Regency

Perceval remained in office. The Regent was watching the King's progress which fluctuated a great deal, and the doctors told him that there were days when His Majesty was almost lucid. The Prince had no desire to make a change which the King, if he recovered, would immediately rescind; for this reason he was prepared to wait a while.

Perceval made no secret of his belief that the Princess of Wales had been ill-treated; and while he remained as the head of the Government the Prince did not change his attitude in any way towards Caroline. As long as she kept out of his way he appeared to be content.

Then one afternoon in May as Perceval was going into the House a man stepped up to him, placed a pistol against his heart and fired. Perceval dropped to the ground – dead.

It happened so quickly and seemed so pointless. When the murderer was caught he proved to be a madman named John Bellingham who had recently come from Russia where he had been arrested for some small misdemeanour. He had appealed to the English ambassador there and as nothing had been done to help him, he blamed the government. His revenge was to shoot the Prime Minister.

About a fortnight after the death of Perceval the London crowds turned out in their thousands to see Bellingham hanged. It was quite a spectacle.

Caroline was desolate, for she knew she had lost a good friend.

After the assassination of Perceval, Lords Wellesley and Moira had attempted to form a government and when they failed to do so the Earl of Liverpool became Prime Minister. Caroline very quickly became aware of the change in her fortunes.

One of her greatest compensations was the affection her daughter felt for her, and the weekly visits to Charlotte were the highlights of her life. Charlotte was now a very forthright sixteen, and being aware that she was the heiress to the throne was not inclined to be forced to anything that she did not want. She was a great favourite with the people and everywhere she went she was cheered. How different it was with the Regent! He was met by sullen silences and the occasional booing. The people took up the case of Charlotte and Caroline, and the general opinion was that the Regent was not only a bad husband but a cruel father. They laughed at his elegance, and his corpulence was exaggerated in all the cartoons. If he had remained faithful to Maria Fitzherbert they would have had some respect for him. But he was constantly in the company of Lady Hertford whose frigid manners assured her an unpopularity to match his own.

It was irritating to him to be given continual proof of the people's affection for his wife and daughter; and in a petulant mood he ordered that Caroline and Charlotte instead of meeting once a week should meet only once a fortnight.

Caroline was furious.

'Oh, what a wicked man he is! What harm are we doing him by meeting? My little Charlotte will be upset, too. Does he think I will endure this? He will see.'

Charlotte was at Windsor and the Queen and the Princesses were also in residence, so Caroline wrote the Queen telling her that she intended visiting Windsor to see her daughter.

A cool note from Her Majesty informed her that it was the Regent's wishes that the Princess Charlotte's lessons should not be disturbed; therefore it would not be possible for Caroline to see her if she came to Windsor.

This threw Caroline into a violent rage. 'Does the old Begum think that she is going to keep me away from my daughter? Charlotte hates her – always has! Why, I remember when she was little her saying: "The two things I hate are apple-pie and Grandmamma." That shows, does it not? And she has not changed. She still hates apple-pie and Grandmamma. And this is the woman who will keep me from her. I am going to Windsor, old Begum or not.'

Lady Charlotte asked timidly if Her Highness thought that wise in view of the Queen's letter.

'Dear Lady Charlotte, I am not concerned with the wisdom but the justice of this.'

So to Windsor she went. But the visit was not a success.

The Queen received her coldly.

'I fear,' she said, 'that you cannot see the Princess Charlotte. We have to obey the Regent's orders, do we not?'

'I am going to see her.'

The Queen looked surprised. 'Perhaps I have not made it clear that these are the *Regent*'s orders.'

Caroline cried: 'I'll find her. I'll see her. You'll not keep me from my own daughter.'

The Queen looked horrified. What could one do with a woman who was so ignorant of the respect and homage due to the Crown!

'I beg of you to leave,' she said coldly. 'I am sure you do not wish me to have you *taken* away.'

And something in the coldness of her manner made Caroline realize how powerless she was. The Queen could call her servants, or even the guards to have her forcibly removed. There was nothing she could do, but return fuming to Blackheath.

As soon as she returned to Blackheath she sat down and wrote a letter:

Sir,

It is with great reluctance that I presume to intrude upon Your Royal Highness and to solicit your attention to matters which may, at first, appear rather of a personal than of a public nature ... There is a point beyond which a guiltless woman cannot with safety carry her forbearance. If her honour is invaded the defence of her reputation is no longer a matter of choice; and it signifies not whether the attack be made openly, manfully and directly – or by secret insinuation, and by holding such conduct towards her as countenances all the suspicions that malice can suggest ...

I presume, sir, to suggest to Your Royal Highness, that the separation, which every succeeding month is making wider, of the mother and the daughter, is equally injurious to my character and to her education. I say nothing of the deep wounds which so cruel an arrangement inflicts on my feelings ...

She went on to write of the implications of such a decree but she signed herself:

Your Royal Highness's most devoted and most affectionate Consort, Cousin and Subject, Caroline Amelia.

This letter she delivered to the Prime Minister, Lord Liverpool, with the request that he should hand it to the Prince Regent. The Prime Minister returned the letter unopened the following day with a covering note:

His Royal Highness has stated that he will receive no communication from Your Highness and sees no reason why he should change that decision.

Infuriated, Caroline commanded that the letter be sent once more to Lord Liverpool. Was she to be the only subject who was not allowed to present a petition? Lord Liverpool had no wish to be embroiled, so he replied that if the Princess would give him a copy of the letter he would communicate its contents to the Prince Regent. This Caroline did, but Lord Liverpool's answer was that His Royal Highness had made no comment whatsoever.

'Very well,' cried Caroline, 'I will publish this letter so that the people may read it.'

Shortly after it appeared in the *Morning Chronicle*.

This naturally had its repercussions in the fury of the people against the Regent and their increased sympathy towards Caroline. But this the Regent ignored: and Caroline received a letter from Lord Liverpool in which he said that in view of the publication of the letter, the Prince Regent had commanded that her next meeting with the Princess Charlotte should be cancelled.

But the mood of the people and the truculent attitude of Caroline forced the Regent to a decision. He called together a committee to decide what the relationship between the Princess of Wales and her daugher should be; and he asked that the papers which were accumulated during the Douglas case be studied again in the hope of proving to the people of England that Caroline was no fit companion for the heiress to the throne.

Caroline was not without friends and now that she had lost Perceval she found two ardent supporters in Baron Brougham and Vaux, a distinguished lawyer and politician, and Samuel

Whitbread, the Member for Bedford, who had made a fortune out of the brewery business.

Whitbread was an earnest idealist who saw Caroline as a much persecuted heroine; Brougham was something of an opportunist who saw in Caroline's case a cause which could bring him fame.

The called on her – separately – and both told her of their admiration for her fortitude in her misfortune and how they would work for her.

With her usual exuberance she welcomed them.

It was fortunate for her that she had these supporters, for those of the Prince were demanding that the Douglases repeat their accusations against her.

Whitbread, aware of this, forestalled the Princess's enemies by asking in the House of Commons that Lady Douglas be prosecuted for perjury.

The affairs of the Regent and his wife were being discussed everywhere. There was no doubt whose side the people were on.

On one occasion riding in Constitution Hill, Caroline's carriage passed that of Charlotte and the young princess called to her driver to turn and follow her mother.

When the carriages were side by side the two embraced affectionately and through the windows engaged in an animated conversation.

A crowd collected.

'Long live the Princess Charlotte!' they cried. 'Long live the Princess of Wales!'

The two smiled affectionately at the people and waved their greetings.

There were loud cheers and grumbles in the crowd too. 'Why should fat George come between mother and daughter? Why should they stand by and allow such wickedness?'

Mother and daughter bade each other a fond farewell, and as their carriages drove away in opposite directions were seen to turn and wave and look after each other longingly.

There were tears in many eyes as well as indignation.

'It shouldn't be allowed,' was the comment. 'Someone should put a stop to it.'

No one was more aware of public opinion than Brougham; so he came down vehemently on Caroline's side.

Meanwhile the Douglases were alarmed, considering the penalties of perjury, and Sir John wrote to the House of Commons on behalf of his wife explaining that the depositions they made on oath before the Lords Commissioners were not made on such judicial proceedings which could legally result in a prosecution for perjury. But as they felt the fullest confidence in their statements they were ready to take the oath and swear before a tribunal, which if they were proved false could mean a prosecution for perjury. They were eager to take these oaths before one which was lacking in these legal liabilities.

Brougham laughed aloud when he heard this.

'Ah,' he cried to Caroline. 'You understand. They're bluffing. They know what this will mean. They will only swear at a public trial in which the Prince Regent would have to appear.'

'They are taking a risk,' suggested Caroline.

'Well, they have to take a risk – but a small one. They're banking on the impossibility of having a public trial in which the Regent would show up in none too good a light. Moreover, all those spies of theirs might have been ready to swear before the Lords Commissioners but would they be prepared to do so in a court of law? Consider the penalties of perjury, dear Madam. No, this is good. There will be no trial. And they don't deceive people in the know.'

He was right. News came that the Duke of Sussex had dismissed Sir John Douglas from his service. This was taken as a vindication of Caroline, and there were bonfires in the streets and the effigies which were burned were those of Sir John and Lady Douglas.

The Duchess of Brunswick died at that time. Caroline was saddened, but her mother's behaviour had not been exactly endearing. The Prince, on attaining the Regency, had offered her an apartment in Carlton House. Caroline guessed that this was to discountenance *her*; and the old lady had been eager to accept and would have done so had she not been prevailed upon by her son to refrain from doing so. So she had declined and continued to hold court in her dark and gloomy old house in New Street, Spring Gardens; but she did seem to take a delight in the humiliations heaped on her daughter, while she declared her dear nephew, the Prince Regent, was always charming to *her*.

Caroline was understandably concerned with the fate of her mother's faithful lady-in-waiting, Lady Finlater, who on the death of the Duchess was left in very dire straits, and endeavoured to get her a pension of five hundred pounds a year.

Caroline was beginning to see that the Regent was too powerful for her. There would always be trouble, and as he was almost the King, she had little chance against him.

Charlotte was to be betrothed to the Prince of Orange, a match which the young Princess viewed with some distaste; and Caroline longed to be with her, to condole with her, to stop her making an unhappy marriage as she had.

But Charlotte had spirit and her father was a little afraid of her on account of that great affection she inspired wherever she went; the greater it became the more he realized that a quarrel between them could be disastrous to his own standing with the people.

He groaned and cursed his wife and daughter. Never was a man such a lover of the female sex, and never was a father and husband so plagued by them.

He blamed everything on to Caroline; he hated her; he could not bear to think of her. The manner in which she behaved disgusted him. She was vulgar; she had no sense of decorum; she was everything that he was not; and to think that she was the mother of the heiress to the throne enraged him.

When the Czar of Russia visited England he was determined to keep Caroline out of his sight, for he could not endure the thought of the Czar's seeing her and knowing that she was his wife.

When Caroline heard that there was to be a state visit to the opera she mischievously decided to discountenance the Regent.

'They may ban me from the drawing rooms but they can't

prevent my going to the opera,' she announced triumphantly.

And while she was dressed for the occasion she grumbled to Lady Charlotte and her women about the manner in which she had been excluded from the Queen's drawing room. ' "The Regent has said he does not wish to see you. And how can I ban the Regent from my drawing room?" ' she mimicked the Queen. ' "I fear in the circumstances I cannot invite you to attend." The old Begum! We have more fun in Montague House in five minutes than they do in a year in the old drawings rooms.'

She laughed gleefully, and gazed in delight at her reflection while Lady Charlotte shuddered inwardly. Could she really be contemplating visiting the opera like that? She wore black velvet and on her head had set an elaborately curled wig so black that her face heavily daubed with white lead and rouge made a startling contrast.

'Come on,' she cried. 'Smack it on. I want to be noticed tonight.'

Her large bosom was generously displayed and she called Willikin to comment on her appearance. He threw his arms about her neck and she gave him several smacking kisses and was clearly contemplating taking him with her.

Oh God, prayed Lady Charlotte, don't let her be as foolish as that.

Fortunately she changed her mind in time.

At the opera the national anthem was being played when she arrived. The Prince Regent was standing to attention in his box – on one side of him the Czar of Russia, on the other the King of Prussia.

The anthem over, the audience seated itself and then someone in the stalls noticed her.

'The Princess of Wales!' the cry went up and the people began to cheer. Here was a situation more interesting than the opera could hope to be. The Princess and the Prince in the house together.

The Czar was looking interested.

'What a handsome fellow,' whispered Caroline excitedly.

'Madam,' said Lady Charlotte, 'the people expect you to rise and acknowledge their cheers.'

'Oh no,' she said audibly, 'Punch's wife is nobody when Punch is there. I know my business better than to take the morsel out of my husband's mouth.'

The applause continued.

And the Prince Regent with that elegance and *saviour-faire* which Caroline could never hope to understand, let alone emulate, rose turning to face her and gave the house and Caroline the benefit of that elegant bow which was the admiration of all who beheld it.

It was an evening of triumph for Caroline and of exasperating humility for the Prince. For when the opera was over she went out to the carriage and found a crowd waiting for her.

They were also waiting for the Prince Regent. 'Where's your wife, George?' they asked mockingly. This was particularly infuriating when he was in the company of visiting royalty.

As for Caroline it was: 'Long live the Princess. God bless the innocent.'

They crowded round her carriage; they insisted on shaking hands with her.

Nothing loath she opened the door and took their hands in her affable friendly way. They cheered her lustily. She was the heroine of the evening.

One cried: 'Shall we burn down Carlton House? You only have to say the word.'

'No, no,' she cried. 'Just let me pass now and go home and sleep peacefully. And God bless you.'

'God bless you,' they cried.

It was certainly a triumph.

But she soon realized the emptiness of such triumphs. The Czar had been impressed or amused by the evening at the opera, and he sent a note to Caroline asking permission to call on her.

How delightedly she gave it! 'We must have a banquet. My word, this will put his little nose out of joint. We'll have such a spectacle as to compete with anything he's ever had at Carlton House.'

That was a wild exaggeration, of course, but it delighted her to think that in spite of her in-laws she was to receive the royal visitor.

She set her cooks to work; she sat with her women while long hours were spent on her *toilette*. She insisted that the rouge and white lead should not be spared.

'That's what he liked last time. Give him lots of it.'

But when she was ready she waited in vain; for the royal visitor did not appear.

Doubtless he had been made to realize by his advisers that he could not in a foreign country visit a princess who was ignored by the Prince Regent.

Caroline took off her wig and threw it into the air.

'Well, that's that, my angels.'

She became very melancholy.

'I don't know why I stay in this country to be treated in this way. What's to stop my leaving it? I can't see anything to stand in the way.'

'There's war on the Continent,' pointed out Lady Charlotte.

'So there is. But if there was not, do you know I think I should go away. It would be the best for everyone, including myself. I'd take Willie with me and some of you dear friends.'

'What of the Princess Charlotte?'

'Ah, my Charlotte! But you know she is in constant conflict with her father and a great deal of that trouble is through her loyalty to me. So perhaps it would even be better for her.'

She sighed. She was certainly in one of her moods of deepest depression.

She left the house she had taken in Connaught Place for Blackheath.

There, she said, she could brood on her troubles, for she was becoming increasingly aware that she would have to take some action – though what she was unsure.

Montague House was always a comfort. There she had had her happiest times. She decided she would send for the Sapios and they should soothe her with their music. It would comfort her considerably and perhaps provide her with the inspiration she needed.

Lady Charlotte came hurrying in with a look of consternation. 'Your Highness, there is a carriage at the door. You are implored to leave without delay for Connaught House.'

'This is too much. I refuse—'

'Madam, the Princess Charlotte is there. She has run away – to you.'

'Get my cape at once,' cried Caroline; and in a few minutes she was on the way to Connaught House.

There she found Brougham, some of Charlotte's ladies, the Archbishop of Canterbury, the Lord Chancellor Eldon, the Duke of York and the Duke of Sussex. And in the midst of this gathering a very defiant Charlotte who when she saw her mother ran to her and threw herself into her arms.

'It's no use,' she said. 'I shall not go back. I am going to live with my mother. I have chosen.'

The men looked helpless and it was Brougham who spoke.

'Your Highness must consider what this could mean.'

'I have considered,' cried Charlotte imperiously. 'I have made up my mind. I am tired of being my father's prisoner. I am going to be free. I am going to be with my own mother. It's what I want. It's what the people want.'

Caroline said: 'Tell me what has happened.'

Charlotte laughed. 'I refuse to marry Orange.' She shivered. 'I absolutely refuse and I have told him so. For one thing it would mean living in Holland which is something I will not do. And why should I? I shall one day be the Queen of England. England is where I propose to live.'

'And your father knows this?' asked Caroline.

Charlotte rolled her eyes to the ceiling. 'The scene! You should have heard it. I will say this for him – he had a fine command of the language. But do you know how he is going to punish me? He's going to dismiss all my staff and provide me with ... jailers. I won't have it. We'll be together, won't we? We'll be a pair of outcasts.'

Brougham said: 'Your Highness will explain to the Princess Charlotte how impossible such a plan would be.'

Caroline nodded. 'They wouldn't let us be together, my angel.

I'd have no power to keep you – happy as I should be to do so.'

'Oh, Mamma, how cruel they all are!'

'Yes, my darling, but we must needs put up with it.'

Lord Eldon was regarding Charlotte with disapproval. He would have liked to deal severely with that tempestuous and bouncing girl; if she were his, he had told the Regent, he would lock her up.

Brougham explained tactfully that the law had to be considered as well as her father. She was very young. She was in the care of the state. She would have to remember this.

'I'd have you remember that I am the heiress to the throne. One day I shall be your Queen.'

'We know it, Your Highness, and it is for this reason that you must submit to the law.'

Charlotte looked piteously at her mother, and Caroline could only nod.

'He's right, I fear, my darling. You'll have to go back. Perhaps when your father knows how strongly you feel he will be lenient with you.'

Brougham, with a dramatic gesture, went to the window and drew aside the curtains. It was dark, being past midnight.

He said dramatically: 'It is quiet out there now, Your Highness; but with dawn the people will begin to gather. If they know that you have run away in defiance of your father it could start a riot – worse still. Who knows? And once these disturbances begin there is no knowing where they will end. You would not wish to start a civil war, I am sure, which could mean bloodshed for thousands of innocent people.'

Charlotte was staring wide-eyed.

'It's true,' he said. 'Everyone here will bear me out.'

She looked round at the assembled company.

And no one denied him.

Brougham knew that he had averted a difficult situation. The Princess Charlotte would return and obey her father.

The allied forces against Napoleon had entered Paris; Napoleon had been obliged to abdicate and had retired to Elba. The French exiles, who had been living in as much state as they

could muster in Aylesbury, had left with great pomp and ceremony for Versailles.

Caroline was thoughtful. The Continent was safe for travellers.

Whey should she not put into practice a plan which had been
formulating for a long time?

Why should she stay in England to be humiliated? Why
should she not travel? She had always wanted to. Next to
children, travel could excite her more than anything in the
world.

There was only one person who could keep her here for she
could take Willikin with her: that was Charlotte. But of what
use was she to Charlotte? In fact now that Charlotte had been
sent to Cranbourne Lodge in Windsor Forest she doubted
whether she would be allowed to see her for months.

No, she was the cause of much of the friction between Charlotte and her father.

She would be better out of the way.

Of one thing she could be certain. The Regent would put
nothing in the way of her going.

She was right. He did not. And so Caroline began to make her
plans to leave England.

The spy at the Villa d'Este

So it was goodbye to England. Caroline's feelings were mixed.
It was sad to leave Charlotte; but she had Willikin to comfort
her; and as she drove to Worthing with the boy and her two
ladies-in-waiting, Lady Charlotte Lindsay and Lady Elizabeth
Forbes, she believed that she had at least some whom she loved
to be her constant companions. Lady Charlotte Campbell had
gone to Europe in advance and would join her later; and in her
there was another dear friend.

The people had cheered her all along the route. It was as though they did not wish her to go. She had their sympathy. She took Willie's hand and pressed it; he was excited, delighted to be setting out on adventures with his dear mamma who spoilt him, as everyone said, so atrociously.

Brougham had not wished her to go; in fact he had done his best to dissuade her. She was not entirely sure of him; in fact she was not sure of any politicians and often wondered how politic their partnership was. Were they for her for the sake of their party – or against her for that reason? She was well aware that numbers of her enemies were such because they wished to please the Prince Regent.

She thought as she had many times of how different her life would have been if she had been allowed to marry dearest Töbingen. Then she would have had a big family of children – not just one daughter whom she could scarcely call her own because the dear child had never been allowed to be with her, and one son who was not her own, much as she loved him. She had been forced to lavish all that great mother-love on Willikin and sometimes she admitted to herself that he was extremely self-willed and not very intelligent. Not that she did not love him. She loved all children. But if she could have had that Töbingen brood . . .

Brougham had said to her: 'Your Highness should never forget that what the Prince Regent desires is to prove you guilty of immorality. He wants a divorce. You are going to be surrounded by spies.'

That had made her laugh. 'I will give them something to report to their master.'

'I beg of Your Highness to take care.'

'Why, my dear friend,' she replied, 'you would deprive me of one of my greatest pleasures in my life which is precisely *not* taking care.'

Brougham was dismayed. What a wild impulsive woman she was, impossible to direct.

He looked at her severely. 'Your Highness should know the worst. Do you know what the Duke of Clarence has told the captain of the ship on which you sail?'

'Well, I should be surprised if he spoke against me. My brothers-in-law have always been my friends.'

'He does not think to speak unkindly. Your Highness knows there has been much scandal surrounding you.'

'Ha. Those Douglases! I'd like to see to them in court. And what has Clarence said of me?'

'He has told the captain that he should have a love affair with you, that he can be sure he would not be repulsed and the Prince Regent would have no objection. In fact would be more likely to reward him.'

Caroline burst out laughing. 'It has come to a pretty pass when Mrs Fitzherbert's husband tries to bribe a noble sea captain to sleep with me!'

Poor Brougham! He had been exasperated with her. And no wonder. After all, his defence of her was going to make him famous. And he believed that her mode of life would certainly lead her into trouble sooner or later, and this was particularly so since the Prince Regent would do his best to bring her there.

But nothing he could say would deter her. She was going on her travels because life in England was no longer endurable. She was to be known as the Countess of Cornwall – a thin disguise, for her face and figure had been made well known by the cartoonists, and her heavy pelisse caught together by fasteners of gold, and her hat of mauve and green, on which drooped a large green feather, were characteristic of the Princess of Wales. She had designed a costume for her gentlemen – embroidered black coats lined with scarlet silk, gold embroidered waistcoats and feathered hats.

She was clearly no ordinary traveller.

From the first there was an uneasy atmosphere in the travelling party, every member of which was aware that they might be called upon at some future time to report on the Princess's actions. Caroline herself seemed to be unaware of this – or perhaps indifferent to it; but there was not one member of her suite who could bear to contemplate giving evidence against the Princess – which would be extremely disloyal, or against the Prince Regent which would be extremely unwise.

There was scarcely one of them who did not wish himself or herself back in England. At the best this was not a pleasure trip; it was banishment, and home began to look very inviting.

Lady Charlotte Lindsay begged leave to go and visit her sister Lady Glenbervie at Spa.

'You must go and see the dear creature,' declared Caroline. 'And rejoin me at Naples.'

By the time she reached Brunswick her chamberlain St Leger had begged leave to return to England, for his health could not stand up to the rigours of travel. Caroline gave the permission and the Hon Keppel Craven took his place. Sir William Gell, who had shared a chamberlain's duties with St Leger, began to suffer acutely from the gout but he remained with her, and realizing now that her suite were not anxious to accompany her – and guessing the reason – she shrugged her shoulders, but she did feel very grateful to the few who remained.

It was a strange feeling to be back in Brunswick. It had changed. After all there had been the occupation. Her brother greeted her with affection and she was delighted to see him back in possession of his lands. She walked through the old palace and recalled memories of her childhood; she lingered in the courtyard where she had often talked with Major von Töbingen. And there was her bedroom where she had staged that disastrous scene when she had pretended she was pregnant.

What anxieties she had caused to her dear good father! She was sorry for it now.

But the more they cage me, she thought, the more outrageous I become. It is not that I am wildly eccentric so much as that I wish people to believe I am. They suspect me and I want to make them go on suspecting. What causes it? Who will ever know? Perhaps wise Madame de Hertzfeldt would. No one else.

She had no desire to stay longer in Brunswick at this time but told her brother she would come back in the spring. Her intention was to spend the winter in Naples.

Before reaching Naples she decided to stay a while in Milan, and it soon became clear to her that she needed an Italian courier to arrange her travelling and he must necessarily be an Italian to overcome the language difficulties.

When she met General Pino at a banquet given in her honour she consulted him on this matter and he in turn consulted the governor of Milan, General Bellegard.

The governor called at the villa she had taken and told her that he knew of a man whom he could thoroughly recommend. This was a certain Baron Bartolomeo Pergami – a man whose fortunes were in reverse through no fault of his own. The Baron Pergami had distinguished himself in the recent campaigns and was something of a hero, but it was true that he had fallen on hard times and although it might be beneath his dignity to take a post of courier in the ordinary way, as this would be in the service of the Princess of Wales he might consider it.

Caroline's attention had already been attracted by one of the loveliest children she had ever seen. This was Vittorina Pergami – a sparkling, vivacious, black-eyed little girl with a mass of dark curling hair. Dear Willie, whom she loved devotedly, was scarcely handsome with his pale eyes, sandy hair and rather petulant mouth. Caroline wanted to know more of this enchanting child and as soon as she heard the name Pergami she wondered if there was any connection. She soon discovered that there was and that the Baron Pergami who was coming to see her was her father.

And as soon as Bartolomeo Pergami stood before her she was attracted by him. He seemed to her to be the complete adventurer. He looked the part with his fierce moustache and his head of thick curling black hair; his eyes flashed; his bearing was that of a soldier; he looked lithe and strong and was six feet in height.

What a man! thought Caroline. If the Prince Regent could know that he was in my service there would be some fluttering excitement among his spies.

For that reason alone she would engage this man. But for purely personal reasons he was such a joy to look at.

He told her of his life, of lost splendours due to the wars, of his own service in the recent fighting. He was gallant and respectful – though not too respectful; he laughed frequently, seeing a joke as readily as she would – her sort of joke – and when he did so he showed beautiful white and even teeth. Caroline was more excited than she had been since she left Worthing.

'I have fallen in love with your daughter Vittorina,' she told him. 'And I wondered how I could keep her with me. Perhaps by detaining her father?'

'That would be a necessity, Your Highness,' he told her. Clever man. He knew who she was although she had now dispensed with the title of Duchess of Wolfenbüttel and had become the Countess of Cornwall.

'While I am in Italy I shall need someone to arrange my travels. It is not a post worthy of you, I know; but if you would consider it for a start?'

'For a start . . .' The bold black eyes were alert with speculation. 'Madam,' he said with a bow, 'it would be a privilege to serve you in any capacity, however humble.'

That settled it. Baron Bartolomeo Pergami was attached to the entourage of the Princess of Wales.

Lady Elizabeth Forbes had left. She had assured Her Highness that she found travelling too taxing and that she had family matters to which to attend in England.

Lady Charlotte Campbell however was returning.

'They are all seeking a chance to desert me, Willikin,' she said.

'Why?' asked Willikin.

'Because they don't love me as you do, my angel.'

Her angel settled closer to her and helped himself to the sweetmeats she always provided for him.

Let them go, she thought. She didn't want them if they didn't wish to stay. Pergami was worth a hundred of any one of them. Very soon he had ceased to be a humble courier and was her chamberlain. He showed exceptional abilities; he was capable of managing the entire household; this brought him into daily contact with the Princess – which was a great pleasure to her. His delightful daughter Vittorina was her constant companion – so it was natural that the dear child's father should not be far off.

Dear Pergami – so efficient, so sunny tempered, so amusing and so handsome! She looked forward to the times when he came to report to her on her household and she would keep him talking of the past – the glorious past when he had been a great baron and had not been forced into service even of so great a lady.

'Poor, poor Pergami,' she would sigh. 'How I feel for you.'

'But Your Highness,' he told her with an ardent look, 'to serve you gives me greater happiness than I have ever known before.'

'These Italians,' cried the Princess later to Lady Charlotte Lindsay, 'they certainly know how to treat a woman.'

'I daresay His Royal Highness the Prince Regent has already heard that the Baron Pergami has joined your household.'

'I hope he has. I see no reason to make a secret of it.'

Lady Charlotte sighed. She never saw reasons – or if she did, she did not care.

And after that conversation she was even more friendly to the handsome Baron.

On her journey from Milan to Naples Caroline startled the people as she passed along. She had ordered a carriage in the shape of a shell and in this she lay over-dressed, over-painted, with enormous feathers rising from her hat and falling about her shoulders; her gowns were always low cut and she liked to sit, most inelegantly, with her short fat legs exposed to the knees. Willikin often sprawled beside her, his eyes round with wonder at the sights he saw; and she had grooms dressed in pink tights decorated with spangles. Everywhere she went she left behind a trail of gossip.

Once, staying at a humble inn, she heard that there was to be a village dance and insisted on going and dancing with the most handsome of the young men. The people laughed and applauded but afterwards they thought this was strange behaviour for a Princess of Wales.

On one occasion the seats of the carriage in which she was travelling were too high to enable her short legs to reach the floor; so she put them on to the lap of a lady-in-waiting who happened to be sitting opposite, and rode along thus to the amazement of all who beheld her and the complete embarrassment of the lady.

The Princess had always been wild, but since she had left England a madness seemed to have possessed her.

In due course they came to Naples.

The King of Naples gave her an enthusiastic welcome. He received her ceremoniously and told her he hoped she would stay in Naples as long as she cared to. Very soon she had set up house and prepared to enjoy the hospitality which was extended to her on all sides.

It was in Naples that she received the first tangible warning. General Matthews, a member of her suite, when strolling through the streets of Naples in the company of an Italian count, met an Englishman whom he knew. He naturally wondered what this gentleman was doing in Naples and greeted him.

'I know you,' he said. 'Your name is Quentin, is it not?'

'That is so.'

'And you have a brother who is a colonel in the Hussars and I believe you serve the Prince Regent in some capacity.'

'I have a post in His Royal Highness's household.'

'And are you here on business in Naples?'

'Er . . . yes. I have been sent by His Royal Highness to look at some horses which he proposes buying.'

When they passed on the count said: 'I'll swear he has not come to Naples to look at horses. It's scarcely the place to do that.'

'It seems very strange, I admit,' said the General. 'But why should he lie?'

'Because his business is such that he does not wish to speak of it. And it is the affair of your Prince Regent.'

'H'm,' said the General. 'A spy.'

'You can be sure of that. I will tell you what I will do. I will tell the King what has happened and he will get to the root of the matter. In a few days' time he will know whether this Quentin has in fact been looking at horses or not. And if not, I think the Princess of Wales should be warned. Do you not agree?'

The General replied that he agreed wholeheartedly.

A few days later the count came to see the General.

'Mr Quentin has not been looking at horses. In fact what he has been doing is asking a great many questions about the Princess of Wales – and talking to members of her household.'

'I shall go to her Highness immediately and report on this.'

'There is no need. The King has taken a great liking to her. And he is annoyed that the Prince Regent should send spies into Naples without his knowledge. He will deal with this.'

The King kissed Caroline's hand; she gave him her large warm smile.

He said: 'My dear lady, I have asked you to come to see me because I have something very serious to tell you. I trust you will forgive what may seem like impertinence on my part but I am concerned for you.'

'Your dear good Majesty! I shall never forget how much at home you have made me feel in your kingdom.'

'But I will not have you persecuted while you are here.'

'Persecuted! Nothing could be farther from the truth. I have been fêted, honoured . . .'

'And spied on, my dear lady. Now this is what I have to tell you. A Mr Quentin has been sent here by the Prince Regent to report on your actions. I thought you should be warned.'

'Ha!' laughed Caroline. 'I trust he carries back a good tale.'

'I shall not allow him to remain if you do not wish him to. He shall be escorted to the frontier and told not to enter Naples again.'

'Oh, don't do that. Poor fellow, he would be so put out and doubtless be in trouble with his master.'

'My dear Princess, do you realize that this fellow is spying on you, that he will carry reports back to England – very likely false ones – of your conduct here?'

'Oh, let him!'

The King was astonished.

'I wish you to know that if any spies come here and you want them to be banished it shall be done.'

'Let them stay. Let them take back their tales. Your Majesty is good to consider me so. But I shall not worry about these spies. So, dear Majesty, do not concern yourself with them.'

The King lifted his shoulders. It was for her to say, he reminded her.

'The dear King,' Caroline told Willikin, 'he is so concerned for me. What a comfort after the way I have been treated in England. I should like to stay in Naples for the rest of my life!'

'You'd be too restless, Mamma. You will be off on your travels again soon.'

Caroline laughed. 'You are right, my dear Willikin.'

It was true that she did not stay much longer in Naples; and the reason was a dramatic one.

Napoleon had escaped from Elba and Caroline deemed it wise to leave without delay and in twenty-four hours was on board the *Clorinde* sailing for Genoa.

Genoa, into which she had a triumphant entry, all spangles and feathers, was excited to receive her and the people came out into the streets to look at the strange English princess.

Pergami had arranged everything with his usual efficiency. 'What should we do without the dear man?' she demanded of Willikin who agreed with her that Pergami looked after them very well. Caroline was becoming more and more familiar with her attractive major-domo and refused to treat such a gentleman, such a treasure, as a servant. Often he sat down to a meal with her alone. 'Just the two of us,' she would say. And this delighted her, because he was so amusing and, as she confided to her servants, she enjoyed a *tête-à-tête* meal with Pergami more than a state banquet where there was too much noise and chatter and people had to shout until they were hoarse to make themselves heard.

Lady Charlotte Campbell arrived in Genoa with six of her children, which was a great delight.

How were the little darlings? And how did they like travelling? And were they pleased to see the Princess again?

They were, and so was their mother though a little shocked at the Princess's manners which had grown even more free and easy since she left England.

And who, Lady Charlotte asked some of the members of the staff, was this man Bergami or Pergami, or whatever he called himself?

There was a little giggling and a little shrugging of shoulders.

'A great favourite with the Princess, Lady Charlotte. He is in constant attention. He's the chamberlain but he's more like her faithful companion.'

Lady Charlotte groaned. What indiscretions! There was talk of her eldest daughter having a post in the Princess's household. Lady Charlotte was not sure that she wished for this.

Caroline, however, was unaware of the gossip. She was delighted to have Lady Charlotte with her and she would arrange for a house in the town for the children and their governess. As for Lady Charlotte she would take up her old duties.

Then came sad news. At the battle of Quatre Bras Caroline's brother, the young Duke of Brunswick, had been killed.

Caroline shut herself up in her apartments and wept for her brother.

But very soon there was shouting in the streets and everyone was rejoicing. Wellington and Blucher had met Napoleon at Waterloo and annihilated the French army.

Peace at last – and this time a lasting peace because Napoleon could never rise again.

'Now,' said Caroline, 'I can continue my journeyings in peace.'

There was startling news however from England.

Samuel Whitbread, who had been her fervent supporter, had died by his own hand.

Caroline could not believe this to be true. He had always been such a vital man, a firm upholder of righteous causes.

He had believed, it was said, that his public career was at an end, and this depressed him. It seemed so pointless; he was rich, having retained a big share in the brewery; he was not old, being in the neighbourhood of fifty, and yet he had shut himself into his bedroom in his town house at thirty-five Dover Street and cut his throat.

Remembering the violent death of Spencer Perceval Caroline said: 'I seem to bring bad luck to those who help me.'

Why was it that people did not wish to stay with her? Captain Hesse, her equerry, who was said to be the illegitimate son of the Duke of York, had come to her when the news of Napoleon's escape was known and told her that he must rejoin his regiment. She fancied this was a good excuse.

Gell and Craven had come to her as she was about to embark at Naples and told her that they must leave her unless she returned to England.

She had told them that she had no intention of doing that and laughed at them because they believed that rather than lose them she would do so.

But when she was alone she was depressed.

Was no one faithful? Few, it seemed; but one who was, was her dear Bartolomeo Pergami. What would she have done without him?

The travels continued to Mantua and Ferrara, Bologna, Venice and Rome.

At each of the places Caroline passed through she behaved with a growing abandon. She dressed extravagantly and was heavily rouged and daubed with white lead; she rode through the streets in her fantastic feathered hats, the abundant curls of her many wigs flowing freely; she was a startling figure. But her conduct was more strange than her appearance. She was over-familiar; she walked the streets – ostensibly incognito – picked up children, squatted on the pavements beside them, embraced them and gave them money; she cooked a meal now and then which she sat down and enjoyed with Pergami; she allowed him to come in and out of her bedroom at will, received him when she was in her bath, and took a great pleasure in shocking those about her in every way she could conceive.

Stories of her incredible behaviour were carried to England and the Prince Regent listened to them avidly.

If only it were possible to rid himself of this woman, how happy he would be! Every tale he heard of her was a humiliation.

That most glorious of victories, Waterloo, was being celebrated. They realized at home what this meant. The name of Waterloo would resound through the world for centuries to come; and it was his great general who had achieved it. It was Wellington's victory. The church bells rang out; the guns boomed forth. It was a victory to set beside Trafalgar and Agincourt.

It was a glorious time; and yet he, the Regent, was pestered by his family. There was intransigent Charlotte who caused him much anxiety by her refusal to obey him; but he could manage Charlotte; and at least she was pleasant to look at.

But Caroline! That loathsome creature to whom they had married him. The First Gentleman of Europe, the most elegant and fastidious of gentlemen, to be married to that vulgar creature!

But for her, he could marry again and get a son. Ha, that would put Charlotte's nose out of joint. The arrogant young woman never forgot that crown she saw in her future. She was already seeing herself mounting the throne, which was unfeeling of her, for how could she until he was dead?

If he could rid himself of Caroline . . .

Good God, should it be so difficult? The Delicate Investigation had been a near thing. He might have managed it then. But now she was roaming about the Continent causing scandal wherever she went.

There was fresh news brought to him by his spies. One of the members of her suite had left her because Caroline was planning a trip to the East and this young man, William Burrell, who was a son of Lord Gwydir, had arrived at Brussels. There he met the Duke of Cumberland; but the important factor was that Burrell's servants had chatted to those of the Duke who had reported to their master.

Cumberland had lost no time when he returned in telling the Prince Regent what he wanted to know.

Something must be done. The manner in which Caroline was behaving with this Italian chamberlain of hers and the way she conducted herself generally must surely supply the evidence he needed. His spies were not working hard enough. There was Quentin, for instance, who had allowed himself to be discovered and this incident had naturally warned the guilty ones. Many people had left her suite; men like Hesse, Gell and Craven. Why? Were they afraid of being implicated?

The Prince sent for Lord Castlereagh and told him that he expected action.

'What do you propose?' he demanded. 'These people who are supposed to be working for us give us nothing but gossip. I want proof.'

'I think, sir,' said Castlereagh, 'that we should appoint a man of some standing to work for us. What we need is absolute proof and someone who actually witnesses misconduct. For that we will need someone who is skilled and able to win the Princess's confidence. I suggest that I get in touch secretly with our ambassador in Vienna. If Your Highness will give me leave to write to him – strictly confidentially – I think he will know the man whom we should appoint to act as our agent.'

'Let it be done with all speed,' said the Prince Regent.

Lord Castlereagh wrote to Lord Stewart and headed his letter 'Most private and secret'.

He must appoint a man whom he thought fit to do this service and this agent must be able to give eye-witness proof. English witnesses would be preferred but it would be better not to involve anyone in the Regent's service. The aim was to enable the Prince Regent to be free of a woman who had no decency and was quite unworthy to be his wife. It would be understood that as the object of the evidence would be to justify a divorce, the proofs must be direct and unequivocal.

When Lord Stewart received this communication he studied it very carefully and cast about in his mind for the person who would be able to perform this very delicate duty.

At last he decided on the Baron Frederick d'Ompteda, the Hanoverian envoy to the Pontifical Court.

He wrote to him commanding his presence immediately, and when the Baron arrived acquainted him with what was expected of him.

'You understand,' said Lord Stewart. 'We must have evidence and witnesses of the misconduct of the Princess of Wales. It should not be difficult to obtain in view of the reports we are receiving.'

The Baron replied that he would do his best.

'It is what the Prince Regent expects,' replied Lord Stewart.

The Baron took his leave and set out for Rome.

Caroline had arrived at Como where she decided to settle for a short time while she and Pergami put their heads together, as she said, and planned a tour of the East.

An Italian countess had a charming house to sell on the lake and when Caroline saw it she decided to buy it and make alterations so that it would be a mansion worthy of a princess. Together she and Pergami planned the alterations; and in a short time it had been greatly enlarged, avenues had been planted and as Caroline said, it was indeed her house. She named it the Villa d'Este. 'For,' she explained to Pergami, 'I am descended from that noble family.'

While she was in Rome waiting for the Villa d'Este to be made ready for her occupation she received a letter from the Hanoverian minister, Count von Münster.

'He is the son of my old governess,' she told the maids who were attending to her as she read the letter. One of these was Annette, a rather flighty girl who spent a great deal of time flirting with the male members of the household, and the other was Louise Demont who was of a more serious turn of mind. 'Ah, what a life I used to lead the old lady! I'm afraid I was a very naughty girl. The tricks I got up to! They would surprise you if I were to tell you.'

Louise said demurely that nothing Her Highness told them would surprise them, which amused the Princess.

'You don't know, you cannot imagine,' she declared. 'Ah, poor Countess von Münster! And this is her son writing to me. He's a very important person now in Hanover and he is telling me that Baron Frederick d'Ompteda will be calling on me and he hopes I will receive him. The Baron is the Hanoverian envoy to the Pontifical Court. Well, we must make him welcome, mustn't we? You have been to tell the Baron Pergami that I wish to see him?'

'Madam, shall we wait until you are dressed?'

'No, no, no! Send him now. He can assist at the dressing. It will not be the first time.'

When the Baron Pergami arrived the two girls left him alone with the Princess.

'What a strange way to behave,' said Louise primly. 'I am not surprised that there all these rumours.'

'Are there rumours?' asked Annette.

'Have you not heard of them?'

Annette shook her head. She had little time to listen to rumours; her great concern was a young German who had recently joined the household. Maurice Credé was very attractive and she was sure he had noticed her.

'My dear Baron,' cried the Princess, 'how good of you to call! My good friend the Count von Münster told me that you would be coming. I trust that you will be frequently with us. We are delighted to have you.'

The Baron bowed and told her she was very gracious and she would find that he would take advantage of her goodness.

'Anyone recommended by the Count von Münster will be well received here. Pray sit down and tell me about yourself. I doubt there is any need for me to tell you about myself. You will have heard stories about me and my goings-on.' She broke into loud laughter.

It shouldn't be difficult, thought Ompteda. One only had to look at her and one could well believe all the stories one heard of her. The loose revealing gowns, the painted face, the over-heavy wig, her very manner of sitting so slovenly, somehow suggested immorality. It would be an easy case to prove, this one.

He talked of Hanover and his work in Rome and while he talked Pergami came in.

'This is Baron d'Ompteda, my dear,' said Caroline. 'Dear Baron, you must meet Baron Bartolomeo Pergami, who is my guide, comforter and very good friend. 'Tis so, is it not, my dear? He looks after my affairs so beautifully. Come, sit down and talk with us. Baron d'Ompteda has had such an interesting life!'

The greatest success, thought the Baron. Why, she makes no secret of the relationship. She even asks him to sit down. She must be besotted . . . or crazy.

And Pergami? Yes, he behaved with a proprietorial air. There was no doubt about it. He was her lover. It was going to be the easiest possible case to prove.

She sent for refreshment.

Good God, thought Ompteda, is he going to be allowed to drink with us?

'Theodore, bring us wine,' she commanded.

The man bowed.

'A very good servant,' she said before he was out of earshot. 'Theodore Majocchi. Such a nice fellow! So willing and so grateful to be taken into my household. Many of my English servants have left me, Baron, but I have been well served by Italians and I have found the country so hospitable. Though I intend to leave it for a while. My dear Baron Pergami is working on a detailed plan for us to travel in the East.'

'And Baron Pergami will accompany you, Madam?'

She laughed at Pergami who returned her smile. 'Now he is not suggesting that I should go without you, my dear!'

'It would be impossible,' said Pergami.

Why, thought Ompteda, they are admitting it! My task will be done in a week.

But he was mistaken. His orders had been: optical evidence. This meant that he must see the Princess and Pergami in bed together, or at least some reliable person must.

Two or three weeks passed and still he had not found what he must have. He had artfully questioned the servants and although they were ready to admit that the Princess's conduct was very strange, no one could actually say that he or she had tangible evidence of misconduct.

Caroline left with her household for the Villa d'Este and Ompteda followed them there. After all, his present business

300

lay with Caroline. It was ridiculous. It seemed to him so obvious but where could he find the tangible evidence he sought?

She was free and easy in her manners. She had been to a ball, during her journey through Italy, dressed as Venus – naked from the waist. This had shocked many but she had danced merrily with numerous men in her semi-nude condition. She was immensely proud of her bosom and saw no reason why she should hide her greatest beauty. There was a great deal of gossip about that costume; there was talk about the manner in which she rode about the town, how she would now and then cook a meal and sup alone with Pergami; how he was allowed to talk with her when she was in the bath; how when he was ill she had made him a posset and sat on his bed talking to him, that she had been alone in the bedroom for some time and was still sitting on the bed when the servants entered the room.

All this – but it was not optical evidence. And that was what he must find.

Quite clearly he must enlist the help of her household and he looked round for suitable people.

First there was the manservant, Theodore Majocchi. He had discovered that before he came to serve the Princess he had worked for Count Pino and had been dismissed from his household for stealing. Perhaps a bribe would tempt him.

Maurice Credé was perhaps a better subject because he was in a higher position and would be easier to talk to. He had seen that Credé was an ambitious man; he was rather fond of the woman, it was true, and was actually conducting a liaison with one of the women. That might be useful. The woman might have easy access to the Princess's sleeping apartments. He would keep his eyes on the woman named Annette and there was another who seemed more intelligent, Louise Demont.

He had selected his tools; now he would get to work.

The Princess was leaving for the East in a week or so. He must get evidence before she left because, through Lord Stewart, he was being made aware of the Regent's impatience.

He encountered Maurice Credé in the grounds of the Villa

d'Este and told him that he wished to speak to him . . . secretly.
Credé looked surprised that such an important person as the
Baron should wish for his company, but as he was ambitious
and always looking for advancement he was flattered.

'If you would come to my room, my lord Baron, we could
talk there in comfort.'

Shortly afterwards the Baron went to Credé's room where he
found the young man waiting.

'You must have a great deal of information as to how life
goes on in the Villa,' began the Baron with a faint leer.

'My lord?'

'The Princess is rather free in her manners, is she not? I mean
there must be few secrets which are not known to the members
of her household.'

'The Princess is a very friendly lady. She is kind and generous
to us all.'

'I don't doubt that she pays you well to keep her secrets.'

'Her secrets? I do not understand.'

The Baron laughed.

'Well, scarcely secrets. Who does not know that Pergami is her
lover?'

Credé looked startled. 'I cannot say—'

'Can you not? Is it not obvious? Is he not in and out of her
bedroom and she in and out of his? Is he not present when she
takes a bath – even alone with her? Oh come, my friend, you
are not so innocent as to suppose there is nothing in their relationship but that between a princess and her chamberlain.'

'I do not understand what you want of me.'

'Then I will tell you. I want evidence of the Princess's misconduct with Pergami.'

'From . . . me, my lord?'

'I mean to get it – with your help.'

'But how?'

'There are keys to the Princess's apartments. I want these
keys. I want to have a witness in her bedroom who can testify to
her misconduct.'

'Who . . . are you?'

'That is no concern of yours. You will get those keys for me, and be paid well for your work. Not only will you be paid but the work you do for me can bring you recognition in high places.'

'I – I cannot do this,' stammered Credé.

'You are a fool. Why not?'

'The Princess has been a good mistress to me.'

'You will find even better masters.'

'I am sorry. You must look elsewhere for your ... accomplices.'

'And you, like the good faithful servant you are, will consider it your duty to report this conversation to your mistress?'

'I – I . . .'

'Ah, you hesitate. You show wisdom at last. I have been discovering certain details about you, my dear Credé. There have been little adventures with one of the women here. Little Annette is charming – I agree with you. And there have been too many kisses in dark corners, too much scurrying along corridors in the dead of night. You see your honour extends only in certain directions. I should not want to have to disillusion those who have a high opinion of you but—'

'You mean you will betray me if I do not work with you, if I do not get those keys?'

Ompteda nodded slowly.

'You have the keys?' asked Ompteda.

'Not yet,' replied Credé. 'I must await my opportunity.'

'You fool. She sails in two days' time.'

'That is what makes it so difficult. In any case Pergami is scarcely ever in her apartments. He is so busy arranging for the departure of the *Leviathan*.'

Frustration! groaned Ompteda. Angry reprimands from London, through Hanover. With all this gossip why was it so difficult to provide what was wanted? It should be simple.

There was talk of nothing in the Villa other than of the Princess's imminent departure.

We shall have to wait now for her return, thought Ompteda.

*

Caroline was excited. Nothing was so entrancing as the prospect of seeing new lands.

'If I cannot have children I will have travel,' she announced. She was sorry that so many of her English suite had not wished to accompany her. It was not that they were afraid of dangers from pirates and bandits – and this was by no means an uncertainty – but they were afraid of being called upon by the Prince Regent to give evidence against her. The fact made her laugh and determine to give them as much cause for suspicion as possible.

Pergami was faithful. Dear, dear man! she thought. He was one whom she could trust; and she had engaged his sister, who called herself Countess Oldi, as one of her ladies-in-waiting. She was already fond of the Countess who however was very respectable and inclined to exclaim in surprise at the Princess's antics. But she was Pergami's sister and that was recommendation enough for her. Little Vittorina was to come, dear child; and she and Willikin would be as her own two children. Dr Holland, her English doctor, had left and in his place she had engaged Dr Mochetti, a most charming Italian. There was one Englishman who had joined her suite. He was Captain Robert Hownam and she had engaged him as her private secretary.

Well, it was a happy little company and what did she care if there were few English among them. The Italians were charming and her friends.

She took an affectionate farewell of Baron d'Ompteda and told him that she hoped he would not stop visiting the Villa d'Este during her absence. She was leaving some servants behind and they would care for him.

He accepted the offer with gratitude; he would certainly take advantage of it. During the time she was away he would have to make a plan so that as soon as she returned he could put it into action.

And so Caroline sailed away on the *Leviathan*.

To Sicily first and there was a short stay in Messina. And after that they would sail to Tunis, Malta and Athens.

Louise Demont, whom she had brought with her, told her she

was writing an account of the journey for she believed few princesses would have made it before.

'How terrified I am, Your Highness, that we shall be set upon by bandits in some of these strange places. And what if pirates boarded us!'

The Princess laughed. 'I doubt not that I should be able to persuade them not to harm us.'

'Your Highness can be most persuasive.'

'You must let me read your account of the journey.'

'If Your Highness would so honour me . . .'

Caroline read the accounts which Louise wrote every day and found them interesting. She walked the decks with Pergami and chatted freely with the sailors. She ordered Pergami to arrange for balls on board, which he did, and she danced with all the men in turn.

There never was such a princess, was the comment. And many of them believed the stories they had heard of her.

There were occasions when her suite was in fear of their lives; she was the only one who seemed unafraid. She thrived on adventure.

When she reached Tunis she was welcomed by the Bey and settled down to enjoy a pleasant stay there. 'For,' she commented to Countess Oldi,' I find these barbarians less barbarous than some Christians I have known.' The Bey sent her the finest Arab horses and she made up her mind that she would stay for some time in his pleasant land.

But this happy sojourn was interrupted by the arrival of the Dutch and English fleets. The pirates whose headquarters were in Tunis had been intercepting too many Dutch and British ships and the fleets of these countries had come to demand a settlement.

In the pleasant villa which had been at her disposal Caroline received a visit from Admiral Lord Exmouth who explained the situation to her.

'I'm not afraid of a little conflict,' Caroline told him.

'But Your Highness,' the Admiral replied, 'it would not be possible for you to remain here while these – er . . . negotiations are going on.'

'Why not?'

'There could be trouble.'

'The Bey is my good friend.'

'Today, Madam, but perhaps not tomorrow. I have orders to ensure your departure.'

She argued but it was no use. Her suite were decidedly nervous and for their sake she gave in. Pergami persuaded her to do so.

'It is wisest, Your Highness,' he said.

'I always do as you say, my dear,' she answered.

So from Tunis to Athens and on to Turkey and Constantinople. The stay there was brief owing to an outbreak of plague, and her entourage was by this time longing for the return to Como; and when she went to the Pyramids and had to take with her two hundred soldiers to guard the party as it crossed the desert, even Pergami tried to persuade her to end the tour.

But she laughed at them all. Her eyes flashed with excitement. It was long since she had been so pleased with life.

'At last,' she cried, 'I am doing what I want.'

Poor Willikin was beside her in all her travels. He was too young to realize the dangers through which they passed and seemed to have a blind faith in her. She was the princess whom nothing could harm and as long as he was close to her, he was safe.

And after Cairo, Nazareth where she decided to found an order of knighthood. She called this The Order of St Catherine of Jerusalem: it was to recompense those who had been with her on her pilgrimage to the Holy Land. Pergami received the Order, so did Willikin and her secretary Hownam.

She must of course visit Jericho, and after that started on the return journey.

By the end of October 1816 she was back in the Villa d'Este.

It was good to be back in the Villa. She called Maurice Credé to her and asked if all had been well during her absence.

'Very well, Your Highness,' he told her.

'You look a little sombre,' she told him. 'Is everything going well with you?'

'Very well, Your Highness.'

'Well, I trust you are pleased to see me back.'

Credé bowed. It was her way of talking. And how foolish it was and how it gave her enemies the chance to do what they had been bribed to do.

Pergami went about the house to assure himself that everything was in order, and in Credé's apartments he was surprised to find an extra set of keys.

He examined them closely and ascertained that they were copies of the keys to the Villa. Now for what purpose should Credé provide himself with an extra set of keys? He could ask Credé. But if he did, that would put him on his guard. No, he would do no such thing. Instead he would watch Credé.

Pergami had long been aware that the Princess was under observation. He was her chamberlain and it was his duty to protect her. He was going to find out what Credé was doing with that set of keys.

He did not at this stage mention the affair to Caroline. She was so indiscreet and he imagined what her reaction would be. She would declare that Credé was a very good servant and she refused to harbour any suspicions towards him. He, Pergami, would watch Credé.

He soon discovered that he was leaving his room at night and prowling about the villa. But this was in search of Annette.

An idea struck Pergami. He would dismiss Credé for seducing one of the maids. It was an adequate reason; and then he would confiscate the keys and would have no more need to alarm himself about them.

He summoned Credé.

'I no longer have need of your services,' he told him. 'You are dismissed.'

'But . . . why – what have I done?'

'You are behaving in an improper manner with one of the maids. I cannot accept such behaviour in this household.'

Credé was dumbfounded but Pergami went on, 'I will take all your sets of keys. I know that you have two.'

Alarmed, realizing that his affair with Annette might not be the true reason for his dismissal, Credé handed them over meekly and Pergami was about to ask why he had had the second set made, but he refrained from doing so. He would not in any case believe Credé's explanation.

Credé stammered: 'Is this not rather harsh to dismiss me because—'

'Because of immorality?' Pergami raised his eyebrows and looked Credé full in the face. 'I do not think so. There is enough gossip about the Villa – all false tales. We have therefore to be particularly careful. I have no wish to discuss this matter further. You will leave immediately.'

With that he turned and left the bewildered Credé.

Dismissed from the Princess's service, where could he find such opportunities again? Credé turned over the matter in his mind and decided that it was certainly not merely because of Annette that he had been turned out. There was another reason.

Could it be known that he had been working for Ompteda? If he made a confession of this, if he explained everything to the Princess, if he told her that he wished to be faithful to her and it was for this reason that he was confessing to her, he might be taken back.

The most important thing in the world was for him to be taken back.

He had the answer. It was confession.

He would not tell Pergami because he had a notion that Pergami would not listen, so he wrote to the Chevalier Tomassio, one of the Princess's equerries.

He was dismissed, he wrote, because of an intrigue with one of the Princess's waiting women and he was full of remorse and hoped that the Chevalier would prevail upon the Princess to reinstate him. He deserved what had happened to him because he had been seduced from his duties by Baron d'Ompteda who was attempting to betray her. Baron d'Ompteda had asked him to procure keys which would enable a spy to be secreted in the Princess's bedroom. He had been threatened by the Baron that if he did not obey he would be ruined and when the Baron had offered him money for his services he had given way. He knew that he had been wicked and he trusted that the Chevalier would have pity on him and give him a chance to show his true repentance in his service to the Princess.

When Tomassio received this letter he took it immediately to Pergami.

So this was the answer, thought Pergami. How right he had been to dismiss the man!

Pergami went at once to Caroline and showed her Credé's letter.

'So Your Highness now has clear proof that we are being spied on,' said Pergami.

'Ompteda!' cried the Princess. 'I should not have believed it of him. So Mrs Fitzherbert's husband has appointed him spy-in-chief. This makes me laugh.'

'Perhaps Your Highness's laughter should be tempered with caution.'

'Dear, dear Bartolomeo, you are right as usual.'

The Baron d'Ompteda was asking for an audience with the Princess.

'Tell the Baron,' said Caroline to Pergami, 'that I am having a reception to celebrate my homecoming. I shall expect him to be my guest.'

Pergami looked unhappy.

'My dear good friend, leave this to me,' she soothed him. 'You know how outrageously I can behave when the need arises.'

So she had not learned the lesson, thought Pergami. She was going to receive Ompteda. She was going to snap her fingers at all the intrigues. 'Where will this lead us?' he asked his sister, Countess Oldi.

'She is too warm-hearted, too forgiving,' sighed the Countess. But Caroline was on this occasion determined on revenge.

When Ompteda arrived at the reception she called for Pergami to bring her a huge cardboard key and this she presented to him.

He looked bewildered. 'My dear Baron,' said Caroline,

'knowing your love of keys I give you this one. I hope it will satisfy you.'

Caroline turned to Pergami who was standing by.

'Please give the Baron one cup of coffee, and tell him that he may leave and that I do not wish to see him again.'

Publicly dismissed! Before all these people he was given the great key and a cup of coffee. What humiliation! He understood that someone had betrayed him and immediately thought of Credé. This was disaster for he had failed in his mission. What hope had he now of secreting himself in the Princess's bedchamber!

Captain Hownam sent a challenge to Ompteda. In view of certain facts which had come to light concerning his behaviour he challenged him to a duel. Ompteda was to name the place and he would inform his seconds without delay.

The wretched Ompteda did not reply; he had reported to Hanover and was awaiting instructions. If ever a spy had made a hash of a mission he was that spy.

Caroline meanwhile had heard about the challenge. She did not wish dear Captain Hownam to risk his life for that worthless creature, she declared, so she wrote to the governor of Naples telling him how her privacy had been invaded while she was in Italy and begged him to intervene on her behalf.

Ompteda was ordered to leave the country; and this he did almost gratefully and with the utmost speed.

Tragedy in England

The Villa d'Este had lost all charm for her. Every time she went into her bedroom she wondered whether anyone was spying on her. Her conduct became even more suspicious. She could not help it. It was her nature to behave more indecorously simply because she was suspected of immorality. She walked about with scarcely any clothes on. She allowed Pergami to be in her bedroom when she was there alone. It was some mischievous spirit in her which drove her to such conduct. It was like that occasion when she had pretended to be in labour, knowing perfectly well that in the future it would be believed by many people that she actually had been.

She was misunderstood. She had always been misunderstood. She was not promiscuous. She had dreamed of love and marriage and a family of children. That was what she had wanted. If they had allowed her to marry Töbingen she would have been a happy wife and mother. But they had separated her from him; they had married her to a man who loathed her and made no secret of his loathing, and her brief experience with him had not made her long for more physical relationships. How could she explain this to people when they so clearly believed the opposite? She was affectionate towards those who served her; she was familiar; but she did not seek the ultimate familiarity. No, she had no lover in the full sense of the word, but she liked to pretend she had. It amused her to pretend, also to deceive her husband in a topsy-turvy way. Deceive him into thinking she was an unfaithful wife. She laughed at the thought. He provides enough infidelity for one family, she told herself. What she enjoyed doing was shocking people, making them speculate about the wild and immoral life she led; let them make up fantastic stories about her and her lovers. They were now linking her name with that of Pergami. Let them! She loved Pergami in her way. He was a good chamberlain who managed her affairs with skill; he amused her; he was a very good friend. But he was not her lover and there was no sexual relationship between them. Nor would there be with any man.

There was something she kept from people. She did not want to think too much about it herself, but there was a mysterious recurring pain in the region of her stomach which at times she found almost unendurable. Then it would pass and she would attempt to forget it. She had mentioned it to her doctor but he could not say what it was and like her, hoped it would pass. She was fifty-two years of age. When she removed her wig and the white lead and rouge she looked like an old woman. Scarcely one to indulge in riotous behaviour with lovers of all classes.

Poor Caroline! she would say to herself. You dreamed of so much and you realized so little. The next best thing was to pretend to the world that one lived gaily, unconventionally and scandalously.

It amused her. So forget encroaching age, alarming symptoms of pain. Slap on the rouge and the feathers, the pink tights and the white lead – and pretend. It was the next best thing.

She left the Villa d'Este and came to Pesaro where she took a villa overlooking the Adriatic Sea.

She missed the Villa d'Este because she had made it so beautiful. How dared he send spies to attempt to trap her! But for that she would still be there. He was not content with refusing to live with her, not content with humiliating her in every way possible; he must make trouble among her friends and servants by setting them to spy on her.

She was angry with him. But if he wanted scandal, he should have it. The more outrageously she behaved the more amused she was.

'He'll hear of this,' she cried gleefully. 'Let him. I want him to. He'll be shocked and mortified. Let him be. Wasps leave their stings in the wounds they inflict. And so do I.'

She was entertaining lavishly. She rode out in her shell-like chariot; she would sit bowing, smiling, exposing her short fat legs in their pink tights. She talked to all kinds of people and when the children ran after her carriage she threw money to them. People gathered along the roads to see her pass; she was the wild Princess of Wales.

The Empress Marie Louise came to Parma and had taken up a brief residence there. She was in a similar position to Caroline, wandering the Continent looking for solace; and with her was her son who had been King of Rome, and as Caroline rarely went anywhere without Willikin in attendance, the similarity was increased.

Marie Louise was different from Caroline in one respect though; she was very conscious of her royalty and loved to stand on ceremony, a trait which aroused Caroline's spirit of mischief. The more regal Marie Louise became the more ribald Caroline would grow.

The climax to their friendship came when the ex-Empress invited the Princess to a dinner party at her mansion in Parma. It was a very ceremonial occasion. Caroline had been rouged and leaded and appeared in multi-coloured feathers.

She was received by the ex-Empress and the guests were made to understand that they should leave the two royal ladies to talk together before joining them in the banqueting hall. She and Caroline sat together before a fire in two ornate chairs. Caroline's short legs did not reach the floor; she was very bored with the Empress's conversation which was mainly concerned with the past grandeur and, as she moved impatiently in her chair, tipped it back and falling with it, remained convulsed with laughter while her legs waved wildly in the air.

The Empress shrieked; several of her suite came running to see what was wrong; and the sight of the Princess of Wales toppled on the floor, her skirts about her waist, her legs waving in the air, so dumbfounded them that they could only stand and stare.

The Empress kept repeating again and again: 'Madame, you alarm me.'

And Caroline unnecessarily prolonged the occasion by remaining in her inelegant and ridiculous position.

She was at length helped to her feet, convulsed with laughter, her face scarlet under rouge, her wig awry.

She insisted on repeating the story at dinner, her accent thickening as she explained the situation.

'I fell mit mine legs in the air. I stay just like this and she—' She nodded to the Empress. 'All she can say is: *"Mon Dieu! Comme vous m'avez effrayé."*'

The incident was repeated. With anyone else it would have been unbelievable, but not with Caroline.

She thought often of her daughter. Dearest Charlotte would soon give birth to a child. She longed for news of her. Charlotte wrote to her now and then and she was always the affectionate daughter. Caroline was melancholy sometimes thinking of her.

She would repeat again and again to Pergami the story of how Charlotte had left her father to run away to her mother.

'She loved me, my little Charlotte. There was no doubt of that. Nothing he could do could alter it.'

Dear headstrong creature, she had jilted the Prince of Orange and married a Prince whom she loved – Leopold of Saxe-Coburg.

Charlotte had written to her of her joy in the marriage. Leopold was handsome and good; he was her choice and she was the happiest of princesses.

Happy indeed! thought Caroline and rejoiced.

She would talk of her daughter to the Countess Oldi with whom she had become very friendly during her eastern travels.

'I'm so happy because my dearest daughter will know a joy that has been denied to me. She loves her husband and he her, and I think that must be the greatest blessing in the world. I missed it, dear Oldi, and I am so happy that she has found it. How can I be sure? Oh, I know my Charlotte. She would never pretend. Her letters overflow with happiness. It makes me laugh aloud just to read them – real laughter this time, Oldi – the laughter that means you are happy.'

The married pair, she learned, had acquired Claremont as their country house and there they were spending the happy months of waiting. For Charlotte had written the glad news: she was going to have a child.

'Dearest Charlotte,' mused Caroline. 'To think of my baby with a little baby. This is all she needs to make her happiness complete. I hope this child will be the first of many. I can imagine the excitement in England about the birth. You see, this child could be a King or Queen of England. The bells will ring; the guns will boom; and there'll be bonfires in the streets. The people loved my Charlotte. And her father – oh, he'll be pleased too and so will the old Begum though she disapproved of darling Charlotte – because she was my daughter, I suppose. And Charlotte disapproved of her. But she'll be glad. And the King – poor mad King. I don't suppose he will even know. I could weep to think of him. He was the only one in the whole family who showed me kindness. Oh, it makes me wish I was there. For the first time, Oldi, I wish I were back in England.'

Each day when she rose she would sit at the window overlooking the sea. 'I wonder how Charlotte is,' she would say. 'Her time must be near. She will write to me and tell me all about her little baby. Poor darling, I hope it is not a difficult labour.'

When any messengers came the first thing she thought of was letters from England.

'Any day now,' she said to the Countess. 'It must be soon. Unless of course she miscalculated. How like Charlotte. But over this I should not have thought so. She has become more serious since her marriage – I sense it in her letters. Fancy! It is three years since I saw my daughter. There'll be news soon. She'll write. I shall hear all the news about the most wonderful baby in the world.'

And still she waited to hear.

She would never forget that morning.

She liked to glance through the English newspapers and had them brought to her. They lay on her table for some time before she picked them up; and then she settled idly to skim through them.

She opened one and stared at the page. No, she was dreaming. This could not be true.

'On November 5 after a long labour the Princess Charlotte was delivered of a fine large dead boy. She died shortly afterwards.'

Birth and death

The whole country was in mourning for the Princess Charlotte. The Prince Regent shut himself in his apartments. He could face nobody – not even Lady Hertford. He wept bitterly. He forgot his disagreements with his daughter; he only saw her now as his beloved child.

Sir Richard Croft, the *accoucheur,* had come to him in an almost demented state. The Prince had tried to comfort him and himself at the same time.

'They tell me the child was perfect . . . perfect . . . and a boy.'

'It was so, sir. And his features were undoubtedly those of your family.'

The Prince turned away and wiped his eyes.

'I cannot bear to think of it. Pray leave me to my grief.'

Sir Richard went away and in the streets the people recognized his carriage and booed him. The rumours were already spreading through the town that he had been careless; he had not done his job as he should; he was responsible for the death of their beloved princess.

The Regent gave way to tears and at the back of his mind was the thought: It is even more important now to rid myself of that woman. It's not too late. But for her I could marry again, get another son. They must bring me news of her misconduct. Why can't the obvious be proved?

But it is necessary now . . . *necessary.*

The Queen was at Bath taking the waters. She had been unwell lately, and her doctors had suggested the visit. Her daughter Elizabeth had accompanied her and they had taken three houses in Sydney Place for themselves and their attendants.

She was glad that her relationship with the Prince Regent was better than it had been for many years. The old battles were done with. He had mellowed, she told herself, and perhaps she was no longer seeking power. It was all his now, and her feelings towards him were like those she had had when he was a child, when he had been her favourite.

He had married that odious woman and she would like to see him free of her; not that he needed to marry now that he had a child and this child was about to bear another. She hoped it would be a boy which would please the people and make them love their royal family again. There was nothing like a child to do that. She remembered how they used to crowd round young George when he was a baby and cheered when he was wheeled into the Park.

How different they were towards him now. Only a few months ago when he returned from the opening of parliament the mob had surrounded his carriage and thrown mud and all sorts of ill-smelling rubbish at it. He had sat in it, ignoring the smell, his scented handkerchief at his nose, a figure of elegance and disdain. Some people said that a bullet had been fired at him although the sound of it was not heard, so loudly was the mob shouting. They found a hole in the woodwork of the coach, though.

Such scenes were frightening. One could never be sure when the mob would get out of hand.

But all that was over for a while. The people would be thinking of the new royal child. The bells would be ringing out and there would be general rejoicing. She hoped she might have a hand in bringing up the child. It certainly should not be left to flighty Charlotte.

She was eagerly awaiting news of the birth. It must be soon now.

Lady Ancaster, one of her ladies-in-waiting, had come to read to her as she did at this time every day. How strange she looked.

'Is anything wrong, Lady Ancaster?'

'Your Majesty—' Lady Ancaster had begun to sob.

'It is Charlotte – is it?'

Lady Ancaster tried to speak but could not do so.

'Something has gone wrong. The child—'

Lady Ancaster looked at her helplessly.

'Born dead . . .' murmured the Queen.

And she knew the answer.

'Charlotte . . .'

Still that look of blank misery.

'No! No!' cried the Queen.

But she knew it was true. Charlotte was dead.

Lady Ancaster was startled into action. She ran to get assistance, for the Queen had fainted.

They were saying in the streets that wicked old Queen Charlotte had planned this. She had always hated her young namesake. Why should one so young and healthy die in childbirth?

And what had Sir Richard Croft to do with it?

Why, the old Queen and the *accoucheur* had plotted together. They were determined that Charlotte should die so they had poisoned her. Sir Richard had neglected her. He had bled her too much. He had weakened her when he should have strengthened her. Who was Sir Richard Croft anyway? The son of a chancery clerk who had become a fashionable doctor.

Wait till they could lay their hands on the old Queen. Wait until they could meet Richard Croft face to face. They had been hoping for a royal birth and the accompanying festivities – and all they would get was a funeral.

Sir Richard Croft blew his brains out and the people were satisfied. After that there was no more talk about the murder of Princess Charlotte and her child.

When the funeral was over the Prince Regent retired to Brighton, there to think of the future. He wandered through his ornate rooms and took comfort from all the splendour which was his creation. And all the time he was haunted by a shadow – the shadow of the woman who was his wife. While he was married to her he would know no peace and he longed as never before to be rid of her.

Why would no one help him? Why was it impossible to find just the evidence they needed?

He was determined that he would rid himself of Caroline. No price was too high to be paid to be free of that woman.

He would marry again. This time he would choose his bride.

He often thought of Maria. The greatest mistake of his life might have been marrying Caroline but to leave Maria was almost as grave. They should have been together. She would

318

have comforted him now. He still thought of her at times like these. Lady Hertford – nor any of them – had ever had the solace Maria had to offer.

But it was too late to think of Maria now. She was older than he was and he was no longer young. But not too old to beget a child. And he must. The country needed an heir and he must provide it.

And how?

Now here he was back to the beginning.

He must rid himself of that woman.

He went to see the Queen. She received him with great affection. It was pleasant to contemplate that the enmity between them was over. Now they were in perfect accord and she knew why he had come to her.

'If I died tomorrow, the Duke of York would be King.'

'With a barren wife who is not long for this world,' remarked the Queen.

'And William – he's living with his large family of Fitz-clarences at Bushey.'

'He should marry and so should Kent,' said the Queen. 'This sad affair has brought home to us how necessary it is for every member of the family to do his duty.'

'I will summon them all,' said the Regent. 'Their duty must be pointed out to them.'

'So many children,' mused the Queen, 'and not an heir among them.'

'If Charlotte and the child had lived . . .'

'Ah, yes, you did your duty, painful as it was.'

'Painful, indeed,' echoed the Prince.

'I always thought it was a pity you took that one instead of my niece Louise. I knew it was wrong at the time. Alas!'

'Alas!' repeated the Prince. Then he added briskly: 'I will speak to my brothers. They must marry without delay. As for myself—'

'As for yourself.'

'I don't give up hope. She is behaving in the most outrageous manner. We must have proof soon.'

'Oh, pray God it will come,' said the Queen piously.

It was not difficult to persuade the Dukes of the need for them to find wives as quickly as possible. They were no longer very young, any of them – and marriage was a duty of which they had been very neglectful. The Duke of Kent was a little disturbed because he was devoted to his mistress, Madame St Laurent, with whom he had been living for the last twenty-seven years; but like his brother, the Duke of Clarence, he was prepared to do his duty.

Very soon the public learned that there was to be a double wedding at Kew. The Duke of Clarence had been accepted by Princess Adelaide of Saxe-Coburg Meiningen, who was very beautiful and thirty years younger than he was, so it seemed likely that they would be able to provide the country with its heir. But just in case they were unable to, the Duke of Kent had chosen for his bride Mary Louisa Victoria, a widow of the Prince of Leiningen.

In the Queen's drawing room overlooking the gardens, the double wedding took place – two middle-aged bridegrooms with young wives; at least Mary Louisa Victoria was not old and Adelaide was thirty years younger than the Duke of Clarence.

It was to Clarence and Adelaide that everyone looked for their heir; neither of the husbands was in love with his wife nor the wives with their husbands; the great purpose behind these marriages was to get an heir quickly, and they knew it.

They were fired with ambition, all four of them; and when the Duke of Kent looked at his comely plump widow he was certain that he and she had as much chance as William and this pretty young girl from Saxe-Coburg Meiningen.

And the Prince Regent aş he led the congratulations when the ceremony was over was sentimentally dreaming of a bride with whom he would defeat the ambitions of these four people: a beautiful woman – a combination of Perdita Robinson, Maria Fitzherbert, Lady Jersey and Lady Hertford – yet subtly different from any of them – young, tender, adoring. He would marry her and together they would produce a son who would be heir to the throne.

There was time yet if only . . .

But here he was back to that perpetual and frustrating matter. He must be rid of her soon.

Marriage was in the air. The princesses saw no reason why their brothers should be married and not they. All this time they had lived under the direction of the Queen, not allowed to stray very far from the closest supervision as though they were children. Their youth was past. Charlotte had married the Prince of Würtemburg and in spite of the mystery which surrounded her husband's first wife appeared to be living happily; Amelia had died at the age of twenty-seven unmarried. It was so unfair, said the princesses, never to have been given a chance of marriage.

Mary announced that she would marry her cousin, the Duke of Gloucester. He was a little simple and known as 'Silly Billy', but she did not care about that. She was past forty anyway and was going to seize this last chance.

The Prince Regent had never been averse to his sisters marrying. Had he been in control earlier he would have done his best to find husbands for them. It was the King who had hated the thought of their marrying. So now no obstacle was put in their way.

Princess Elizabeth was determined not to be left out and when an opportunity came from Homburg she made up her mind to take it. The Prince of Homburg was very fat – but Elizabeth was by no means slim. 'And at least,' she said to Mary, 'he is a husband.'

The Queen was against the marriage. She saw her daughters disappearing one by one. She had grown so accustomed to having them all about her; and they had made up to a very large extent for the trouble her sons had caused her.

She reasoned with Elizabeth, but Elizabeth for once opposed the Queen who at length agreed because she knew that the Regent would be on his sister's side and would say that if she wished to marry she should do so.

So the marriage took place.

The ceremony in the throne room was very formal and the Queen felt very sad to lose yet another daughter.

The Prince Regent was unable to attend the ceremony because he was ill, and there was no doubt that Charlotte's death had upset him greatly. He would be well again, thought the Queen, if only he could be rid of that odious woman. If it were *his* marriage we were celebrating to a young fertile woman how pleased I should be!

The waters of Bath had done little to alleviate the Queen's illness and although she had attempted to ignore this during the various marriage celebrations she knew that she was very ill indeed.

I'm getting old, she thought. I'm seventy-five and have had my life. I must expect now to prepare myself to go.

She wished that she could have been with the King. He would have been most sympathetic. But he, poor sad man, was living through his clouded days at Windsor and he would not understand if she talked to him. And if he did, it would only upset him.

He never loved me, she thought; but he had some affection for me. He respected me. He knew that like him I tried to do my duty.

She thought she would go to Windsor in any case because she would like to be near him; but first of all she would go to Kew. Dear little Kew, the palace which she had loved more than any because it had been like home to her. Yes, it was fitting that she should first go and say goodbye to Kew.

She was comforted in some degree to be there again – the dear Green and the Strand and those houses where the members of the household had lodged because there had been no room for them in the Queen's Lodge. Oh, those little rooms, the numerous cupboards and cubby holes! How draughty it had been in the passages and the rooms had always been overheated. The chapel had been icy too. In the winter everyone had caught cold there. Why did she love the place? Because it was unlike a royal palace, because it was homely, because it would always be 'dear little Kew'. Here the children had been young. The Prince of

Wales – what a bad boy – creeping out of his apartments after dusk to meet young women in the garden. He had always been a source of delight and trouble to her: her first-born, her favourite. Now, thank God, they had at last come to an understanding.

She would be loath to leave Kew. She would not say this to anyone, but she felt that if she did so, she would never see it again.

She was glad that the Princess Royal seemed to be making a success of her marriage; and Elizabeth wrote happily from Homburg. The girls should have been married before. But the King would not have it and she must confess that she encouraged him in this because she wanted them about her. The sons they had been unable to control. They had gone off and had their matrimonial adventures – disastrous ones – but the girls had been denied those opportunities. And now Elizabeth and Mary as well as Princess Royal were married, but none of them young.

It was no use regretting now. What was done was done.

She was ill . . . seriously ill at dear little Kew. She was aware of her daughters, Mary and Augusta, constantly at her bedside. The Prince Regent came too. He held her hand and wept, and she was happy.

More than anyone in the world she had loved him. The period when they had hated each other and had worked so violently against each other seemed now like a temporary madness which had come to her and to which he had responded.

It was love really, she told herself. I wanted him to love me and I was jealous because he loved others more, and so I pretended to hate him and I behaved as though I did.

But that was all past and now he was with her, at her bedside, holding her hand.

Sophia was not there because Sophia was ill. Otherwise she would have been there with her sisters.

Her sons came to visit her and she was vaguely aware of them: the new bridegrooms whose wives might well give birth to an heir to the throne.

But in her heart she hoped George would be the one to do this. If they could get rid of that woman . . .

She knew how that matter occupied the mind of her dearest one.

All though the week the Prince Regent's carriage was seen going to and from Kew, and it was recognized that the Queen was nearing her end; and on a dark November day her family gathered in her bedroom for the physicians had warned them that the end was very near.

She had insisted on being put in her chair and she sat there breathing heavily. Her family was with her and the Prince Regent was seated beside her; her hand was in his.

And so she died.

It was fitting that it should be Kew Palace where she should lie in state. The Prince Regent was so affected that he had almost fainted at the moment of her death. He was overwhelmed by remorse for all the enmity which had been between them, sorrow that he could no longer let her know that she was restored to his affections and a great relief that they had parted good friends.

He wished that she could have lived longer to see him parted from the woman he had married. He believed that if she could have seen that, if he could have married, she would have forced herself to live and see his heir.

But it was not to be.

Her coffin was carried by torchlight from Frogmore to Windsor and there she was buried in the royal vault.

This was a period of momentous events in the royal family – for births and deaths must be so called.

The Prince was tiring of Lady Hertford. She was frigid and no one knew whether or not the friendship was platonic. What he needed in his life was comfort and affection. He did not get this from Lady Hertford, whose greatest concern was to protect her reputation and to lead him in politics.

For a time he had been fascinated, but with the loss of his mother he needed a woman who could be loving, affectionate and uncritical.

He thought often of Maria. He would always think of Maria. But Maria had retired from the scene: she wanted no more upheavals in her life. She had diverted her affection to Mary Seymour, little Minney. She was old – older than he was and although young girls had never appealed to him and he had chosen one grandmother after another, he wanted someone whose beauty could inspire him.

Marriage! He thought continually of it. Which always brought him back to the same problem.

There was another birth in the family. Not, it was believed, a very important one this. In May of the year 1819 the Duchess of Kent produced a daughter.

She was called Alexandrina Victoria.

The Clarences had not been so fortunate as the Kents. The Duchess had borne two children neither of whom had survived. Meanwhile the Duke of Kent gloated over his plump, healthy little daughter whose looks already showed her to be a true member of the House of Hanover.

He was delighted, he remarked to his Duchess, that little Victoria had a chance – a very fair chance. York could not produce an heir now; and it seemed that Clarence could not. And if they did not there was nothing between their own little Victoria and the throne.

'But a girl,' said the Duchess, her eyes sparkling at the prospect.

'The English are not averse to women rulers. There was Elizabeth. There was Anne. They were both more popular than any George has ever been.'

He spoke regretfully. He had wanted to christen Victoria 'Elizabeth', but the names had been chosen for her and she was Victoria after her mother.

'I have a feeling,' said the Duke, 'that what I hope might well come to pass. It's just a feeling but it's very strong.'

Shortly afterwards he took his wife and child to Sidmouth which he thought would be healthy for little Victoria. It was a rainy season and on several occasions the Duke, who was fond of walking, was out in torrential downpours, as a result of which he caught cold; inflammation of the lungs set in and in a few days he was dead.

Little Victoria was fatherless but a step nearer to the throne.

And within a few weeks she had taken even another step forward. The King, whose mind had given way so many years ago but whose physical health had remained very, very good, suddenly became ill.

He had no will to live. In those rare faintly lucid moments when he was aware of what had happened to him, he had always wished for death.

He need wish no longer.

Six days after the death of the Duke of Kent he too was dead.

The Prince Regent had become George IV.

Return to England

Since the death of her daughter Caroline had lived a little more soberly. She often reproached herself for not being in England at the time of Charlotte's confinement.

'A mother should be with her daughter,' she told Lady Anne Hamilton who had joined her and was proving to be one of her most faithful attendants.

'It was not easy in Your Highness's place,' Lady Anne reminded her.

'I wonder whether I should have stayed.'

She was not at all sure and it was a question no one could answer.

She had heard, long after the events, of the marriages in the family and of the Clarences' disappointments and the birth of the Kents' little girl.

'That is our trouble, my dear,' she said. 'Everything is political. My brothers-in-law married because they must, not because they wished to. They were happier with their mistresses. Sometimes I think it is a mistake that royalty should marry royalty, for royalty often hate each other. My father hated my mother because there was a woman he loved and whom he would have preferred to marry. As for the Prince of Wales he was already married to Maria Fitzherbert and would have been a happier man if he had stayed married to her. But royalty demanded that he marry me – and you see what a merry pickle we have got ourselves into.'

Messengers arrived from England and Caroline, eager for news, had them brought to her at once.

'A letter from Brougham?' She turned pale. That must mean that something very important was happening in England.

She read it through and said: 'Oh, my God.'

She gazed at Anne and went on: 'He tells me that the King is very ill and not expected to live. It may even be that at this moment our Prince Regent is King of England.'

Lady Anne looked startled and Caroline could see that she was thinking that she was talking to the Queen of England.

She laughed. 'Oh, yes,' she said, 'it may well be that I am your Queen, my dear. That poor man! How he suffered! And he was so kind to me. No one else was. He was a good man. You see I say "was" for something tells me he has gone. It is not bad – for him at least. He will go to heaven to meet his old Begum – if she arrived there, which I much doubt. She could be a wicked old woman at times. Oh dear, but think what this means to us who are left. I – the Queen of England! That is why Brougham writes to me. He will be in communication he says. You can be sure he will. He has my interests close to his heart. Only because they are your own, my dear Brougham. *You* have never deceived me. Ah, my dear, I can see that our travels will soon be over.'

'You would return to England?'

'My dear, if I am Queen of England is not my place in that country? You doubt it? Let me tell you this, when the Prince Regent becomes George IV he will have to understand that he has a Queen. I shall certainly go back to England for I am indeed the Queen.'

Brougham knew a great deal more than Caroline. He knew that the new King was going to do everything in his power to obtain a divorce. He was a very ambitious man and one of his great stumbling blocks to advancement was the Lord Chancellor Lord Eldon who refused him a silk gown. Brougham saw that if he became the Queen's attorney he would automatically take silk and there would be other advantages too. He was therefore determined to act as Caroline's legal adviser and to be in at the start.

While she was aware of his ambitions Caroline was not blind to his talents. He was a brilliant man and it was purely the animosity of the Chancellor which was preventing his rising in his career. While she knew that he would be working for Brougham rather than her, she realized the advantage of such a man's advice and was ready to appoint him.

She had learned of the King's death through Brougham; she realized that she would never have been officially told, which was an indication of what treatment she might expect when she reached England.

All the same, she insisted, I shall go.

The King was happier than he had been for a long time, because he was in love. He had found the perfect woman in the Marchioness of Conyngham. Fair, fat and fifty, mother of five grown-up children, easy-going, gentle, adoring – she was exactly what he had been looking for. She was completely uncritical and content only to listen and admire.

He was behaving as he had in his youth. He would sit and gaze at her in wonderment. He might have been a boy of seventeen. That this was a rather ridiculous attitude for an extremely plump and ageing monarch was left in no doubt, for the cartoonists and lampoonists were soon busy. She never argued, only agreed; she looked pretty; her blue eyes were still beautiful and her brow had never been wrinkled in concentration. How different from the waspish Lady Jersey, the frigid Lady Hertford and the hot-tempered Maria with her obsession about her religion and right and wrong.

Yes, he was happy. And the Marquis of Conyngham was the most complaisant of husbands. He raised no objections. He accepted the honours handed lavishly to him and his children as graciously and gratefully as his wife accepted the jewels which the King delighted to give her.

He begged her to make full use of his palaces, his carriages, his horses. They were all at her disposal.

'Do everything you please,' he entreated her, 'and then you will please me.'

And Lady Conyngham replied as he would have expected her to that only if she pleased him could she be pleased.

He wept. She did so much to make him happy in the most trying circumstances, he told her.

And the trying circumstances were across the Channel threatening to arrive and break his peace at any moment.

Queen! Why should that woman have that proud title? How much better it would suit dear Lady Conyngham. And yet even she could not give him children.

He struck Caroline's name from the Liturgy and he reiterated to his ministers: I must have a divorce.

A divorce, thought Brougham. That would involve a case – a costly case, a case in which he would defend the Queen and as he reckoned himself to be the ablest lawyer in England, he would win. What fame that would bring! He could laugh at Eldon then for denying him silk.

A case for divorce. It was a situation greatly to be desired.

Meanwhile Caroline had appointed him her attorney-general which meant that he was now called to the Bar. This was the first step forward. Lord Liverpool who was Prime Minister pramptly called on Brougham and told him that the King was very anxious that the Queen should not return to England.

'As her attorney you should advise her to remain abroad.'

Accusations had been brought against Her Majesty, pointed out Brougham. Did the Prime Minister suggest that she should make no attempt to clear her name?

'The accusations do not appear to be without some foundation,' was the grim reply.

'They are of such a grave nature,' was Brougham's answer, 'that it is unwise to speak of them. It might be that it will be necessary to have Her Majesty's name cleared publicly.'

Lord Liverpool understood. That was what Brougham wanted. Clearly he was visualizing a *cause célèbre* with himself in the centre of it – a chance to show the world what a brilliant lawyer he was.

'Do you realize that if it came to that point it would be the Queen versus the King?'

'I do not see what else it could be.'

'It is not easy to stand against kings.'

'Not easy, I agree,' said Brougham.

'I bring a proposition to you. You may offer her £50,000 if she will live abroad.'

'£50,000!' said Brougham, lifting his eyebrows.

'A comfortable sum of money.'

'Very comfortable.'

'If she is wise she will take it. I look forward to hearing her comments.'

When Liverpool had left Brougham thought: £50,000 and no case.

That did not suit him at all. He decided he would not pass on this information to his royal client.

Caroline was making her preparations to return to England. There had been a subtle change in the treatment which had been accorded her by those who had hitherto been her friends. She guessed what had happened. It had been suggested to them that their hospitality and friendship for her meant that they were behaving in an unfriendly manner to the King of England. How he hates me! she thought. How he hounds me!

And what was he doing at home? Rumours came to her and she did not really need to be told. He was preparing a case against her because he was going to attempt to divorce her. 'Let him,' she cried. 'He'll not succeed.'

She laughed in her usual way with Lady Anne Hamilton. Dear creature, she thought, she had served her well in England and when she knew that her English attendants had made excuses to desert her had come out to be with her. Lady Charlotte Campbell had married a Mr Edward Bury two years before and she could not expect her to desert her new husband to serve an old mistress. But she was delighted with Lady Anne, for in her she found a true friend.

She discussed her thoughts freely.

'He will try to divorce me, dear Lady Anne. He's going to try to prove my adultery and he'll fail. I'll tell you a secret. I did commit adultery once. Shall I tell you with whom?'

Lady Anne looked startled and Caroline burst into loud laughter. 'It was with Mrs Fitzherbert's husband.'

Lady Anne was relieved. Like everyone else in the Princess's suite she had feared that her indiscretions meant she had at last taken Pergami as her lover.

If she is innocent, Lady Anne reassured herself, they will be able to prove nothing against her.

She felt very relieved.

Caroline's party had left Italy and were travelling through Burgundy when Sir Matthew Wood arrived. She received him with great pleasure for he had been a friend of Sir Samuel Whitbread and since Sir Samuel's suicide had written to her frequently.

Here was a man whom she knew she could trust. He had sent his son William Page Wood to her some weeks before because young William was a linguist and Sir Matthew guessed that while some of her Italian staff stayed with her, she would not bring Pergami to England with her, and that she would therefore need an interpreter.

Caroline was well aware that the scandals which had been circulating about her mainly concerned Pergami and she realized that to bring him to England would be construed as an admission that he was her lover, for in England she would naturally have no need for an Italian chamberlain. Pergami was well aware of this and was reconciled to the parting. He had planned to accompany her to Calais and then return to Italy.

Therefore the services of young Wood were very desirable, particularly as he was a charming boy who had been told by his father to serve her to the best of his ability.

So now it was doubly pleasant to greet Sir Matthew.

He had come, he said, to escort her back to England.

'My dear, dear friend. I know I can rely on you.'

He was a little shocked by her appearance. She looked as rakish as ever but even the lavish application of rouge could not hide the change in her. Sir Matthew believed that the reports she must have heard were giving her sleepless nights.

She was even more talkative than usual; she laughed louder. She was aware of this. It was because of the pain which was recurring more frequently.

Sir Matthew told her a case was being prepared against her and she would have to answer it when she returned to England.

'I'm ready,' she replied.

'The people will be on your side,' he reassured her. 'I am certain of that. The crown has not brought His Majesty popularity.'

'That's strange. They like me better than they like him. And what he wants more than anything is to be loved. That's what we all wish, I suppose. But he more than most.'

And she thought: I might have loved him. He might have loved me.

Why was it we never had a chance? And now it can never be. We have come to a sad pass when he so wishes to be rid of me that he will take up the fight against me in public.

Brougham had arrived in St Omer. It now seemed to him imperative that the Queen should not return to England . . . yet. They were unprepared. He wanted time. Moreover the King's ministers had now made an offer of £50,000 a year and for this there were conditions.

He could no longer hide them from Caroline and set them before her.

'The conditions,' he told the Queen, 'are that you are no longer named Queen of England and that you have no title which belongs to the royal family. You shall not live in any part of England. You shall not even visit England.'

There was a note in this letter which was ominous: 'If the Queen sets foot in England proceedings will immediately be taken against her.'

When Caroline heard this she was furious. How dared they! They had always treated her unfairly but this was insulting.

Did they think to frighten her?

Brougham, who now wished her not to hurry back to England yet, tried to persuade her not to be rash.

But her anger was aroused.

She was going to return to England. She was going to claim her rights.

She sat down and wrote a somewhat peremptory note to Lord Liverpool:

I now take the opportunity of communicating to Lord Liverpool my intention of arriving in London next Saturday the 3rd June. And I desire that Lord Liverpool will give proper orders that one of the royal yachts should be in readiness at Calais to convey me to Dover; and likewise he would be pleased to signify to me His Majesty's intentions as to what residence is to be allotted to me either for a temporary or a permanent habitation ...

Caroline the Queen

On the sunny noon of 6 June Caroline arrived at Dover.

She had said goodbye to Pergami, who had returned to Pesaro where he bought a house and busied himself with clearing up Caroline's affairs there.

Sir Matthew Wood had taken over Pergami's duties and she was now as affectionate towards him as she had been to Pergami.

No one at Dover had been advised of her arrival and when the commander of the garrison came down to the shore to discover who this important personage was and found her to be the Queen of England he ordered a royal salute to be fired. The people came running out of their houses and when the rumour went round that the Queen had come they cheered her and were determined to give her a good welcome.

She had not come to stay, she told them in her friendly manner; she was on her way to London. And after a brief stay in town she set out for Canterbury.

News had reached Canterbury that the Queen was on her way and as it was dark by the time she and her suite arrived the townsfolk had lined the streets and stood with flambeaux to light her way and cheer her as she came. The landlord at the Fountain Inn had prepared a feast for the travellers and there they stayed the night. As they ate Caroline heard the shouts: 'Long live the Queen.'

'Ah,' she cried, 'at least the people are glad to see me.'

The next day there was waving of flags and more loyal greetings as she set out for London.

All along the route she was vociferously welcomed. At Gravesend and Deptford eager helpers were waiting to change the horses. The people of Blackheath were particularly determined to show her how glad they were to have her back. Many remembered her kindness to them when she had lived among them.

Some of them joined the party and rode with her into the capital.

She had received no reply from Lord Liverpool and no place had been put at her disposal. Sir Matthew however had suggested that she make use of his house in South Audley Street until some suitable residence was offered her.

Into London she rode, triumphant and acclaimed. Next to her in her open carriage was Sir Matthew Wood and opposite her Lady Anne Hamilton. In the first of the carriages which followed sat Willikin, and other members of her entourage followed, some of them Italians, who looked on the scene with wonder.

Flags were waved and the people shouted long life to her.

This was indeed an affectionate welcome home.

There was one spectator who looked on in horror. The King had gone to one of the small windows on the top floor of Carlton House where he would be able to watch unseen. He had asked his sister Mary to accompany him so that he would have a member of the family at his side.

'Oh, God,' he whispered, 'how vulgar she is – even more so than I remembered! I cannot accept her as the Queen. The thought that she is considered to be my wife nauseates me.'

Mary whispered comfort and the magic word: Divorce.

'We'll get the evidence,' he said. 'There can't be a doubt of it. Soon I shall be free.'

On trial

The King was determined that no time should be wasted. On the very day Caroline had set foot on English soil, Liverpool in the House of Lords and Castlereagh in the Commons read a message from the King.

This stated that His Majesty thought it necessary to give to the House of Lords certain documents concerning the conduct of the Queen. This was a painful thing to do but the conduct of the Queen gave him no alternative.

Brougham, who was present in the Commons when the message was read, lost no time in seeing Caroline and compiling an answer in which she stated that she had been induced to return to England to clear her name for she was aware of the calumnies which had been invented against her. Her name had been omitted from the Liturgy; she had been denied a royal residence; she had been insulted at home and abroad. Efforts had been made to prejudice the world against her and she had been judged without trial. Only trial and conviction could justify what had been done to her.

Liverpool and members of the Government were disturbed by her attitude. They could see that a trial could bring the monarchy into disrepute. The King's private life had been far from moral and it was not so long ago that across the Channel the people had risen in their wrath and annihilated the monarchy.

Liverpool suggested a compromise. The £50,000 a year, a royal ship for travelling abroad and the honours due to the Queen of England should be accorded her.

This Caroline scornfully refused: There was nothing to be done but go ahead and on 5 July – only some few weeks after Caroline had set foot on English soil – Lord Liverpool introduced a Bill to be read. This was known as the Bill of Pains and Penalties. Its object was:

To deprive Her Majesty Caroline Amelia Elizabeth of the Title, Prerogatives, Rights, Privileges and Exemptions of the Queen Consort of the Realm and to dissolve the marriage between His Majesty and the said Caroline Amelia Elizabeth.

The Bill set out that Caroline had engaged Bartolomeo Pergami to serve in her household and that a disgraceful intimacy had sprung up between the Queen and Pergami. This licentious relationship had brought disgrace on the King and the royal family. Therefore it seemed right and proper that the Queen should be robbed of her privileges and the King granted an annulment of his marriage.

Under the guidance of Brougham Caroline likened herself to Catharine of Aragon and demanded a fair trial.

The people of London were intensely interested. In the streets they talked of nothing else. The King's great unpopularity meant that they were all on the side of the Queen. Caroline only had to appear for the crowd to sing her praises and cheer her.

The King's carriage was pelted with mud. They saw him as a wicked old lecher. He could be as promiscuous as he liked but they would not accept his cruelty to his wife.

It was exciting. Nothing like this had happened for a long time. The funerals had been depressing occasions; but this was amusing. They had someone whom they could champion; they had someone whom they could hate; and they did so with enthusiasm.

Mobs went about crying 'Caroline for ever'. They stoppped carriages and demanded: 'Are you for the Queen?'

They even stopped that of the great Duke of Wellington – such a short time before, the hero of the crowd.

'Declare for the Queen!' they cried. 'Declare for the Queen!'

The Duke was furious that he, the great Wellington, should be drawn into this undignified squabble. The hero of Waterloo to be forced to 'declare' for a woman like the Queen. But the mob was ugly. They carried brooms and pickaxes, and who could say that there was not a gun or two among them?

'All right,' cried the great soldier. 'The Queen – damn you all. The Queen! And may you all have wives like her.'

That made the crowd laugh. Trust Wellington to give as good as he got. A laugh went up. A cheer went up. He had after all saved them from Old Boney.

And the day of the trial approached and the excitement was intense.

Everyone was asking what the outcome would be.

Caroline left Brandenburg House, where she had taken up residence, for the court. She was dressed dramatically for the occasion in a dress of black figured gauze with enormous white bishop sleeves decorated with lace. A heavy lace veil was swathed about her head and beneath this were seen the curls of her wig. She was heavily painted and leaded. She looked, remarked one observer, like a toy which was called a Fanny Royd – a product of Holland with a heavy round bottom so that in whatever position it was placed it jumped upright. She came rushing into the House in a most ungraceful fashion and made a bob at the throne before seating herself, short legs apart, her dress falling in an ungainly manner over her chair.

Sir Robert Gifford, the Attorney General, presented the case for the Crown with the Solicitor General Sir John Copley. The Queen's leading counsel were Brougham and Denman who were opposite numbers of Gifford and Copley. General opinion was that the Queen had the better men on her side.

The first two days of the trial were devoted to legal arguments and then the first witnesses were called.

This was disastrous for the Queen because to her amazement the first witness for the prosecution was Theodore Majocchi, one whom she had always regarded as her faithful servant. The knowledge that he had come to give evidence against her made her cry out somewhat incoherently. Some people said she denounced him as a traitor and what she said was 'Traditore'. Others that it was his name that she spoke. But in any case she was so overcome emotionally that in her usual impetuous manner she rose and left the court.

There was a gasp of astonishment. How guilty was this woman who was afraid of a servant's evidence!

It was easy to see why she was afraid as the court listened to Majocchi in the hands of his interrogators. He began by explaining the position of the Queen's and Pergami's bedrooms in Tunis. They had been separated only by a small chamber. He gave the impression that there could be no doubt of the liaison between the Queen and Pergami. Her maid Louise Demont was called – she who had served the Queen well and had kept a diary of her travels in the East and written only praise of Caroline in that diary. But having lived close to the Queen she was recognized as an ideal witness against her if she could be persuaded to give the damning evidence that was required of her. Temptation was too much for Louise and she agreed to become a witness for the Crown. So with the evidence of Majocchi and Louise Demont, the case looked very black against Caroline.

But it was a situation which Brougham and Denman found stimulating. As they sifted the evidence they began to believe that the Queen was innocent of all but an indiscretion so great that it was the utmost folly. But innocent she was of that which the Crown was trying to prove. And with innocence *and* Brougham, thought that gentleman, she must win.

It was easy to deal with Majocchi for the man was clearly lying. Captain Hownam was called to prove that the Queen's and Pergami's bedrooms in Tunis had not been on the same floor. Majocchi had stated that the Queen dined in her bedroom with Pergami who sat on her bed while they ate together. Captain Hownam assured the court that this was absolutely untrue. The whole suite had always dined together.

So under fire Majocchi withered. He took refuge in the phrase 'I don't remember' – 'Non mi ricordo.'

The people who followed the trial day by day were immensely amused by this witness and a song was soon being sung in the streets:

To England I was trudged
Nor cost me a single farden
And was safely lodged .
In a placed called Covent Garden
There I eat and drink
Of the best they can afford O
Get plenty of the chink
To say Non mi ricordo.
To the House so large I went
Which put me in a stew

To tell a tale I was bent
Of which I nothing knew.
There was a man stood there
My precious brains he bored O
To which I wouldn't swear
I said Non mi ricordo.

There were many verses and these were added to hour by hour. People were singing them everywhere.

'Their witness,' said Brougham chuckling, 'is our witness.'

It was the same with Louise Demont. How easily the liars could be discredited in the hands of men like Brougham and Denman.

There were other Italian witnesses, all eager to earn their money and testify against the Queen. There was a certain Ragga-zoni who admitted that he had seen indecent conduct between the Queen and Pergami. This had caused some concern to Brougham until Hownam was able to tell the court that it was impossible for the man to have seen this from the place in which he described himself to be.

Another witness, Sacchi, said that on a journey from Rome to Sinigaglia the Queen had insisted that she and Pergami travel in a coach and that he was riding beside the coach in attendance when he saw an act of misconduct. There were other witnesses to prove that the Countess Oldi had travelled in the coach with them and that Sacchi had also ridden in a coach and not on horseback.

Rastelli, another bribed witness, had further stories to tell. These Brougham was not able to refute at the time but he had hopes of doing so.

He called on the Countess Oldi who had come to England with Caroline and knowing her devotion to the Queen – and moreover she was the sister of Pergami – he thought she would be a good witness.

She was distressed because of the cruel things which were being said about the Queen.

'So untrue,' she cried. 'So untrue.'

It was clear that she had a great affection for Caroline.

Should he call her? She was a foreigner, and it would be good to have an Italian who had a good word to say for the Queen. But she was Pergami's sister – what effect would that have?

'Of course,' said Brougham, 'people did go in and out of the Queen's bedroom.'

'Never at any time,' declared the Countess.

'I thought the manners of the country might make this permissible.'

'Never on any occasion.'

'But it has been proved that people did wander in and out of Her Majesty's bedroom rather freely.'

'Never at any time.'

She had learned her phrase, he realized; and she was going to stick to it, having decided that only by denying everything could she serve the Queen. Brougham imagined her in the hands of the Crown.

She would do as much harm to his cause as Majocchi had done to the other side.

He decided not to call her.

His great opportunity came when he proposed to recall the man Rastelli and heard that the Crown had sent him back to Italy.

What a sensation when the cry went up 'Call Rastelli' and the Crown had to admit that he had returned to Italy.

Brougham was a man to make the most of his opportunities. He wondered why the man had been sent back. He had questions to ask him which he very much doubted the fellow would be able to answer to the satisfaction of the court. Was it not strange that he should have been sent away at such a time?

It was indeed strange, Lord Liverpool admitted. It was highly culpable; it was iniquitous.

From that moment Brougham knew he had won his case.

Denman summed up the case for the Queen brilliantly until he came to the end of his speech.

'I know that rumours are abroad of the most vague but at the same time of the most injurious character. I have heard them even as we are defending Her Majesty against charges which compared with these rumours are clear, comprehensible and tangible ... There are persons and these not of the lowest condition, nor confined to individuals connected with the public press – not even excluded from this august assembly – who are industriously circulating the most odious and atrocious calumnies against her Majesty ... To a man who could even be suspected of so base a practice as whispering calumnies to judges – distilling leprous venom into the ears of jurors – the Queen might well exclaim: "Come forward, thou slanderer and let me see thy face. If thou wouldst equal the respectability of an Italian witness come forth and depose in open court ..." ' Denman gazed contemptuously at the King's supporters. ' "As thou art, thou art worse than an Italian assassin." '

He went on declaiming the injuries the Queen had suffered and he had the sympathy of the court for he spoke with touching eloquence; but unfortunately as he neared the end of his speech he gave his listeners the opportunity to ridicule and this they seized eagerly.

He who the sword of Heaven will bear
Should be as holy as severe.

'And if your lordships have been furnished with powers which I might almost say scarcely Omniscience itself possesses, to arrive at the secrets of this female, you will think that it is your duty to imitate the justice, beneficence and wisdom of that benignant Being who, not in a case like this when innocence is manifest but when guilt was detected and vice revealed said: "If no accuser can come forward to condemn thee, neither do I condemn thee. Go and sin no more." '

It was a brilliant speech; no case had been proved against Caroline but Denman could not have chosen a peroration which would have so delighted the people.

There was a new song now to replace that of 'Non mi ricordo'. It was:

Gracious Queen, we thee implore
Go away and sin no more.
But if that effort be too great,
Go away – at any rate.

Poor Denman was furious with himself. But Brougham was not displeased. He knew he had won.

There was still the Bill of Pains and Penalties. It passed through the House of Lords with a majority of twenty-eight.

If, reasoned Brougham, that Bill was passed in spite of the fact that the Queen could not be proved guilty of adultery, the first part of the Bill to exclude the Queen from her rights might still be put into force.

He called on Lord Liverpool.

'If this Bill is passed,' he said, 'this will not be the end. We have had an inquiry into the Queen's private life, what if there is an inquiry into the King's?'

'He has had his mistresses – as most kings have,' began Liverpool.

'This is not so much a matter of mistresses as of wives. There is a strong suspicion that as heir apparent the King went through a form of marriage with Maria Fitzherbert, and in the Act of Succession since the lady is a Catholic this could mean losing the crown.'

Liverpool understood. The Bill must not be passed.

On its next reading it received only a majority of nine in the Lords.

'This is the end of the Bill,' said Brougham to Denman. 'We've won, man. They'll never attempt to pass it through the Commons.'

He was right. Lord Liverpool withdrew his Bill.

The Queen was acquitted.

Through the cheering crowds she drove to Brandenburg House.

Return to Brunswick

Caroline called Lady Anne Hamilton to her.

'You see me ... triumphant ...' she said, and she smiled wryly.

'Is it the pain, Your Majesty?'

She nodded. 'Give me the magnesia.'

Lady Anne brought the drug and Caroline mixed it with water herself.

'And I'll add a little laudanum,' she said.

'Your Majesty – is it wise to take so much?'

'Well, my dear,' she laughed. 'When have I ever been wise?'

The King was humiliated by the findings of the court. The Bill had been thrown out. And he was still tied to that woman. Even Lady Conyngham found it hard to console him. He was not feeling well; he was far too fat; he had the crown but life had lost its savour.

He stayed at Windsor. He wanted to shut himself away. He had no desire to ride through the streets of London and suffer the further humiliation of having mud thrown at his carriage and overhear the remarks he guessed the people would make at his expense.

How different, he thought, from what he had dreamed in his youth. Then he had been Prince Charming and everywhere he went the people applauded him. They had preferred him to his dull old father. What a King he will make! they said. And here he was – the king – skulking at Windsor afraid to enter his capital, thinking sadly of the trail of scandal which marked his progress from Prince Charming to Prince Regent and King George IV.

It was dear Lady Conyngham who brought him comfort as usual.

She had changed the furniture in his bedroom a little and confessed to him that she had been very bold.

'Change what you will,' he told her fondly. 'What pleases you pleases me.'

She sat beside him and they played a game of patience.

She said: 'I have heard that the people are not so much for the Queen as they were. They all believe she *was* guilty, of course.'

'They cheer her wherever she goes.'

'They are singing "Go away and sin no more".'

'Then they have changed.'

'They always knew she was guilty only it wasn't possible to prove it. I think they would like to see their King.'

'You imagine them all to be as fond of him as you are,' he told her indulgently.

But as they retired to bed he thought: The public is fickle. Perhaps they are changing towards her. The enthusiasm was due to the impression that had been given by her supporters that she was a persecuted woman.

Surely they must see that she was not the woman they would want for their Queen. Whereas he was, in spite of his corpulence – and his doctors had persuaded him to abandon his corsets which he knew was for the best while he regretted the result – a magnificent figure.

It was time he had a coronation. Perhaps he would go to the theatre and see how he was received.

'Your Majesty is thoughtful,' said Lady Conyngham.

He patted her shoulder. 'As usual, my dear,' he said, 'you have succeeded in comforting me.'

It was a magnificent occasion when the King attended Drury Lane.

The people were pleased to see him and because they now began to believe that Caroline was guilty of infidelity and that he had come rather badly out of the trial they felt a little more affectionate towards him. He was a splendid figure and always would be; and he did look grand and imposing with the great diamond star flashing on his chest.

It was time he gave them a coronation and coronations were great occasions when there was feasting and revelry and everyone enjoyed life.

So cheers for the King and let him be crowned soon, and they would all turn out to sing: 'God save the King'.

He was deeply moved. He smiled and waved and showed his pleasure – and the more he showed his pleasure the more they cheered.

He stood in his box at Drury Lane and received the ovation. Bowing, his hand on his heart, the tears of emotion visible on his cheeks, he loved his people. And, temporarily, they were prepared to love him.

Preparations for the Coronation had begun and London was in a state of excitement.

'And what of the Queen?' they asked each other. 'She is not going to be crowned. More trouble!'

When the King rode out they called after him: 'Where's your wife, George?' But it was asked with bantering affection and no mud was thrown at the royal carriage.

But Caroline in Brandenburg House was determined to attend the Coronation. She wrote to Lord Liverpool to tell him so.

Her Majesty feels under the necessity to establish herself in England and communicates to Lord Liverpool that the Queen intends to be present at the Coronation and requests him to present the enclosed letter to His Majesty.

Caroline R

The letter to which she referred was addressed to the King and in it she asked him to command which ladies he desired should attend her on Coronation Day and in what dress he wished her to appear.

Lord Liverpool replied that it was the King's determination to receive no communication from her and that she was to form no part of the ceremonial of the Coronation.

Caroline's reply was curt and to the point:

The Queen is much surprised ... and assures the Earl that Her Majesty is determined to attend the Coronation; the Queen considers it one of her rights and privileges which she is determined to maintain.

This was the state of affairs as Coronation Day grew nearer. The Queen was determined to attend; and the King was determined that she should not.

*

19 July 1821! The day when His Majesty King George IV was to be crowned. The previous day he had left Carlton House in a closed carriage to spend the night at the Speaker's House, and next morning the procession assembled in Westminster Hall for the walk to the Abbey.

When the King appeared there was a gasp of admiration. One observer remarked that he was 'a being buried in satin, feathers and diamonds'. He could always be relied upon to give a good performance on occasions such as this and the people who had waited in the streets since the early morning were not going to be disappointed.

The procession was led by the King's herb woman and six of her assistants. They threw down flowers on the path which the King would take to the Abbey. Under the canopy came the centre of attraction: King George IV; and the crowd roared its approval. His crimson velvet train decorated with gold stars was nine yards long and on his head was a black hat with ostrich feathers.

The people went mad with joy. Trust old George to give them a good show. The manner in which he walked alone was worth watching, and it was said no one on earth could bow as he did.

He was a king, all said and done, and if he had had a few wild adventures, who could blame him?

God save the King.

An open carriage drawn by six horses was making its way from Brandenburg House to the Abbey.

'I am going,' Caroline had cried, her eyes alight with purpose. 'I have said I shall go to the Coronation and no one is going to stop me.'

Painted more heavily than usual – it was necessary, she told Lady Anne, for her face was a peculiar shade of yellow under the lead and rouge – dressed in outrageous colours, her jewels flashing, she rode through the crowd.

'The Queen!' they cried and ran after her carriage.

They surrounded it, impeding its passage towards the Abbey.

What now? Everyone knew that the King had forbidden the Queen to come to the Coronation.

She was surprised to detect a note of jeering laughter. Someone started to boo. She did not believe that could be meant for her. The people had always been on her side and she had just been acquitted.

She had been warned against coming to the Abbey by all those who wished her well. It would be considered bad taste, they told her. This was after all the day when the King was to be crowned. But she had been determined and had gone against them.

At the door of the Abbey her way was barred.

'Madam, no one is allowed to enter the Abbey without a ticket,' said the stalwart doorkeeper.

'I am the Queen.'

'No one without a ticket, Madam.'

She turned away. Someone in the crowd laughed. Flushed beneath her rouge, her head shaking so that her enormous hat was jerked rakishly to one side, she ordered her coachman to drive to another door.

'No entrance without a ticket, Your Majesty. Those are orders.'

She stood dismayed. The pain started to nag. A voice in the crowd called: 'Go home.'

She looked wildly about her as though she were about to speak and someone cried: 'Go to Como. Go and enjoy yourself with the Italian.'

Gracious Queen we thee implore
Go away and sin no more.
But if that effort be too great
Go away – at any rate.

They were jeering at her. They no longer believed her. They were suggesting that she was guilty when she had been proved innocent.

They had been right. She had been foolish to come . . . foolish, foolish. Foolish as I ever was, she thought.

She gave instructions to be driven home.

And as her carriage passed through the crowd she heard the jeering laughter.

The next day she was very ill.

'I pray you give me the magnesia quickly,' she cried to Lady Anne; and she mixed such a dose that it was like a paste so that she had to eat it with a spoon. 'And laudanum too,' she added. 'It will deaden this pain and perhaps let me sleep.'

Lady Anne was alarmed and tried to dissuade her but Caroline took the stuff and after a while slept.

A few days later she recovered and talked to Lady Anne about that humiliating experience.

'I should never have gone. I should have listened to advice. But then I never did listen to advice, did I? I shall go to the theatre. I said I would go to see Edward Kean and I will go.'

'Your Majesty is not well enough—'

'Nonsense, my dear Lady Anne. I wish to see how the people treat me. They were very unkind on Coronation Day. They have changed. They quickly change, I fear. The play is *Richard III*. Don't try to dissuade me, my love. I must go.'

And so to Drury Lane with a fearful Lady Anne.

She fainted half-way through the performance but recovered by the time the play was over. The audience was neither friendly nor unfriendly. This was Coronation time – and George was their King.

When she returned to Brandenburg House she collapsed on to her bed. Magnesia could bring her little relief and even laudanum could not give her sleep.

'I fear,' she said, 'that I am very ill.'

The doctors came and bled her. They gave her more magnesia and castor oil.

She had been ill for some time, her doctors said. It was an inflammation of the bowels which she had tried to pretend did not exist.

She sent for Willikin and embraced him.

'You have been a great comfort to me, dear boy,' she told him. 'We have had some good times together, have we not?'

Willikin wept and said that was so.

'Do not fret, my little Willikin. You will not want. I have taken care of that.'

Brougham came to her bedside and she laughed at him. She began to talk of all the places she had seen during her travels and of the strange life she had led. She had grown animated and seemed unconscious now of pain.

'Your Majesty is going to recover,' said Brougham.

'No,' she said. 'I shall not. Nor do I wish to. It is better for me to die. I am tired of this life.'

Believing that she would recover, he left her.

But she asked for her friends to come to her bedside. There was Willikin and Lady Anne, Sir Matthew Wood and one or two more.

'My friends,' she said, smiling at them. 'Bury me in Brunswick. It is better that I should return to the home which perhaps I should never have left. In my will you will find the inscription I wish to be engraved on my coffin. Will you see that it is done?'

They assured her that it would be; and she smiled and died.

According to her wish her body was to be buried in Brunswick, and the King, suspecting trouble as the cortège travelled through London on its way to the coast, gave orders that it was not to pass through the City.

The rain was streaming down yet the people had come out in their thousands to pay their last tribute to Queen Caroline. Now that she was dead she had again become a heroine and when it was discovered that the procession was to be diverted that it might not pass through the City the crowd decided otherwise.

As it came down Kensington Gore and Knightsbridge the mob surrounded it and insisted on leading it to Temple Bar. There was a clash between the soldiers who had been sent to guard the cortège, and in the mêlée two men were shot.

But the people had their way, and the crowds waiting in the City madly cheered the departing Queen.

She was buried in Brunswick. Willikin and Lady Hamilton were among those present. They stood solemnly thinking of her and the strange life she had led; and the words she had asked should be engraved on her coffin were:

> 'Here lies Caroline of Brunswick,
> the injured Queen of England.'